Praise for

SHOGGOTHS IN TRAFFIC

"Tobias Buckell's speculative fiction is a revelation: honest and wry, characters and situations fresh and unexpected, all the action my ADHD soul craves, proudly Caribbean to the core, and every so often, moments of sheer human vulnerability so poignantly expressed it brings tears to my eyes. Enjoy."

NALO HOPKINSON, SFWA GRAND MASTER
AUTHOR OF *MIDNIGHT ROBBER* AND *SISTER MINE*

"Incisive, thought-provoking, and profound, *Shoggoths in Traffic* is an astounding collection of wonders by one of the finest practitioners of short form science fiction and fantasy working today."

JOHN JOSEPH ADAMS, SERIES EDITOR OF
THE BEST AMERICAN SCIENCE FICTION & FANTASY

"World Fantasy Award winner Buckell delivers a collection of speculative shorts that are both timely and timeless. These 24 subversive, bite-sized pieces explore an array of settings and tones and excel in convincing readers to look at the world from new perspectives . . . Most captivating are the stories that offer unique spins on current events: the pandemic response is turned on its head in "A Different Kind of Place" when a zombie outbreak forces the residents of a small town to debate whether or not to put up a wall or get a vaccine to protect themselves. And in "The Alien from Verapaz," ICE raids a day care to take in the children of an alien superhero, El Fantastico. Buckell shows his chops in a range of subgenres with a keen focus on diversity and humor. Even the busiest readers will find it easy and worthwhile to take a few minutes out of their day to dip into this collection."

PUBLISHERS WEEKLY

"An enigmatic cover heralds the best start ever to riveting story-telling. Opening with 'A Different Kind of Place,' a zombified San Fontaine and fuckwit antivaxxers, you quickly get Tobias S. Buckell's distinct voice in subversive text that's also a curiosity. *Shoggoths in Traffic and Other Stories* is the darkest, the most fun Black writing you'll ever read. Buckell draws from his Caribbean roots in 'Spurn Babylon' and steps the reader into a strong sense of place inside an ancient slave ship with its black characters questing for a new future.

"The theme story 'Shoggoths in Traffic' stuns a pair of car thieves and the reader with a time-travelling wizard rocking a bikie vibe in a carnage of traffic, unrouteable in his quest to save a patterned universe. The deeply unsettling 'Death's Dreadlocks' and its Old Ma unveils the eeriness of friendship and the power of story. Meet a demon-possessed Karen in a novel story 'Brickomancer,' where policing takes its own turn, and find how running over a white girl in 'Four Eyes' opens up a taxi driver to a whole lot of weird.

A third into the collection, you know how much you love this shit. This book is ace. It's ribboned with Patreon deliciousness and titillating stories from an award-winning author who dexterously borrows from the everyday to slip the reader into other worlds and the occult. Buckell is knowledgeable in a nerdy sort of way as he tackles racism, vaccination, otherness, togetherness, even deadness . . . with a diverse cast of orphans, single mothers, communities, immigrants, taxi drivers, shamans, entities in the city grid, and more."

EUGEN BACON
AUREALIS MAGAZINE

SHOGGOTHS IN TRAFFIC

AND OTHER STORIES

ALSO BY TOBIAS S. BUCKELL

<u>Novels</u>
Crystal Rain
Ragamuffin
Sly Mongoose
Arctic Rising
Hurricane Fever
Halo: The Cole Protocol
Halo: Envoy
The Trove
The Tangled Lands (with Paolo Bacigalupi)
A Stranger in the Citadel

<u>Collections</u>
Tides From the New Worlds
Nascence
Mitigated Futures
Xenowealth: A Collection
It's All Just a Draft

SHOGGOTHS IN TRAFFIC

AND OTHER STORIES

TOBIAS S. BUCKELL

FAIRWOOD PRESS
Bonney Lake, WA

SHOGGOTHS IN TRAFFIC AND OTHER STORIES
A Fairwood Press Book
November 2021
Copyright © 2021 Tobias S. Buckell

First Edition

Fairwood Press
21528 104th Street Court East
Bonney Lake, WA 98391
www.fairwoodpress.com

Cover image © Dabeen Lee (A. Shipwright)
Cover and book design by Patrick Swenson

ISBN: 978-1-933846-18-7
First Fairwood Press Edition: November 2021
Printed in the United States of America

For Emily

CONTENTS

A DIFFERENT KIND OF PLACE

AFTER THE ZOMBIE outbreak in San Fontaine was put down, Zadie treated herself to a new hair color as a way to get away from constantly watching the news. At the Clip-n-Curl, a modest house turned into a salon tucked away behind the gray and green brick building of Zippy's Pizza, the conversation took a turn for the *oh-shit-really?* when Carla loudly announced she would not allow anyone in her family to get the vaccine.

"It's full of mercury," she said. "And all sorts of other chemicals."

It was like someone tossed a stink bomb into the middle of the salon.

Not that the ladies, and occasionally Phillip, were averse to talking politics. The Clip-n-Curl might not be an overly functional barbershop with clipper buzz and Fox News blaring away on the flat screen, but the Clip-n-Curl hosted some of the more intense round tables in the town regarding the topics of the day.

But San Fontaine was just a few hundred miles down the interstate from Chester. Zadie wasn't in the mood. She wanted to get away.

Abigail Jones, eighty years young and getting purple highlights in her ghost-white hair, looked up. Her eyes glinted with—Zadie wasn't sure—anger, or possibly disgust. Abby was eighty, she didn't pull punches. She had a tattoo on her right bicep, a shield and something in Latin. Someone told Zadie it said "don't let the bastards grind you down." Abigail Jones said what she thought and if you were on the other end of it . . .

"You've got to be fucking kidding me," Abby said.

Carla, forty years old, frequent volunteer at the annual fish fry for the town beautification committee, member of the garden club, and mother of three, returned the dagger stare. Zadie and the two stylists, Eva and Whitney, were just bystanders.

"The government's in bed with those pharmaceutical companies. I mean, this company that makes the vaccine, did you ever hear of it before all this?"

Zadie knew the conversation that was incoming with all the certainty of an infantryman hearing the whistle of an incoming shell. Abby, a retired professor who had traveled the world, would explain there wasn't any goddamn mercury in the vaccine. Carla would counter by talking about the model Onisha, whose kid had some sort of palsy that appeared right after the vaccine was administered and now campaigned against it. Abby would ask if Carla wanted someone in her family to turn into a zombie. Carla would talk about that one kid who had been Turned after he'd been bitten just the day after getting the vaccine. Abby would talk about herd immunity.

So Zadie, tired, nerves slightly ragged from a lack of sleep from staying up all night to watch CNN, politely interrupted. "It's a public-private partnership."

The two women turned to face her. "What?"

"The company, it was created by the government to pass the vaccine around, but the CDC found the vaccine." She'd seen a report on MSNBC. Apparently the company had then tripled the price of the vaccine. The CEO was living in a floating offshore cruise ship with a private security force.

No worries about a zombie wandering into *his* living room.

Carla didn't take too kindly to the interruption or the correction. She doubled down. And suddenly Zadie was in the middle of an exhausting verbal fight about whether the vaccine caused palsy. How was it, she wondered, that Carla was the one getting more and more upset at Zadie when it was Carla that just announced out of the blue her strong opinion?

Some folk didn't see their opinion as opinion, but after they surrounded themselves with their beliefs mistook them for common sense. And most folk didn't want to argue like this, so they just quietly suffered through a tirade, like the two stylists were.

But speak up and suddenly you were such a bitch.

Zadie ended it by laughing, crossing her arms, and saying "Well, when you're trying to chow down on Rick like he's a half-off steak from Gina's Deli, I won't give a shit because I got the jab."

And that finally cut Carla down because she mumbled something about agreeing to disagree, paid up, and left.

Everyone pretended nothing had happened and moved conversation on to the new development on the edge of town. It was double gated, and rumor was that someone on the village council was going to move in.

The houses were gaudy monstrosities and way overpriced.

On Friday, Zadie got an email to go see the superintendent over in the high school building. Shit. Someone had noticed her hair color and complained, she figured. So she packed up at lunch and crossed the road to walk the four blocks to her destination, past the post office and dry cleaners, waving to a few folk who passed in minivans or pickups.

Zadie loved Chester. She hadn't when she was in school there. Her mother, an immigrant from Trinidad, had met her father a few towns over. He'd left one night to go pick up a six pack of Coors and just keep riding on past the Spin Thru with the beer cave until he ended up somewhere in Montana a week later, leaving them all alone in a leaky trailer on the edge of town. One of their neighbors blew his convertible van up because he was cooking meth. The other raised chickens and rabbits.

Zadie's mom worked like someone possessed. Zadie had wondered if it was some first-generation immigrant hoodoo. Everyone she'd ever met who had an immigrant parent said they were like that. She'd never appreciated it as a child, but as an adult now Zadie wouldn't have worked three jobs and every weekend. Couldn't hardly imagine it. Let alone the sort of back-breaking cleaning that her mom did day in and day out. Izelda had been a force of nature.

By middle school, they'd moved to Chester. Izelda had saved enough to change location. Better school. Walkability. "Everyone there smiles," she'd said. And all her cleaning clients spoke so highly of Chester.

And everyone did smile. But there was a certain distance, and Zadie had never been sure if it was the fact that she was brown-skinned, a child of a single parent who cleaned people's toilets, or if it was just simply that she wasn't someone who had been born in the town from day one.

But Zadie had missed Chester. Missed walking down to the grocery store with its limited selection and walking back with her grocery bags on each arm. Missed filling up a prescription on her way to the post office. Missed the half mile of antique stores along Main Street and the weary tourists driving out from the big city on the weekends to go hunting for something "real" and "authentic" to clutter-charm their million-dollar apartment's entry way with.

So she was back to teach third graders math—before their elders taught them that football was the way out of the small town, instead of an accounting degree—and reading before it became labeled "uncool."

Standing outside what used to be the principal's office made her feel just as intimidated as back when she was a half foot shorter and much younger. When she nervously stepped inside, preparing for a chewing out about the change in her appearance, the superintendent didn't even look at her hair but passed her a printed out email.

"There was a complaint about the content of your lesson yesterday." Holt was an older gentleman, silver in his hair, proud grandparent, and a patriarch of the community. He stood every day out amongst the high school parking lot, watching kids drive out and cautioning them to watch out for the little kids biking and walking home. He'd been pleasantly surprised when Zadie had applied to come teach, something about needing a diversity hire. Zadie, knowing full well that Chester had once been a sundown town not that many generations ago where brown or black-skinned folk were not welcomed, had just nodded.

"A complaint?"

"About the, uh, not-dead awareness."

Oh. Zadie stiffened. She should have seen this coming. "The children are asking a lot of questions, Mr. Holt."

"I'm sure they are," he said patiently. Then he leaned forward, as if sharing a secret. "But, if they start asking you how babies are made, you're not going to start telling them about the birds and the bees, are you? There are waivers, and appropriate times. And this community prefers to teach . . . sensitive things . . . in their own home."

"Well, sure," Zadie said carefully, realizing her job could be on the line. "But I was sent this by the CDC. The US government is recommending that all children understand what happens if a zombie attacks. That they shouldn't try to save their friend, but get to a safe place. To help cut down on reinfection and spread—"

Holt leaned back, his smile strained. "Look, this won't fly with the folk in Chester. I talked to the parents for you. But it needs to not happen again. Folk around here, they want to decide for themselves how to educate their children. And they have a right to do it in their own way without interference. You see what I'm saying?"

Zadie did, but still had one more play. "They're terrified about San Fontaine."

Holt nodded. "Well, that's understandable. Kids shouldn't even be allowed to see such things on TV. But San Fontaine, it's not Chester. This is a different kind of place."

A different kind of place.

That was echoed at the Wednesday night town hall, which was more packed than usual. The San Fontaine effect. Only a single video clip had come out of the town before quarantine by what looked like thousands of National Guard: it was video of an old man, face buried deep in some teenager's chest while the kid writhed and screamed.

"We are not going to have an infestation," the mayor said. "This is a different kind of place."

Councilwoman Maggie Dobresh had been talking about a new grant from both the Department of Defense and the Department of Transportation to help smaller towns build walls and fund an increase in police and volunteer armed patrols.

"This kind of money," the mayor explained, "comes with strings attached. Remember when the state helped build the new road through Pine Street? After that we had to change all the sidewalks to match federal regulations."

That created a murmur of discontent. A lot of people in town hated the fucking sidewalks, with bump outs that had damaged at least ten different vehicles when turning too tightly onto Elm. Zadie occasionally drove over them in her little Chevy sedan, swearing when the unexpected bump rattled the whole car.

"With a wall we can check who comes into town," Maggie said.

"More likely shut us in if there's an infection," someone from the rows of citizenry muttered.

Someone stood up, hands in their blue jeans. "Look, San Fontaine is the kind of place where people from all over pass through. It's not a surprise they had some kind of outbreak, of some kind. We are not San Fontaine."

Everyone agreed, Chester wasn't San Fontaine.

But Zadie saw a few sidewise glances. Well, shit, she thought. That's how people were thinking infection spread. An odd, chilly feeling prickled her back, and she really wanted to *not be here*.

"If we create walls, it's gonna kill the antiques shops up and down Main Street," one of the store owners said. "No tourist wants a stop and frisk on the edge of town before coming in for an ice cream and a browse. And the edge of town is all gas stations and fast food from truckers."

Zadie decided to bounce out of the town hall while everyone was thinking about the loss of jobs, and Iggy was standing up and saying that building walls around a town was something the damn Europeans did and that walls were a UN plot to make the heartland more like Sweden. Something to do with Agenda 21.

"I love this town," she confessed to Wendy the next night over a bottle of cheap red from the local Spin Thru. Not the one her father had driven past but the Chester one. "But Jesus Christ: they voted down the wall. Carla was telling me she won't vaccinate her kids against zombiesm, and principal Jenners told me the vaccine rate was likely barely half."

"Oh, honey." Wendy refilled her glass, even though Zadie tried to wave her off. She had to drive two miles back into town and her small apartment over the glass trinkets shop. "It's only a few attacks. I know they're scary, but we really shouldn't change our towns and way of living just for that. It's too expensive. Can we really afford to put up walls around every single town and city in the country over, what, a dozen incidents? The deficit is so high. Unemployment is up. It would wreck the economy, sweetie."

"It's a few outbreaks now, but what happens as it keeps doubling? It was one at first, then two, then four. In no time flat that suddenly becomes attack everywhere, all the time." The human mind, Zadie thought, was ill-prepared for thinking logarithmically.

Exponential growth always seemed to come out of nowhere. Doubling would keep happening for months, then in a week hit the steep growth curve and overnight . . .

Suddenly the night outside Wendy's house looked menacing. The acres of mowed grass out in the country somehow a massive target.

"Well, I'm not worrying about it," Wendy said.

Zadie stared at her old high school friend. "How?"

"If this is what God wants, it'll happen." Wendy drained her glass. "Not much I can do about it."

"But we could build a wall," Zadie said plaintively.

Wendy smiled, and leaned forward. "Even if they come, Bob has us covered."

"How?"

"Guns. He has a lot of guns in the basement. And food. We'll be fine. Besides, Bob doesn't think there are such things as zombies. He has the guns in case, well, things just get generally chaotic. You never know."

Zadie took another sip. She shouldn't, but if she stayed on the county road she'd skip the speed trap by the highway. She could have a third glass.

"Bob's been watching this show, and they have a man on across from the CDC people, and *he* says there isn't any such thing as zombies coming for us. It's just special effects and the government throwing their authority around."

"So you think the government shut down ten small cities, doubled the National Guard, and faked around-the-clock coverage for every incident to convince us there were zombies so that they could better control us?" Zadie grabbed the wine bottle, somewhat in shock, for another pour.

"When you put it like that, it sounds crazy. But, sweetie, have *you* ever seen a zombie?"

Zadie had to concede that, other than on the TV and listening to CDC experts, she hadn't.

"Well, if they try to force their way into Chester it won't be so easy, not like San Fontaine. This is a different kind of place."

Zadie wanted to laugh. San Fontaine, with Las Rojas dealing drugs out of the suburbs so heavily? They had guns too. Hadn't helped them.

She was hit by another car on the way home. A white SUV that clipped her before she even realized what was happening. Her reflexes too slow, Zadie spun off the road in a confusing haze of cornfields spinning around her and asphalt slamming against the roof of her car until it spun slowly to a stop.

This was it. This was the end. She'd be cited for driving over the limit. She shouldn't have had that last glass. But Wendy had been talking craziness, and the wine had helped Zadie keep her mouth shut.

Always holding it in.

Zadie staggered out onto the grass berm, staring at her upside down car.

The SUV that hit her had skidded out and struck a tree. Smoke trickled from under the hood. *Oh god*, she thought. She'd driven drunk and killed them.

A pickup slowed and pulled over. A tall and familiar burly shape jumped out.

"Zadie, that you?"

"Hey Bobby." She waved at him. A silly thing to do, but, the entire scene felt ridiculous. "I was on my side of the road, I swear. I had three glasses. And I think they're hurt."

Bobby. She hadn't called him that since high school. And he'd barely talked to her since, that one time under the bleachers after the homecoming game sophomore year. Her fault, she'd pushed him too far and he'd gone all shucks and shy and . . . limp. Could hardly look her in the eye since. Always found a reason to be missing whenever he knew Wendy and Zadie would be meeting up.

He put an arm around her. "You got a bad cut to your forehead, Zadie." And he was getting a shirt out from under the seat. It smelled of grease and campfire when he wound it around her head.

He hadn't been tall and large, a bear of a man, the last time she'd been this close to him. He'd been all ribs and elbows.

"I haven't called anything in. Let's check the SUV first, see what's what. We might be able to buy you some time before we call Sheriff Peterson."

They crossed the dark country road, the wind sifting through corn softly, to the line of trees near the ditch against a soybean field where the white SUV had fetched up. The license plate on the rear had a sticker that said SAN FONTAINE BUICK AND CHEVROLET.

"Hey, Bobby, I mean, Bob . . ." Zadie started to say. "This might not be a good idea."

Bob, because that's what he preferred since graduation, shook his head. "We gotta see if they're okay. I'm not going to be part of any hit and run type thing. I mean, even though you're Chester, that isn't the thing to do."

"No, that's not what I'm saying." Zadie took a step back and pulled out her phone. Drunk or not, she wanted Sheriff Peterson here.

Bob pulled the driver's side door open. "Everyone okay in here?"

The driver lunged out. Zadie screamed as the man bit down on Bob's forearm so hard that blood briefly spurted and the bone cracked. Bob punched the man in the face and stepped back.

As he reversed, the woman from the passenger's side crawled over the driver and shrieked as she struggled to get free of the seat belt. There was a hunger, no, an anger to her that froze Zadie to the spot.

Then her head exploded. Two shots.

Then the man likewise jerked in place.

Bob look across at her, the gun in his hand still smoking. "Oh god."

"Please tell me you got the vaccine," Zadie said, her voice shaking. "Bobby. Wendy was telling me you were talking about it all being fake news. Tell me you got the goddamn vaccine."

He nodded, finally, no longer staring in shock at her. "I got it. I mean, I wasn't sure, but, I thought, just in case. You know?"

A small animal pushed through the tall grass around the SUV. It was barely the size of a dog, and until it latched onto her, Zadie didn't even process that a baby could move that fast. A few tiny teeth dug deep into her ankle. "Fuck!"

She kicked at it, then freaked out. You can't kick a baby! And like its parents, it didn't *look* like a zombie. They must have just Turned. Like, right before they'd hit her. They still looked human. Pale, but human.

It turned for Bob.

Bob couldn't do it. Couldn't bring a gun to bear. Not after the shock of killing two humans. And for a lucid, brief second, Zadie wondered if the fact that they'd been trying for a kid so long made this too much for him.

The baby ripped his throat out. Nothing a vaccine could do about that.

Zadie ran to the still-running pickup, slammed it into reverse, turned, and headed for town. She picked up the phone and dialed nine, and then a one as she was still driving, then stopped.

Yeah, she was a partially drunk, brown-skinned woman in someone else's pickup truck roaring into town and calling the police. No.

She was drowsy by Pine Street and rolled through the intersection's four way stop. The wine was too much. She was all but asleep at the wheel. The world seemed at a remove and she was just mulling over the week.

Carla. Fucking Carla. And it wasn't just Carla and people like her refusing the vaccine. It was the people like Jason who ran Town Health of this world, too. He'd told her the other day that there was a concentrated lemon juice cleanse diet that changed the body's acidity so that it dissolved zombie infection.

A fast-acting, DNA-hijacking virus was going to surrender to fucking lemon juice?

And all those folks who'd refused the wall. If they were out there taking this seriously, patrols could have stopped that family of infected. But no, no government was better than government intrusion.

And this was a different kind of place.

A place that had never really stopped being cool to her, even when they were all smiles.

God she had loved it here. She was going to miss it.

The lights, red and blue and flickering, made the inside of the pickup feel like a disco.

Herd immunity, Zadie thought. Not everyone who had the vaccine would resist the bite.

The pickup truck rolled to a stop on Main Street of its own accord, right near the Bean Express. Zadie felt hot, flushed, and her mouth felt so dry. She heard a far-off door slam.

An eternity later, Sheriff Peterson flashed an entire sun's worth of light right down her pupils and into the back of Zadie's brain. A distant part of her noticed his reaction as he realized she wasn't Bob. And his hand went to his gun. And then he smiled. "Goddamn, it's Zadie. Jesus, girl, what have you been drinking? You look like shit."

She wondered why he was smiling.

Happy that he was going to help her out? Or happy that she was going to lose her job, and end up having to leave.

A small part of her was sorry it would never get to answer this fundamental riddle about Chester. It fumed that she would never know if they just smiled to smile and stabbed her behind her back, or if they genuinely were just that insular. Wondered why it took five years for Wendy to invite her over to her house when Zadie moved back.

And all this pent-up anger, frustration, and rage bubbled up as Peterson leaned into the cab. "Let's just put that in park, shall we?"

Because, fucking Peterson was Carla Peterson's husband, and

something inside Zadie was screaming because it *knew*, it knew he smelled just right when she bit down on his forearm and heard the crunch.

She couldn't speak, she was infected, she knew it as the last small bit of consciousness fled.

And this was all so avoidable.

But Chester was a different kind of place.

SPURN BABYLON

EASING BACK ON the throttle of the company's yellow Scarab powerboat, just clearing the rocky point of Hassel Island, I found myself stunned by the lack of yachts. Usually St. Thomas's Charlotte Amalie harbor was a forest of masts and a rainbow of hull colors. Now only two ships sat at anchor, looking lonely and out of place. The recent hurricane that had closed down the island's airport, forcing my company to send me here by boat rather than plane, had swept this anchorage clean.

Even more incredibly, a three-masted square-rigger lay lopsided on the waterfront's concrete shoreline.

"Where'd that come from," I wondered aloud.

I shook my head, wishing I had a camera.

It didn't seem like things were all that bad, I thought later, sipping a Red Stripe and relaxing underneath the flapping awning of the Greenhouse Restaurant. Even only two weeks after the worst hurricane in the Virgin Island's recorded history, things looked okay. Maybe even "irie," as my supervisor seemed to glory in saying, trying to imitate local dialect. I distantly understood that half the houses on the island were uninhabitable, and I could smell seaweed no matter where I walked. But these islands were well known for recovering quickly.

I let the condensation roll off the side of the brown bottle and down the back of my hand, a cold contrast to the heat shimmering off of the concrete all around me. In the distance a generator hummed, keeping even more beer cold. Life went on.

"Evening," someone said.

J. Ottley sat down into the seat across from me. The plastic hinges squeaked. He removed a well-worn straw hat and set it on the table. His long sleeved shirt was soaked under the armpits. He ran the St. Thomas cell of B.E. aerospace division, one of three sections.

"Evening to you," I replied, handing Ottley the keys to the Scarab. Sombrero Island held our main launch pad complex, weathering the storm with minimal damage. St. Croix supported additional docking and shipping facilities for our sea-launch sections and shipping for the launch complex. St. Thomas housed even more shipping facilities. I'd spent the last week running around St. Croix helping rebuild damage to the sterile clean-rooms that prepared satellites for launch. Cutting edge. Now it was time to check in and make sure our warehouses here in St. Thomas were okay. "Ottley, what is that?" I pointed at the ship across the street from us. Now I could see a thick patina of silt hung to its sides.

Two brown-skinned men with dreadlocks and baggy gray trousers stood around, poking at the hull. A few uniformed students in red trousers and white shirts from the local public school had climbed aboard. They hung from the long wooden pole that stuck out of the front of the boat. The bowsprit, I think it would be called. The topsides seemed about seventy feet long. It looked just like my mental image of a traditional old wooden ship.

"An old ship," Ottley said. "Very old. From under the sea."

And that was all he would say. He gave me folders with pictures of the damage taken to our warehouses. Roofs ripped off, boosters inside damaged. There was water damage to a few satellites.

Yet my eye kept wandering from the pictures of fractured com-
posites to the silhouette just on the edge of my vision.

A waterspout spawned by the recent hurricane must have
sucked the ancient wooden ship up from the silted bottom of Charlotte Amalie harbor. And then set it next to the asphalt road in a
pool of stagnant seawater and gray harbor mud. But even as I tried
to envision that, I struggled. There should be more damage. What
strange force had preserved it from decay?

I spent the next day coordinating the recovery efforts. We had
a warehouse near the airport, more or less on the west side of St.
Thomas; one in Red Hook, the east end; and an office in town. I
tackled Red Hook first. Later, as the sun began to shimmer and kiss
the distant salty horizon, I sat down exhausted on a lounge chair
next to the pool and bar of the Marriott Hotel; Frenchman's Reef.
From the pool I could see the entire curve of the harbor and the
whole waterfront skyline.

Charlotte Amalie is a beautiful little Caribbean town. Its Dutch
architecture is mostly symmetrical, and the facades of the stocky
two-story buildings reflect that with arches and squared windows
in even numbers. The colors of the walls are vibrant bright yellows,
pinks, clean whites, contrasted with red shingled roofs. Similarly
colored tiny houses cluster all over the steep mountainside.

And sitting there I realized a familiar wooden shape was still
up on the waterfront.

I took out my surveyor's monocle and zoomed in. The dark-
skinned crowd still surrounded the ship, and they had tools. I could
see them hacking away at the hull. It seemed an inefficient way to
move the ship.

Another sip of Margarita later I left to find my room.

*

I hired a taxi to take me out to the warehouse near the airport. It was a blue Toyota pickup with bench seats and a large canopy strapped onto the bed. "Safari bus." I sat in front with the driver, who had what sounded like reggae thumping away in the cab. A harsh scratchy voice in a strong accent swore and belted out angry lyrics.

"Buju Banton," he said, turning it down.

"Sorry?" I didn't understand. He pointed at the tape and I understood; the name of the singer. "Airport."

"Right."

New York taxi drivers had nothing on island driving. We took off out the driveway and onto the road. Every corner seemed the last, with the pickup leaning, the contraption on the back shifting as we turned. Particularly since I couldn't shake the conviction that we were driving on the wrong side of the road, the left. The driver honked and waved at every other car or pickup going the other way, and at the pedestrians along side the street.

The road took us down gently into town, and there we slowed down to a crawl with all the other cars. Finally I could get a close look at the ship. Crowds still surrounded it, but I didn't think they were government workers. Children, old women, a Rastafarian with long dreadlocks and tattered jeans; some of them wielded tools, scraping away at the ship. Others stood around, singing hymns, or just watching. Many had tears in their eyes.

Some of the wet planks were pulled away to expose ribs. I could see the dim gleam of white inside. Skeletons? It suddenly dawned on me that this was an old slave ship. Horrible. I shivered. St. Thomas had been one of the center points of the trade, being one of the best natural harbors in the Caribbean. Had a pirate ship fired and sunk this slaver in the harbor? Divers often searched the bottom after large cruise ships stirred up the silt, looking for history. But here it had been brought straight to land.

I leaned over and tapped the driver, who was just as fascinated as I was.

"What are they doing?" I asked.

"Taking care of it," he said. He had a strong accent: "Tekkin' cyare af it."

"What is it?" I whispered.

"It old," he told me. "Very old."

I had lunch again with Ottley. It was nice to relax and talk business with the skinny round-faced local. We reviewed plans on fixing the warehouses. Afterwards I walked out onto the concrete walkway that extended across the bay, following the old shoreline.

"You goin' ah see it?" a passerby asked me.

I nodded.

I left my beer on the table, feeling that standing there and looking at the ship with a beer in hand would be sacrilegious. I felt this strange, deep tugging that called me closer.

The crowd around the ship parted and let me through. I could see a full range of color. From the darkest black man to the pale and grizzled yachtsmen, they all stood around watching me. Work paused. The wind kicked up a haze of dust that brushed past, tugging up my shirt and cooling the sweat on the small of my back. Someone coughed.

Placing the tips of my fingers on a plank, I looked at my tan hand and wondered how I fit in. I pressed against the wood, and it gave slightly, soft with age. Beyond that I could feel something else beneath the surface. A sense of history, the past talking directly to me. It was a knot in my stomach.

And yet, I still remained distant. Maybe because my ancestors were mixed, and I could never bring myself to identify with either side. It was the same struggle I had with deciding what "race" box to check off on paperwork, or applications. Black? Definitely some: there's my unnaturally easy tan. White? During winter I would blend in with the average mall crowd, an easy anonymous decision. Or even maybe a little Latino, and some Oriental thrown in for good measure. I was trapped in dispassion. In the end, I always chose "other."

I pulled away, and an old graying Rasta next to me nodded.

"Hear it call," he said in a deep voice. His muscles stood out as he grasped and ripped a plank away. I looked into the heart of the ship. Sometime during the night the bleached remains of the scattered skeletons had been removed, but the chains and manacles still hung from the bulkheads and partitions, the iron blacker than the skin of the man standing next to me. They should have had barnacles on them, or been rusted, yet they gleamed at me as new as they day they were made. What force was at work here?

Then the moment passed, and the crowd began to attack the hull of the ship again. I wandered off and found a stand selling Johnny Cakes, fried dough of some sort. Pates were a rolled up pastry with meat inside. One of each and a Coke made for a good lunch.

Early the next morning I went through the motions of moving our office to a building in better shape. But even in the back streets of town I was near enough the ship that it dominated my thoughts. At lunch I wandered through the alleys with small shops and cool shade until I ended back up at the ship.

"Eh, white-boy. Hyere."

The same old Rasta greeted me. He'd been waiting. He handed me a pick and I joined him at the hull, pulling off the old planks. We spent a sweaty hour ripping off old wood and stacking it up near the sidewalk. After that we took a lunch break, eating pates, squatting on pieces of wood. Two skinny old fellows slapped dominoes on a table, and Soca music drifted over from a small tinny speaker.

Eventually three other men joined us. The Rasta passed around a joint, and the five of us sat in silence for fifteen minutes, seeking enlightenment, drifting to the warbling in the air.

"Come." The old Rasta got up, and I followed him around to the other side.

Here I found my surprise. They weren't just taking the ship apart; they were rebuilding it. New waterproofed lengths of wood replaced the old. I hadn't paid attention before, but the sound of sawing I'd heard while pulling planks off was not that of the old planks being broken apart.

"Why are you rebuilding it?" I asked. "Will you make it a museum?" I was trying to understand. The Rasta shook his locks.

"The whore of Babylon fall soon, we have ah be ready."

"The whore of Babylon?"

"Babylon America," he told me, shaking his locks. "Jus' like in Revelations." Revvy-lay-shons. "U.S. Virgin Islands part of Babylon, is time for we to spurn Babylon."

My head spun from the sweet smoke in the air, and I blinked. The ship hummed.

It scared me. The wooden planks, the manacles, the calm intensity of the people working at restoration. Yet they didn't plan to restore it. I would have understood restoration. I wanted to help with that, to rediscover a hidden part of myself, make peace with myself. Just like the Jewish I read about who returned to Auschwitz.

These people were planning something different though. I didn't understand what. So I drank alcoholic drinks with umbrellas back at the hotel. Every time I visited the bar at the pool I could see the waterfront, and I couldn't push the ship out of my mind. It was a relic, a reminder, and a key, and I didn't understand how to use it.

I wandered through the silent corridors looking for anyone, until I found a single busboy. He sold me a packet of his best red. I lit up on the porch of my roof and smoked until I feel asleep on the cold tile.

I dreamed of naked and emaciated black specters rising out of the muddy waters of Charlotte Amalie harbor, thousands of them, marching in force up through town, and then swinging out towards the point that the hotel sat on. They picked me up and carried me back down into the sea with them.

There were lines up and down the waterfront. Islanders lined up and waiting to see the restored product, I thought. The taxi driver dropped me off, and I found the Rasta.

"'Ere we ah go," he said, smiling.

I noticed someone had painted a name on the rear: *Marcus Garvey*. One of the founders of the back to Africa movement a long time ago. I paced the length of the ship, trying to come to figure out what exactly it was they were doing.

"This is insane," I protested. The Rasta nodded again.

"Massive insanity," he agreed. I briskly walked away to get a better view of the deck.

An old woman in a green shawl stood just under the forecastle. A young boy in a green and white uniform from the school just up the street stepped in to the front of the deck. Her old withered hands reached out to give him a sip from the green gourd she held. He shivered and fainted, crumpling in on himself, then rolling onto the deck. I could see the tiny chest rise with a slowing rhythm of breath, until the child fell still. My stomach flip-flopped with memories of stories of mass suicides.

The woman next in line, maybe his mother, took the liquid just as calmly. Behind her a policeman waited his turn.

As soon as they lay limp on the deck two men would bear the unconscious down into the ship's holds.

The silent ritual repeated itself. I whirled upon the Rasta by my side.

"What is this? What are you doing?" I demanded, heart pounding.

"They sleep zombie-style 'till we ah come there."

"Where?" I asked.

"Land of milk an' honey." He shrugged. "Or anywhere else.

A new place. They will wake in Zion."

"But why *this* ship?" I wanted to know.

"We ah bring we history with we. We face it, not run from it."

I made my way to the hull and touched it. It sang now, full of energy. It sounded like a temple of Buddhist monks, an *ooom* sound that hinted at deep power.

My dispassion faltered for a moment. I was trying to think about work, rational facts, anything but deal with what was happening around me.

"I have to go," I said. I was expected to return soon back out at Sombrero Island; I had to leave tomorrow. What could I do here, when even the police were lined up?

"You missin' it," the Rastaman said. He looked disappointed.

I turned away and walked back to the taxi. My hand trembled as I opened the door.

A slave ship could hold maybe four hundred bodies stacked in the worse imaginable manner. Yet it seemed that most of the population of the island stood waiting their turn to be led into the hold.

Impossible.

I slept fitfully that night until the deep *ooom* called me. I sat up, stood, and walked to the pool. The night was deathly quiet, and the clouds twisted in long strands above. The moon shone full on the shimmering harbor water, and lights blazed across the massive natural amphitheater of the harbor and curving backbone of the island's mountains.

Anchored in the air above the town was the ship. As I watched it cast itself free and floated up over the hill. The long streamers of cloud that usually just scraped the tip of Crown Mountain, the highest point on the island, seemed to reach down and take the ship up into their depths and out of sight.

It's a dream, I told myself, grabbing the railing. The cold metal railing told me different.

*

I woke up the next morning nervous. Today I was to take the water taxi from the hotel's dock into town where Ottley was to be waiting with the powerboat's keys. From there I'd go back to St. Croix. Then fly to Florida.

Now, waiting by the dock, the taxi already late, I knew I hadn't been dreaming. I couldn't see the slave ship way off in the distance on the waterfront. Only bare concrete. No cars moved through the street.

Hours later, after wandering throughout the deserted hotel to find something to eat, I walked down to the waterfront. The entire island had gotten into the boat yesterday and left. I understood that. Where they were going I still was not sure. I sat on the concrete rim of the waterfront, trying to explain to the wind why methane booster rockets were more efficient than kerosene, but I couldn't remember, and it didn't matter really. The entire waterfront, loud and bustling, lay dead quiet. I remembered other busy cities I'd lived in. I remembered production deadlines and dirt-free clean-suits, laptops and cellular modems, and being asked to have the numbers on the desk by the next morning.

A tiny wooden skiff bumped up against the large truck tires hung off the edge of the concrete to protect the ferries. I looked down. The green, red, and yellow letters read *Little Garvey.* My hand started to tremble again, and I wished I still had another joint with me.

The skiff had a bench in the middle, and two pegs on either side to put the oars between. It bobbed and hit the tire in rhythm with the swell. I carefully clambered in, untying the rope, and pushed off from the waterfront. Somehow they had all managed to subvert that horrible legacy, the slave ship and what it represented from the past, and take it with them proudly into a new future.

How?

I wanted to try.

I set the oars between the two pegs, closed my eyes, and leaned back. The oars bit into the water, the small boat began to move. Trust, I figured, was important. And belief.

I began to row.

SHOGGOTHS IN TRAFFIC

WE STOLE THE cherry red 1984 Corvette at noon, when Random was inside the strip club for Tuesday's Wings and Things and otherwise occupied. At one we stopped behind a Denny's to swap the plates, even though it felt dangerous to have paused, knowing that Random would be standing in the badly maintained asphalt parking lot staring at where he'd left the 'vette and coming to certain conclusions.

"It's okay," Abony said as I held the license plate in place and she screwed it on. "Take deep breaths."

"We stole a car from a fucking drug dealer," I said, voice quavering.

Technically we'd repossessed the damn car. Abony had jimmied the car door and popped the lock in a second. She'd worked a roadside assistance gig for five years and had gotten pretty damn quick at it on older model cars. I went in with the screwdriver and hammer to crack the ignition open and jumpstart it.

Not gonna lie: the adrenaline kicked in pretty hard when I swung out onto the road, rear tires smoking under the faded GIRLS GIRLS GIRLS sign.

By the time the letters in the mirror were too small to read, I wanted to throw up.

The goal was to get the car from Chicago down to Miami. Twenty hours straight shot, each of us taking turns to drive. Bathroom stops only. Once there: turn the car over, collect our fee, then vanish for the West Coast.

"Random is going to kill us," I said to Abony as she stood up.

"He doesn't know it was us. As long as he doesn't catch up to us." Abony's hair clips tinkled against each other as she turned back to me. "A hundred grand, Trent. We just have to get to Miami."

As long as he doesn't catch us, I thought.

South of Gary and halfway down toward Indianapolis on I-65, we pulled over because I had the shakes. Abony took the wheel.

"I'm scared, too," she said.

I couldn't stop looking in the mirrors. We'd agreed to drive exactly two miles over the speed limit. Not exactly the limit—that was suspicious. Not just under it. Couldn't risk being pulled over, as our plates and registration wouldn't hold up under a computer check from the cops. We were rolling dice here.

Abony's glasses glinted in sunlight as she looked over at me.

"A hundred grand."

It was our mantra. Our guiding light.

She'd first named the sum while we were inches deep in mud alongside a freeway, the tow truck behind us stabbing the night with its yellow emergency lights, struggling to replace a blown out tire on some Iowa grandma's 2016 Corolla.

The rain was seeping through my poncho, dropping long streams of ice cold water down my back and ass crack. I slipped. Jammed my hand against the hubcap in the mud and sliced it open. I'd scattered the lug nuts in the puddles.

While we'd both swore and grubbed about in the mud looking for the bolts, she'd looked at me. "Man, I'm tired of this shit. I've been out here, inches away from being run over by these fucking idiots. I'm still living in my aunt's spare room and I can't hardly pay my student loans."

I found four of the five nuts. I bled all over them as I threaded them back on to get the replacement tire in place.

"What would you do with a hundred grand?" Abony had asked me.

"I'd go live near the ocean. California."

"That money won't get you shit out there. That's for rich folk."

"I just want to live near the ocean for a bit. You know, like Venice Beach." I dropped the old lady's car back down.

"You're gonna run out of money in weeks."

"Spent most of my life in trailers on the edges of dead-ass towns," I told her. "Even just a few weeks of beach would be worth it. You going in on lotto tickets with me?"

She'd shaken the water off her glasses. "Nah."

We'd gotten coffee at a diner a few miles up the street to dry off and wait for another call from dispatch. After a while of watching something eating at her, she'd leaned forward. "I hear you did a few years for GTA, right?"

I stared at the coffee. "Left Pennsylvania to try and start over after I got out. It's not good money. It was just part of the hustle." Meth, cocaine, weed, hubcaps, radios, and then one day whole cars. The older shit I stole barely ever made more than a few hundred a vehicle.

Abony and I had been driving the tow truck as a team ever since Olaf had been jumped and mugged when out by himself last year on a call. She must have come to think of me as reliable, because she leaned over the table. "I know where to get a hundred thou by repossessing a car."

"Repossessing or stealing?"

"It's complicated."

Now I looked across at her, jaw clenched with determination. I'm sure a lot of folk assumed Abony would know how to steal a car, but she only knew how to jimmy a door because she'd worked roadside service. She'd started out answering the phones, the only job she had found after college. Then one night Craig didn't show up to ride and she offered to go out with me because miles out in the dark on the late shift paid better than phones.

Fifty thousand would let her pay off her loans. Let her help her aunt with the house in Chicago. The neighborhood was getting gentrified. The taxes were getting jacked up.

My cheap Android phone chirped. The GPS began giving us alternate directions, routing us off I-65.

"Think we should stay on?" I asked.

She glanced at the phone. "How long a delay?"

I had been looking up ahead at the highway, trying to see if there were stopped cars up ahead. Looking back down I read the screen. "It says we save half an hour if we get off the highway."

I could see her doing the math. We were maybe an hour ahead of Random, who would likely be racing out along the most direct route to Miami. He knew where the car was headed. He would be breaking speed limits. We'd spent, what, five minutes changing the plates?

We couldn't afford delays.

Abony took the exit, the Corvette happily hugging the curve of the offramp as we slowed and spiraled onto a two-lane county road.

She hit the brakes and slowed to a near stop. "What the hell is this?"

A burly man in a leather jacket, chaps, and the usual long beard waved at us from a row of orange traffic cones in the middle of the road. I spotted a Harley off to the side of the road with a small trailer attached to the back.

"You need to go back!" the man shouted. "Back to the high-way!"

I rolled down my window. "The phone says there's an accident?"

"Ain't no fucking accident, brother," the man said, starting to wave at a semi coming along down the ramp after us. "Get back on the highway."

"That's no highway worker," Abony said. "Something's . . ."

The semi behind us didn't slow, it swerved around us. Maybe the driver hadn't been paying attention and didn't realize we were stopped. Tires screamed, the trailer wobbled, and I instinctively pulled back against the chair and waited for the impact.

Metal and rubber whipped past my window, and burned rubber floated into the Corvette, making us cough. The semi downshifted, roared, and then continued on down the road through the cones.

The biker lay on the side of the road, arms and legs outstretched.

Abony was out of the car in an instant. "It clipped him!"

"Shit!" I crawled over her side of the car and out onto the side of the road.

The man groaned. There was blood all over his leather jacket, and dripping from his beard. He gurgled a bit and I wanted to throw up.

"Shit," I said again. "What do we do? We call 911, right?"

"Uh . . ." Abony looked around. "We're in a stolen car. You have a record."

"Jesus." I grabbed my head. "Jesus. But we gotta call 911."

Abony suddenly looked cold and distant. "Even if they don't think to run our details, you want to be standing here when Ransom and his crew get routed through by the same GPS. They got phones just like you, Trent."

"Fuck. We can't just leave him there. That ain't right."

She stood up. "No, we take him to the ER. Drop him off, and take off. We're in the middle of fucking children of the corn territory, right? It'll be faster to get him there ourselves then wait for an ambulance. This isn't the city, there won't be flashing lights here in five minutes."

Relief flooded me.

Then I looked back at the car. "Abony, ain't no back seats in that car."

She was already walking back to it, though. She popped the

hatchback and started throwing the extra food, water, and other shit for the twenty hour drive out onto the shoulder, right by the $1,000 fine for littering sign.

"Help me lift him in," she said.

The biker was short, heavy, and we hit his head twice getting him there. We had to curl him up, fetal position. I'd watched enough medical shows to know that if he had internal injuries that wasn't going to help him much.

It occurred to me that if he died back there, we'd have a dead guy in the hatchback trunk of a car, with a window and all.

"What about his bag?" I asked, pointing to a backpack that had been knocked clean off the man farther down the road.

"Toss it in the back with him," Abony said.

But we didn't have the time to wait for an ambulance or police to ask us questions. Abony was right. Out of breath, something in my back tweaked and screaming from the awkward angle of trying to shove the biker into the trunk, I asked the phone's GPS for directions to the nearest ER.

It give us a route straight ahead.

The truck had already scattered the cones or crushed them. We drove past them onto the country road.

The biker groaned and stirred, his head right behind my head rest. I'd rested it against some bags of chips for cushioning. They crunched, releasing the smell of salt and vinegar into the air as one of the bags burst.

"It's okay, we're getting you to a hospital," I said.

"Check the phone again," Abony ordered, voice tense. Ten minutes following the 3D map and we were way out on a flat plain of skeletal recently-harvested corn fields. "I think we were closer to a town back at the off-ramp."

I started fiddling with the phone, trying to zoom out of the map while it kept giving us instructions. "I hate it when the GPS does that."

"Yeah. It feels like it's taking us around the edge of the town," Abony said. "We're just making a big loop. It's confused."

Normally, it'd do my pride some harm to be taking orders so much. But Abony had the college degree. I may have constantly tried to mess with her, show her that some elite book smarts didn't mean shit out here in the greasy real world. But after a year working as a team, I'd stopped giving her shit and started giving her my attention.

I'd driven hundreds of miles to run away from my past in Pennsylvania. I'd sworn to stay on the straight, even if I was always broke. Abony said I needed to learn some self control.

Well, I hadn't ended up in drugs and stealing cars because of my moderate nature.

But I'd turned it around. Cleaned up. Learned my lesson.

So I'd told Abony to fuck off the first time she told me about the car. Her cousin had done a job for Random and heard the story. That the car had been taken from a big drug dealer in Miami. It had been his dad's car, and a project they'd both worked on. It was *important* to the man. And Random stole it after some falling about a smuggling corridor coming up from Miami through Kentucky.

Random drove it around Chicago, through the salt in the winter, and potholes. He drove the damn Corvette everywhere until it looked like an old piece of shit, but kept it running. A trophy.

Javier, in Miami, offered a hundred thousand dollars to anyone who got it back to him.

A repossession to the rightful owner, Abony said.

She was supposed to be the smart, college educated one. But a month of idly talking about the money and how we could get the car wormed its way into my brain. At first, it had been a running joke as we drove from stranded motorist to stranded motorist.

Then it became something we nervously laughed about.

And finally, I told her about the strip club and Random's love of Tuesday's Wings and Things. And blushed when she asked how I knew.

"This is taking us around the town," Abony said, more confident as the GPS routing had us take another turn. "Look up the hospital on your phone."

A bloody, hairy arm grabbed my shoulder just as I was raising the phone up. I screamed and dropped it, Abony swerved as she looked back. The biker, head crammed against the glass of the hatchback, pushed himself between us.

"That damn thing won't ever take you to the hospital until it's completed the symbol you're driving," the man said, blood misting the air inside the car as he spoke. "Once the summoning pattern is complete, you'll be released. You have to stop the car, or everyone in this town will be in dire . . ."

He started coughing blood everywhere.

We stopped by the side of the road again. Abony grabbed my phone and started hunting for the hospital as I unbuckled.

The biker was shifting around and had popped the hatch. Blood smeared the glass from his coughs.

"Man, you're hurt, you need to stay here. Let us get you to the hospital," I said.

"No, I'm okay," the man said.

"Don't let him out," Abony shouted.

He tumbled out onto the grassy shoulder before I could get around the Corvette to stop him.

"Sir, you need to come with us. You can sit in my seat," I offered.

He staggered and collapsed, sitting on a mound of mud and gravel. "It's not too late to save people," he told me, his voice calm. He had grabbed his bag. "How far are we from the bridge?"

"The bridge?"

"There's a bridge over there. We can still stop the traffic from completing the summoning if we blow it." He opened the bag between his legs and I jumped back. Those little foil-covered bricks, the wires. That was like, C4, or something.

This guy was some kind of biker terrorist.

"Abony . . ." I said, backing up.

"There's a hospital just . . ." she saw the open bag from the car window. "Oh fuck."

"No, no," the biker waved his hands and coughed more blood down that crazy long beard. "I need to explain. I need you to help me blow that bridge."

"I seen this," I said out of the corner of my mouth to Abony. "It's like, bath salts, right? Some crazy heavy shit he's on. I mean, he's hit by a truck and talking about blowing up a bridge."

"Look," the biker said. "I'm a wizard, got it?"

"You mean like the KKK?" I asked. "They had a biker crew like that the town over in—"

"No, not the fucking KKK," the man said, visibly frustrated. "I'm a goddamn magician. Like . . ." he started coughing blood again and folded forward. He pushed himself back up to sitting with visible effort.

"Get in the car, we gotta go," Abony said. "This is some fucked up shit here and we gotta go. We can't be involved in this."

But the old biker reached into the grass and scratched out a circle with his finger, digging at the grass until his fingernail popped clean and began to bleed. He drew more symbols into the grass, then spat blood into the palm of his hand and pressed it into the dirt.

I was rooted in place, the madness of what I was seeing holding me in thrall. Abony was frozen as well.

The biker began to run his thumb along the pattern drawn in the mud and blood. He traced the whole thing once, then started it over and traced it again, compulsively.

He was mad.

But each time he pushed his thumb around the sigil, he sped

up, energy flowing into him. Seven times, eight, he kept repeating the motions.

The pattern lit up with blue fire. Like when you poured grain alcohol out onto the table and lit it up for laughs.

But the fire didn't fade out. It strengthened. Turned white hot. The ground burned but didn't catch fire. And inside the complex swoops and swirls something flickered in the dark.

For a brief moment, a tiny swirl of tentacles and otherness hung in the air over the road's shoulder. It looked like something you'd see on a deep sea expedition special that ran after Shark Week.

The moment the creature appeared the biker threw a handful of mud into the corner of the sigil. The lines broken, the fire that wasn't fire guttered out. A tiny howl of frustration from inside the circle hung in the air between us all.

We got the biker, the wizard, into my side of the Corvette. He put the C4 between his legs. I cleaned up the blood from the hatch and back of the car as best I could and curled up in a ball and let Abony shut the hatch down on me.

It was claustrophobic as hell.

"You see a lot of biker gangs rolling the highways," the wizard wheezed. "But what you don't know is that a lot of them are wizards. The long beards, their steeds a bike, and the nomadic ways, it all works."

The wizard's name, he said, was Ozymandias. "Yeah to answer the obvious question, I knew Shelley," he said. But I didn't know who Shelley was, though Abony nodded as if that meant something.

"What the fuck was that thing you made in the air?" I asked from behind them both.

"It was a summoning. A pattern. You know how you can draw a cube on paper, even though paper is flat. Two dimensional? You can do the same with higher dimensions."

"Like a pentagram?" I asked. I'd seen a lot of that stuff on some goth kids.

"Kind of. That's an abstraction, not an actual higher dimensional summoning pattern." He paused to wipe blood from his chin with a handkerchief. "You also need to charge it with motion to crack the space between worlds. In the past, you had to do that waving your arms and following the drawing. Took a lot of training. It took me almost a hundred years."

"Oh come on, you're not that old," I protested.

Our wizard, or insane biker, shrugged. "In the old days, it was hard to find the patterns and charge them up. But, as technology began to change and get better, folks started summoning things from behind the veil with machines. We do our best to hunt down and stop the worst. Occasionally things get out. Zodiac Killer, Highway of Tears. Things that go bump in the night."

Abony caught my eyes in the mirror. "Why were you stopping traffic?"

"GPS," the wizard said, stroking his long beard.

"The alternate route?" Abony nodded.

"Wait, what?" I wasn't following.

"It's traffic, Trent. Think about the roads from above the air, like a clover leaf exit."

I did that. Then thought about the pattern the wizard had drawn in the ground. Motion. Patterns. Summoning. "Holy. Shit."

The wizard was breathing deeply. "We started noticing that apps, GPS, were creating patterns. Test routes, routine things. But someone is either hacking them, or the companies are in on it. Whatever the reason, we're not sure about it yet, they're charging summoning patterns using diverted automobile traffic."

I thought about all the times a GPS would offer an alternate route and I'd take it without thinking.

"If I could summon something dangerous with just a foot-wide pattern, what do you think a fifteen mile wide pattern could do, in terms of breaches to another universe?" the wizard asked.

We were all silent.

"You were trying to stop it with those cones, turning traffic back?" I asked.

"A big pattern takes a lot of traffic to charge it. It's not active yet. I tried to stop it with the cones. But I could also blow the bridge just another mile down the road. Look, I'm not asking you to help me. Taking me to a hospital won't do me any good if the fabric of reality gets ripped apart while I'm there. Drop me off on the bridge. I can interrupt the pattern, stop it from being charged. Do that, and we can save an entire town from something monstrous."

We drove on in silence.

It would take two minutes to get to the bridge.

I had the hospital up on the map, but no directions to it. I could get us there.

Abony's fingers gripped the steering wheel tightly and I looked up at the sun through the hatch's glass I was curled up tightly under, grateful for my tiny, bony frame. Was it my imagination, or did the sun just waver slightly?

Ten minutes later we left the bridge as Abony revved the Corvette up and we risked breaking the speed limit to put craziness as far behind us as we could.

"Did we really see that . . . thing?" I asked.

Abony bit her lip and didn't say a thing.

"We did the right thing, right?" My voice cracked slightly.

"I'm just thinking," Abony said. "That the truck that hit him, it was one of those new automated ones. The self driving trucks that they just started allowing on the roads."

"Jesus." If what happened was real, it could get way worse when the cars just drove themselves. Apocalyptic, even.

"And I'm also thinking," Abony said, proving once again that she was the smart one, "that Random is only five to fifteen minutes behind us after all those stops. And his GPS will give him the same route as the one we took."

In the mirror, there was a flash of light.

I didn't know if it was a bridge exploding or another universe folding itself out over the small town we left behind us.

Either way, it was eighteen more hours to Miami.

DEATH'S DREADLOCKS

SOMETIMES, **LATE INTO** the dead night, Old Ma takes the long locks of my hair and massages them between her callused yellowed palms. Such fine dreadlocks, she tells me. Such fine young shoulders they rest on.

But some of the old people are scared of dreads, she whispers into my ears. Don't mind them.

And I know why.

There was an old, very old, bush tale about the shadowy man some called Death. He was a fat giant who lived deep in the forest, teeth stinky with the smell of rotted flesh. In all of time he had never brushed his hair, and the knotted locks grew out into the underbrush for people to find.

It was a good story.

When I was young, out of the corner of my eye, sometimes I could see the long root of a tree, and just past it, I would just see the edge of a long creeping dreadlock. I would avoid that space.

Once I got older, and times became hard, I saw more and more dreadlocks that sat right out in the open of the land. Old Ma's gift, and curse, to me.

And that is how I know why the few old ones left look at me with a strange eye.

*

Times, the old men said, were getting hard.

Really, we replied, mockingly. They were easy before?

Old Ma lifted us up and away from the old men, their wrinkled faces host to patient flies immune to leathery handed swats, and she told us to "hush."

Outside the bush the dust came and hung over the camps. And the wheels of Toyota mini-trucks with Kalichnikovs welded to their beds and our brothers manning the wicked heavy guns with wide grins, the wheels of these vans kicked up even more dust.

Ho Kuabi, we shouted.

Hey little brothers, he yelled.

Good day, Mouwanat, we shouted.

Mouwanat ignored us, sitting with his new friends around a barrel with AK-47s spilling over the side. They spit in the dust and spoke of grown up things.

That is the way it is with older brothers.

On the way home we passed the relief tent, dusty red cross on the side almost ready to lose itself in the gray fold flapping in the wind.

One of the workers, a pretty but very white lady with a red nose asked us if we know about the Lord Our God. Many of the relief workers had little pieces of paper with pictures waiting in their pockets. I'd even read one once with Old Ma, and we'd giggled and giggled. Who else but a white man would believe in a god born in the east, describe his looks in their holy writings as if he were an Arab, and then paint him as if he was what one of the older relief men called a hippy?

And apparently old white men don't even like "hippies," Old Ma told us. Why would these men both love and hate their god so? I wondered.

Anyway, the relief workers didn't understand. Old Ma and us would never insult any god by believing in just one god, because that would leave all the other gods out. So like most other times, we thanked the worker for her interest in our souls, but pointed out that our own souls were really our own business, and none of hers. Which I think offended her, but no less than her own words offended us.

When we left with the rice, Old Ma said, well, at least they don't kill us for saying no anymore.

I'd laughed, thinking she was being funny. Then I remembered Old Ma was . . . very old. Maybe she remembered different times. I swallowed. Did they really used to kill people to accept their god? Would their god even accept such souls?

Would you even want to spend time with a god that such people worshipped?

I shuddered.

Old Ma, I asked. Were times better, back then?

Old Ma shifted the rice on her head and didn't look down.

Times, she said, shift around, go from here to there, and are often what you make of them. We've had worse times, we've had better times. No matter what times they are, there are always people outside the land who come in and tell us what times to have.

And with that she walked faster, her bare callused feet slapping the ground hard, kicking up small puffs of dust.

Old Ma was old. Very old. But she could walk like a demon. Sweat poured from my forehead and I felt faint when we found our tent. There were many other tents all around us, and some men in jeeps asked us who we where, and were we where going.

They walked us to the tent, winked at Old Ma, then turned to me.

You are a little old to be walking with an old woman. You should ride with us. Be strong. Kill our enemies.

Who are our enemies? I asked. Old Ma smiled.

The men conferred among themselves, but could not come up with a single enemy. The enemy, they finally announced, are all who oppose us.

Then since I . . . I would have said: oppose you; I must be your enemy. But it was a foolish thing to say. Old Ma saw my words even before I did, and spoke.

This one looks old for his age, she said. And I clamped my mouth shut.

The men laughed at us, then left to climb into their jeep and harass someone else. Old Ma shot me a nasty look, then crawled into the tent to start a dung fire and make us rice.

It is a hard thing to eat rice over and over and over again. The little brother and I left to hunt birds with a slingshot. A woman in red stripes stopped us at the edge of the tents.

Where is your mother? She demanded. She looked at my dreads with suspicion.

We have no parents, little brother said.

Then who takes care of you?

Old Ma.

Who?

Old Ma, I interjected. The old lady in the tent cooking rice. And we pointed Old Ma out, sitting with her legs crossed in front of the fire.

The witch takes care of you? The woman shakes her head. You should not go out past the tents, you will die.

Not that easily, I protested. We can both see the dreadlocks.

The woman looked at us sideways, her hands on her hips, mouth slightly open.

Why do you think we never walk in a straight line? Little brother laughed. And we ran out into the dust, leaving the woman to forget to scream at us.

*

Old Ma came out of the jungle during one of the wars, when Mom and Dad died. She took us under her flabby arms and told us stories, dried our tears, and fed us some soup. She tried to take us back to the forest one night, but Mouwanat started crying, and the relief workers found us.

Later, men in trucks packed us up and took us to the tents. There were explosions in the trees, making us so scared we cried until our lungs hurt, and Old Ma looked back out past our village clearing and cried with us.

The tent people didn't like her, because she had a necklace with bones and things on it. They would spit in her face, and Old Ma ignored them, muttering things under her breath and sighing to the old gods. The problem with casting at them, she told me, is that they don't believe, and so I cannot affect them.

But I believe, Old Ma, I would say.

I know, child.

So she would explain to me and little brother why, just under the surface of the infertile land, we could see the long snaking black strands, the dreadlocks that coiled around everything.

When I saw them push into the trees and jungle, she told us, I knew Death came for me, and I had to follow them out. And that was when I found you! She would tell us about the old gods, and the story about Death and how his dreadlocks now draped out across the whole land like a spider's web.

We didn't find any birds to kill with our stones, and other boys were out looking. Tired and dusty, little brother and I returned. On our way back we heard gunfire, and the crackle of tents in flames.

Dreadlocks, black and sinewy, moved just under the ground away from the relief tents.

Stepping carefully over them, we walked to the tents. Men in jeeps rode around, and one of them recognized me.

See, he said. Ride with us little one, and you will vanquish our enemies.

All around, the white relief workers lay with dreadlocks curled around their bodies, the tightly wound hair soaking up the red blood oozing from their torn bodies. I recognized the pretty lady who asked about our souls.

The men in jeeps spun more dust into the sky.

Late, late, into the night, I woke little brother up.

Times are going to get worse, I said.

He agreed with a nod.

The relief tents fed us, but now the rice is in flames. We are many miles from Old Ma's jungle. People are being crazy. I don't think any more relief people will come if they keep getting killed, and so we will starve.

Little brother agreed.

So I must go out and find us a new place, or food, I said.

I will go with you, little brother declared.

No. I will go alone.

So little brother helped me pack, then gave me a small portion of dried beef he had stolen from somewhere in the tents and hidden under his bedsack. I tried to make him keep it, but he insisted, and we cried together and hugged. Then I left.

Far from the tents, on my own in the morning cool, I watched the great ochre sun rise above the distant mountains, and paid homage. I crouched on the sand and waited, and waited, for a plan.

As I watched, two vans chased a jeep across the flat dust. They shot and shot until the jeep exploded. They fired at it some more, then left. When I reached the jeep I recognized the men.

One stirred and looked at me with one eye.

Dreadlocks circled around and sniffed.

Is Death the instigator of all this, I wondered, or merely just circling around like a buzzard?

I followed the locks. I started at the burned out jeep, and ended up near the foot of the mountains. They stretched up towards the heavens above me. There was even some scraggly jungle around.

The dreadlocks all converged here. They all wound themselves towards a large bunker. The concrete was the same color as the hard earth around it.

When I walked in, the smell of rotting animals dizzied me. I steadied myself and walked on through many rooms. They were sumptuous rooms, tall and gilded with glittering objects, jewelry that must have once adorned beautiful men and women.

I followed the thick shanks of dung-smelling hair into a grand pit of a throne room. The air was dark, and dust hung still on everything. The hair all ran up into the center of the room, up the back and shoulders of a giant, as dark as the shadows. The giant's belly had rolls and rolls of fat that overflowed onto his crossed feet, and when he stirred, all the dreadlocks leading to the room shifted and coiled around the corners like snakes. It made me shiver, and I wished that times were different, and that I had never seen all the things that I had seen this day.

Hello, children, he said.

Who else is here? I demanded in a shaky voice. A small form stepped out from the hallway behind me.

My name is Kofi, the boy whimpered. Please don't hurt me. I followed. I was hoping I could steal some bread, or rice.

The giant, his dreadlocks shifting about us, laughed the deepest, most fetid smelling, belly laugh. A thousand TVs fastened to the walls flickered on, bathing everything in a cold blue light.

Of course I have bread, and rice, he said. But why would you want such boring and tasteless foods, when I have much better.

He took from his side two large brown paper bags. They were stained on the bottom with grease. Kofi ran forward and snatched the bag, impossibly small against the giant's hand.

The bags smelled heavenly, and Kofi pulled a meat sandwich from his bag. There were more inside. He began to eat them rapidly. The giant flicked the other bag at me, and I caught it. As I opened it, my small stomach growling with excitement, I thought; if those are Death's dreadlocks, then this giant is obviously Death. And if he is Death, then there is no doubt that something is not right about this food.

I decided I would wait and watch what happened to Kofi. And as I watched Kofi, the giant, Death, also watched Kofi. Kofi ate, and ate, and ate, until he grew heavy with all the food, and lay down against the side of the room.

If you will not eat, the giant said, why don't you enjoy yourself. And the TV closest to me started to show movies. Pick a movie, the giant said. Any movie.

So I watched men leap around buildings and fight each other, until the flickering made my eyes heavy, and against my will I drifted to sleep.

When I woke I found my wrists bound with a heavy iron. The giant chuckled to himself in the corner, and my heart thudded with fear.

What is going on here? I demanded.

The giant chuckled some more, and picked his teeth with a bone. He smiled at me, and his smile carried a rank, rotten smell. Like that of a man left in the desert to bloat and be picked at by carrion.

You have pretty dreadlocks, just like me, the giant said. He leaned forward with a blast of a belch, and touched the top of my head with his smallest finger. I wanted to vomit as the giant leaned back, still picking his teeth with the piece of bone.

Where is Kofi? I asked.

He went to play, the giant said. He snapped the bone in half and tossed it aside. I shuddered, for I knew it was most surely Kofi's last remains. I shook even harder, imagining what it would be like to die under the giant's greasy, chubby, fingers. More than anything I wanted to run from the dank bunker out into the hot dust outside. But I was trapped.

Please don't eat me, I cried out, holding my manacled wrists into the air.

Why not, the giant demanded angrily. I can do with you as I please.

I thought hard and quick, looking to save my skin.

I have brothers! I yelled.

The giant was interested. His eyes gleamed, and I saw my chance.

I said: my brothers are warriors, and plump with victory and full of life. They are young and strong, with supple dark skin and tight curly hair.

The giant drooled and swallowed noisily. He pulled at my manacles with a dreadlock, like it was a tentacle of some sort, and I stumbled closer. I did not breathe, scared to smell his stench, as his nasty breath wet my face.

Bring them to me, he declared with moist lips, and I will spare your life.

When I returned to the tents, my skin was dry and dusty, and my ribs showed beneath my skin. Little brother grabbed my legs, and all my brothers stepped out from the tent. They hugged me and gave me water, then hugged me more.

I was surprised to see Mouwanat cry and hug me the most.

That is the way it is with older brothers.

Where have you gone? Kuabi asked.

Who did this to you? Mouwanat demanded.

And little brother said in a small, wavering, voice, the Old Ma is gone. She walked out into the night and never came back. We think men have killed her. Then we all hugged and cried again.

Brothers, I said, after grieving Old Ma. I was captured by a giant that showed me shows on TV, and gave me food in a paper bag.

Little brother took the bag I pulled from my waist and looked at it. He wiped his forefinger on the grease and sniffed it.

Is that a bad thing? my brothers asked.

In response I opened my robes, and showed them the dreadlock that had lodged itself in the hollow place in my chest, just below my heart. For Death was not stupid; he had me just as surely as if I were still in the bunker with the blue light.

All raised by Old Ma, my brothers saw the dreadlock, and cursed and swore.

What shall we do? they all asked me.

You should follow me, I said. We will face Death.

For I had made something of a plan during the long trip back, all the while ignoring the evil-sweet smells of the bag on my waist. Old Ma told us stories of tricksters who had been trapped by Death, and jabbed him with spears to kill him. We would do the same.

We drove back to the bunker, after bribing a warrior with our bag of evil-sweet food. The man never saw the faint dreadlock clinging to the bag, and though we felt sorry for him, our compassion fled as we saw him eat the food so fast he grew sick.

As we drove we sang together. Old songs, new songs, and some in between. We kicked up dust, and drove over dreadlocks bravely. Here they were thick in the ground, and we could hear the sounds of war in the distance, feeding the ever-hungry fatness of Death. And when we drove up to the bunker with our truck, my brothers leaped from its sides and ran down into the darkness to face the giant, defiance in their eyes.

Ho, the giant said, dreadlocks squirming with eagerness among the sides of the walls. Little brother's eyes opened wide, and he looked around at the TVs. A table filled with food and fruit sat near the giant.

Come, eat, the giant beckoned to us.

I turned to my brothers and nodded. We all turned weapons onto the giant. I fired a small pistol at the giant's face, and watched his cheek shatter with a great gout of blood.

Kuabi threw grenades into the folds of the giant's belly, and the flesh flew apart with a great fart of sludginess.

Little brother threw stones.

Mouwanat held his flamethrower forward and a great stream of fire leapt out and struck the giant. Fat burned and slid to the ground, and the giant's arms beat against the sides of the walls. His dreadlocks slid up into his body, and kept sliding and sliding. Mouwanat turned his flame to them, and the dreadlocks lit up and spread crackling blue fire all over the bunker.

We burned and shot until there was nothing left to burn and shoot, and we walked out with smiles on our faces. We have killed death, we celebrated among ourselves.

And saved our brother, Mouwanat said.

Outside the dreadlocks had dried up, and were rusting into the sand.

If we killed Death, Kuabi thought out loud, aren't *we* immortal?

From by us came a loud chuckle. We turned, and there stood Old Ma, barefoot and sweaty, by the side of the jeep.

You can't kill Death, children! She walked over to me and put a hand on my chest. She ran her hands through my locks, and kissed my forehead. She put a salve on my chest, and it raised my spirits and let me breathe easier.

My brothers embraced Old Ma, and shouted and cried to see her alive.

But Old Ma, little brother cried, what about the stories you told us? Where they killed Death with spears?

Those, Old Ma said, turning away from me. Those were just stories. Stories to teach you, stories to help you be brave, stories to warn you, but still, just stories. Everyone tells stories. All over the world they tell stories, to help explain why things are just the way they are. Death will always be with us.

Kaubi said, if these were just stories, how could we see his dreadlocks?

Just stories? Old Ma snorted, as she shooed us all back into the jeep. Kuabi started to drive us off across the land. Crowded around her, we listened as she spoke.

Stories can build up an empire, or strike down a people. You can spell the most powerful spell, ease a friend's hurt, or break an enemy. Stories make you believe.

But how can we fight Death, little brother shouted, his eyes misting.

Old Ma took his hand. I told you a story to help you see the ugly Death in our land. But now you have to look for it on your own. There are other Deaths to face, other stories. Ones more cruel, others hopeful, kind. You have heard mine.

I looked around the jeep. My brothers had left their weapons with Death. We jounced on through the dust.

I nodded.

Old Ma was right. She had helped us, come from the bush to guide us. And now we had our own story to tell.

Many miles passed, and Old Ma waved us towards the forest, where we could hide and be safe. As I looked all around us, the world seemed eerie and still. A dead quiet had fallen. Even the dust hardly dared stir.

We had been brave, and faced Death. Now we had to be even braver and face the things that Death fed off. We could not fight

Death with weapons. Death was not something we could burn, or knife. These things made it stronger, harder to see.

And we could never kill Death. We could only make it gentler, kinder, a friend who came after many years. But this Death would only come to us when we changed the current story, the one with Kalichnikovs, dreadlocks, and fear, with the dust heavy in the air as it was kicked up by wheels.

BRICKOMANCER

THERE'S A DEMON-POSESSED Karen stalking you as you set the waxed canvas ruck down on the sidewalk with a clink. She thinks you're here to tag one of the walls out behind her remodeled brownstone, and you can see the self-righteous anger brewing in her posture: back rigid with indignation, Ray-Bans pushed up over the blonde highlights, and a confused but redolent Maltese pants from the heat of the Manhattan asphalt from its throne inside a chunky Graco stroller.

"I called the police," the woman snaps.

The Maltese growls at you, and one of the yellow bows holding its hair back flops to the side.

Adorable dog.

"What do you have in there?"

You look down at the bag.

"You have spray cans in there?"

Her voice shakes. She's scared. Looks on the edge of tears, and she's pushing them down by shoving the white hot poker of superiority, nosiness, and entitlement up to buttress the rigid, royalist bearing she projects out onto the world around her.

You look back at the canvas bag full of cheap Krylon cans.

This is going to make painting the anti-summoning symbols

onto the corner of Chewie's bodega really fucking hard.

"You're live on video," the woman says. Her head tweaks back and forth to emphasize her words. "This is why property values suffer here. There's no pride of place—"

She has a lot to say, but you tune her out like you do the Mad Russian when he starts wandering up and down the D train. One hundred streets up the line and a thesis on satellites that take control of your minds. Fun stuff the first few weeks, you split rent with five roommates, but after a while it's just the background noise of the commute, like metal on metal screeches, the sway of the car, and the tired look on the faces of all the houseworkers and nannies from seventeen different countries on the way back up the island to cook dinner for yet another set of hungry mouths.

You look down at the Birkenstocks you scored off the boutique thrift shop around the corner. All the best stuff in the used stores around this place now. Rich people toss out the best stuff. Nice shoes. You found a Gucci purse there that could hold a can for emergency touch-ups, but the ruck is best for more complex work.

But despite the comfortable shoes, you know if you leg it she's gonna send your video to the local police and they'll come knocking at the already-busted-in door on 205th, take you in, and then Yesse's gonna fucking bail you out and tell you all about how you're disappointing your poor, departed mother, God bless her soul and the Mother Mary—

No.

"It's okay." You fold your arms. "Let's wait for the cops."

It's a gamble. A big fucking gamble. Where, you wonder, is Chewie? Because, you swear to God, you're going to shit on his mother's grave if he doesn't show up soon.

You hear the siren warble around the corner. You feel the pit of your stomach lurch. You're imagining all the brutal shit you've heard, and now in this day, you've seen with everyone else on shaky handheld videos. This Karen might yet be setting up to record the next horrible beatdown.

Or worse.

And if those sigils don't get touched up soon, well, the evil gnawing at the back of this Karen's eyes, that dead look behind the colored contacts, that evil would spread out even farther into the world again.

So in the ruck are a set of spray cans and a book of Enochian summoning scripts that your mother spent half her life reverse engineering from the 1500s occultist John Dee's books of angelic script. You'd spend half the day down at the New York Public Library, the Main Branch, past the magnificent lions. She'd read, take notes on a battered old Moleskine, while you colored with crayons and watched the tourists noisily clump on past to take photos against the hand-carved, wooden backdrops.

Sometimes an old white man would stop and stare at you both, your skin as dark as the varnished bookshelves holding the weight of human knowledge. Stuff you thought was old and musty at the time. Mom paid them no mind. "Mija, listen, we have work to do, and getting distracted by them is what they want. They can't touch us in here."

At the time you thought she meant tut-tutting racists couldn't touch you all in the library, so you hid in libraries whenever you could, as if a book could hide you away.

Much later, you come to realize she meant the demons had no power there, because the Main Branch ceilings project nullifying energy that dissipated demonic interventions.

In third grade she got called in because you drew a set of pentagrams and a perfect summoning grid on a poster board for show and tell. When you connected the final Enochian binding call to the fifth cell, the power to the school flickered out.

Just a coincidence, the teacher said. But you couldn't be bringing pentagrams to a Catholic all girls school. No more. They'd put up with this immigrant stuff enough, and young souls were at risk.

They are at risk, your mother agreed. Very much.

Never mind that Becky had a sleep over two weeks ago where everyone used a Ouija board to find out if the boys over at the Episcopalian school liked any of them.

"I don't want any of this for you, Julia," she whispered to you on the subway home. "You shouldn't have been reading those books."

But they're everywhere in that small apartment. When the power went out because she couldn't afford the electric, the candles sat in little dishes on top of books about the occult, flickering away. They seemed more malevolent and mysterious in that yellow light that could never be pinned down, locked in some back and forth eternal struggle with the shadows.

You'd give anything to spend a night again in that old apartment over the widow Lester's creaky old house with no power, the mold crawling back up the wall behind the toilet, the heat baking you so hard the windows warped, and eating baked beans straight out of the scratch and dent can as a curtain of her dark hair fell over whatever occultic book she had ready for the evening.

"I always remember, Mama," you whisper whenever you load the spray paint into your scuffed up ruck. "I'm still doing the work."

"You think you're some kinda fucking Banksy?"

The cop is out of his air conditioned car and already sweating in the heat. The wards are getting battered down, and you can feel an oppressive weight in the air.

This patch of sidewalk behind the bodega and the brownstone is balanced on a knife edge. The people in front of me don't have the tattoos etched in cremated ashes that let them see the tall creature just behind the brick. An armored shell of a demon, a core sigil burning it into being.

It wants souls. It wants to suck the life out our husks.

It wants blood on the street.

You could have run. You could have let it ooze out of the brick and fully possess the people here. But you're betting on Chewie. Because, even though you want to slap the twitch of that woman's lips right off, and you fantasize about taking that cop's hand off his holster to snap it in two, you know it's the energy swirling in the air that has the back of your mouth acidic, your heart hammering, and your vision blurring.

Add more rage into the loop and it'll spin up enough energy to snap the veil between the worlds.

"What the fuck is this?" The cop holds up your notebook, open to a grid diagram.

"Art," you say, voice level. He cuffs you, has you against the car. You shiver with indignation, because none of this should be happening.

He steps forward. That dominating pose, and mirrored sunglasses frame your round, tired face back at you. The fourth-wheel earrings, their pattern just barely able to hold back the demonic energy that spills into the air between you, flash and twinkle.

Those patterns run all over the island. All over the world. Hundreds of years ago, Masonic planners in shadowy rooms behind taverns met to layout the city grid using occult patterns to create energies that would hold entire cities in their grip. In ancient times, they burned cities to the ground for practical reasons: to destroy the portals and energies unleashed by their street grids.

Since the time of Sumer and ancient Babylon, whole populations had been held in thrall by the patterns laid into the corner stones of the first cities. It had never been farming that dragged humanity out of the hunter-gatherer mode, but shamans, their minds grasped by entities far out the guttering lights of dying stars, that established cities long before farming came.

Why did witches live in forests and holy men in caves outside the chaos of cities? Why did Jesus have to live in the wilderness, or the Buddha seek out a tree far from the teeming masses of his India?

Even white people know that here in New York City, Robert Moses and modern day city planners lowered bridges so that buses couldn't go certain places in NYC. The cities today haven't changed much about it redlining, carving up the land in their patterns, they just feel guilty about it and talk about it a lot.

Your mother fought a war in the seventies. "See that car," she'd say, and point out a tagged up, omni-colored subway car with almost no silver poking through the bubbled sigils. "Every time it makes a loop around the city, it reestablishes a closed circuit that protects us."

Once you saw the protective shapes, buried in the work of a generation, you saw that the island was covered in protection.

Now, gentrified block by gentrified block, you had all lost so much of it.

From the finance district out, those people once holding the knowledge, the Romani, the brujas, the old world witches from Ukraine, the hippy crystal-loving artist grandmothers cooking up a cauldron in the back of a squat in the Garment District . . . all forced out by redevelopment.

"We'll lose the soul of the city again, one day," your mother said.

But not here, Mama, you think.

Not entirely yet.

"Oye! What's with the cop?" Chewie shouts from around the corner.

He looks out of breath, his face red, and hovering somewhere between apologetic, which you think is aimed at you, and angry.

The cop sees angry, and pushes me to the side. He's been buried in his rage, and only just now realizes that more people have spilled out onto the street to stare at the scrum of people.

Phones are out. Even retired old Narovka from across the street has the new phone her grandson gave her in hand, and she's shakily recording everything.

"Chewie! Slow down," you snap. You try to get to him, but also, project calm.

"That's Julia!" someone else says. "Why he got Julia handcuffed?"

The rage has spread. The brick wall pulls at them, like a vortex. And the helplessness, the hurt from past arrests of friends, family, people that look like them, it boils around us.

And the thing on the Other Side wants that. It used the Karen at first. Racism was its favorite fuel, an art perfected in the 1800s by its kind. And the cop has been trained to fear us, to use violence as a tool. He's spent his life being told we're the enemy, that any second things could turn.

You can see his eyes dart about. You can see the far back erosion of soul, a lifetime of drip, drip, drip that left the once innocent boy who may have played with a black friend in Kindergarten, but is now surrounded by neighbors who say Those Things, and watches a single news channel that preaches from the dark sanctification of Fear, Subjugation, and Order, and he's trapped in a pattern laid out by suburban planners of swirling ticky-tack developments that created who he is now: someone who comes in from outside of this block to patrol and occupy it.

"I told you," you say calmly, like talking to a wild animal. "I have permission. This is the bodega's wall. That's Chewie."

"Don't film!" the cop shouts at someone. "Get back, you're interfering with an arrest."

But they all have the phones out.

And for all that hatred in the air, you can taste love. Community.

Yeah, you know, it's a whole lot of woo-woo.

But if there is hatred, there must be love. And if there is an individual, there has to be the opposite, right? Community?

These are people you've known your whole life. You've pledged to your mother to keep this block safe. To keep the bodega a castle against the unseen forces that want it gone in favor of a chain. A chain grocery store that would take this point on a line, a pattern that stretches over this country, and complete another part of a dangerous grid that would snatch a small piece of a person's soul every time they stepped into its repetitive similarity.

"Please," Chewie begs, taking a deep breath. "I hire her to

paint my store's logo up there. She's family. Please."

You hate that we have to beg for dignity, beg to be allowed to do what others never even have to ask for.

But the cop shakes his head, broken from the spell as Chewie gets close to him. Chewie's an empath, a healer. He'll get you the right herbs, the right medicine, or listen to you talk at the end of the day about how bad it was. He'll send you on your way with a lightness in your step and a bag of groceries. You can pet his familiar, the bodega cat, on the way out.

"Okay," the cop says.

"Are you fucking kidding me?" The woman rails at the cop, shouting, almost spitting at him.

"Ma'am—"

"Do your *fucking* job!"

Her dog barks at him.

People drift away, a few stop to rub your arm, commiserate. The moment has passed. Chewie hugs you, sweat and Axe deodorant choke you for a moment. "It keeps the small demons away," he claims.

Some day, Chewie won't be here. Narovka will pass. You certainly can't afford to live here anymore. E Pluribis Unum used to be a motto for the land. It's not a bad one, and for a moment, here, it was again.

For now.

You get your on-sale Krylon cans back, and re-tag the protective wards on the side of the bodega, and the Karen glares at you in deep hatred from her stoop.

Fuck her, she doesn't know what she's missing. Chewie invites you back into the store, and you all hold an impromptu potluck lunch. Friends and family cluster around, gossip, and hug.

It's not a bad life if you have a community.

You can get through it with a good pattern.

Tomorrow you'll be over in the Flatiron District to fix the tags on a playground at the invitation of Rabbi Hoffman. You have to keep fighting the fight, building alliances, or the darkness would break on through.

But like your mother, and her mother before you, you'll carry on. Every little bit moves the world forward.

FOUR EYES

MANNY HAD BOB Marley cranking on the stereo, his van was full of passengers, and the air conditioning was working after a long week of giving him trouble.

The sun beat down on the wet-looking asphalt road that ran along the harbor, next to the concrete waterfront. It curved along in front of the brightly-colored Dutch Colonial warehouses of Charlotte Amalie, which were now converted restaurants and jewel shops. Tourists in day-glo shirts and daubs of sunscreen rubbed over peeling skin crowded both sides of the waterfront road. Manny slowed somewhat, keeping an eye on them.

On the sidewalk by the shops, a tall black man stood by a food cart. The hand-painted wooden sign hanging from the cart's side had faded letters. The man wore a grand suit with tails, like an orchestra conductor, and a top hat perched on his shaved head. A cigar burned in his mouth. For a brief second he held Manny's attention. Then the food cart's owner stepped forward, and the strangely dressed man disappeared.

Manny looked at the other side of the road. A white girl with oval shaped sunglasses and pink leather pants stepped off the sidewalk into the road in front of his van.

He slammed on the brakes, trying to dodge her, but the van

couldn't respond that fast. Her ponytail flew up towards the windshield and her head struck the star-shaped hood ornament. She bounced along the asphalt. Manny weaved the van to a stop, with swearing from the passengers in the back.

He opened the door and stepped out into the heat. Get up, stand up, the radio cried out, and that was what Manny hoped would happen. He hoped that she would at least just stir and be okay.

But she just lay there.

Manny's stomach pulled itself tight and began to hurt. He looked back at the van. One of the passengers, an elderly lady with a straw hat and sunscreen on the tip of her nose, stepped down through the sliding door. She covered her mouth with the back of her palm.

"Oh my god," she said.

A trickle of blood ran down from the girl's head, muddying the dust in the gutter.

A passenger with a large belt buckle, working boots, and a southern accent, crawled out the sliding door with a cell phone in his hand. A mahogany-skinned man in khakis and a floral print shirt followed close behind.

"An ambulance is on its way here," the southern man said.

The man in khakis walked over to the girl and squatted. He held a small piece of rope in his hand, tied in an elaborate weave of knots. He shook his head.

"She dead," he said.

"How you know?" Manny demanded. The man in khakis said nothing, but looked sad.

The southerner closed his cellphone. "He seems to know about these things," he said. "I met him on the plane here. His name's Jimiti. I'm Stan."

In the distance, Manny heard the low wail of an ambulance start, fighting its way through the snarl of waterfront traffic. The world rippled, and Manny swallowed hard. He hoped she was alive.

"It's a shame," Stan said.

"I never knock into no-one before," Manny said, still stunned.

A bystander, an old lady with a large handbag, called out from the bench she sat on. "Don't fret so, man. She walk right out in front of you. Nothing you could do."

Manny looked down at the girl, the trickle of blood from her head growing. The man in khakis, Jimiti, nodded. He put the knotted rope in his hands back into his pants pocket.

"Nothing you could do," Jimiti agreed. The wail of the ambulance began to drown out the din of traffic and town noise.

Jimiti stood up and walked over to Manny. He put a small length of knotted rope into Manny's hand, as well as a business card. The card was simple. Plain white. JIMITI, it said in black letters. Obeah and other practices.

Manny started to put the card and rope in his pocket, but Jimiti's leathery hand grabbed his wrist.

"Keep the rope out in you hand. It suck up you fear."

"Look . . ." Manny said, annoyed. He met Stan's eyes, though.

"He means well," Stan said. He had a similar piece of knotted rope around his wrist. "He gave me one when I met him on the plane coming down here."

Manny slipped the knotwork over his hands.

The ambulance pulled in front of them, killing its sirens and bringing back the usual wash of background noise. Manny watched as two men jumped out of the doors in the back and knelt by the girl.

Please live, Manny hoped.

Manny revved the engine and turned into his driveway. He parked to the right of the out-of-control hibiscus bush and just to the left of the brand new Acura he hardly ever had time to drive. The Acura was painted a glossy gold, fully tricked out with rims, low ground effects, tinted windows, and a spoiler. The twelve-inch speakers in the back had once cracked the rear window.

He knew the car was an extravagance. He had bills to pay, large ones that he owed doctors who had done surgery on his granddad. But since he'd been a kid Manny wanted a car like this. Something that said he was someone, not just a taxi driver ordered around by tourists.

When he got out of the van, Manny took a deep breath.

The sun disappeared just over the galvanized tin roof. It sent streamers of clouds out in all directions, and random bands drifted around the sky like streaks of brilliant-colored cotton candy. They started rosy at the horizon, and graduated all the way to off-white over his head.

"Manny," his grandfather called from inside the house. "You late."

"Yes, G.D."

Manny walked up to the door. The house needed painting. Jagged flaps of aquamarine made the outside walls look like they'd caught some sort of scaly disease. His grandfather backed the wheelchair away from the doorjamb as Manny walked in.

"What happen?"

"Some white girl step in front the van."

G.D. picked up his glasses with unsteady hands. Once they were on he looked out into the driveway and blinked his super-magnified eyes.

"The girl okay?"

"No." Manny had stood with the police and answered question after question, and signed his name to documents. And strangely enough he stayed calm throughout it all, despite the shaky feelings he was sure would come later.

"You supper up by the microwave."

Manny shook his head. He emptied his pockets and tossed everything into a decorative terra-cotta dish at the edge of the kitchen counter. He pulled the stupid piece of rope off his wrist and threw it on top of the card the Obeah man had given him.

"I don't feel hungry," he said. He walked out of the kitchen and passed the door to the guestroom. Still locked, he saw with relief. He and G.D. stayed out of there. Ever since last year. Ever since after his grandmother's funeral.

The continuous whine of the wheelchair just behind him gave Manny the feeling that G.D. and the machine were stalking him. He walked the rest of the way down the hall, past G.D.'s room to his bedroom. The doorknob felt cool to the touch.

When the door creaked open, wind sucked in and slightly moved the drapes.

The white girl, in pink leather pants, Gucci sunglasses hanging by her neck, sat motionless on the chair next to Manny's bed.

"Oh god, oh no," he said. Suddenly unable to breathe, he stepped back and tripped over the wheelchair. The concrete wall smacked him in the back of his head and the world jumped to the left.

G.D. pulled his cane out of the side of the wheelchair and pointed it at Manny's throat. He held the business card up in front of him, the name JIMITI still large in the center of the card. G.D. glanced quickly into the room. He licked his lips.

"She the girl you run over?" G.D. asked, his voice wavering.

Manny nodded.

G.D. pushed the card forward at him.

"The card here, it for real?"

Again, Manny nodded. He glanced into the room. The girl hadn't moved. G.D. reached out with the cane and pulled the door closed with energy Manny hadn't seen from him in years. His eyes bulged behind the glasses, and a bead of sweat ran down his papery cheek.

"Go call the man on the card."

"Why?" he asked, still fuzzy.

G.D. smacked Manny's leg with the cane.

"Ever since you was just a little child you had go around vexing people with you questions," G.D. hissed. He lashed out with the cane again, and it bit down into Manny's shoulder. "Just call the man."

Manny grabbed the cane and wrenched it away from G.D.

Still breathing heavily, he walked back to the kitchen. He ran the tap, water pooling in his cupped hands until it spilled over his fingers into the sink, and splashed water on his face. He looked down at the card.

JIMITI, the card still said. But in the corner it now showed the words: DUPPY REMOVAL AND OTHER SERVICES.

Days passed for Manny. Days of driving taxi, but not paying attention to the small winding roads around the coast. He drove all up and down the fourteen miles of St. Thomas, up the spine of the mountains into the small patch of rain forest, and back down again into dry and dusty town. Days that built and mounted onto Manny's shoulders. He began to wonder if the Obeah man would ever respond.

He even spent one night in a motel, tired of waking up on the couch with crusty eyes and a cramped back. Too scared to walk into his room. Too scared to see the motionless statue sitting by his bed.

When Manny came back and parked his Acura, G.D. threatened him with the cane the moment he passed through the kitchen.

"Where you been?"

"Out," Manny said. "Leave me alone."

G.D. pointed out the window.

"You should sell that ugly car. You can't self afford it."

"I never had anything nice like that, ever," Manny said. He was tired. He looked around for the keys to his taxi-van. Another day of following the roads for money lay ahead.

"You just a taxi driver, you can't afford no fancy car. You ain't rich."

Manny found the keys and clenched them.

"You think I don't know that!" he snapped. "I feed you, I pay you bills. I been keeping you alive all them years, and all you do is trouble me so. I pay the doctor-man. What you ever done? You useless, that's what you do."

G.D. rolled his chair away. Manny continued.

"Yeah, I just the taxi-driver. And I all you got, old man. I ain't selling the car unless we poor, you hear?"

Manny stopped and faced G.D. His grandad's tears ran down his cheeks, magnified by the glasses. G.D. rolled away, and Manny angrily made sandwiches for the two of them.

Afterwards he checked the porch looking for G.D., then cautiously peered into his room and shuddered. The ghost still sat there patiently, hands in her lap.

But no G.D.

Manny walked to the guest room. He took the key from over the door and, with a trembling hand, unlocked it. The room swarmed with dust that made slow, lazy spirals and patterns in the air.

In the corner of the room sat the still figure of an old lady with a veil over her face. Her hands were crossed politely in her lap, just like the dead girl in Manny's room.

"I should have gone with she," G.D. said from next to the doorframe. Manny jumped, heart pounding. "Caroline . . ." G.D. cried. "I miss you so, dear."

Still angry, still feeling he'd been caught between everything and everyone, Manny wanted to both yell and hug G.D.'s frail body.

G.D. wheeled out past him. Manny closed the door and locked it.

"You right," G.D. said to Manny. "What I ever done?"

Manny leaned his head against the wall.

"I have to go work, G.D.," he said.

He drove more. From Red Hook, on the East end of the island where the ferries left for St. John, to Brewer's Bay on the West End. He drove over Crown Mountain and down onto North side to let tourists take their pictures with the donkey by Drake's Seat.

At the end, when he counted the day's take, he had a bit. But not enough.

He sat with a bottle of soda and a pate. He wondered if it was faulty memories that made it seem like he was making less and less, and that fewer and fewer tourists were coming to the islands as the years passed.

He'd once had other things in mind for himself. University. Stateside. Computers. But driving taxi brought in money for G.D. and living. Manny had left those plans far behind.

The radio interrupted to tell him he had a last pickup for the day.

"At Magen's Bay?" Manny complained. "I'm in town."

"They had ask for you special."

Manny sighed and shut the door. He drove up the mountain from the back end of town and down into the cooler air of the North Side.

Magen's Bay stretched out, a white crescent in the dimming light. The last clumps of people were leaving, knocking the sand off their feet and getting into cars and taxis to leave.

The sun's last streamers of orange pastels dripped behind the islands off the North Side. The last few vehicles coughed on, then drove off. Manny was alone, slightly nervous that he was about to be mugged.

Instead, Jimiti stepped out from behind a coconut tree, barefoot, his red floral shirt unbuttoned.

"Sorry I took so long," the Obeah man said. "I had a lot of things to reflect on."

"Okay," Manny said.

The Obeah man's hands hung loose by his side.

"Walk with me."

Manny took off his shoes and socks and followed Jimiti. They walked down the long beach until the water sucked and splashed at their toes. The darker it got, the whiter the beach seemed. Manny slapped at bites to his exposed arms. Mosquitos and no-see-ums hungry for his skin.

"You got duppy?" Jimiti asked.

"That a ghost?"

Jimiti sighed. He stopped walking and faced the huge bay.

"A ghost," he confirmed, with sadness in his voice. "I don't self understand what I doing here. I would have prefer to stay in Florida, helping all them old people over, giving them some company. Instead, I explaining what a duppy is."

"Who you talking to?" Manny asked, because Jimiti spoke to the water.

"You see duppy often?"

Manny hesitated.

"Never mind." Jimiti took one more step towards the water. The steady roll of waves against the beach began to slow, almost to a crawl, and then died away. The wind dropped, the air hushed.

One lone rogue wave washed towards them. It broke, a miniature froth of salty mist spinning off from its top. And from that, Manny saw it wash against a form.

"You see her?" Jimiti asked.

Manny blinked. The wave died, but a lady stood out of the water. Her skin glistened with rivulets of water that dripped down between her breasts, her stomach, her inner thighs, and then back into the ocean. Her features never stayed in focus, but wavered like a reflection in a windy puddle.

"Yes," Manny breathed.

"This La Llorona," Jimiti said. "We meet often at places like these: beaches, rivers, small ponds in parks with ducks paddling around the middle."

"Who is she?" Manny stood frozen in place.

"My spirit guide." Jimiti nodded. "You won't find her on any Vodou altar. And until a year ago, I never seen her. I think all the believing Latinos in Miami that make her strong. Or maybe the world changing this year. I don't know." Jimiti chuckled. "I once tell her she ain't even the right mythology for me to see. And she had ask me 'what the right mythology, Jimiti? You a two hundred-year-old blend of cultural mess! What in you vein? Kikiyu? Ashanti? Grandmammy rock you to sleep talking 'bout Ananzi, or

Brer Rabbit? It don't matter where I come from, only that I exist to you.'"

Jimiti stepped forward again.

"I old La Llorona. You tell me everyone here lose they culture. You right. Look this one here. Don't self even know what a duppy is. My coming back useless. You hear?"

The watery figure spoke. It sent shivers down Manny's back. He had never heard a ghost speak.

"So because they don't know, you won't try bringing it back to them."

Jimiti sucked his teeth. "They young. They don't care. Too busy with they nice car, big building, money, technology. I don't have nothing to share with them. The world change past me, and I don't understand them."

La Llorona looked at Manny. Her eyes cleared with a ripple.

"You are right. The world has passed you. But they still need understanding. Compassion."

Jimiti spat. He looked at the amazed look on Manny's face and pursed his lips.

"Compassion. What you know of compassion?" He looked angry, and hurt. "Let me help you understand this spirit here," he told Manny. "La Llorana . . . better known as Bloody Mary."

"Please don't," La Llorona asked.

"Haunting, crying, river spirit," Jimiti continued. "At the youngest age she had take her two children to the river. She grabbed them by they little young neck and pushed them both under river, and hold the both of them there until their palms stop hitting the water. Then she let go and watch them still body float away."

La Llorona looked down at the water by her waist.

"And after she killed herself," she whispered, "she searched the edges of waters everywhere, hoping to find her two lost children." Her voice hardened. "Thank you for telling him this, Jimiti. You are such a kind old man."

Manny felt the water around him vibrate and surge against his legs.

"Please," La Llorana asked him. "Don't think those things about me." Silent tears rolled down her face. They mingled with drops of water hovering on the edge of her chin and fell down into the ocean.

"I'm sorry," Jimiti apologized. He had tears of his own.

La Llorana shook her head.

"Take care of yourself, Jimiti," she said, putting a wet hand to his chest. "I will see you again, soon enough. You know this. Go do what you have to do."

A wave broke against La Llarona's legs. She dissolved into the water with a sigh. A single strand of seaweed that had been wrapped around her small breasts floated free and grounded itself on the sand in front of Manny.

Out past the small reef he could hear her calling for her children, a small plaintive voice lost in the rustle of coconut palms.

Jimiti put a hand on Manny's shoulder.

"You know what they does call the men that could see duppy?"

Manny shook his head.

"Four eye," Jimiti said. "Not hardly any four eye anymore. Just you and me and G.D." They began to walk back up the beach. The mosquitos and no-see-ums returned and started biting. Manny hadn't noticed they had stopped.

"I will come to your house tomorrow," Jimiti said sadly. "We take care of things then."

He left Manny looking out at the sea, puzzled.

It rained the next day. Manny didn't drive anywhere, but waited in the kitchen for the Obeah man to show up.

Jimiti came to the door well after lunch. His soaked shirt clung to his thin chest, and he looked far older than he had last night. He opened a case on the table and pulled out a laptop.

He took a bracelet of rope knots and hung it off his wrist.

"What that?" G.D. asked, watching the process from his wheelchair. "That thing on you hand?"

"Celtic knotwork," Jimiti said.

"Don't sound like no Obeah I ever see."

"It a form of white man magic. From the English. And my spirit guide is Latino." He looked at Manny. "What the duppy doing? Raising cain?"

Manny shook his head. "Just sitting there."

Jimiti made a note on his laptop, carefully pecking at the keys.

"That a computer?" G.D. asked. "How come you need a computer?"

Jimiti sighed and turned to the old man.

"I could leave, you know? I could leave you to deal with the Duppy you self. Then what? How many Obeah-man you know? Where is you respect?"

G.D. wheeled backwards.

"Sorry. I just . . . I just a little crazy right now."

Jimiti handed the old man a knotted bracelet.

"Maybe that go ease you some . . ."

"Uh-huh."

". . . because you a little stress out with the Duppy . . ."

"Right," Manny said.

". . . and you go need to be calm, seen? We almost there."

Then Jimiti pulled a small bag out of the case and started walking around the house carefully. He stopped in front of the guest room.

"The duppy here, right?" Jimiti asked.

Manny looked at G.D.

"No," they lied together.

"Nothing in there," Manny said.

Jimiti looked at the door and nodded. "Okay."

They opened the door to Manny's room. Jimiti looked at the girl by the bed. She hadn't moved. She still sat exactly as Manny had first found her. G.D. left the room, chair whining.

Jimiti began to poke and prod at the apparition. He sat and studied it. Then he finished and stood up.

"I need a second," he said. He sounded tired. "Hold this, it will calm you."

Manny took the piece of rope. He sat and stared at the girl's pale skin for as long as he could. Where had G.D. gone? With Jimiti? Suddenly worried, he got off his bed and walked into the hallway.

Jimiti stood there waiting for him.

"You tried to keep me from that other room," he said. "I ain't stupid, you know. I could sense you had more than one duppy."

Manny looked at the guestroom door. It was ajar.

"That Caroline," he said, slowly. "My grandmother."

"She waiting for you grandfather." Jimiti put a hand on Manny's shoulder. "She there to help him die. I explain that to them."

"Die?" Manny shoved Jimiti aside and ran into the guest room. "What you do? You and you stupid spirit stuff. You kill him!" he wailed.

The last outline of a dress faded from beside the curtains as he ran inside. The only body in the room was G.D.'s small frame lying peacefully on the bed.

"What you do?" Manny cried out. "What you do!" He grabbed G.D.'s hand, pushed his face into the sheets, and wept.

Jimiti knelt by him.

"For some, is time we pass on," he explained.

Manny leapt up and raced into the kitchen. He called an ambulance. When he put down the phone Jimiti stood in front of him.

"I can't make you duppy leave," he said. "Only you can do this now. I am old, failing. I don't have the strength. I can barely even see her."

"Then what you even doing here? You useless," Manny snapped.

"I here to offer it to you, Manny. I know it a hard time, but I have a diary and notes. They all on that machine," Jimiti pointed at the laptop. "All my knowledge I spoke into the laptop these last few years. I hear my guides, and my gods, and they are calling for me one last time.

"Everything I have, everything I am, is now yours."

Jimiti walked out the door. He turned into Manny's garden and headed out in the rain. He walked into the bushes past a tree.

"You go catch a death of cold," Manny shouted. He got no response.

He ran out into the rain after Jimti. But Jimiti had disappeared. His footsteps ended by a large puddle of pooling water.

"Jimiti left, gone for good," said a man from Manny's side. Manny spun around. A tall thin man in tails, cigar lighted despite the rain, smiled at him.

Manny heard the ambulance coming up the hill and ran back up his yard towards the house. Nothing today made sense. He was beginning to fall apart. It was as if he were standing at some sort of crossroads.

After the paramedics came and left, Manny threw the laptop into his car. He left the house resolving not to ever go back. And he left the van in the driveway, telling himself he would never drive it again.

He drove all the way to a point where the rocky edge of the island butted out against the ocean, not far from Magen's Bay. Here water hurled itself against the rocks, shaking the ground with booming explosions of saltwater spray that perpetually hung in the air.

"I want nothing to do with spirits, or ghosts, or witch doctors," Manny muttered.

He walked as near to the edges of the wet rocks as he dared, and flung the laptop out into the air. It arced slowly down into the foaming water and sunk.

"Please," a voice implored. "You must help."

Manny looked down at the rocks beneath him. Massive waves

roiled up, swept over the boulders, and retreated. A man sat on the top of a dripping rock, the water passing right through him. He wore a suit, and glasses, and held his shoes in his right hand.

"I think I slip down into the rocks. But my son still here. Help me find him?" The man stood up and began to look around.

The next wave crested the boiling waters around the rocks, reached up into the crags, and the man disappeared. A spirit, Manny thought. Another duppy only he could see.

For a moment he stood still, then he sighed and cupped his ears to see if he could hear a child calling for help.

He heard the child crying behind him. It took only a few seconds for Manny to search through the rocks and find him. A small child, his hands cut, crying for his dad. Manny picked him up and took him back to the car.

"Where you live?" Manny asked, leaning over the back door. The child wouldn't say anything, and kept sobbing.

Manny got in the front seat. He almost jumped out of his skin to see the tall man with the cigar sitting across from him. Somehow the smoke failed to fill the inside of the car.

With a deep breath Manny started the car and turned around. He would take the child to the hospital.

As he drove he ignored the apparition in the other seat. He would not speak to it. He would not acknowledge it. He would give it no control over him.

But finally the man spoke.

"The child name Timothy. He mother waiting for him and she husband. She real anxious, you know. You won't do them no good if you take him to the hospital, because tonight all the doctor there from stateside. They won't hardly understand her when she call, and they go treat her like she dumb. You would make an easier messenger. You like to know where they live?"

Manny drove on, clenching the steering wheel. He bit his lip. Still not willing to speak, he nodded.

The tall man smiled and gave him directions, and fifteen minutes of tense silence later they pulled into a sloping concrete drive lined with palms. Manny pulled the parking brake up, and Timothy in the back seat stopped crying.

"Okay, what is it you want from me?" he asked the man next to him.

"To do things like this for me." The cigar was waved in a long gesture. "Some things little, some things big. Sometimes you go like it, other times you go hate it. But you always guiding people in this world."

A screen door banged. A thin, worried-looking woman peered hopefully around the edge of it at the car.

"I can't," Manny said. "I ain't right for this. What I know about helping people? Plus, I throw away that laptop already."

The man shook his head. The top of his hat poked through the ceiling of the Acura.

"Look under you seat," he said.

Manny felt around and grabbed the edge of something plastic. He pulled the laptop out and set it on his lap.

"Okay," he said. "Okay. But only because I want help people." He looked over the man, who was fading away. "But who you is?" he demanded.

The thin man smiled again.

"Most call me Eshu."

Then he was gone. And Timothy's mother was walking up to the car. From the look on her face Manny could tell she suspected something was wrong.

He took a deep breath and opened the door.

Later that night Manny returned to the house. Inside he wandered around, laptop in his hands.

There was no girl sitting next to his bed, or any other ghosts in his house.

Outside the crickets made their song. The wind rustled the

leaves outside, and cars passed by his house on the nearby road. Manny closed the window and turned out the light in his room.

Tonight he would start to become more than just four eyes. Tonight he would become Obeah.

He sat at his desk and lit a single candle.

Then he carefully cracked the laptop open and turned it on.

TRINKETS

GEORGE PETROS WALKED down the waterfront, the tails of his coat slapping the back of his knees. An occasional gust of wind would tug at his tri-cornered hat, threatening to snatch it away. But by leaning his head into the wind slightly, George was able to manage a sort of balancing act between the impetuous gusts of wind and civilization's preference for a covered head.

The cobblestones made for wobbly walking, and George had just bought new shoes. He hadn't broken them in yet. But the luxury of new shoes bought the fleeting edges of a self-satisfied smile. The soles of his new shoes made a metronomic tick-tick-tick sound as he hurried towards his destination, only slowing down when he walked around piles of unloaded cargo.

Men of all sorts, shapes, and sizes bustled around in the snappy, cold weather. Their breath steamed as they used long hooks to snatch the cargo up and unload it. George walked straight past them. He did not put on airs or anything of the sort, but he hardly made eye contact with the grunting dockworkers.

His destination was the *Toussaint*. George could tell he was getting closer, the quiet suffering of the New England dockworkers yielded to a more buoyant singing.

George detoured around one last stack of crates, the live chickens inside putting up a cacophony of squawks and complaint, and saw the *Toussaint*. The ship was hardly remarkable; it looked like any other docked merchantmen. What *did* give people a reason to pause were the people around the ship: they were Negroes. Of all shades of colors, George noticed.

Free Negroes were around the North. But to see this many in one area, carrying guns, talking, chatting, flying their own flag? It made people nervous. Ever since the island of Haiti drove the French from its shores for its independence, their ships had been ranging up and down the American coast. George knew it made American politicians wonder if the Negroes of the South would gain any inspiration from the Haitians' visible freedom.

The crew stood around the ship, unloaded the cargo, and conducted business for supplies with some of the New England shopkeepers. George himself was a shopkeeper, though of jewels and not staples of any sort. He nodded, seeing some familiar faces from his street: Bruce, Thomas. No doubt they would think he was here for some deal with the Haitians.

The smell of salt and sweat wafted across the docks as George nodded to some of the dockworkers, then passed through them to the gangplank of the ship. One of the Haitians stopped him. George looked down and noticed the pistol stuck in a white sash.

"What do you need?" He spoke with traces of what could have been a French accent, or something else. It took a second for George to work through the words.

"I'm here for a package," George said. "Mother Jacqueline . . ."

The man smiled.

"Ah, you're that George?"

"Yes."

George stood at the end of the plank as the Haitian walked back onto the ship. He was back in a few minutes, and handed George a brown, carefully wrapped parcel. Nothing shifted when George shook it.

He stood there for a second, searching for something to say, but then he suddenly realized that the tables had been turned, and now *he* was the one who wasn't wanted here. He left, shoes clicking across the cobblestones.

In the room over his shop George opened the parcel by the window. Below in the street horses' feet kicked up a fine scattering of snow. When it settled by the gutters, it was stained brown and muddy with dung.

The desk in front of him was covered in occasional strands of his hair. He had a small shelf with papers stacked on it, but more importantly, he had his shiny coins and pieces of metal laid out in neat, tiny little rows. George smiled when the light caught their edges and winked at him. Some of the coins had engravings on them, gifts between lovers long passed away. Others had other arcane pieces of attachment to their former owners. Each one told George a little story. The jewelry he sold downstairs meant nothing. Each of the pieces here represented a step closer to a sense of completion.

He cut the string on the package and pulled the paper away from a warm mahogany box lid. The brass hinges squeaked when he opened it.

Inside was a letter. The wax seal on it caught George's full attention; he sat for a moment entranced by it. The faint smell of something vinegary kicked faint memories back from their resting places, and Mama Jaqi's distant whisper spoke to him from the seal.

"Hear me, obey me . . ."

George sucked in his breath and opened the seal to read his directions. *There is a man*, the letter read, *right now sitting in a tavern fifteen or so miles south of you. You should go and listen to his story . . .*

There was a name. And the address of the tavern.

Who is Louis Povaught? George wondered. But he didn't question the implicit order given. Layers of cold ran down his back, making him shiver. Automatically, without realizing it, he pulled something out and put it in his pocket, then shut the box. As he donned his coat and walked out of the shop to find a carriage, he told Ryan, the shop's assistant, that he would be back "later," and he should close the shop himself.

Hours later, the sky darkening, George's cab stopped in front of "The Hawser." A quick wind batted the wooden sign over the door around. George paid and walked through door. It was like any other tavern: dim, and it smelled of stale beer and piss. He looked around and fastened his eyes on a Frenchman at the edge of the counter.

Frenchman, Negro, Northerner, Southerner, English . . . to George, all humanity seemed more or less the same after he met Mama Jaqi. Yet even now he could feel that he was being nudged towards the Frenchman. This is the man he was supposed to meet, as irrational as it may have seemed. George carefully stamped his new shoes clean, leaned over to brush them off with a handkerchief he kept for exactly that purpose, then crossed the tavern to sit by the Frenchman.

The Frenchman—who would be Louis Povaught, George assumed—sat slouched over. He hardly stirred when George sat next to him. The barkeep caught George's eye, and George shook his head. When he turned back to look at Louis, the man was already looking back at him.

Louis, unfortunately, hadn't spent much time keeping up his appearances. A long russet-colored beard, patchy in some places, grew haphazardly from his cheeks. His bloodshot eyes contained just a hint of green, lost to the steady strain of enthusiastic drinking.

"I think, not many people walk in here who do not order drink," he declared. "No?"

George pulled out his purse and caught the eye of the barkeep. "He'll have another," George told the barkeep. George looked down and pulled out paper money, leaving the shiny coins inside.

"And you," Louis said. "Why no drink?"

"It no longer does anything for me," George explained. He reached his hand into the pocket of his undercoat. Something was there. Like something standing just at the edge of his vision, he could remember picking it up.

Now George pulled it out. It was a silver chain with a plain cross on the end. He held it between the fingers of his hand and let the cross rest against the countertop.

"I have something for you, Louis," George heard himself saying. "Something very important."

Louis turned his tangled hair and scraggly beard towards George. The chain seductively winked; George locked his eyes with the entwined chains and followed them down to the rough countertop. Such beautiful things human hands made.

Louis' gasp took George's attention back to the world around the necklace.

"Is this what I think it is?" Louis asked, reaching tentatively for it. His wrinkled hands shook as they brushed the chain. George did not look down for fear of being entranced again. He did not feel the slightest brush of Louis' fingernail against his knuckle.

"What do you think it is?" George asked.

Louis turned back to the counter.

"My brother Jean's necklace," Louis said. "On the back of this, it should have engraved . . ." Louis waved his hand about, "J.P. It is there, no?"

George still didn't look down.

"I imagine so."

Louis leaned back and laughed.

"*Merde.* So far away, so damn far away, and that bitch Jacqueline still has talons. Unlucky? Ha," he spat. "Do you know my story?"

"No," George said. "I do not."

The barkeep finally delivered a mug of beer, the dirty amber fluid spilling over the sides and onto the bar top where it would soak into the wood and add to the dank and musky air. Louis took it with a firm grasp and tipped it back. It took only seconds before the mug contained nothing but slick wetness at the bottom.

Louis smacked the mug down. "Buy me another, damn you," he ordered. George tapped the counter, looked at the barkeep, and nodded.

Stories, George thought, could sometimes be as interesting as something shiny and new. He would indulge Louis, yes, and himself. He handed Louis the necklace.

"Jean was much the better brother," Louis said. "I think it broke my father's heart to hear he died in Haiti. My father locked himself in his study for three days. Did not eat, did not drink. And when he came back out, he put his hand on my shoulder, like this—" Louis draped a heavy arm over George and leaned closer. His breath reeked of beer. "—and he tells me, he tells me, 'Louis, you must go and take over where you brother has left off.' That is all he tells me. I never see him again."

Louis pulled back away. "And Katrina, my wife, she is very, *very* sad to see me go away to this island. But I tell her it is good that I take over the business Jean created. I will make for her a better husband. My brother has left me a good legacy. Hmmm. I did good business. I made them all proud. Proud! And you know what," Louis said, looking down at the necklace, "it was all great until Jean walked into my office three month later. It was unnatural . . . I'd seen his grave! There were witnesses . . ."

"Business was good?" George interrupted Louis. "What did you do?"

Louis ran a thumb around the rim of his glass.

"It didn't cost much. A boat. Provisions. We bought our cargo for guns . . . and necklaces, or whatever: beads and scrap." He opened a weathered palm. There was nothing in it.

"What cargo?" George interrupted. This was the point. It was why Mama Jaqi had sent him.

"Slaves," Louis said. "Lots of slaves."

"Ah, yes," George said. Mama Jaqi had been a slave.

"I made money," Louis said. "For the first time I wasn't some peasant in Provencal. I had a house with gardens." Louis looked at George. "I did good! I gave money to charity. I was a good citizen. I was a good *businessman*."

"I am sure you were," George said. He felt nothing against Louis. In another life, he would maybe have sympathized with Louis' arguments. He remembered using some of them once, a long time ago. A brief flash of a memory occurred to him. George had desperately blabbered some of the same things, trying to defend himself to the incensed Mama Jaqi.

George shook away the ghostlike feel of passion to prod Louis' story along. "But what a shock seeing your brother must have been." George was here for the story. He wanted it over quickly. Time was getting on, and George had to open the shop tomorrow. He would have to finish Mama Jaqi's deed soon.

"I thought some horrible trick had been played on me," Louis said. "I had so many questions about what had happened. And all Jean would do was tell me I had to leave. Leave the business. Leave the island. I refused." Louis made a motion at the bartender for more beer. "I was still in Haiti when it all began. Toussaint . . . the independence. I lost it all when the blacks ran us all off the island. I slipped away on a small boat to America with nothing. Nothing." Louis looked at George, and George saw a world of misery swimming in the man's eyes. "In France, they hear I am dead. I can only think of Katrina remarrying." He stopped and looked down at George's arm.

"What is it?" George asked.

Louis reached a finger out and pulled back the cuff of George's sleeve. Underneath, a faint series of scars marked George's wrist.

"Jean had those," Louis said. The barkeep set another mug in front of Louis, and left after George paid for it. "Do me a favor," Louis said, letting go of George's sleeve. "One last favor."

"If I can," George said.

"Let me do this properly, like a real man. Eh? Would you do that?"

"Yes," George said.

Louis took his last long gulp from the mug, then stood up.

"I will be out in the alley."

George watched him stagger out the tavern.

After several minutes George got up and walked out. The distant cold hit him square in the face when he opened the door, and several men around the tables yelled at him to hurry and get out and shut the door.

In the alley by the tavern, George paused. Louis stepped out of the darkness holding a knife in his left hand, swaying slightly in the wind.

Neither of them said anything. They circled each other for a few seconds, then Louis stumbled forward and tried to slash at George's stomach. George stepped away from the crude attempt and grabbed the Frenchman's wrist. It was his intent to take the knife away, but Louis slipped and fell onto the stones. He fell on his arm, knocking his own knife away, then cracked his head against the corner of a stone.

Louis didn't move anymore. He still breathed, though: a slight heaving and the air steaming out from his mouth.

George crouched and put a knee to Louis' throat. The steaming breath stopped, leaving the air still and quiet. A long minute passed, then Louis opened an eye. He struggled, kicking a small pool of half-melted snow with his tattered boots. George kept his knee in place.

When Louis stopped moving George relaxed, but kept the knee in place for another minute.

The door to the tavern opened, voices carried into the alley. Someone hailed for a cab and the clip-clop of hooves quickened by the tavern. George kept still in the alley's shadows. When the voices trailed off into the distance George moved again. He checked

Louis' pockets until he found what he wanted: the necklace. He put it back into his own pocket. Then he stood up and walked out of the alley to hail his own cab.

The snow got worse towards the harbor and his shop. The horses pulling the cab snorted and slowed down, and the whole vehicle would shift and slide with wind gusts. George sat looking out at the barren, wintry landscape. It was cold and distant, like his own mechanical feelings. He could hear occasional snatches of the driver whistling *Amazing Grace* to himself and the horses.

Mama Jaqi had done well. George felt nothing but a compulsion for her bidding. *Obey* . . . no horror about what he had just done. Just a dry, crusty satisfaction.

When he got out George paid the driver. He took the creaky back steps up. He lit several candles and sat in his study for a while, still fully dressed. Eventually he put his fingers to the candle in front of him and watched the edges turn from white, to red, to brown, and then to a blistered black. The burnt flesh smelled more like incense than cooked flesh.

He pulled them away.

Tomorrow they would be whole again.

George pulled the silver necklace out with his good hand. He set it on the shelf, next to all the other pieces of flashy trinkets. Another story ended, another decoration on his shelf.

How many more would it take, George wondered, before Mama Jaqi freed him? How many lives did she deem a worthy trade for the long suffering she knew as her life? Or for the horrors of George's own terrible past? George didn't know. She'd taken that ability away from him. In this distant reincarnation of himself, George knew that any human, passionate response he could muster would be wrong.

Even his old feelings would have been wrong.

Long after the candles burned out George sat, waiting.

THE PLACEMENT AGENCY

IF I WERE smarter I would have just served out the last three months of my job contract and I wouldn't be hiding inside a crook in a corridor that is a three-dimensional representation of four actual dimensions, holding my breath as the warden floated through the air just several feet away.

The child next to me, barely eight years old, is also holding his breath.

I hope he doesn't make a sound. Doesn't stir. Doesn't fight the screaming desire to let out that breath that comes as the carbon dioxide inside starts to build and triggers the most ancient of our reflexes, the one buried deep down in the lizard brain.

The crook, or nook, or eddy in space time that we're crouched in, is a black shard of even blacker disquiet that the eye slips across. It's an unsettling thing from the outside, like a piece of glass that slides across the eyeball without causing pain.

Being inside of it is even more upsetting.

My back presses against something that isn't really a wall, that both gives and doesn't. My back of my shirt is both a million miles away and a billion years behind me. Sweat takes an epoch to slide down the small of my back, which is a world away.

And then the floating orb of the warden has passed us, humming its way deeper into the labyrinth of ultra-black, monolithic walls around us. Above us, the heavy skies of when the Earth was still being formed, thick with fire from cometary impacts. Below, the floor is a mirrored plane of dimensional space that can't be accessed, so forms to us mere mortals a solid surface.

Pretty messed up?

Yeah, my first several weeks here I was on Xanax and would curl up into a ball in my room with the drapes drawn shut and just cry.

But when you're broke you'll take just about any short term contract that pays well, offers room and board, and has a five thousand dollar sign up bonus that pays the moment you sign the contract and gives you a week to spend it.

I had thought I was getting away with something.

"Can we run, now?" the child asks.

"Yes. We can run."

I hold his hand and we run down the corridor. Each step is ten thousand years towards the future. Luckily we've been running for three hours already. Ducking into hiding places, turning off into rooms. The child's eyes still taking in the skies above and the infinite black walls. I'd told him what to expect, told him what lay outside the commons.

Now he was scared.

So was I.

The ad had been buried in the middle of a number of other similar listings. A temp agency located in the middle of a failing strip mall outside the rust-belt town of Lincoln.

SIGNING BONU$$$ FEEL GOOD BY HELPING OTHERS.

I had half a tank of gas, an ashtray full of quarters, a duffel bag full of clothes, and a fuzzy, stuffed cat to my name. Guff, the cat, had been with me since the beginning. Since back when I'd had family and long before . . . before things got worse when I was a kid.

I'd been considering taking my friend George up on that job helping build the new nuclear plant.

I figured I'd try one last time to see if I could make Lincoln a go. I had experience doing menial work in an assisted care facility, which fit with the job description. And George was never good for me. Always had some scheme or another up his sleeve, even if a buck was a buck.

So I'd pushed through the double glass doors, scuffed my boots on the faded industrial carpet, and stared at the scratched formica-topped counter wondering if I'd come to the wrong place until a middle aged, pencil-thin woman in a gray suit came out and handed me a clipboard.

"Take the test, sign the application."

There were a lot of questions. None of them, it seemed, related to medical work. Names of family. Names of friends. Was that a kind of background check? Coworkers. Pet names. I had briefly wondered if it had all been a way to get my personal info to hack any of my online accounts.

But I didn't have any money, and I figured I had nothing to lose.

WHAT IS THE MOST EXCITING THING YOU'VE DONE IN YOUR LIFE?

What strange questions.

"They said there was a bonus?" I had asked loudly. "Who are they again?"

The woman looked at me. "It's a five thousand signing bonus. We're the placement agency."

Oh. Just contractors.

I had looked at the strange questions, and then set about answering them.

Five hours later, I had a five thousand dollar check and instructions to go to an empty warehouse in Lincoln. When I stepped through the doors I fell into a time vortex that closed behind me as I screamed in incomprehension.

*

More running.

"How do you know we can get out?" the child asks. His brown eyes search me, looking for any hint of guile.

"Food," I tell him. "It's about food."

The skies above us are no longer burning. They're a swirl of brilliant stars.

"I don't understand," the child says.

"Every week the fridge gets stocked, and there's bread in the cupboards."

"And milk!" he adds.

"Milk. You're right."

"New DVDs."

"Where," I ask, stopping him from listing all the things that come in, "do you think all that comes from?"

He frowns. "I always thought it was magic, really."

I shake my head. "No. It isn't magic. They're things. Made by people."

He sort of remembers people. Grown ups that aren't the Caretakers like me. But for children younger than eight, few of those early memories persist. I remember straining to remember my parents. I'd lie on strange beds in homes that weren't homes, closing my eyes and willing my parents' faces back from the murkiness. But I only ever had impressions, or a faint snatch of a smell.

I could remember that I once knew them, but I couldn't remember them.

"Maybe we shouldn't keep running," the child suggests. "We're very far away from the Commons, now. We don't have any food."

"We're almost there," I reassure him. "Would you like a water?"

I hand him a bottle from my small pack, and he takes it after a moment's consideration and chugs it loudly. When he's done he looks down at it thoughtfully. "Will they have bottles of water where we are going?"

*

The child is innately curious. That's what impressed me at first. It took my mind off the madness of my situation. Asked about the scar on my upper arm. The one I try never to look at.

There were fifteen children in the Commons, which hung in the middle of a bubble of milky nothingness, spiky vines of solid black reaching from it off into the cells of other potential fractals of space and time. I fear I'm not describing it well, but the entire structure, sealed off away from space and time, was hardly comprehendible by tiny minds like my own.

What I *can* describe is that the great platter of the Commons was a garden five miles across, with gently sloping hills in the center. A modern apartment complex, clearly ripped off from Frank Lloyd Wright (or, knowing what I know now, maybe even designed by him!), hung over a babbling river.

There are basketball courts. Two treehouses built in the carefully maintained forest behind the hills. It reminded me when I first saw it of a college campus I'd visited once. A mini city, but with many clear areas for physical pursuits of the not-yet-adult.

I liked the beach by the pond. As long as I didn't look up. I *preferred* the forest, because there, wandering among the paths, with the trees blanketing above, I could pretend I was actually in a normal forest.

I use the word campus, because then I can only describe myself as a resident advisor of sorts. I never went to college myself, but I saw movies. When I arrived I was shown to a large apartment in the center of the first floor of the apartment complex.

The old man who took me to the Commons called himself the Keeper of Souls. He'd been waiting for me when I hit the bottom of the timeless vortex. He had been wearing an old overcoat, a raggedy fisherman's hat, and he'd held out an old oil lamp to cast a beam of light in the infinite darkness.

"You're the new contractor," he'd said in a papery-thin voice.

"Come with me, the Commons is just a short walk."

I'd said nothing, my mind quaking at the assault of passing through time and space, and then recoiling at the sight of the green disc of the Commons held by the tendrils of super-compressed dimensions in the void. The old man had held out an RFID-chipped keycard and said in a whispery voice, "If there's anything you need, anything at all, just ask. There's a phone by your microwave. My extension is zero. Only use it if you . . . absolutely must. The children are in the theater room; they'll be expecting you."

And that was how I became Wendy to my tribe of little Peter Pans.

Though my name is actually Riley.

"So what does food have to do with getting out?" the child asks, handing back the water bottle.

A water bottle might as well be magic to the child. They arrive in the refrigerators in the kitchen in the first floor when we're asleep. Hell, it's magic to me. I'm responsible for making dinner for the fifteen, but most of the deep freeze meals are fairly easy to defrost, and the palettes of the under-ten are fairly straight forward. It is no problem for me to bake chicken fingers and microwave fries.

For breakfast, they have varieties of cereals and milk. I host pancake Fridays, even though days of the week don't, as such, exist. I'm trusting my iPhone to keep time, even if it hasn't had a signal in months.

Lunch is whatever they want to scrounge from the fridges. Usually peanut butter and jelly. They almost never tire of it.

I have basic first aid training. I can dial zero for anything more than that.

I counsel them after fights.

But mostly they run in the forests, play in the lake, and eat voraciously when they return to the apartments. They play video games or watch movies in the theatre until they are too tired to stay up. Though I note the movies never have violence, or have anything to do with history.

I carry stragglers up to their rooms if they fall asleep.

I wonder where plumbers come from if something goes wrong with my toilet.

"How does food help us leave?" the child asks again, frustration creeping into his voice. I realize I'm losing myself in thought. It is easy to do here, where time is folding in on itself and so vast. As soon as the second week in the Commons, staring at the sky, I realize I was becoming prone to long stretches of silence and contemplation.

"The food," I say. "If I'm contracted to take care of you, then someone must be contracted to deliver the food."

The child smiles. "You followed the man in the little van."

I startle. "You know about the van?"

He nods. "It comes when the quiet creeps over the Commons and everything stops." The clocks, the motion of the river, the swaying of the trees from the alien wind. It happens when I'm not looking for it, out of the corner of my eye, just before I fall asleep, but before I can stop myself.

I took a caffeine pill right before sleep. An accident. Or maybe something in the back of my mind *knew*.

"I followed it," I tell the child. "I found a way out."

The van had been an old, museum-looking thing. The man in it wore a blue uniform, complete with a cap. He drove and drove down these corridors, and I struggled to keep up. But hours later, sweating and exhausted, I was rewarded by seeing it pass through the last of the horrible corridors and vanish into a vortex just like the one I'd come through to get here.

"What will we do on the other side?" the child asked.

"I don't know." I cannot leave him to the foster system. I

tasted that myself. I have barely planned that far ahead. I have only known that I have seen something wrong, and have tried to fix it.

At first, I'd only done what I'd been told. Kept an eye on the children.

They ignored me. I was not the first Caretaker. I was just the latest. They obviously had lives and plans of their own. A tree-house extension. A large tunnel they were digging. Levels in video games to be beaten.

But then one of them wandered up to me. Stared right down through me and into my soul and asked, "What is it like, outside?"

And that had shaken me. Because until then, I'd assumed none of them knew there was anything other than the Commons.

Day by day, he'd kept asking small questions. Did I have family? Did I remember the sky? Instead of falling into my routine of day by day, ignoring the reality I was in, he would remind me there was something else. That I was just here temporarily.

That he was a prisoner.

That I was working with his captors.

Did I think of myself as a kidnapper of children?

No.

But somehow, after two weeks, without this child ever suggesting as much, I started to believe I was.

After all these hours of walking, after all this time and space kicking up under our heels, with the skies shifting overhead, light pollution slowly fading the stars out, we arrive. I've been keyed up, waiting for the warden to reappear.

The child had called it that, I remember. Said they floated around the Commons, watching the children. Stopping them from leaving the island suspended in nothingness.

"Riley!"

I freeze.

It is the Keeper of Souls. This is the first time I have seen him since he took me to the Commons.

He does not look threatening, but his voice is firm. I notice that he has ink-black eyes, and I had thought he had a beard under those wrinkled cheeks, but it has never been there, I realize. He is clean-shaven.

"You cannot stop me," I tell him. I place myself between him, the warden, and the child. The vortex, which makes our eyes water with incomprehension, swirls just a few yards away. We can almost jump into it.

"I know," says the Keeper of Souls. He crooks his fingers, waves, and the orb fades away. It suddenly . . . never was. Much like the beard I had thought he had. "I am not here to harm anyone. You are safe."

He gestures again, and I stagger back to jump. But my feet land on the balcony of my apartment. I am looking out over the river, the forest, the large pond. Children are screaming and splashing among the artificial beach. Two girls are playing badminton on a freshly mowed lawn.

The translocation twists something in my stomach. I throw up into a potted hibiscus.

The Keeper of Souls opens the sliding door and limps into my apartment. He busies himself making tea as I try to regain my bearings.

"I'm sorry I had to do that," he says, setting a hot cup down on the coffee table where I find myself sitting. I'm unsure if he has warped time and space around me again, or if my mind is stuttering. "It's an unpleasant sensation, even for the most prepared and familiar."

"The . . . the child?"

"Yes . . . the child." The Keeper of Souls strokes the several foot long beard that hangs over his chest. He props dirty feet up on my coffee table. "He is back in his room. Riley, we talked about this."

"We did?" I'm horribly confused.

But so is the old man. He looks pained. "I'm so sorry. It's, swirls of time, maybe things got dislocated. But, this should have been a part of your briefing. Do you not remember?"

There's a hazy recollection.

"It's the nature of this place," the Keeper of Souls says, not unkindly. "Memory can be complicated as well. Particularly for contractors. It's your first time. And only a short stint."

"It's not fair, what you're doing to them," I blurt. "You've ripped them from their families, their places."

I realize I'm crying.

The Keeper of Souls moves next to me, wipes a tear from my cheek with the cuff of his robe. He sighs. Pulls back his hood. He hasn't shaved in a few days; a dark stubble makes him look a bit tired. "I think I understand. We missed something very important. Do you remember your parents, Riley?"

I swallow. "No."

"Do you remember when your mom took that knife?"

"No."

The Keeper of Souls shakes his head. "But you do. You remember. No matter what they wrote down, you remember. She didn't try to kill you, she tried to protect you."

Time fractures again, but this time it is definitely my mind. A place I have tried to avoid for a lifetime. A woman screaming. A man's anger. And so much blood.

Murder suicide, they called it.

"Do you remember what your father did?"

I do. I don't want to, but I do.

"Imagine the people worse than him. The ones who killed more than just a mother. Imagine the mass killers. If you could go back in time, Riley, to that moment, right now, would you try to stop him?"

I look up at the Keeper of Souls. I nod, tears dripping from my chin. "I'd kill him," I hissed.

His ancient eyes harden. "What if you could go back in time to when he was a child? Would you? Would you stop all that pain, save your mother? Could you do that?"

I stare.

Could I?

I look at the children playing throughout the Commons. "Is that . . . ?"

The Keeper of Soul's eyes soften. "Your father is not here. But if he were, would you do it?"

I let out a deep breath. "I . . . I don't know."

"They used to call it the Hitler dilemma."

"Who?" I ask, puzzled.

The Keeper of Souls smiles. "If you can go back in time and stop a great mass murderer by killing his child self, would you? Far at the end of time, amazed at having survived, we asked that question. We bent time and space, and came back. But, who among us are killers? Would we be no better than the ones we are sent to judge?"

For a moment, the Keeper of Souls sips his tea thoughtfully.

"I will not do it," I say.

"No one asks you to." He smiles sadly. "Who would murder a child just for its potential when one could just give it to another family for adoption? Maybe even in another time. You'd be amazed what a good pre-school and decent social safety net does to a dictator, or a good psychologist can do for a serial killer. Most of our worst killers are scattered among time and space for rehabilitation. But a few, a select few, the greatest abominations . . . even where I come from, we cannot risk letting them out into the general population."

The sound of children's laughter rises to my balcony. The splash of a cannonball.

"He figured out your vulnerability. Got you to navigate the corridors of space and time. Tricked you, so he could hide in the glitches where our eyes can't make sense of what they see, all to get you to try and take him back to where he came from." The Keeper of Souls smiled sadly. "There's a reason our contractors are drawn from different times and places, for short periods of time."

I stand up slowly and walk toward the balcony. I look up at the void above.

"Take heart," the Keeper of Souls says. "It's only another month, and then you'll be back in your time. You'll have enough money to avoid having to work that construction job and avoid cutting some corners with George. Trust me, it'll save a lot of lives."

And then, he's gone.

I'm alone, on a couch, watching the children slowly melting out of the woods toward the apartment complex.

It is dinner time.

And I shiver.

Only a month.

How much longer will that be in a place where time and space swirl above me in the sky?

SUNDOWN

C OLORADO, 1877

Willie Kennard rode into the town of Duffy dangerously late, looking back over his shoulder at the height of the sun
and squinting. He dropped down from the old mare he'd borrowed
off Wilson Hayes and hitched her to a post.

Every step shifted two days' dust and grit off his long coat, and
his thighs ached so bad it felt like he'd been punched in the groin.

"You're a fool to walk into Duffy," the old Pawnee man Willie
had hired as tracker muttered when they'd split up outside of town
on the bluff. "Once night comes, you won't need to be worrying
about your quarry. It's the town that'll get you. They'll string you
up. Whether or not you're wearing a silver badge."

Judging by the stares the white folk sitting outside the hotel
gave him, Willie knew it was truth.

"Help you?" an older man with a long beard asked in a hard
voice.

"Looking for the sheriff," Willie said. "I need his help finding a
man that might be hiding somewhere around these parts."

"What kind of man?" the old timer asked. It was a pointed
question.

"The murdering kind," Willie said.

"Sheriff's at the Longfellow Ranch," said a dapper man crossing the wooden slatted walkway. He looked to be a store owner of some kind, in his carefully pressed suit.

"Now why'd you go tell him that?" spat the old man.

"Cuz he's a Marshal, Pat. You see his star?" the shopkeeper said. "And cuz it's getting late."

They glared at each other, and then the old man pointed a wizened, crooked finger down the other side of town. "Ranch is down that way."

Willie looked down the dusty road, sunk deep with wheel tracks and horse shit. Then he looked back over his shoulder at the sun, moving toward the horizon.

Best to get on with it. He sighed.

He tapped a finger to his hat at the younger gentleman and made his way back to the horse.

As he rode past, he asked, "What's the Sheriff doing at the ranch?"

"Indians mutilated the cattle," spat the old man. "Damned heathens."

Willie spurred the horse into an awkward gallop, the best it could manage, leaving a plume of dust in the air that set the old man coughing.

Willie rode up onto the ranch hard. The damned horse was heaving and bitching about the work, but he didn't pay it much mind. Dropped out of the saddle while the mare still trotted down to a slower pace, left it with a muzzle flecked with foam and turning circles in the dirt.

His boots scuffed up dust as he ran for the door, glancing around.

"Hello Longfellow Ranch!" he shouted, right hand dropped low to brush aside his coat. He put a palm to the Colt's grip.

The faded gray wood of the door creaked as it opened slightly. "Who's that?"

"I'm looking for the Sheriff of Duffy," Willie said. "I'm Marshal Willie Kennard."

"Marshal?" A ruddy face frowned from the gap in the door, looking out at Willie. "Never seen a negro Marshal before."

"Don't imagine there're many of us," Willie said. He tapped the silver star. "But here I am, nonetheless."

The dark green eyes flicked down, noted his draw stance through the crack in the doorway. "You seem agitated, Marshal Kennard. Mind if I ask why?"

"Been tracking a murderer through the scrub a couple days," Willie said. "Tracked him to Duffy. Hoping I could rely on your help."

With a horrible creaking sound, the door opened the rest of the way. "I'm Sheriff Bostick Keen. Come on in. I'm talking to Dr. Longfellow here about what happened to his cattle recently."

Willie'd seen them on the way in. The cattle ripped open, ribs exposed and drying in the sun, tongues lolling.

"Dr. Longfellow is getting us a drink of water," the sheriff said.

Sheriff Keen had a puffy, round face but was a stick of a man, really. Wind-swept lean. Meant he didn't hide in his office, but walked out in the windy grit. Did his job.

Willie respected that.

Dr. Longfellow came back into the room with a tray of glasses and a pitcher filled with water fresh from the well. Beads of sweat rolled down the rounded belly of the pitcher.

The ranch owner bent forward to pick up a glass and fill it.

Willie stared at the man's neck.

Before the sheriff could move, Willie drew. As Dr. Longfellow straightened, he looked at the barrel of the Colt, as if for a second fascinated by it.

The gunshot filled the room with its violent crack, and Dr. Longfellow's brains splattered out across the wall behind him. Only, the brain tissue was all wrong. Black goo, filled with insect-like fragments that dripped down toward the ground. No blood.

What looked like a wasp's stinger, but was the size of a thumb, was stuck fast in the plaster.

Sheriff Keen screamed like a child, raising his hands in front of him, then recovering and reaching for his gun. "What the hell . . ." he started to say, then stopped and looked at the oversized stinger. It twitched and wriggled slowly. Not a slow man, he realized something wasn't right. "What in the hell?"

Willie pulled his left piece out and aimed it at him. "Turn around," he ordered.

The sheriff took a deep breath, his eyes wild and wide. "No."

Willie cocked his head. "No?"

"If you gonna kill me, do it right to my face."

"Most likely, I won't kill you," Willie said. "But I do want to see the back of your neck. If you don't show it to me, chances are you do end up dying. I gotta make sure you're not like him. You understand?"

Keen's face scrunched up in defiance and anger. Finally, after several short breaths, he screwed up his face in disgust and turned around.

He trembled a bit, expecting the shot.

But Willie nodded. "You're all right." He slid the two Colts back into their holsters. "I apologize for drawing on you."

Keen yanked his own, overly large revolver out, but Willie ignored him. He moved around the house, kicking open doors and looking into rooms as the sheriff followed him, gun aimed. Willie paused in front of a storeroom in the back. Looked at the bodies on the ground.

"See that?" he asked Keen.

The sheriff's green eyes took it all in. Shattered human ribs poking through broken skin. Glazed eyes staring at the ceiling. The wife, the two children lying in her arms. "Like the cattle," he said.

"Like the cattle."

"How'd you know?" Keen asked.

"Seen it before. Some men attacked a camp I was providing

protection for. Wasn't pretty." Willie remembered muzzle flashes and glazed eyes, men with broken legs dragging themselves toward him.

"Would he have gone for me?"

"Guessing so."

"Then I owe you my life," he said. "But I still gotta take you in."

Keen waved the gun at Willie, pointed outside. There was a horse and wagon waiting.

Willie looked at the old mare. "Sheriff, I got the impression I wouldn't be welcome in Duffy after sunset. That was the word. You telling me I got that wrong?"

The sheriff shook his head. "Putting you in jail. For protection."

Willie raised an eyebrow incredulously. "Protection?"

"The cattle. It isn't just Longfellow's farm. They're all over the place," he said. "All around town."

All around town.

"There's a Pawnee tracker I hired to help me get here. He's just outside the other side of Duffy," Willie said. "If you don't mind, I'd like to pick him up or let him know to run like hell. If that's all right with you."

Sheriff Keen nodded. "After what I just saw, I'd say that's fair. But my shotgun'll be resting here on my lap, and you're still coming with me."

Willie nodded. He had time to think about what to do next on the ride out. Time to decide whether it was better to lay in with the people of Duffy or leg it out into the dark wilds knowing there were strange things out there.

He got up in the back of the wagon, looking around the farm.

The sheriff urged his horse forward, and they rumbled out over the dirt road in the dim light of a nearly setting sun.

"Damn."

Willie stood on the edge of the wagon and looked down at the tortured body of the Pawnee man who'd led him here. They were well into dusk, the last sliver of sun slipping down under the trees. Residual orange light dappled the scrub.

"Never even got his name," Willie said, a bit of anger touching his voice. "What a thing."

The sheriff looked over at the horizon. "Figure we got time to bury him?"

"No difference to him now, and I doubt that's a good idea, tarrying here. I think it's time we got moving along," Willie said.

"What are they?" the sheriff asked. "I know I saw what I saw. Enough to turn my wits shaky."

Willie nodded. "You saw what you saw. And I don't know what they are either. I just know they overrun us. We set up camp for a night, on the way to the goldstrike outside your hills. They killed the men I was being paid to shotgun for. Murdered them before I understood what was going on."

"But why? What did they want? What demonic thing is happening out here?"

"Never really had a chance to ask," Willie said. "Been moving behind them and trying to get my revenge since they hit."

He'd been turning over the idea of overpowering the sheriff and walking out into the desert. But to do that he'd have to steal the man's horse and leave him without a gun here.

Not a fair thing to do to a man in these circumstances. Not with what might be out in the dark. And Willie was a man of the law. Sure, most hated him. But there was a respect he'd come to expect, and that had been earned by being a stickler for rule of law. Drilled into him even earlier by the army and his years in uniform.

Sheriff Keen was a fellow officer; leaving him out here alone was not a brotherly thing.

And the murderer who'd escaped Willie's camp was somewhere around Duffy. Willie had sworn he'd bring justice.

Willie sat down on the bench in the back of the wagon and tugged his hat down lower. "Sheriff, what kind of trouble are your townsfolk going to make for me?" he asked.

Keen shifted uncomfortably in his seat. "Well . . ." he said. "I've been thinking on that. I can pass you off as someone I caught and lock you up, keep you under watch. But that could end up going the wrong way. I'd rather explain to the mayor what's happening. Because if those things are all around Duffy now, what happens when they start coming in? Either way, I'm getting you to safety and standing outside with a shotgun."

Willie thought about the shambling forms ripping through the darkness of the camp toward him. It might be dangerous back in the cell. But certainly not as dangerous as it certainly was out here. In the dark.

"Promise me something, sheriff," he said.

"What?"

"Put a key to the cell in one of my boots, and my guns in a box under the bed. No one has to see them, but I want them there. In case."

Sheriff Keen thought about it for a long moment.

Then he nodded.

The mayor glared belligerently at Willie through the bars of the cell. He didn't say anything. Quirked the edges of his mouth, then stalked back to Keen's desk. They started arguing.

Willie sat on the wooden bench and leaned back, sighing.

He could see where this was going.

The mayor wasn't about to let some "darky" tell them all how some possessed people were out there lurking in the dark. That maybe they'd come attack townsfolk.

Didn't make no sense, the mayor insisted.

"I don't care how deputized you are," the well-dressed mayor hissed. "You don't come into my town spouting half-crazed bullshit like that and expect any of us to believe you. You killed Longfellow. You may well have killed his family, too. And that

Indian the sheriff saw. I think we keep you locked up in here and locked up good."

Willie didn't say anything. That was always the better course in these situations.

He just eyed the man levelly until he swore and walked out.

The sheriff checked his shotgun, then sat at his desk. "You think, whatever those things are, they're going to come for the town?"

Willie leaned back against the wall, relaxing a bit. "Hope they don't," he said.

"That all you got? Hope?"

"All any of us ever had, Sheriff," Willie said said as he lay down on the bench and pulled his hat down over his head.

He woke at night to the sound of the sheriff cursing.

First he stretched, worked out the kinks in his arms and back, and then splashed water on his face from a small jug Keen had put inside the cell with him.

"They are gathering outside." Keen drew the rough burlap curtains closed against the flicker of torchlight in the dark outside. "And I cannot see their necks," he said, clearly exasperated.

"So we don't know whether they are here to lynch me for being in Duffy after dark, or to kill us and fill our heads with insect parts," Willie observed.

Keen looked back at him, horrified.

"I'm just saying, either reason is a messy one," Willie said.

"You're right. We need to get out of here," Keen said. "If they're here for a lynching they're likely to come after me for trying to help you."

Willie was already pulling the box out from under his bench. He holstered up and took a step toward the metal bars, and right as he did so the front doors busted open. Three townsmen stumbled in, and Sheriff Keen wracked a round into his shotgun. "Now there!" he shouted. "You stay back or I'll shoot."

"Sheriff," Willie muttered through the jail bars, key in hand as he tried to unlock the door. "I'd get in here with me quick . . ."

They didn't look like the hanging type, the three that stepped forward. They looked drunk. Vacant eyed. Although once they saw Willie, their heads tracked him.

Sheriff Keen stepped forward. "Get outta here," he growled.

"We want the nigger," they growled right back. Willie stiffened. Lowered his hands to his belt.

Keen aimed the shotgun at them. "I'll shoot," he said. "Jamie, Nicodemus, Alex, you know I mean it."

They swung their heads to regard Keen. Willie scuttled over to the edge of the cell. "Sheriff, I—"

Keen fired. Buckshot ripped through all three men, and both Keen and Willie swore to see the black ichor and chitinous pieces mixed with skull slap against the wooden doors. Jamie and Alex slumped dead to the ground, but the one Keen had called Nickodemous jerked forward like a sped up marionette.

Willie fired from between the bars of the cell, got him twice in the chest, but the man kept on. It took a third shot to get him in the head, and by then the rest of the mob was kicking through the door.

"Keen!"

The sheriff never even backed toward the cell. Stood and reloaded his shotgun, fired, moved to reload again, then pulled a pistol. He threw his keys with his spare hand back toward the cell without a word.

He went down, covered by townsfolk ripping him apart, limb from limb, with one last muffled shot.

And then when they were done, they stood up and looked at Willie.

There were more of those possessed townspeople out there than he had bullets for. And he could hear more of them shuffling around in the dirt outside. They pawed around the sheriff's remains, looking for the keys to the cell with those vacant eyes as Willie watched them.

He figured he'd shoot as many as he could as they came in, once they figured out how to break through the cell.

Willie dragged the bench out to the middle of the cell, pulled the blanket off it, and set his spare bullets down on the hard top. Checked his two Colts.

Twelve in. Ten loose on the bench.

Thirty townsfolk.

"Marshal, sheriff, you still in there?" shouted someone in the street on the other side of the mob. "Lie down flat! I am opening fire!"

Many other men would have paused or asked a question back.

Willie did no such thing. He dropped and kissed the dirty floor without a second thought, and as he did so the *chack chack chack* sound of a multibarreled Gatling gun ripped through Duffy's main street. The windows exploded, wood cracked, splinters flew around the room. Black ichor stained the bars, Willie's hat, coat, the floor.

The barrels wound down.

Wounded townfolk scrabbled around the floor.

"I'm standing up!" Willie shouted. He shook black goop from himself, and then shot the nearest man still stirring. He let himself out of the cell, dispatching anyone that even groaned, and stepped through the door warily.

There was a wagon parked in the middle of the street with a Gatling gun mounted to the back. A grandfatherly black man in a duster with a marshal's star on his lapel stood behind the still smoking and crackling barrels, reloading the ammunition belt by himself. When he saw Willie, he swung the gun at him. "Show me your neck," he said.

Willie leaned forward and exposed it.

"Good enough," the stranger said. He had a shock of white hair that he'd left long. It framed his lined and strong face, off which a strong snowy white beard hung. The eyes glinted in the firelight of the street's torches.

"Sheriff's dead," Willie reported. "My name's Willie Kennard. Who're you?"

The man looked around the town warily. "I'm Frederick Douglass," he said.

"The abolitionist?"

"Yes."

"Thank you for the assistance," Willie said, surprised. What was Douglass doing out west? And at this particular moment? "Do you know what in hell is going on?"

Douglass looked down the street. Now Willie heard a faint buzzing in the dark distance of the night lurking around the edges of the town. Like a hive of bees, but lower pitched.

A beam of light lanced out of the sky and illuminated the scrub. Strange, haunting shadows danced and moved across the horizon.

"We'd better get up into the crags and hills," Douglass said, pointing Willie toward the rider's bench and the reins. "They'll have a harder time catching up to us amongst the rock. I'll tell you what I know as we ride."

The team of horses ran like the devil and dragged the wagon along over the rough dirt road leading out of Duffy. Willie could hardly hear Douglass over the racket of hooves, the creaking wagon, and the bouncing of his chair. Douglass was cleaning the mounted gun and arranging belts of ammunition, grunting with the effort.

"I've been appointed a marshal of the District of Columbia, by President Rutherford B. Hayes," Douglass shouted. "Ostensibly it is so I can bring more of our folk into civil service. And with those strong jobs previously denied to them, we might rise in our stations. I'm the first negro man in this position. We have had many firsts since President Lincoln—God rest his soul—passed emancipation. I see you, and I see a marshal. All over this land, even despite the fact that President Hayes agreed to end Reconstruction in the South, we are making great strides, Mr. Kennard. Great strides."

That flying beam of light stabbed out and lit up the world like a second sun.

"I know. I served with the Seventh Illinois Rifles," Willie said, urging the horses on faster. The droning sound, a hellish one if he'd ever heard it, had grown louder. It was associated with that infernal light in the sky. "What is that in the sky?"

Douglass shielded his eyes and looked up. "They've spotted us." He swung the Gatling gun up and squinted through the sights.

The howl of the machine behind Willie deafened him. Shells bounced around the wagon's floor, smoldering as they struck wood.

The droning sound lessened, and the light dimmed.

"The marshals report directly to the president," Douglass said, clearing the gun and awkwardly loading a new belt of ammunition. "Sometimes they're used as instruments of executive policy. In this case, I was asked to find the lost crew of an airship. And the airship, too, if possible. The president chose me because most cattle hands or cowboys in these western territories are either black or Mexican, and he felt I might better navigate these parts with my team."

Willie blinked. "An airship?"

"You've heard of hot air balloons? Lighter than air travel?" Douglass asked.

"I saw one once. In the war. Used to spot troop movements." The great globule had hung impossibly in the air, tethered to a pine tree by a rope over a bloody meadow growing a black gunsmoke cloud that soon obscured the machine.

"Our army built a rather advanced version of a balloon, one capable of moving under its own power. Like a steamship of the air. A wealthy count from Prussia who observed balloons here during the war and was quite taken with the concept of using lighter than air machines for military purposes worked with the army to help build an experimental hydrogen airship. Perfect for avoiding the treacherous and snowy grounds of the territory of Alaska."

"Alaska?" Willie glanced back at Douglass. "The territories we purchased from the Russians after the war?"

"Yes. President Hayes demanded a modern day Lewis and Clark expedition. We hardly know what, if any, resources lie in the territory, after all."

Willie looked up into the sky at the pursuing beam of light. It must be like a lighthouse signal, focused to become a spotting light. And behind it, a floating machine.

"The army is chasing us?" Willie asked.

"No, Mr. Kennard. It looks like they lost control of their machine when they were overrun, just like this town was." He looked up into the sky and pulled the Gatling gun into position. "I need to fire off another belt to keep them farther back from us again, I'm afraid. They're trying to get close again."

An ember landed in the road ahead.

Willie squinted. Then slew the horses off the road as hard as he could. He reached back with a hand to steady Mr. Douglass, who pitched to the side. The whole wagon tilted onto two wheels and the horses screamed.

And then the world exploded in a rush of dirt and violence that blew Willie off the wagon.

"Can you hear me, Mr. Kennard?"

Willie looked off into the night and blinked. Shook his head.

"Are you well?" Douglass asked. The old man was holding him up, helping him stumble through the stunted, scraggly trees and toward a cut in the foothills. Blood ran from one of Douglass's nostrils.

Willie looked down and saw the front of his shirt stained with dark blood. "Am I hurt?"

"Was the horse," Douglass said.

"I don't remember any of it," Willie said.

"We took a violent tumble thanks to that damn dynamite they were tossing from the airship," Douglass said. As if to underscore his point, a nearby explosion filled the air with a cloud of sharp-smelling dust. "Fortunately they've lost sight of us again, and are randomly tossing the stuff out in hopes of hitting us."

They hobbled together, helping each other over rocks and up scree toward the cut. The beam of light had died out—maybe they'd run out of fuel for its light. Willie could discern a large, cigar-shaped shadow gliding between the stars and him. Which meant that at any moment a lit stick of dynamite could land near them.

"The last thing I remember is you telling me that airship thing was made by the army," he said.

Douglass grunted. "One of the last reports before the machine went missing was that they'd found a crater. With a large metal object buried in the center of it. One of the officers sent back a simple sketch via carrier pigeon."

Both men winced as another stick of dynamite exploded. But this one was farther away than the last, and Willie breathed a sigh of relief. That old instinct to shelter he'd learned from being shelled by artillery hadn't gone away, but there was no betraying whistle of an incoming shell to help him here.

"There's a book by a gentlemen by the name of Jules Verne called *From the Earth to the Moon*," Frederick Douglass said, "where some men from Baltimore build a gun large enough to shoot a sort of bullet with men inside of it to the moon."

"I have not heard of it," Willie allowed.

"Well, the illustration the officer sent to us could have been taken right from its pages. It was a scarred and burnt tip of a bullet, nestled in the center of a crater it caused. I believe, from what I've pieced together since arriving here, that the creatures that infected the crew of the airship above us, and the townspeople of Duffy, are creatures from another world that arrived on it. That arrived via some kind of machine, like Verne described."

"These are moon people?" Willie asked incredulously.

"I do not know whether they are from the moon, or from Mars. There is an astronomer, Giovanni Schiaparelli, who said just this year that he has seen canals on the face of Mars. Maybe these things come from there. Maybe from farther away. I do not know. They do not parlay; I lost the men I traveled here with when I tried that futile initial gesture. The creatures are violently hostile."

Willie nodded as they struggled up loose rock and into the safety of the narrow crevices of a valley made by carved cliffs. He found himself a bit relieved they were not facing demons, but creatures. Even if otherworldly ones. Creatures could be shot. And hunted. "But why are they here?"

"Our world? I don't know."

"No, I mean, why Duffy?" Willie asked. "Why did they take the airship? Why did they fly all the way down here?"

"That I can't tell you," Douglass said wearily. "Come, there is an abandoned mine just ahead of us. It is stocked with supplies and weapons, and should be easy to defend from the entrance."

They passed a trio of fresh graves just inside the mouth of the mine, which was located in a natural cave entrance at a high point in the rocky canyon-like area of the foothill. A very defensible spot, Willie noted with pleasure before he walked deeper inside. Willie had been around a few gold strikes before. Enough to tell that the timbers looked thick and recently placed. This one had been dug in quick for exploration, then abandoned.

Several crates were stacked deeper inside.

Not surprising to find a mine here, he thought. Just ten miles away was a bustling hill full of prospectors who all used Duffy as their nearest town. The camp he'd been hired to protect had been planning to try their luck there.

"Only one way out," Douglass said. "But it means we can stop them from coming in if they find us."

"For a while," Willie observed. "But we'll be the rats. And they have dynamite. Better off for us to get our ammunition and stay out front to hold them off than try to hide. How did those men out near the front die?"

"I brought them here. Three other marshals I took with me for this mission. They may have become those . . . things. But the men I'd travelled with deserved a Christian burial," Douglass said. "Listen, we just need to last until tomorrow afternoon. Can we defend this mine that long, do you think?"

"In a pinch," Willie agreed. "But what happens then?"

"Cavalry stationed at a fort forty miles away. I sent for them via pigeon." Douglass levered open a box full of rifles and ammunition. Willie looked in with approval. He picked up a small pistol that he didn't recognize.

"What's this?"

"A Very pistol. It's a Navy signal device they just designed. It shoots a burning flare into the sky. I'll be using it to signal the cavalry where we are."

"And what do you think the cavalry will be able to do against that airship?" Willie asked.

Douglass looked at him with troubled eyes. "Shoot it down with the rockets I ordered them to bring."

"Rockets?"

Douglass sang, "'And the rockets' red glare, the bombs bursting in air?' They'll get high enough."

It sounded possible. If the airship was still around.

But a stick of dynamite boomed somewhere in the distance. The possessed crew of the airship seemed obsessed with finding and destroying the two lawmen.

Willie had a feeling they would still be out there.

They broke open a case of canned food and levered it open by candlelight, risking the flicker since they were deep in the mine for right now, and ate cold canned beans with wooden spoons that Willie quickly whittled out of a piece of the crate's top.

"How'd you end up deputized to be a marshal?" Douglass asked.

Willie tapped a piece of hardtack against the side of the can of beans, an old habit. The long-lasting, brick-like biscuit was fresh though, as nothing wriggled out. "After the war I came out west. Did this and that for some years. Four or so years ago I fetched up near the town of Yankee Hill. They needed themselves a new marshal."

Douglass raised an eyebrow. "What happened to the old one?"

"Up and died," Willie said, picking at the hardtack. "Lost two marshals to a gunslinger by the name of Barney Casewit. They tried to bring him in for the rape of a girl of fifteen years' age. And killing her father when he struck out for vengeance. As well as other murderings. I figured, with the war over, our folk voting and getting jobs, that I would ask for the job. Particularly as they were a town of very scared white folk desperate for a solution, I allowed myself to think that maybe they'd overlook the color of my skin in their desperation for a marshal."

Douglass laughed. "This man, Casewit, though?"

Willie didn't laugh. "As hard a man as they come. But then, he'd never been on the other side of a Confederate line of soldiers facing a company of fellow negro rifleman, knowing that they'd never give you surrender."

Douglass's smile faded.

Willie continued, "The town's councilmen asked me to arrest Casewit right there that minute. I don't know if they were looking for entertainment, or desperate to end that despot's reign. But I agreed. Took the star, pinned it, and made my way across the street to where Casewit was playing poker with two of his hands, where I then told him he was under arrest."

"Just like that?" Douglass asked. They both stopped, though, and cocked an ear. No more dynamite had exploded since Willie started his recollections.

The airship was backing off from the hills. Maybe finding somewhere to drop down its crew. Douglass blew out the candle.

They'd need to move out front to defend their spot soon.

Willie grimaced and continued. "Just like that. Casewit's sitting there and he asks if he's just supposed to follow me. I told him it was his choice: jail or hell. So he stood and reached for a pair of Colt .44s. I shot them both in the holster."

"What? Why?" Douglass was engaged, but didn't take his eyes off the entrance to the mine. With his night sight coming back, Willie could see where starlight seeped down to faintly illuminate the wooden frame.

"The councilmen told me to arrest him, not kill him. I was trying my best to do it," Willie said. "Casewit's two partners draw, and since no one told me nothing about whether they were to live or die, I shot them both between the eyes. Casewit put his hands up and surrendered. I hanged him the next morning after the trial for raping that girl and his murderings. Bastard kept trying to shimmy back up the pine tree I hung him from, but after twenty minutes or so he finally gave up and hung."

Douglass nodded. "And then you became their marshal, just like that?"

"Some didn't much like me as marshal," Willie said. "Some tried dueling me to get rid of me."

"Yeah? What happened?" Douglass asked.

"They're not here to talk about it, are they?" Willie said, leaning back against a crate. If that airship had dropped off more attackers, he needed a rest to get ready for them. "Think I'll take advantage of your hospitality, old timer, and take the first sleep while you cover the entrance."

Willie settled down with one of his Colts on his chest and closed his eyes.

The sound of a Winchester firing and the lever-action reload snapped Willie awake with his Colt coming up in the direction of the shot. He ran up from the depths of the mine in time to see movement down the hill in the scrub. After fetching a Winchester of his own, he joined Douglass and leaned against a large slab of rock.

"You let me sleep all night down there?" he asked Douglass. "Or did you fall asleep on watch?"

"I wanted the gunslinger you told me about last night to be as fresh as possible for the morning," Douglass said with a tired smile.

Willie sighted down the scree and rock. "Miners," he said.

"What?"

"You're holding off a band of miners. That one's got a pick-axe." He looked up at the morning sky and squinted with a sour expression. "Means that airship's gonna be floating around any moment."

One of the miners made a stumbling run up at them. Willie's Winchester cracked, and the man stumbled and dropped. He began to pull himself along with his hands, fingers digging into the hard soil to drag the rest of him toward the two marshals.

Willie snapped the lever down, back in, shot again, and the body fell still.

There were more coming up from the scrubland. How many miners had been out at the strike outside Duffy? He couldn't remember.

A bullet whined and struck the ground to the left of the mine opening. Willie moved in toward the rock for better cover.

Douglass reached inside his jacket and checked a pocketwatch on a long chain. "Six or seven hours to go, Mr. Kennard," he said, patting the signal gun in his waistband.

The droning sound Willie'd heard last night returned. The cigar-shaped airship passed overhead and floated over the canyon. Steam and black smoke poured from slanted, sideways stacks in a metal basket underneath the massive gas bag.

Willie stared, the miners momentarily forgotten. The thing was the size of a large city building, floating lightly through the air.

"What a thing," he said to Douglass.

But Douglass was more focused on the crowd lurking behind

cover, trying to advance on them. His rifle cracked out, dirt puffed, and the possessed miners hung back.

For now.

"I count a hundred figures," Douglass said, his dust-flecked face lined with exhaustion. Red eyes betrayed the man's lack of sleep. "I was not expecting so many, so quick."

And despite a full night's worth himself, Willie was already tired of shooting at shadows.

"They're massing for a charge. They'll be easy to shoot when they come over that open ground, but they're just too many," Willie said. "And without a Gatling gun or something as serious, I don't see how we kill them fast enough."

"I just had the one," Douglass said. "I was tracking the airship after I sent the pigeon for the cavalry. When I saw the mob, I thought I'd lend a hand."

"Was the gun damaged? I can't remember after the dynamite," Willie said.

"Dirty, on the ground. And not here," Douglass said.

The murmuring of the crowd shuffling about the loose rock downhill had been growing.

"If we climb up over the rock, the airship will see us in the daylight and shoot at us or drop dynamite. And if we go down there we'll face these miners," Willie said. "If we stay here, we will be overrun before noon."

"It is a despicable position we are in," Douglass agreed. "I can bring more rifles and ammunition up for our last stand. But I'll understand if you want to make a run for it. I, however, will make a stand and fire off the flares before I fall. I cannot imagine what these things would do if they were to get into a city. Think of New York or Philadelphia falling to them. It makes me shudder."

Willie leaned against the rock and thought of that for a moment, and then decided it was best to focus his imaginations on the present.

"Mr. Douglass, we should take our chances heading over the hills and staying alive," Willie said. "If we do that, we can alert the cavalry."

"The airship . . ."

"It'll be dangerous, but I think it best we engage with it if we have to," Willie said levelly. "I will smite these goddamned possessed men out of the sky if I must. But hopefully we can keep running long enough for the cavalry to save us."

They crawled out of the canyon with difficulty, hauling rucksacks with ammunition and several rifles with them.

And the signal guns.

Willie stopped twice to fire back at the horde behind them. Any of them able to climb with any precision dropped off the high hill face.

The horde waited patiently for them to make their climb.

Sweat drenched their dusty, tattered clothes by the time Willie and Douglass topped the hill and began to leg down into the next canyon. For another hour they hiked it, stopped to drink water, and then climbed up the other side.

It felt pointless skirting the foothills of the mountain, but once they had a canyon between them and the horde, they sprinted downhill, back toward Duffy.

"This way," Willie muttered after a half hour of fast walking.

Douglass said nothing. He looked focused on his breathing, and Willie eventually offered to take the man's rucksack. Douglass refused with a snarl.

And that snarl turned into a chuckle when the older marshal suddenly realized where they were. "Hell, Mr. Kennard. You wanted an old friend back, didn't you?"

Horse flesh littered the ground and draped off scrub. Flies buzzed. Pieces of the wagon were scattered around, and the Gatling gun was buried upside down in the dirt.

"We don't have much time," Willie said. "Help me drag it into the clear area."

That horde of mining men would not be too far behind.

The gun was mounted in such a way it wouldn't tilt up to aim into the sky. Why would it? No one had designed it with airships in mind.

But the Gatling would let Douglass hold his own.

They could hear the trampling march of feet in the distance. See some heads wavering over the low-lying scrub. The dust and desert made it easy to spot the first elements of the charge.

Willie grabbed the rucksacks and opened them up, pulling apart a knot and unrolling them. Set on the rock, their small arsenal was at the ready.

He picked up a pair of the signal guns.

Douglass glanced at his pocketwatch. "It is eleven. We still have an hour with even the most optimism."

Willie paid the time no attention. "I'm not thinking about your cavalry," he said.

"Then what . . ."

The airship swooped in from the hills with a buzz and swoosh of steam and smoke.

"Shoot at it with your rifle," Willie said. "Let them know we're down here."

Douglass looked reluctant to let go of the Gatling. He picked up a Winchester and fired off at the airship. It adjusted course, bearing down on them.

It vented something from the gasbag and lowered. Willie eyed it as being some five hundred feet off the ground.

"Come lower," he said sweetly.

And it did, responding to the crack of Douglass's Winchester.

It passed over the masses of miners advancing on them, some of them shooting wildly in their direction. A brown whale, shifting slightly as the wind bumped at it.

"Mr. Kennard?" Douglass asked. "What do you plan to do?"

"It's easier to shoot if you wait until you can't miss," Willie said, and fired the Very pistol. The flare sparked and fizzed as it arced out toward the airship.

Willie picked up the next pistol and fired. Same arc, slight adjustment based on the course of the last shot.

The first shot still hadn't hit as he picked up and fired the third.

And then one, two, three flaming orbs of light struck the gasbag.

The first one hit the nose and bounced off. People in the metal understructure were running back and forth, and already the airship was beginning to change course. Lift.

The second ball of light hit a piece of rigging. And stuck. It began to burn merrily.

Willie sighed and picked up the fourth Very pistol. The last one. He looked at the three rifles waiting beside them. The backups for the last stand.

The third flame, the last adjustment, arced over the nose of the airship and toward the area he'd seen the venting. There was enough left over gas in the air still.

It caught.

A wild, dancing flame ran along the top of the airship, and then like a devil it lanced downward. The entire envelope began to glow like hell itself, and then flames burst out from every corner and seam.

The cigar-shaped inferno staggered out of the sky and dropped to the desert floor before them.

When the hesitant crowds of miners walked around the remains of the airship, Frederick Douglass and the Gatling gun raked them with a withering volley of gunfire, while Willie stood on a tall rock and sighted with a Winchester, picking them off one by one with shots direct to the head.

*

Willie walked from body to body, examining them. Douglass followed him.

The cavalry had arrived, following the smoke. They'd help flush the town out. Drag the dead bodies to the street. They'd done the same to the mining camp.

Now Willie could look for the murderer that he'd tracked here. Make sure his job was done.

"I wonder," Willie mused as he walked down the line of carnage. "Why here?"

"What do you mean?" Douglass asked.

"Why Duffy? Why did creatures from some other world fly their airship all the way from the Alaska territories to Duffy? It was the mine, wasn't it? Just like everyone else coming here?"

Douglass thought for a moment. "If their machine was damaged, they could have been looking for metals."

Willie nodded. "That was what I wondered." He stopped. And squatted. Looked into a familiar face.

Well that was that, then: He'd found the man that had come into their camp. Killed his employer. Killed the other men.

Willie stood up. "Thank you, Mr. Douglass. I'll be on then."

"I have a counter-proposal," Douglass said abruptly. He waved his hand around at the uniformed cavalry stacking dead bodies. "There are still possibly other infected out there, in the countryside. You are a steady man with a gun, and with flint in his heart. We could use you, out here. And elsewhere. With . . . other things that pose a threat to the nation out here in this country."

Willie nodded. "I understand. But I was headed east, hoping to find myself a good woman."

Douglass leaned forward. "Now, I don't take you as the settling down sort. I asked around about you via telegraph yesterday," Douglass said. "Learned about you and Billy McGeorge. How'd you bring him in?"

Willie scratched his chin. "Offered a reward. Met him in town when he rode up to discuss the matter with me."

"He came to you?"

"Well, he wasn't too happy about the reward," Willie explained. "Everyone else was offering north of $300. I figured $50 was good enough for him. He figured that was insulting."

"Insulting?" That smile had come back to Douglass's lips again.

"Yep. Met his whole gang when they rode into town right in the middle of the street with my shotgun. Ended up shooting one of his men when they drew on me. Led the rest of them off to jail. Hung McGeorge from the same pine I hung Casewit on."

"Just like that?" Douglass asked.

"Just like that."

Douglass looked easterly, down the main street. "No room for a man like you back east, Kennard," he said softly. He gave him a business card. "If you don't find that woman, you call on me."

Willie nodded.

They gifted him a swift horse on Douglass's orders, though they grumbled about it. Willie left, riding east, leaving Duffy as the sun began to sink toward the horizon in the west.

THE SCAR THAT STAINS
RED THE GULCH

I **CAME TO** town, as begged by telegraph, as speedily as I could, to see about the problem of the women who'd all thrown themselves to death off Rushtown Gulch. I rode on the back of a sturdy chestnut mare with a crisp wind pummeling our heels and whipping up swirls of dirt. Rushtown wasn't more than a few streets of store facades, eagerly set up to drain the miners of their gold. In the evening's waning light, as the lamps began to flicker on, those windows looked as soulless and vapid as the men sitting about outside to stare at me.

The sheriff came out right away to demand any weapons I had on my person and demand my name.

"John Scobell," I told him. I gave him the rifle from my back, and the two pieces of hot metal on either side of my hip.

Even gave him the Remington under my seat, that he hadn't spotted, just to let him know I was cooperative.

Also gave him the sword I'd taken from that Lieutenant after I'd slit his throat, watched red stain gray, and then turn to black.

"What are you doing here?" he asked.

"Pinkerton," I said, and showed him identification. "Came to retrieve Moll Smith's remains, take them back to her sister."

The sheriff frowned.

"Moll . . ."

I leaned forward, made my voice all conspiratorial as I lied. "Turns out, she was from high quality folk. Fell from grace. Came out here. They want to bring her body back to the family plot."

The sheriff thought about that for a while. Again with the frown. He chewed at something non-existent for a while. "You sure you're a *Pinkerton*?"

"Last I checked." I sat back up fully. It was the skin color. They were used to the cowboys roaming around the west, Mexicans, free blacks, the ones coming up from the south after the war. But the law was usually white. And Pinkertons were . . . *kinda* the law.

Whole new world now. There was a black senator back down south now that the federal troops occupied the separatist states. When I have a kid, his name'll be Hiram Rhodes. Because to the day I die, that shit will always be amazing to me.

Now this sheriff was staring at me like the way I figured the white folk down in Mississippi stared at portraits of their new representative to the congress.

"Well we don't want no trouble here," the sheriff said.

"I'm a Pinkerton," I said.

"Right," the sheriff said, glancing around, stumbling as he fell off his script. "Right."

"Anything else?" I asked.

"No," the sheriff said. "Just . . . we don't want—"

"No trouble. Got it."

I looked over at the saloon doors and thought about fetching myself a whiskey. But no whiskey had ever tasted so good as the bottles we smashed to burn down George Albert's farm. Shipped all the way from Scotland, and tasted like leather.

Instead I went to find White Charlie.

*

White Charlie stopped at the edge of the gulch and tied his horse off on one of the gnarled trees that seemed to huddle into itself against the wind.

"That's where they did it, John," he said, pushing against the wind to get to the lip of rock. He yawned mightily before continuing. "Just jumped on right off like they was gonna go for a swim."

Only there was nothing but jagged rocks down in the old, dried up streambed, like the shattered teeth of a gaping mouth.

I sat there with my legs over the edge, trying to think about what would make a bunch of white women walk all the up the trail, past all the cactus and scrub and boulders and howling coyotes, to jump off into that certain death.

"I was sweet on the one called Jane," Charlie sighed.

"And I bet she was sweet back to you for a fistful of dollars," I said.

Charlie smiled and shook his head. "Weren't doing it like that. Just, looking for friendship. She had some secrets. She guessed mine. We looked out for each other."

And she hadn't been sad, or abused? Charlie didn't think so. He hadn't seen or heard anything.

"I read the doctor's report," I said, turning my back to the mouth of the gulch with a shiver. Somewhere in the back of my mind I remember my mother whispering the story of when she'd been back in one of the Caribe isles, before they had ripped her away north.

Telling the story of the Ibo warriors who had thrown themselves against the plantation owners to get free. They'd thought they were on a great land, the western equivalent of the coast they had been taken from.

"What would make them jump themselves off into that?" Charlie asked me.

When the Ibo, and the Yoruba and Iwe they had freed with them, had gotten to the edge of the small island, they had realized

the horrible truth. With torches flickering in the distance and flint-
locks firing into the night like lightning to reveal angry white faces
behind them, they'd scrambled their way to the top of a cliff.

They'd jumped.

A leap of faith, his mother had called it. Even the plantation
folk called it Selwin's Leap when his mom had worked the house
there as a child.

These white women, they'd been free. The doctor who exam-
ined them said no lesions to their brain, no disease other than the
ones he expected, no lasting marks of abuse.

White Charlie lived in a hut near the back of the saloon that
seemed to want to slump over to the right a bit.

"Saloon's life can't be easy," I said to him. "Handful of them
women, and all these men with gold in their eyes and dreams."

"I been all up and down and around the territories," Charlie
said, washing his face. "They ain't any worse treated than others.
No one went and done that before."

I ate some jerky and thought about it some. "What do you think
happened? You think someone did it to them?"

"I had any stirrings toward thinking I knew who did it, you
know what I woulda done already."

We lay down in the bed, the ropes creaking underneath from my
extra weight. It smelled of Charlie, and the mules he trained for the
miners. The air was bitterly cold and I could see it hanging above
our heads as we breathed, like a spirit drifting up from our bodies.

"You talk fancy now. Like one of them," Charlie said.

A flame of anger kindled in me, and my back straightened.

"It ain't a bad thing," he said quickly. "You got a job with the
law folk. It suits you. You were smart. It's why I telegraphed you.
You get the thing. You always went and figured it out when we
were down there."

The last time we'd lay under a blanket trying to keep warm

Charleston was burning in the distance. We were wandering the land, Charlie holding papers that said I was his. I had the eye for what was important, what the generals back north wanted to know. I could tell them where to head for the jugular. And Charlie, well, he looked white.

We were both useful.

The North, they acted like it was all battles and tactics that ended it. They never crowed about the folk who risked worse than death to slow production, sabotage crops, lose shipments, smuggle out information, and more.

There were a people that pulled the brakes of the train until it all came to a screaming halt, just sitting there, waiting to be overwhelmed when the armies marched south.

Can't fight if you can't eat.

"After, those Quakers asked me to go to their college," I told Charlie. "Get an education."

"You were good with a pen. I bet they loved you."

I snorted. "They loved the idea of free men, in theory. When I actually showed up on their white campus they shit themselves. They rioted. Freeing us in the South was an idea they worked hard for, but they sure as hell didn't want me showing up in the North."

"I shoulda done it. No riots for me. After, I coulda gone and said 'Boo, I'm really a darkie.' Good laughing there."

"You're a horse man," I said. "Always and forever. Nothing for you in those halls."

And Charlie, a good man, would never have told them about the secret stain. Can't say I blamed him.

Sometimes.

Other times, I hated him for it. Not him being born as he was, but that he kept it hidden.

In the middle of the night the bed creaked. I half woke, waited for that sound of piss hitting the pot.

When it didn't come I opened my eyes.

"Jesus, Charlie," I muttered. I pulled on the blanket, shivering.

White Charlie stood near the one small window in his hut, the view outside warped and twisted from the cheap glass. His skin gleamed in the moonlight, pale as a corpse.

"Charlie, what . . ." I trailed off. It wasn't anything I could put my finger to, but, a sense of unease tugged at me. A feeling that pressed down on me from around the edges of the night.

Charlie stared at the window, as rigid as a marble statue.

Through the window, I saw figures move. I grabbed my overcoat and leaned over my bags to find one of the pistols I had hidden away.

When I stepped outside, cursing mightily, I halted in my own tracks like a man struck by a club.

They were all out on the dusty street between the store fronts. What seemed like every living person in the town. Their eyes, unseeing as I passed between them, all stared toward the far edge of the town. The direction of the gulch we had just sallied back from at sunset.

Something howled in the distance, and it sent fear prickling down the back of my neck.

When the folk moved, and many of them did, it was as if some terrible child were playing with a mannequin, jerking their sorry limbs this way and that. Those that stumbled like this staggered their way off away from the town, while others milled about, staring toward something that I could not comprehend.

I stood there, pistol out, as the sheriff grunted and flailed past me without even so much as a glimmer of recognition.

I took White Charlie with me at high noon back to the gulch, now understanding his deep yawning for the symptom it was.

We pulled one of his mules along with us down the steep sides, kicking rock loose and sliding along the path that so many had already trod. Then we wound our way through the jagged boulders, still black with blood from the women that had fallen to their deaths on them as it had yet to rain.

"They all sleepwalked to here?" Charlie was dubious.

"Seen them do it. Followed the sheriff step by step."

The gulch's walls began to cast a shadow over us, and I felt a cool chill on my neck. I pulled my collar up against any wind, but the chill was still there, something of a cold hand on my nape.

"Here."

We tied the mule off to a gnarled tree with roots that made a fist around the broken rock it made a stand upon. The smoothly worn wood of its twisted branches held the rope, and I would have thought it a good hanging tree.

It shivered slightly in the wind that crossed the top of the gulch.

I broke out a cannabis cigarette. A habit I picked up from the cowboys out here, who were more often Mexican than not. It steadied a nervous hand, and when I faced the shaft dug into the side of the gulch, I needed that.

CAIN'S CLAIM, it said on the wooden beam across the top.

I stared at it for a long time.

"This where they come?" Charlie said. He was looking around for footsteps, but the ground was hard and baked, mostly stone.

"Yep," I said slowly.

"And they all walked on down in there?"

"Yep."

I'd slapped the sheriff across the face so hard, the outline was still there when I saw him at my breakfast. But last night, he hadn't blinked, just walked right on through me with a determination fueled by some sort of deviled animation.

No one could be stopped, until I'd tied up the doctor with a leash. He'd pulled at it so hard I got scared he'd hang himself, so I let him go.

Off into the dark of the mine.

I felt a coward for not following any of those damned souls in there. But there was only so much you could ask of a person. The rest is between him and his god, and I know mine would not pass judgement on my hesitancy.

There was no way in hell I would walk into that hellmouth of shadows without more than just a pistol and a sense of curiosity.

Charlie had licked his lips and shook his head when he found me sitting on his hand-carved chair just staring at him when he woke up. I'd told him what all I'd seen, with plain honesty, and he'd called me a fool and a liar.

Until he saw the tremor in my hands when I lit a cheroot to hand to him.

"Sometimes, I took to thinking you didn't think much of my ability to mentate," he told me after a deep lungfull. "Here I was, the one who could walk you through the valley of death, and yet sometimes, I see things in your eye."

"Brother . . ." I trailed off.

Charlie handed the cheroot back. "Don't matter. I know your mettle. What we seen, what we been at. I could pass through them's world, and I knew they would kill me just the same as you."

I knew.

We smoked a bit as morning made its way on the world, and Charlie looked closely at me.

"You're not funning me."

"I didn't travel all the way out here to make jokes, Charlie. We need to go back out to the gulch."

As we probed the dark with our lanterns and left the rectangular entrance and its promise of light behind us for the gloom of shadows and hard rock, my heart fluttered. I did not know if we would find the hand of whoever murdered the women, but in my time as an investigator for the Pinkertons, I had come to learn to leave no coincidence alone.

There were numerous digs of which we found several dead ends to. I wasn't sure of how far we'd walked, but we did several hours of it by my pocketwatch.

We stopped to eat and drink from the heavy packs I'd carried in.

"Pinkerton," Charlie said. "You stayed with the old spymaster?"

"He hired us. He saw us. He was an abolitionist." I threw several of the heavy crackers to the ground, not interested in picking out the weevils. Was a time I'd eaten them all up and been grateful for it.

"Lot of hate for them breaking the leaseholders out by the new rail."

"Pinkerton's as good as you hire him to be," I said.

Charlie snorted at that. We left our refuse, reshouldered our packs, and got to moving again. This time, we seemed to be following a main shaft. Or so Charlie said, who knew such things from being around the types who did that work.

The rock started to glitter by our light.

"Is that gold?" I asked, struck with a moment of wonder.

"Pyrite," Charlie grunted. "Fool's gold."

"And what's that?" I asked, looking further down where our lamps did not penetrate, where a sickly green glow seeped out of the walls.

Charlie did not know, but I scraped at it and came away with some sort of soft algae. The green light died in my fingers.

We pushed on, and the light grew to the point where we extinguished our lanterns. From there, it led us deeper and deeper into the heart of the earth, and to a great chamber within it, all lit in the eerie green glow of the living walls.

At the heart of the chamber was what I could only describe as a cocoon, gray and fibrous, a bulb of dessicated husk that stretched as tall as the two storeys of the saloon.

It resisted our tools.

I even shot it with the shotgun from the pack. A spray of noxious dust sprang into the air, and green sparkles filled the space around the cocoon. But there was barely any crater to the shell of the thing.

"What is it?" Charlie asked.

"I have no idea," I said. I checked the pocketwatch. The sun had set above the rock we were deep inside. I eyed Charlie warily, but he showed no signs of becoming entranced.

"We oughta get the doctor," Charlie said. "And the priest."

"And lots of dynamite," I added. There was a pressure building in the back of my head. Tension in the neck. And something else. A presence. A compulsion to do . . . something.

Ever had that feeling you forgot to do something but you can't quite remember what it was?

We camped after we climbed out, and I made a fire. I wanted to observe the night's activity from on high, from a safe place.

"I don't want to sleep," Charlie said. "If what you said is true, I don't to sleep."

"We all gotta sleep, Charlie. I'll look over you."

He drank coffee, committed to fighting the urge. But by ten he pitched over. I saw him struggle against it, but something came up over him and his eyes rolled back.

For a while, it was just normal sleep. Some snoring.

At midnight he sat bolt upright.

Only this time, he began to flail and churn toward the cliff's edge. I tackled him like a calf and roped him quick. I'd learned my lesson from last night, so I tied his feet and hands off, then hung him from a nearby tree.

He spent the whole night bucking about, much to the mule's annoyance.

Wasn't like when he was back in town. Being closer to the source, that left him more under the hand of the controlling force in that mine than he had been in town.

Down in the gulch, fifty people from town walked on toward the Cain's Claim, just as they had previous. Only this time, I noticed that they were carrying things. I hadn't cottoned to that last night.

I saw jars of chemicals. Sacks of cornstarch. Oils. Handfuls of nuts and bolts.

What would a demonic source need metal bolts for?

I could think of nothing, but as I sat and watched, my mind wandered. I'd slept little the night before, and as I mulled the problem, my eyes slipped closed.

"Jesus!" I cried out as I woke on the end of a rope leash I'd made for myself. I stood near the edge of the cliff, looking down, saved by a faint suspicion that even I would not be immune.

The ladies of the saloon were the most recent to town. I found this by asking about. And from old man Trevor, I was told the tale of a young boy who had gone missing from a camp on the gulch side of the edge of town.

"The effect must be more powerful the closer you are," I told Charlie. "Like a magnet."

And the longer one lived in town, the greater the effect.

The owner of the claim, one Cain Jenkins. Well, the last he'd been seen was three weeks ago.

"Most of the town came up just two months ago," Charlie said. "That's when Cain sent word to his brother he found a big old vein. Asked him for money. Word spread. People came to start digging. Big claims all around."

Charlie got here three weeks ago.

Those poor women, their limbs twitching and jerking about, must have been marched off the cliff by whatever lay deep beneath the earth there in that gulch. Or maybe, recently come to the town, some small piece of their minds had rebelled, and like the Ibo at Selwin's Leap, they had jumped rather than let themselves be enslaved to the malevolence in that mine.

*

The learned men of the town marvelled at the cocoon.

Charlie had worked the magic that he was best at when my mind and his skin were married, convincing them that they needed to go looking for the missing Cain. We spread rumors around town, each to the purpose of getting folk to hunt the man down. I found a way to move the pieces around the board where I needed.

Some men hacked at the cocoon. The doctor poured acid on it. It was impervious to their hands.

Of course, dynamite was suggested, but with so many in the chamber the sheriff put a stop to it.

I was disappointed.

"Where'd it come from?" the sheriff asked.

One of the rock-men said it might have been here millions of years, like a fossil, and Cain had uncovered it. But another pointed out the rock above looked congealed. As if the cocoon had melted through it from above. In that case, maybe it had fallen to earth in great heat, and melted through to land in this cavern.

They would have to call out for scientists, and they would need to notify authorities higher up, and maybe even the army. There was a division sixty miles away.

Plans were made, but it was near sunset, and everyone hurried back to town.

"We should tell them," Charlie said. "About the walking."

"The army gets here, and scientists, they'll know soon enough. I can't go around saying I was slapping the sheriff, can I?"

I tied Charlie up to the bed, and I took the chair and a great pot of coffee.

My last night? I intended to spend it wide awake and ready for anything.

*

I saw the fire through the thick panes of the hut's window.

"Mr. Scobell," I said out loud. "Do not investigate this thing. Leave it be."

But I did not heed my own counsel, and instead took my Winchester and some pistols with me. I heaved on my overcoat and stepped out.

The telegraph office burned merrily in the night.

Then the horses started screaming. I found a scene of butchery and horror in the stables, as the poor animals were being ripped apart by the very people who owned them.

Whatever force this was, it had woken to the threat against it.

I went back to the hut where Charlie strained against his bonds.

"I think I have to solve this one myself," I told him, grabbing my pack full of weapons and slinging them over my shoulder.

I broke into the general store, jumped the counter, and in the back, found the crates of dynamite. The horses were dead, and I'd seen men moving on the mules as well.

So I filled the inner pockets of my overcoat with dynamite, the outer pockets as well, and then joined the flow of people heading for the gulch, their arms full of knickknacks and oddities, their faces as vacant as a madman in an opium house.

I debated for a long time about taking in the explosives myself or hanging the sticks on someone else, but I felt it would be cowardly to hang the dynamite on some poor soul to walk it in and die with no consent on their part.

So I merged with the lines of people staggering down into the mine.

With no light, I panicked for a while as we shuffled in the dark. But I could feel the press of others near me, and soon the green glow greeted me.

It was stronger now. Not brighter, but it pushed against my

mind with a persistence that made me want to shout back at it. And as I approached the chamber, I had to gasp. All around, my vision wavered, as if my eyes could not properly reflect what I saw.

There was no cocoon now. Instead there was a rippling lack of nothingness that was something, a vastness in a tiny space, that made my head swim in confusion.

I wanted, more than anything, to drop to my knees and crawl in obesience.

But I was awake, and strong. I had kept my own voice to myself when lashed with a whip. I had remained calm as Confederates questioned me, suspicion in their eyes. I had ridden under the hell of artillery slamming from overhead.

I huddled against the wall, tears streaming down my cheeks and lit stick after stick of dynamite in my coat.

When I last walked out of the mine, I had timed how long it took with my pocketwatch out of a sense of general curiosity. That gave me a sense for how long to cut the dynamite's cord before I lit it.

And after I threw the coat into that warped, shifting, changing place that wasn't really there, I turned and ran.

The explosion happened before I got to the gulch. Either I miscalculated, or I hadn't been running as fast as I thought. A hot wind slammed up through the mine, and I felt a shiver go through me.

Fear.

Anger.

Confusion.

And the eyes of people looking at me. Faces turning. Faces *seeing* me.

I ran then. Ran hard. Ran from the hands grasping at my shirt, pulling at my hair. I leapt over feet that tried to trip me.

They ran after me. Everything surged to catch me, and then I burst free of the mine. Up ahead, the gulch was closed off. Lined with angry faces that had dropped whatever they held and picked up rocks or sticks.

I'd left the pack hanging from the great tree near the mine's entrance, and with half the town on my heels, I grabbed it. Without hardly a thought, I scrambled up the old tree.

The force within the townsfolk seemed to focus, and their movements became less spasmodic, more fluid.

I watched as old man Trevor grabbed the nearest branch to pull himself up after me. And then the sheriff came. And then more, until the tree shook and leaned with the weight of all the bodies crawling with malevolent intent toward me.

As they did, I calmly hung my pack on the branch to the right of my head, taking comfort in the ammunition and weapons I'd stored inside.

That night I killed thirty seven white men who tried to climb the tree to kill me. I bathed its limbs in their blood, and I figured, come morning, I would likely hang from the same tree for what I had done.

But before dawn, the force that animated them gave up. It needed living bodies for something, and this did not suit it. There was a grand plan that I could not perceive from behind my human veil.

As the first birdsong echoed through the gulch, my pulse still pounding from fear, I climbed down and stepped over the corpses I had made as I headed cautiously back to town.

I packed what I had and didn't even bother to go to the deputy to ask for my weapons back.

White Charlie and I left on our own feet.

We walked the whole day with no rest. And the next. But Charlie broke free of his ropes while I slept, and I couldn't go after him. I couldn't go any closer back without becoming one of them. I didn't have any spirit left for resisting.

I wept for Charlie, I sucked on raw coffee beans, chewed them, and I kept walking. I had survived many things in this world. I determined to survive this as well.

I didn't stop until I saw the Pacific Ocean.

I had nervous occasion to pass back through that damned town a year ago when the train linked up nearby and I knew I could be well away while it was still light out. I found a ghost town, and a hermit living in the ruins of the saloon.

"Never anything in any of those mines that I could find when I came here," he told me after I gave him some cheese and liquor. "Never even a bank in town for their gold. Strange gold rush that, one with no bank."

That was something I realized hadn't even pierced my conscious nature the last time here. I wondered, not for the first time, just how much of a pall I had been struggling under here.

I still wake up from time to time with random things in my hands. And to the day I die, I will always sleep with a rope around my waist, hitched to something solid just like a horse.

There are some experiences that stain you, that you can never escape.

Something from that gulch still lingers deep within me, a scar in the back of my mind. I hope to never again pass the ruins of that town in my lifetime, even though I am sure that whatever came to dwell there seems long gone today.

TIDES

IT WAS MOONLIGHT-TIME and the second sun, orange and stately, slipped into the inky depths of the Roranraka sea. The first sun had been quenched for well over a tide. Siana played in the silver pools the tide had left behind, looking for spiraled shells that she could decorate her new room with.

She didn't skip from pool to pool. On the crumbly, wet coral, skipping could cause a slip and fall, and Siana had learned about falls the hard way. She had fallen face first into a patch of firecoral when she was very little. Her mom said she'd cried so loud, half the tall-village came looking for her. And the wickedly fierce burning left small patches of Siana's left cheek discolored.

Siana had to time her excursions for shells well. Her tall-village sat in the middle of the ocean, on the tallest mid-ocean peak where reef had grown and sand had collected over time. Several times during the day the Roranraka receded, and Siana could look for shells. But during the rest of the day the ocean lapped at the pillars of her entire village.

So Siana carefully stepped her way between the pools.

In a funny-looking kidney-shaped pool, she paused and squatted to try and peer through the mirrored surface. The hem of her gray skirt touched the water and turned even darker. It stirred ripples into the surface as she shifted.

Although Siana couldn't see very well through her reflection, she was the best at finding beautiful shells. It wasn't a case of looking, she knew, but reaching her hand out over the surface and feeling through the water for the perfect shell.

There! Just tucked into the corner of the pool was a mahogany-brown cowlie. Rippled stripes ran in wedges around the spiral, and clean bone-white patterns twisted in between them. How beautiful. Siana carefully reached down and picked it up. Ah, and she was lucky, nothing had moved into the empty shell.

It sat large in her hand, dripping salty water down her palm and tickling her wrist when she held it up into the moonlight. This will go above the doorway, Siana thought. Right next to Toffhey, her stuffed dolphin.

A large shadow passed in front of Mainmoon: a long, thin, airship. Siana stopped admiring the cowlie. She'd never seen an airship before, though Mum talked about them sometimes in a sad way. Teamdroves of enormous wrinkled birds squawked and complained as they pulled the large silvery craft against the wind.

It was going towards her tall-village! Siana tucked the cowlie into a wet, dirty, canvas bag along with all the other shells she'd collected. She walked back home, but slowly. No matter how excited Siana got, she refused to chance the firecoral.

When Siana finally got home, she stood and looked up at the four massive wooden posts that kept home above the high-tide level. All the lanterns were lit, flickering a warm yellow light. Her new room, hanging off of the side of the main hut and propped up on the south post, also had a lantern in the window.

Even stranger, Siana could smell cooking and the excited rumbling of Dad's voice. Strange because they'd just had supper, and Mum had let her out to go look for shells while the tide was well out.

Siana grabbed the first rung of the ladder and climbed up and up. She paused halfway to catch her breath. When she reached the hatch of the entryway, she clambered in and closed it behind her. She carefully set the canvas bag of shells down.

"Siana? Is that you?" Mum called, peeking around the corner of the door.

"Yes."

"Come in," she said with a big smile. "There's someone we'd like you to meet." Mum smelled reassuringly of bread and saltfish stew. She wore her apron, and had her long brown hair carelessly pulled back in a ponytail. Her hair, Siana thought, was almost the color of the cowlie in her bag. And so was her skin. Tanned and weathered.

Siana walked into the room. Dad sat in his driftwood armchair. He was also grinning. And next to him stood a woman. The woman looked a lot like Mum: the same brown eyes, and the sharp cheeks. She looked the same age as well. But even though she smiled when she saw Siana, the woman's eyes looked really tired, like Dad's when he'd been out after a whale for many weeks and come home without a catch.

"Hello, Siana," the woman said. "I can't believe how big you've grown. Look at you!"

Siana smiled politely. Adults always said things like this in a high-pitched voice. It actually annoyed her, but Mum would get angry if Siana got smart with the guest.

"Thank you," Siana said.

"Do you know who she is?" Mum asked excitedly.

Before Siana could hazard a guess, though she was thinking that the visitor was a cousin to Mum of some sort, the woman spoke.

"I'm Miasia. I'm your sister."

Siana pursed her lips.

"No you're not. Mum says my sister died in the Coastal War."

Mum made a half strangled sobbing noise, and Dad looked angry for a second. Then he grinned ruefully.

"No, Siana." He reached out with his long arms and pulled her closer. "No, this is really your sister, Miasia."

Siana regarded Miasia for a moment.

"Sorry," Siana said. "You looked old. You look just like Mum. But even older."

Miasia looked at Mum and shrugged.

"I've been through a lot," she said. There was a large duffel bag by her feet. She picked it up and opened it. "But, I do have a little something for you that I bought back from over the ocean." Miasia pulled out a small wooden box and gave it to Siana. It was made of old, dark wood, with brass hinges that creaked as Siana opened it.

Inside sat a purple and pink conch shell. It was stunning.

"Thank you," Siana breathed. She moved away from Dad and gave Miasia a quick hug. "It'll go well with the other shells in my new room."

Dad tapped his fingers on his chair.

"Siana, Miasia's going to sleep in your new room tonight." He glanced at Mum. "Until we figure out how things are going to work. Okay?"

Siana stood stunned. She knew how "temporary" things like this worked in a tall-village. Where could Miasia sleep except here? She'd just come back, and it would take her a long time to get settled on the island. And Dad couldn't afford the wood for another new room; it had taken him years to work for the extra wood to build the small addition to their tall-house.

There were few islands scattered on the ocean, and even fewer building resources traded between them and the Mainland. And tall-villages all across the Roranraka were fighting the Coastal War for access to forests, so that they could build their homes that barely stuck out of the ocean. Siana's Mum often told her it made everyone sad to lose so many children, and brothers and sisters, for the sake of wooden pilings.

Siana looked at a sister she had almost forgotten. Her return was a good thing, Siana thought, but losing a room! Children in tall-villages dreamed and prayed for a room of their own most of their lives. And now . . .

She started to get a pout ready, but Dad gave her a stern look, knitting his eyebrows together. Siana sighed.

"It's not fair," she declared. "I'm going back outside."

"No you're not. Easytide comes in a few hours," Mum said.

"It's only a few inches," Siana started.

"No."

Siana bit her lip.

"I'll go to bed then."

"That's a good idea," Dad said. Siana changed into her night-clothes and crawled back into her old bed, the one next to the kitchen. The bed she'd spent most of her life in. Her elbows hit the shelves on one end, and her feet the other. Bulbs of onions, dangling parsley, garlic, all swung in planters above her. Siana listened to the distant murmur of everyone talking while she mulled over various ways of running away from home.

None of them would work. There weren't any big vessels she could stowaway on besides the whaler Dad worked on, and the tides prevented anyone from walking to any of the other islets near hers. The nearest other tall-village was a week away by boat. The only other land was Mainland, hundreds and hundreds of miles away, where the world came up out of the ocean, and green trees grew, and people lived without worrying about tides. It sounded like a fairy-tale.

But the Mainland was crowded with people. And they guarded their precious trees with their lives. Tall-villagers were not welcome. The only way Siana could get there was if she got involved in the Coastal War. Children were not meant for that kind of fighting.

The thought of the Coastal War made her think of Miasia again, and got Siana even angrier.

Just before Siana fell asleep, she heard someone walk carefully up to her. Siana feigned sleep, but peeked. Miasia stood there as if wanting to say something, but then apparently thinking Siana was asleep, left. Her footsteps creaked on the floorboards.

At least someone was getting their own room tonight, Siana thought. She turned back the other way, trying to get comfortable.

Siana followed her friends to the edge of the tall-village the next midtidemorning, and everyone kept questioning her about Miasia.

"Where has she been?"

"What does she look like now?"

"Why does she look so old when she is only a little older than you, Siana?"

"Did she use up all her magic?"

Siana looked at the excited faces, their hair blowing in the wind. The sand sucked under her feet as she walked.

"And how is Siana today?" she asked, annoyed. But even her close playfriends didn't find it all that horrible that Siana had lost her room.

In fact, most of the children in the tall-village weren't very nice to her. Siana's family had only been in this tall-village since her grandfather had fallen on hard times and been forced to leave the Mainland to become a whaler. So still, when they played war, Siana had to be the Evil Coastie.

"Really, Siana, it must be so neat to have a sister back from the wars," they all said. Then they rolled their eyes when Siana slurped off down the sandtrails in a huff.

It had been her room. Why did Miasia have to return at all?

Siana asked Mum that same question with a calculated foot stomp. Mum looked down at her, then leaned over. Her shell necklace tinkled and shifted.

"It's not always easy," Mum said softly. "Sometimes we have to adapt. I wish we could just live on the beach, not on the poles. It would be so much easier to build a home."

But that was silly. Mum was being strange. The tides would wipe out a house without stilts in an instant. Its owners would never be heard from again.

Mum's silliness didn't change Siana's rage.

She stomped towards her bed. She looked at the shells on her shelf above her bed, and the cowlie she had picked out for Mum but hadn't given her yet. She was might regret this later, but . . .

Siana swept the shells onto the floor with a shriek.

"I hate it! It's not fair."

"Siana," her mother yelled. "Your shells!" The fragile pieces lay on the floor, most of them okay. Shells were tougher than they looked. Some had chipped their spiraled edges, or the little horns sticking off their sides.

But the beautiful cowlie, Siana's new pride, had shattered against the little table by her bed.

"Siana," her mother pointed. Miasia's gift, the conch shell, also lay broken. "Why?"

Siana swallowed.

"I don't care," she declared, lying. "I don't care." She ran out of the kitchen and down the ladder.

Siana sat against one of the pillars of the tide-caller's station. It was the highest building in the tall-village, and the furthest out. She let her last few tears dry on her cheeks and sat watching the second sun rise as the first sun dipped below the horizon to fire the sky and clouds with patterns of deep red and purple.

Miasia crossed the sand with a slight limp. Siana scuffled to face the other way as Miasia got close.

"Hey," Miasia said.

Siana didn't answer.

"Mum says the conch shell fell off the shelf and you're pretty upset about it."

Siana looked at Miasia.

"No she didn't. You're just saying that."

Miasia leaned back in mock horror.

"Caught in my own lie! Okay, I'm sorry. I couldn't think of anything else to say that would be more comfortable for the both of us. Can I sit?"

"I guess."

Miasia scooped out some sand and then wiggled into the side of the pillar. She turned a bit to look at Siana. Siana resolutely stared ahead. Miasia pulled out a wooden bead with tiny lines of blue painted around it in a wiggly pattern. She held it up to the sun. Siana watched out of the corner of her eye, still trying to pretend not to.

Then Miasia opened her palm and dropped her hand below the bead a few inches. And the bead stayed where it was: in the air, just above Miasia's palm.

Siana couldn't not look. She shifted around to face her sister.

"How'd you do that?"

Miasia grinned.

"It's not that hard. You could probably do it. According to my teachers, the talent runs in blood."

"Wow," Siana breathed. The bead spun in the air. "But what about the price?" She'd been taught in school about it. Using magic was dangerous. Miasia sighed and the bead dropped into her fingers.

"Each little bit of magic takes a proportionately sized piece of your life," she said. The corners of her mouth tugged down briefly, and she looked past Siana's shoulder, out at the sand that went on and on into the distance.

"Miasia," Siana asked. "Is that why you look old like Mum?"

"Yeah." Miasia stood up. She grunted as she did so. But Siana was still thinking.

"You shouldn't have floated that bead," she said. "That cost you."

Miasia smiled and ran a finger through Siana's hair.

"It only cost me a few seconds," she said. "It's the least I can do for taking your room away from you."

Maybe, Siana thought, maybe Miasia wasn't so bad.

They stood up and started to walk slowly back to tall-home, Siana delaying to look for shells, Miasia limping. Halfway there, Siana paused at a leftover pool of water and looked in. There was a small shell she couldn't quite reach, but Miasia quite deftly leaned over past Siana and plucked it out of the water, only slightly wetting the edge of her sleeve.

"What did you do in the wars?" Siana asked, a bit bold, as Miasia dried the shell off on her dress.

"I made shells. Invisible shells, like bubbles, to protect the officers." Miasia shut her eyes. "Before battle ten or twenty of us spellcasters would stand in the tent. The officers came in one side, their uniforms bare to the danger of gunfire, and they came out the other side protected by my magic. I had to make the bubbles big for them, to give them enough air to come back and have the bubbles unlocked so they could breathe. I had to repair damaged shells, not far from the fighting. All the time around us soldiers died of horrible things, Siana, and I grew old quickly."

"Oh."

"One day the Coasties attacked the tent." Miasia looked around to see if anyone was about, then pulled up the edges of her skirt and showed Siana the angry red scar that ran down the front of her leg.

"Why didn't you have your own bubble?" Siana asked.

"They don't teach us that version of the spell. The rulers decided to take all the books about magic that spellcasters owned a long time ago, and only the rulers can decide what spells they should teach each spellcaster. That way no spellcaster gets too powerful, like they used to be in the barbaric Old Ages. But then the rulers still get to use the powers to help them. So other than that one powerful spell they taught me for the war, all I know are some simple little tricks."

Siana digested this all.

"Why did you leave the tall-village?" Siana asked. "If the magic was going to do this to you."

Miasia looked off into the distance.

"You know Dad promised the rest of his life to the whalers to afford our tall-house? Just because those on the Mainland drive the price of wood so high. I wanted to help Dad."

Siana scratched at the sand. Dad always looked glum. Always sea-tough, tired, and yet so proud of her shells.

The thought of fighting Miasia for the room suddenly seemed extremely selfish and petty. Siana realized she had much growing up to do. Her sister was drained and old from war, her father chained to the whaling ships for life, and Mum did her best to find part time work around the tall-village, cooking and cleaning for established families.

But Siana didn't want to think about sober things. It was still a pretty day out, with the salt heavy in the air. All those adult things seemed so far away.

"Would you teach me the bead trick?" she asked.

After all, what were a few seconds of her life in exchange for the ability to really impress her playfriends?

But Miasia turned away. All the joy dropped from her face. Siana realized how old Miasia looked: her face had wrinkles, and some of her hair had begun to silver and grow wispy.

"Let's go back," Miasia said.

It took Siana several days to get Miasia to ease up and show her the bead trick again. And Siana tried to look through Miasia, just like she looked through the pools of water to find her shells.

Miasia handed Siana the bead with a smile.

"Okay, you try."

Siana let the bead sit in the crease of her folded hand. It felt slightly hot. She scrunched her forehead and stared at the bead, willing as hard as she could for it to rise.

Nothing happened.

Miasia put her hands underneath Siana's and smiled. The bead began to rise into the air.

"Oh," Siana giggled. The bead hovered, then it slowly began to spin, gyrating like a top on the floor, wiggling all over the place. The little lines of blue painted onto the bead created a smooth mesmerizing pattern in the air. "I wish I could do it," Siana said, frustrated.

"You are," Miasia said. "Now." She pulled her hands away and the bead continued spinning, for a second. Siana gasped in surprise and the bead spun out from her hands and landed in the sand.

Miasia laughed and tousled Siana's hair.

"Not bad you little egg, not bad at all."

Siana looked at the little bead in the sand.

"Can I try again?"

Miasia leaned over and picked the bead up.

"Sure," she said.

They spent the rest of the hour laughing and together making the bead dance over their hands.

Siana's guilt at the smashed shells was weighing on her mind, and she decided she should find a good shell for Miasia and Mum as a way of making up. She left after one of the littletides, just before the rushtide, to go out and look for the best shells. The best shells were to be found just beyond the edge of the tall-village, past the lookout towers who would no doubt call Mum to come and fetch Siana back into the tall-village because she was wandering too far out. Again.

She squelched out eastwards over the sand, and then after a while started picking her way over rock as the ground slipped downwards. Walking around great round pieces of brain coral that were orange-gray, wrinkled, and covered in mucus, Siana began to zero in on a few tide pools that felt promising.

Mainmoon sat gray in the sky, along with first sun. This was farther than Siana usually went.

Siana found the perfect pool. She carefully squatted at the edge, then waddled down in. Her careful movements sent ripples across the peaceful surface. Despite her caution Siana's foot slipped in between two rocks and she fell into the tide pool.

The cold water shocked her, and for a moment she floated there. Then her foot began to throb and Siana started to cry. She was scared, her foot hurt, and she knew she'd definitely walked too far away: she would get into trouble from Mum.

"Hey, hey," came Miasia's voice. "Don't cry. It's okay." Her sister's face appeared at the edge of the pool, and Siana stopped crying.

"Miasia?"

"Yep. The lookout sent someone to fetch Mum to bring you back. I decided to come instead. Figured you'd get into less trouble." Miasia reached over and grunted as she helped Siana out of the pool.

Cold water streamed from Siana's dress and she shivered, glad to be out in the first sun's warmth.

"I'm sorry," Siana said. "I was trying to find the best shells for you and Mum."

"Well, that's sweet of you," Miasia said. "But come on, let's go home, rushtide is coming soon."

"My ankle hurts."

"All the more reason to leave now. We'll go to the nearest lookout."

Siana grabbed Miasia's shoulder and they both slowly hobbled back towards the tall-village. They passed the brain coral step by step with Siana stopping to rest when her ankle hurt too much.

Miasia tried not to look worried, but Siana knew she had done something very bad. Miasia kept looking north when she thought Siana wasn't looking. They both knew rushtide was coming soon. Siana had been hoping to find her shell and walk back, with just enough time, to the nearest lookout. Any tall-villager knew the tide schedule instinctively; their lives revolved around it in every way.

Siana should have made it back to the tall-village already. And because they were on the slope, no one from the lookouts could see them to come out and help.

She tried to hobble faster, but it only hurt more. She tripped and fell, and Miasia couldn't move quickly enough to catch her. Siana's chin hit a piece of rock.

"Oww . . ." She forced tears back. "Miasia, I'm scared."

"It's okay," Miasia said. Her feet began squelching in sand that had become slightly wetter. "I'm going to try and carry you."

Siana got on Miasia's back and grabbed her thin shoulders. Miasia grunted and began slowly walking.

"Mum's going to be really mad at me," Siana said.

"Maybe not," Miasia said, out of air and panting the words. "If we don't—" She shifted Siana's weight. "—tell her."

They walked a little while longer, then Miasia set Siana down, breathing heavily.

"I'm sorry," she said, her voice breaking, "I can't do it. I'm too spent. I'm too old."

Siana, scared, grabbed Miasia's hand.

"Come on, I can keep walking. We have to make it."

She hobbled on faster, leaning on Miasia, but after a minute the ankle began to give out, and Siana was hopping. And in the sand and rock, every hop was almost a disaster. She flopped to the ground twice more, once bringing Miasia down with her.

Siana tasted salt water. A thin trickle was beginning to flow up the slope with them.

Miasia sat down and ripped at the hem of her skirt. She took the strip of cloth and bound Siana's leg to her own.

"Now try," Miasia said.

They began to walk in tandem. It took a few tries. They started slow, splashing through the water, then got into a good peg-legged rhythm. But the water was beginning to trickle louder around them, and Siana heard a familiar distant roar.

"Faster," Miasia ordered, an edge in her voice.

They cleared the rocks and stepped onto wet sand. Siana lost her step and they both tumbled. Siana could see tall-village. The nearest lookout was frighteningly far away. If she'd been able to jog she could have made it in time.

Siana struggled to get back up, crying out from the stab of pain in her ankle, but she couldn't. Miasia was still sitting. She had a distant look on her face. She started unwrapping their legs.

"What are you doing?" Siana asked. The cold water swirled around her lap and tugged the strip of cloth away when Miasia let it go.

"Pay attention," Miasia said, "to what I'm going to teach you."

Siana's heart thudded in her chest and her mouth went dry.

"Now," Miasia said. "I'm going to create a bubble around that rock, and then teach you how to unlock the bubble on your own."

"No, that will take too long." Siana said. "Teach me how to make a bubble and we can make them on each other."

Miasia looked at Siana, the lines in her face crinkling as she smiled.

"It took me weeks and weeks of training, sister. This isn't just a bead trick you can learn in a day. The unlocking trick is hard enough, but I know you can do it."

"No," Siana said again. "If you put me in a bubble without teaching me how to unlock then you can run back to the lookout tower and come get me after rushtide."

"What if I don't make it? Who will come unlock it? You will run out of air and die as well."

"Don't say that," Siana begged, starting to cry again. "You will, you have to. You just got here. I'll lose you again."

"Stop it," Miasia said. "Pay attention." She grabbed Siana's hands. "Please. Pay attention."

And maybe it was just her ability to stay calm that she'd learned abroad, at war, but Siana responded to Miasia's calmness by falling quiet.

"Okay."

Miasia spread her hands and murmured some words. Siana

didn't understand them, but she could feel them coming out of Miasia and caressing the rock. The rock shimmered, half in and half out of the rushing water. Then a clear bubble formed around it, trapping the air and protecting the rock. The water rushed around it.

The spell was powerfully subtle, and Siana could not grasp what Miasia had done no matter how much she strained to hear and see and understand.

She had to learn to save Miasia with a bubble. But the understanding never came to Siana. Miasia sighed and relaxed. She looked tired.

"Okay. Now feel with me as I unlock it."

Miasia took Siana's hands in her own and Siana followed as they both reached out and felt the bubble around the rock. There was a spot Siana could feel, a spot where she could put in her finger and twist. Miasia twisted the bubble and it collapsed. Water rushed around to fill the empty space. It burbled over Siana's belly now, threatening to sweep her away.

"Now I'm going to put one around you," Miasia said. "And make it large enough to last through the tide."

"No," Siana begged. "Please . . ." she trailed off and began to cry. Miasia hugged her.

"I love you, little sister," she said. She stood up and stepped back, and Siana closed her eyes and cried some more.

The water around her quit rushing.

She looked back up from inside the now massive bubble surrounding her and saw Miasia moving through the water back towards the tall-village. Through the ground she could feel the vibration of rushtide, and the wall of rapidly rising water took Miasia's shrunken figure.

Siana ran over and slapped the wall of the bubble with her small fists and cried until it hurt, then cried some more, and still the pain didn't go away.

Eventually she slipped into the now tepid water floating around in the bottom of the bubble. The water level all around her rose until she was totally underwater. The surface lay many feet overhead, and torpedo-shaped scudderfish began to nose around the edge of the bubble. Every breath sounded loud inside the bubble, and the light that filtered down to her danced and rippled around her.

The tall-village now stood alone in the center of the Roranraka Sea, alone for hundreds of miles.

At times the tide threatened to wash the bubble away, but Miasia had grounded it well, including a great amount of sand and water in the bottom. She had put it near a large rock, so it moved a little, but stayed still.

After the many hours of rushtide, the people for the tall-village emerged from the houses and came to look for Siana. When they found the bubble, they gathered around and began hammering away at it with whatever they could find. Hammers, chisels, axes.

Mum and Dad pressed up against the side with frantic faces, but Siana ignored them. She pressed her cheek against the bubble, trying to touch that last piece of her sister that lay deep in the filmy nothingness between Siana and the outside.

No one outside understood what Siana could feel and understand; that when she unlocked the bubble Miasia's presence, contained in the bubble which she had given a piece of her life to create, would dissolve. Siana's tears ran freely, and she pressed her fingers against the bubble.

"I'm so sorry," she sobbed as she found the lock with her mind. When she put her finger in and turned, the bubble fell apart. The water in it burst out and soaked everyone around it, and the pieces of bubble whisped out at them in little filmy fragments that passed harmlessly right through them and evaporated in a flash of rainbow colors.

And inside Siana, something else broke, and her tears stopped cold.

Siana flinched when Mum and Dad hugged her. She was

looking far, far off into the unseen distance, to where there was real land, land that didn't have the tides. She felt hard inside, and friends, fun, and shells fell from her mind.

After she had been carefully tucked into the new bed in Miasia's room, Siana looked at the broken conch shell on the floor. It would be a long time before the next airship touched at her tall-village, but Siana knew she would leave with it. Out there, she could learn the magic that would have let her save her Miasia. She would practice what little she knew, and try to learn what she couldn't. She would erase anything of herself to lose the pain of Miasia's memory.

And all the village who saw her in the days, and months after, whispered to each other. Though they didn't think she could hear them, Siana could. They whispered that she seemed different from the village folk. They said that she was no longer a wild, young child, favored by her parents. They thought she had a far off look in her eyes, and that she seemed . . . older.

THE WIDOW'S CUT

IN THE SEVENTH year of the reign of An, four thousand spearmen marched on the Okland edgetowns in the south. None stood against the bristling march of death. The small folk fled before the death and destruction with tales of woe and slaughter, and words passed on to the Great An by fast-flying scouts from the Kairin mountain pass.

Great An, my childhood friend, the one who'd held my hand as we waited for my father's heavy breathing to finally finish in a fading gasp, called for me. I ran through the oak doors carved to look like wings to the common room where he waited with his electors.

"Take three of our fastest skyknights," An said. "Go east until you see the Heron tribes. I've sent messages ahead; they will let you pass. Once fed and rested, make for the coast and petition for a meeting with Ibbisal."

"Ibbisal?" I couldn't believe what I was hearing. Their slow, silk skyhawk ships had clashed with the Heron tribes so often. "The Heron hate him. He's a rising threat to all we built in the east. Some think the spearmen are his."

"If that's the case, and they are, find out what Ibbisal wants, then see what you can do to stall him. But the scouts say the spearmen are wearing Condor colors."

Okland fought them in a great war three years ago, and we'd burned their rookeries, smashed their eggs, and hunted their skyknights down. We'd ignored them since. They couldn't fly, so what threat were they to us?

Our pride had left us vulnerable.

The electors had a plan. Two hundred of our archers assembled outside, and An would lead them to the river island Riket. It would serve as a fortress.

"We spent so much time building our defenses against the air, we neglected our ground troops," one of the electors said bitterly. "We need time to fix the mistake. We can harrass them by air with our fifty rocs and with our archers until we have the numbers needed to push them out."

An gave me four papyrus rolls, each with his seal on them. "Here's an offer to Ibbisal to help us. We leave for Riket as soon as you fly east. Will you do this?"

Every assignment was voluntary. I could refuse.

A whole full moon ago I'd told An I wouldn't fly again. I'd been training skyknights for three years now. It hurt to climb up onto the back of a flying creature, and I could barely pull a bowstring anymore.

I would give lectures, and teach theory, and live in one of the turrets. I'd see the young nights off and wish them luck.

That had been the plan.

"Of course I'll fly for Okland," I said.

We hugged. An kissed me on the cheek. The electors wished me luck.

I took Gar, Lain, and Silv with me. They met me at the rookery, all of us in our fur-trimmed flying leathers and smoked glasses.

"Again into the air?" Gar asked.

"For the Heron lands."

Lain pulled the skydoors open on the balanced weights. The

vets had already left to fly the other rocs off to Riket. That left only
the four meanest, strongest birds for us.

"Skyknights," I said, "every league counts, every minute matters. Okland lives or dies by our wings in the days ahead."

"It's five days around the Spine to get to Heron," Silv said as
she snapped on her gloves. Rumor said she lost her three fingers
to the ice in the clouds. It wasn't true. That only happened to bal-
loonists or crew on a skyhawk. A roc would die, or freeze, just
like a human.

I knew Silv lost her fingers to knife fights. One reason I'd
chosen her for this. Silv had ridden tailfeather with me in a battle
against a pirate over Fallen Gorge. I'd dropped her onto the ship's
balloon, and she'd cut it from stem to stern, and when she slid off
the side I'd flung my roc into a dive to catch her.

We'd thrown each other into our beds for nights after that,
young and invincible, lords of the sky. Now she'd married an elector, wore an emerald rank necklace, and slept in an eerie with running water supplied by a spring.

I'd never go on a mission without her.

We slapped our forearms together. Looked at each other with
a warrior's grin. Okland called for us, and we would answer that
call again.

What retirement? We would save our country yet again.

"We go over the Spine," I said. "I'll find the Widow's Cut. I
won't say you must do it with me. You can fly around."

Silv nodded. "I'll fly it."

Gar and Lain nodded as well. My youngest instructors, they'd
flown with me through the trickiest rising winds. Steady men, with
the slight build needed to be a skynight. Gar, in particular, an almost child-like sized man with a vicious mind for flying. And Lain
could hit a target with a bow and arrow while in a swooping dive,
leading a roc with just nudges from his knees.

The other reason I liked Gar was that he didn't speak much, but
he was a calm flyer.

The massive rocs snarled and shrieked at us as we crawled up into our wicker saddles. We waddled them over to the balcony and they leapt off into the air. My stomach plunged, as it always did, from that inevitable moment of weightlessness.

Then came the steady beat of the vast, feathered wings.

The spires of the Elector's Castle hung off to my right as the roc found rising air, then spiraled up. Then I adjusted the reins until the compass on my pommel showed due east.

I glanced once more behind me, right before it all disappeared behind the clouds that always fetched up against the mountains the castle nestled up to.

We called them the Spine because they ran down the center of Okland. From here Okland had risen on the wind the mountains flung into the air, to rule the lands for four days flight in any direction.

I'd trained hard to become a skynight, sworn to the electors to protect our way of life.

Now it was in my hands and I couldn't be more terrified.

The Spine's peaks hid inside of the clouds ahead of us. The Widow's Cut lay ahead, unseen.

Five sightings I had. Land beneath me in gaps that showed me the land below us as clouds parted for a brief moment. Then there was the count.

The moment we'd turned and crossed the eastern flight marker, I'd started counting. My old music teacher drilled rhythm into me, and now I kept a second by second count in my head like a human metronome.

But I also knew I was no machine, and every second, I introduced a slight mistake in the count.

At the ten minute mark, I shouted and pointed. Close.

My roc had beaten for as much height as it could, and I could see Gar hung just below me when I looked back.

The mountain loomed ahead, but we couldn't tell, unless you paid close attention to the wind.

Buffetting, whipping winds and my roc's reluctance to keep an easterly course all told me the wall of rock sat right in front of us.

"Higher, Gar, higher!" Lain shouted. I couldn't see Silv anywhere.

Then the clouds broke, and we flew right at jagged stone shards that wanted to rip us apart.

I had no time to look around me, only to yank on my reins and fly. I banked and spun, fluttered, and rock passed just winglengths away from me.

A scream. Feathers exploded into the air. Silv had dived ahead of me and struck a peak. Her roc tumbled across our flightpath, shrieking as it tumbled in a mess of broken wings, and then Silv pitched free of her saddle.

Her body pinwheeled off rock, then hit a crevice with a splatter of blood.

My roc and I rose on the wind and skimmed the Widow's Cut. As the roc banked, using the violent rising winds, we made the turn before striking another pillar of rock. And then we did it again, this time well high of them.

There was more mountain nearby, but in this tight plateau, surrounded by crag, we gained height.

The air grew bitter. So cold I couldn't think. My skin cracked, tears froze to my face.

And then we burst into sunshine, far over the Spine.

The roc tried to dip out of the rising winds, but I pulled it back in to keep circling.

"Not yet," I whispered. "Trust me."

I looked back and saw Gar and Lain break out of the Widow's Cut behind me. We all kept circling higher and higher.

Now I could barely breathe.

"Higher," I said.

The higher we rose, the farther we could glide before coming back to land. The closer to Heron territory we could get on the first day's ride. Only Gar kept up with me. I saw Lain's roc twist and break off as Gar and I kept rising.

My roc bucked and threw itself out of the rising wind, refusing to rise any further. Wings spread clear out, we began the glide.

I couldn't argue, my vision had spots. My fingers barely held the leather straps of the reins. I slumped forward, only correcting the roc when I noticed the compass twitching away from east.

Below me, so far below me, were the clouds.

Had any skynight risen so far?

Maybe in stories, drunkenly told around fires. I knew of none who rose this far above the Widow's Cut.

We found a stablery as the sun dipped over the flat land and forests of the east.

"The featherhand says it's a half-day to the Heron territories," Gar said. "He has a flightmark map he can copy for us while we sleep."

The rocs tore at the carcass of a cow while the hands watched on, excited to see the massive rocs and the skyknights who rode them. The invasion was a distant threat to them, something happening on the other side of the Spine.

I led Gar to the small pond out back. I stood and looked at the fields of barley and tried to get my shaking hands to hold the roughly hewn wooden railing.

"Can you continue?" I asked him.

Gar nodded. "My roc is well. My lungs burn, but the rest of the journey is just hops over the trees. There are few rising winds out here, and the roc will tire quickly from flapping with a person riding it."

"But you should be close to the Heron, and then the rest of our mission."

"Thanks to you," Gar muttered.

He flexed his fingers. One of them didn't move quite right.

"I'm sorry," I whispered. "Maybe I shouldn't—"

"No," Gar said earnestly. "The price was high. But you cut three days off the trip. Days that will matter when we seek Ibbisal's help. If we hadn't taken the risk, Okland falls."

Silv.

"You're young, Gar. I remember thinking, every battle, every action I did, it was the fulcrum on which everything pivoted on. But the truth is, everyone else thinks the same. You, Lain, Silv. Right now each elector is trying to save us. Each bowman who will put their life on the line, every skynight who dives on the spearmen at Riket, they all think that."

"But three days," Gar said. "It speaks for itself. And I never would have dared to fly that high if you hadn't been up there ahead of me. I was terrified the sun would sear me, but instead, I froze!"

I made a fist and lightly tapped his back. "I have images of flying back to Riket at the head of relief force of Ibbisal's skyhawks and rocs, and maybe some Heron? Maybe An will look at me and think, there is a great man, I should make him my prince!"

Silv's body would hit that rock in my mind forever. Her blood had erased that noble image I'd started with.

All the people I'd lost, fallen from the sky, hit by arrows, and Silv had been the final feather lost that dropped me from the sky.

"I don't regret the choice to make for the Widow's Cut," I said to Gar. "But to bring you all with me. It was careless."

"Let history and Okland judge. But tomorrow we fly."

"You will fly. I'm staying here.

Gar raised an eyebrow. "I—"

"I taught you to fly, Gar. I know your skill, and more importantly, I know a roc will go further for a man of your build than mine. Particularly once I give you my roc. It will follow you on a lead. You will swap them out when it tires. Do this, and you will reach Ibbisal on your own far faster than if we both fly."

Gar looked stunned.

"Go rest, Gar. You will hold Okland's fate on your shoulders tomorrow."

I had to let my pride die.

For Silv.

For my country.

I would not be leading a flying army back to save An. Gar would.

Getting us over the cut, that was my contribution. From here on, Gar would be Okland's hero.

I spent the night watching the rocs sleep, then watched Gar rise up into the sky, the heavy roc wings blowing straw and dirt into my face.

And then my own bird rose to follow him, hundreds of feet of tight silk rope between them.

Many days later, when the flocks of Ibbisal's fleet pulled his great warships over the stable, I shielded my eyes and looked up. The fleet of airships and birds turned south, making their way around the whole length of the Spine. I hoped they made it.

Lain had offered to fly me up to one of the skyhawks, so I could join the battle.

Instead, I'd taken the supplies I'd purchased and made her drop me off in the foothills.

It would take me many days to climb the Spine without a roc, but I had the papyrus maps strapped to my forearm to guide me, and a travel bag full of food.

Walking the foothills, it was strange. Everything took so much longer than the quick jump between marks I was used to.

But I would make it back up into the Widow's Cut, on foot.

I would find Silv and bring her body back off the mountain while the war raged on without me.

ON THE EVE OF THE
FALL OF HABESH

HABESH, YOU BEAUTIFUL stinking whore of a city.

I love you so.

The sun is grim this morning from the street. There's a haze in the air giving the glowing ball its grit and waver. My brother says the Sea Peoples are burning the Kopach just five miles north. Which means the haze comes from the cinders of huts, crops, and burned flesh.

Thus do we inhale and exhale the destruction of our cousins outside the city walls.

But Habesh goes on, as always.

I glance upward, up the thick stone towers of Pophis where I'm headquartered. Cheap to live in, as most people near Market remain convinced that the towers, once part of the original city walls and its watchtowers, would fall at any moment due to their age.

But I know they are as solid as the foundations of Habesh itself, sunk into the granite of the cliffs of Elkatoa.

This city is going nowhere.

The towers will stand.

At least, I think, until the Sea Peoples burst through like water through a dam.

And even then, the city will abide.

But this morning won't. Not with this dallying.

I sweep my long cloak around me and check the small piece of paper a runner delivered me last night.

The consignorii have a target for me.

My target begs in an arterial street feeding into the heart of Habesh: the Market. The leaders of the city have marked him.

And here I am.

But first, the Market.

It's not a square, like in many cities. It's a great oval plaza. And even the oval isn't so much dedicated to the Market. The Market is flexible. There are some pit houses, dedicated to the city patrons, scattered throughout. The House of Defensive Arguments, marble columns rising high, crowned with the fires of Justice blazing at their tops, sits on the northwest loop.

Other civic institutions stand against the flood of the Market, but the consignorii relocated most of those to Ruling Hill.

So the Hall of the Gods no longer hosts the ancient objects of worship, but now the tall building is host to half a mile of stalls. Shouting merchants, screeching birds, bartar, and the smoke of thousands of animals and roots and cooking fires replace the brazen fires and sacrifices of supplicants. There are warehouses and common grounds and temporary tent cities and minstrels and plays and priests of every belief shouting their truths in exchange for alms.

That is the joy of Habesh. A single-minded dedication to the selling of everything you can ever imagine.

Out on the rim of the oval the ferocity of the commerce of thousands and thousands fades. But the traffic of incoming and outgoing via cobblestone is like a river, the trickling sound of feet over stone replacing a brook's babble.

Vendors sell meat on a stick or in a pie alongside the roads, and beggars lie along the gutters.

I'm looking for a particular beggar.

"Hello, Bruse," I say, coming up behind him. "I'm invested to take back the powers granted to you by the All, as taught and allowed to you via the Defensive Council of Habesh. This is due to the use of them in a cowardly, criminal, and consistently rogue-like manner, as confirmed by the Princips of the House of Defensive Arguments."

Bruse's head barely reaches my chest. He turns to look at me with oversized, rheumy eyes even wider with startlement.

His skin is wrinkled and loose, pale from spending too much time in the shadows, and his hair is patchy. But he moves swiftly against me. A faint blue aura twinkles in the air around him, and then a blast of air strikes me true in the stomach.

It is strong enough to throw me back several feet into a wooden cart, and I bounce off the oversized iron-rimmed wheels with a grunt.

All I can see of my quarry is a foot disappearing around the corner.

What looks like an old lady helps me to my feet. "Hello, contragnartii. What a blow you took," she croaks.

I instinctively grab my belt and the tiny purse wrapped to it, catching her withered little hand. I twist it, and she half sobs out a scream.

With a sigh, I squat before her. "How old are you?" I ask gently.

A grubby, nervous face regards me. She hasn't washed in days, and I can see bruises from where other beggars have hit her to chase her away from the prime spots. Like this street corner. "I'm nine, contragnartii."

It is young. They seem to be getting younger all the time, the progeric refuse spit out of the spellyards and magic workhouses.

I finger out several coins into the palm of my hand where ancient-seeming nearby eyes won't spot them, and with a touch almost as deft as the most skilled pickpocket in Habesh, pass them into her hands. "Make it last," I whisper, and take off in pursuit of Bruse.

Any contragnartii worth his salt or silver has a network of informers, spies and grifters. I know where Bruse is headed: the soup tents.

Our greatest villians are often our daily habits.

Bruse's arch-enemy is the comfort of potato and leeks swimming in a salty broth and a cup of wine in a soup tent along Dinner Row. I walk along the backs of the tents, in the gutter, my boots slushing through excrement and piss and garbage.

He thinks it's safe because it is in public, packed among hungry people, and even if the exits are closed off, he can rip a hole through the thick canvas of the tall tent with a knife to make his escape.

He thinks, no doubt, to himself, that an altercation would bring the Street Guards.

But this is all good defense against the street. No one in the tents gives a damn about what a contragnartii is up to. The official cape and the seal of the city on the clasp under one's throat meant they'd leave me the hell alone.

And not just because I work for the city, but because I can summon up a spell that rips the ability to do any magics right out of their skulls.

That's why Bruse is running. The ability to throw airblasts in the dog-eat-dog world among Habesh's fallen is a useful talent. And Bruse doesn't want to lose it.

But he's attacked someone important, or been accused once too often of using magic for ill gains.

Which leads to me, carefully slicing the back of the tent open, peeking through the slit, and ducking inside.

I stand right behind Bruse once again.

Wooden benches wobble their way down the old brick street,

now the inside of the permanent soup tent. People fill the darkened areas between the poles with their flickering torches, moving around, conversation bubbling. Most of them sit at the tables, slurping soup and watered down wine. There is a kitchen nearby, made of mortar and stone, with a chimney at the top that pokes up through the tent fabric and is stained by the leaks from around that joint.

The air is moist and warm.

This time I don't have to Announce to Bruse. I raise my hands, reaching deep down inside myself, and let slip a tiny bit of my life-force as the air around my hands and forearm twinkle.

There is a small sense of loss. I have sacrificed a small measure of my life's essence to fuel this piece of magic. Is it five minutes of my life? Or an hour?

When my fingers touch the back of Bruse's neck, he gasps and twists away, but I can see by the horror in his eyes he knows the reaction is too late.

"You pig's dick!" he screams, raising his hands, then realizes there is nothing he can do.

"You knew this was going to happen," I retort. "Why run and make a scene? Now everyone knows you've been stripped of your talent."

He's breathing heavily, something running through his head. And then he pulls his knife out and leaps for me.

This is not unexpected. Loss, grief, they take many expressions among peoples. Ennui, tears, rage . . . action.

The tent is crowded: slipping away from the rusty point of his knife means shoving a burly man away from me as I draw a pair of short swords.

I parry Bruse's first and second thrusts easily. He's depended on his magical blasts of air for all his fighting life. He may have once served on the city walls, as most do who are taught a fighting magic, but only ever learned the basics of fighting with a blade.

It isn't hard to hit him with the flat of one of my blades and move in to disarm him.

"No! Let him live!" Two young boys and a girl break out of the door of the kitchen. The youngest raises his hands and strikes me with a mild bolt of fire that hits the tip of my swords.

I drop them both before the heat can burn my palms.

"Stop there," I shout, holding my hands up. "I do not have to touch you to strip you of your magics, I can do it as long as I can see you."

"We know, but you're naturally old," the girl says. She has oak-brown eyes and skin and silky black hair. "You conserve yourself: I'll bet it *costs* to do what you do, the farther away you are from your prey. Just like it would cost more for Aylei here to burn you alive, rather than just startle you."

She's right. "I wasn't going to kill him," I say. "Just disarm him and stop him from killing me. You are willing to interfere with the city's business?"

That gets me a haughty look. "The city is dying. The Sea People will be at the walls soon enough. Habesh has other things to worry about than Bruse. Leave him to us. Please."

I think about defending my honor for just a moment, then laugh. My job is done. I have no desire to spend on magic. "What do you want with Bruse?"

"We're leaving Habesh," the girl says. "And Bruse is helping us."

"He'll cut your throats for your money the moment your back is turned," I tell her.

Surprisingly, to both Bruse and me, she nods. "We know, and we have anticipated that. But now, more than ever, I doubt it. He needs us almost as much as we need him."

"Well then, don't let me stop you," I say.

The girl looks just behind me. "Okay, Liat, let's go. We got what we came for."

I twist around, a cold rivulet of fear in my gut. The space behind me shimmers blue, and out of the air forms another little girl with blue eyes and ratty hair.

Liat walks past me, tapping the sharpened dagger in her hand against her forehead in a mock salute. "G'day, contragnartii."

Everyone stares at the group of children. It's not something you see anymore in Habesh. Most of the children are drafted to serve on the city walls, or sent to defend the Kopach. The rest work the Spellyards and factories. Or they fled the city the day the Great Sea Fleet arrived on the horizon of the Roranraka Sea.

I pick up my short swords and leave through the back of the tent, annoyed by thinking about the impending war. But it's in the air, literally. The black pall of the burning Kopach is always an upward glance away.

The Sea Peoples, scattered across their archipelagos and island chains all throughout the Roranraka, are subject to the whims of storm and tide that brew in the Roranraka. They'd never attacked the Elkatoan coast before. Usually they trade exotic foods, spices, and rare metals along Elkatoan harbors in order to get access to the forests.

That is how things worked, until two years ago, when the meta-consignorii of the four greatest Elkatoan cities plotted together to deny them access to the dwindling lowland forests. The cities wanted to guarantee the survival of what forest was left. The meta-consignorii thought the varied islands and traders weak and non-militaristic.

Everyone thought this, until several hundred ships appeared on the horizon. Each ship represented an island, or a tribe, of the Sea Peoples. They brimmed with warriors. Trade failed: now they take the land they need by force.

They need the wood to build their stilt villages to protect against the daily floods of the Roranraka. They need it to build their massive ocean-crossing, island-connecting ships.

But who could have known there are so many Sea Peoples, and that the Roranraka is so much larger than any person suspected, containing in its vastness all these Sea Peoples?

Ignorance is the death of many, I guess. And that includes cities and countries as equally as men.

At the edge of Dinner Row I stop at a wooden pavilion with lace curtains and rain drapes.

Only the most powerful and rich eat here. Though judging by the empty tables, most of them have left the city, fleeing for the mountains.

I walk to the back, where the cook is stacking his pots in crates.

"I want a meal," I demand.

"We are done. There is no one left. The Sea People are here. Go to the soup tents."

I know I'm taking my anger at being beaten by the kids and having to chase Bruse out on this man, but it does not change my response. "Look at who I am, cook. The rich are addicted to your beatiful little meats and your sauces. Maybe it's because you slip a little spell over each meal. I'm not sure, but I'm willing to try stripping whatever it is you have from you if you don't give me a damn meal, you traitor to the city."

He looks startled, but understands. "Fine, why not. I'm leaving the food anyway, I can only take the tools of my trade. The city is dead."

My eyes narrow. "You shouldn't talk like that."

"And you're scared. At least I have a talent I can use anywhere. What you do, it is only for the city's leaders. And soon, they'll be dead. You can't flee, there is nothing else for you."

"Do you know who you're talking to?" I hiss.

"Of course, contragnartii. You can strip me of my magic, and it would make no effect on my ability to cook great meals." He waves his hand around the kitchen. "But still, take whatever you want, anyway, threats aside."

My mouth waters: there are racks of lamb and other delicious meats and still steaming breads.

I'd bring my brother home a feast he would never forget.

But heavy boots tramping the wooden floorboards get my attention. Five City Guard in full armor and helmets walk up to me.

One of them is holding his hands out in front of him: he's a Locator.

"Contragnartii Jazim?" the Locator asks.

"I am Jazim, yes."

"Come with us."

The Guard clusters around me as they march me away from the rich smells of the kitchen.

There is a whiff of ominousness to Ruling Hill, I've always felt. Even as contragnartii, walking into the crooked alleys of government edifices and climbing the stone stairs toward the center of power in the city, I always feel . . . nervous.

That Ruling Hill is built on the charred remains of the previous rulers' final stand, its flagstones the walls of their forttress, is an irony that is today not far from my mind.

An irony I need to banish quickly from my thoughts as I approach the large moat that leads to the stone behemoth where the consignorii dwell.

The spiked gates swing aside with a soulful shriek, and grim mercenary soldiers, not Guardsmen, wait behind them.

A short and wizened inquisitor stands by the atrium. He grasps my forehead with ashy hands, green eyes looking deep into mine, and declares me loyal to the consignorii.

Once he does that, Yamis and two consignorii I am unfamiliar with stride out to face me.

"Your Allness," I say politely, and bow, then kiss the extended thumbtip.

"Tell us about the children," Yamis says, his voice sizzling like rain on an outdoor cookfire.

I recount what happened, talking up my skill at tracking down Bruse, but Yamis could care less. "The children!" he shouts. "Have they left yet?"

"I don't know," I reply honestly.

Yamis sighs and grabs my forehead. He is another inquisitor, but like anyone important, only uses his taught skill sparingly, less he hasten himself toward his own end, like Bruse.

But now Yamis is digging his way through my head. I can feel it, a ripple across my thoughts. Memories of the day are springing back to me, then stopping, jumping around, and stopping again until Yamis has seen everything he wants.

His fingers twinkle blue as he lets go of my head. "It is true," he tells the other two. "It is them."

I'm not sure what is going on here, but I realize they don't care a bit about Bruse: they're focused on the children.

It makes a sudden sort of sense. All the children not already drafted to defend the city have fled, either taken by their families or friends, or escaped by their own means.

These children are late to the game. An oddity. The consignorii want to press them into service, or get them into a weapons factory.

Yamis must have some faint touch with my mind still, as he shakes his head. "You're only partially correct," he growls. "They're all escapees from the factories. Maybe a hundred. They've been sharing skills back and forth, *teaching* each other magics."

I try to hold in my shock. Magic is a gift from the All, the chance to tap into the raw power of life. Lest it consume us any further than it already has, the Nariaad specifies that no one should learn more than a single spell.

To do otherwise is to claim yourself a god.

The Songs of Demiurgiastes tell of the Novidei who dared to become gods, back when the world was a whole land. Men who learned all, then died as it consumed them like a fire from within. Their battles against the All, and the gods who protected it, cleaved the land, and water poured from under the earth rivers and filled the chasms, giving us the oceans. These were things everyone knew from near-birth.

Here in Habesh, one of the duties of the consignorii is to listen and watch for teaching, a sin graver than any other.

These children lived once in the same Spellyard, but came from the high foothills of the mountains, the peninsular areas, and all up and down the coast of Elkatoa, as well as the gutters of Habesh. And somehow, despite the close eye of their guards and the brutal atmosphere of the yards, they had collaborated in snatched moments and taught each other.

To escape, they'd killed guards, and magically dug tunnels under the Spellyards. They'd created shields to stop pursuers, and cast mental confusion to slip away into the streets.

An entire dormitory of children has been lost to the city, the consignorii explains to me.

"We will hunt them down and hang them," I promise, knowing this was what is expected of me. It still tastes sour, though. Only the consignorii teach magic, and the one skill you are granted, if it is needed, is the only skill you'll ever be granted. Who would risk ending the world, ending magic, and all else, by teaching another their own skills? The Nariaad made clear the consequences, through stories of the beginning of the Roranraka Sea and the history of the lands.

Yamis shakes his head. "It sounds heretical for me to say this," he sighs. "But we need them back in the factories to help defend the walls. Habesh must stand. After we repel the Sea Peoples, then we will hang them all."

It does rank of heresy.

But then, for Habesh, it is a dark time.

"Go find the children," Yamis orders me. "And bring them back to us that we may bind them to the factories. And this time, they will not break their shackles."

There is dark certainty in his voice.

I'm hoping he doesn't look into my thoughts right now. I'm scared of what heresy they're proposing, and what it means for the survival of the city. Surely the All will not tolerate a violation of this sort.

It is right there, in the atrium with the consignorii, that I realize Habesh is doomed for sure.

And I am doomed with it.

*

Just in the hour since I've left the streets, something has changed. There is a sense of panic. Any moment the last chances to escape will be shut off, with the roads out of the city dominated by the Sea Peoples.

Habesh will fight for its life like a cornered animal.

But for those who are not willing to stand behind it, they must leave now.

Furtive groups move quickly through the streets toward the distant walls with packs strapped to their backs. They do not meet the eyes of anyone else walking the street. They are like awkward gray ghosts, sidling along the alleys, trying not to be noticed.

For it's a certain kind of treason. Not that the Guard has time to deal with them and their cowardice. The walls are shut, but that doesn't mean there aren't small gates designed to let scouts and smugglers out.

A high fee is all it takes to get someone with access to these areas of the wall to let you out. And then you just have a fast jog to skirt the advancing armies.

And the children are mixed into one of these nervous crowds.

It will be a tough exercise to ferret them out.

Just to hand them over to be used as magical automatons.

Yes, there is some strong seed of doubt in my mind. And it troubles me to look into my soul and find someone different staring right back.

I have to shake it away, move over the cobblestones faster than the dispirited cowards around me, and make my way to one of the sharks poaching on them.

His name is Kish. A terrier of a man, who looks like he should be digging around the inside of a small hole hunting rats. I find him in one of his many haunts, and he stands up to run when he sees me, but I shake my head. "I need your help."

"Your help usually costs me more than I make," Kish complains. Rightfully.

"You don't make a profit," I tell him. "You help me, and then you get to keep your powers of persuasion. If you do not help me, I decide you are using them in a matter that does not honor the All and the City."

I've never put it quite so bluntly. Kish licks his lips and moves from one foot to another, like a nervous messenger.

I glance over at the small cart next to him. "You're leaving, I see."

"Leading one more group out under the Trumpet Gate," Kish says. "I'd offer you a place, but your brother . . ."

"Let's get back to why I'm here," I snap, cutting that piece of conversation down. "There's a street tough, Bruse, used to run up and down the edge of the market. Know whom I'm talking about?"

Kish does. He has a mind for those things.

"If he's leaving the city, where would *he* do it?"

"Well . . ." Kish looks thoughtfully up the pall of dark smoke over the city, then quickly looks back down at his feet. "The old King's Road, by the Spellyards."

In a flash, I understand why the children chose Bruse. Who would think that they'd use an escape route near the very place they'd once been trapped inside?

The Spellyards are heavily guarded and gated, the compounds filled with squat, square buildings with massive granite plinths that would look like civic or religious buildings, if not for their featurelessness. No paint, no carvings, no nothing.

Tough, brutish Guardsmen in full armor stand on the tops of the Spellyard walls, looking out over the courtyards and buildings, ready to stop escapees.

Through a set of gates, in the distance, I can see tiny bodies trudging from one building to another.

Whether it is swords of fire, or magical shields, each of them gives up a piece of their life, their connection to the All, to create these things.

Wasted potential and failed spells waft continously out of the massive chimneys, the blue sparkle of life disappating over the city as the winds take it for themselves.

The sight weighs heavy on me.

"*That's* why you're congragnaritii," says a voice from by my elbow. "I see."

I jump, whipping around toward the blur in the air, and pull one of my short swords.

The ratty-haired Liat drops her invisibility and holds her hands up in the air. "Truce," she says, rope bracelets sliding back from her wrists to expose manacle marks burned into her skin. I stare at them for a long moment.

"You read minds and hide from sight," I say, still startled, wondering if I was about to be ambushed. Then I realize I am standing right in front of a Spellyard gate. Liat is the one in danger. My confidence returns, and with it, a righteous anger. "You sin against the All."

Liat looks over at the Spellyard and holds up her burned hands. She begins to walk away, and I follow her. Let her talk, let her lead me closer to her friends. "My brother used to sing me the Songs of the Demiurgiastes and the Naiad: it said there we were given our talents freely as gifts from the All, and should gift others with their benefits in the same way. My family were hillfolk shepherds; we came to the city during a drought. We knew no one in the city, so when my family died, I was taken and forced to use my talents to create things for the city. That is no gift. And it troubles you as well, watching your brother slowly die, all his life used up, living in that little dark tower you call home . . ."

"Stay out of my mind," I hiss, my voice breaking. "Please." I should rip her abilities from her right now. I can feel the tingle in my hands as I get ready.

"We know."

But there's a commotion in front of us. It's Bruse. He's getting the life kicked out of him by four over-muscled thugs.

He has no way to defend himself, other than to curl up into a ball of rags, his wrinkled hands over his face.

"It's Bruse," Liat says, and runs toward him.

This is not my problem.

This child has seen the inside of a Spellyard, a tougher place than any street.

I watch her slam into the nearest man, and he backhands her with a casual fury that leaves her folded in half on the dirty cobblestones, a tiny thread of blood trickling down her nose.

The smart thing to do is walk away.

But is it? The consignorii will rip into my mind, just like the child did. Then I will be shackled and working on the inside of a Spellyard.

I'm doomed. Whether it is the Sea People or the consignorii.

One of the men is standing over Bruse, ready to kick his skull in as I walk up to them, my fingers crackling. "Leave," I say, my voice strident and calm and full of authority, as if I have the skill of convincing.

The four of them look at me, and pause.

"*Now.*"

The city is on the edge of chaos, but they don't want to lose their connection to the All, whatever skill it is they each possess. They grudgingly step back.

And I am left with the fruits of my treachery and heresy: A child and a broken thief.

Why do it?

I think about that as I walk along the street, my boots echoing off the facades of taverns and cramped buildings around us.

Bruse is slung over my shoulder as he weighs next to nothing—no more than some feathery skeleton. Liat limps along by my side, still dazed.

We're passing into the Tannery district where the smell of curing leather is strong enough to make you gag.

But here, on this particular road, it begins to fade.

Stunning godesses of women stand in open windows, on balconies, and by the doors to winehouses. Their hair is long and trussed in perfect knots, their bosoms massive and pert, their long legs slipping out of carefully cut dresses. The air smells sweet, of flowers and incenses and things I can't identify that make my head swim. I find myself missing steps as I walk by, and women coo at the three of us.

Liat's eyes are wide.

We stop in front of a shop advertising quality hides, where I barely recognize the two figures before me, until they realize who I am.

And suddenly the magic is gone, fading away into a faint turquoise in the dark tavern. The two grandmotherly women in front of me curse. "Jazim, we paid you already!"

I wave her cautious indignation away. "Yelena, Doria, this child and man need somewhere to rest. They were attacked."

"So you come here? What are you going to do, sell the child to the Spellyards?"

They have no reason to trust me. I am not the helping type. They're suspicious. "Do it or the next time you walk out the door looking to get someone in here to sample your "hides" they'll only see overdried leather," I snap.

It has the effect I want. They'd stab me in the back, if they dared. But the city's oldest trade relies on convincing the clients through illusion. The illusion that these women are flawless creatures.

And I can rip that ability away from them in the blink of an eye.

So Liat and Bruse get a room in the back. It is a quiet place, with thick walls and luxurious drapes. It is clearly normally a refuge for Yelena, Doria, and the others.

"The consignorii will disown and kill you for this, won't they?" Liat says.

I look over at the bruised and broken Bruse. "Yes."

Liat sits down on a purple padded wooden chair in front of a mirror lit by tens of small, wavering candles. "You could come with us. We need older allies to guide us through the countryside. You have talents we don't, you could share them, we could share with you. We are of all ages, and came from all over Elkatoa before we were taken to the factories. Our leader, Gull, she was once a captive of the Sea People. She doesn't lord over us, we're all free, together. We just want to get away from the city and try and start a small village of our own. We don't care about your past. You can bring your brother . . ."

It is an offer that brings with it a sliver of hope. Since the Sea People took their beachhead, since the allies of Habesh dallied at the foothills of Mount Oribeas to wait and see how strong the Sea People really were as they dashed themselves against the walls, I've thought of my fate as tied to the city and the consignorii.

Maybe there is another way.

Liat takes my hand and looks at me with a depth of seriousness that no child should have, but all in Habesh do. "I will get our Healer to come help Bruse. We will be leaving the city tonight, at midnight, by the old King's Road."

"You shouldn't have told me that," I say softly. "I knew where you would leave, but now I know when. The consignorii could take that from me. Or I could betray you."

She nods. "That's true. But I've looked into your mind, Jazim, and you are not nearly the horrible thing you make yourself out to be. I have faith you will do right by us, because the reason you've done these things is to protect those like us, and your brother. Not because you have a wicked heart. You strip away our magic so that we don't use it up, like Bruse, and end up used and begging on the streets. Not just because the consignorii manipulate you to do so."

"I wouldn't be so sure . . ." I start to say as I look down at the thick carpet, unable to meet her piercing eyes. Until now, people have always feared me. Here is a child who forgives and understands me.

Liat gets up and stands in front of me. "Go and get your brother. But be careful. You know what you'll have to do to bring him with us."

And then she hugs me. Like a little sister, wrapping her arms around my stomach before she turns to leave.

Outside, on the street, my mind is heavy with a black pall, and so is the sky.

The city is like a man who takes his last meal the night before his execution. People are dancing in the streets, drunk and fearful. People are slinking in the shadows, trying to escape. People are grimly preparing for war, sharpening blades, dousing their rooftops with water, and hammering their windows shut.

In the squares, the Patriots are preparing the city for its stand.

They are tall, proud men with booming voices that make your insides quiver. They are illusions, these particular mouthpieces of the consignorii, much like the women of the Tannery district.

Here they stand, defiant against the Sea People invasion. "What manner of men are the Sea People?" they shout. "Inferior ones! Habesh is the greatest city on the coast of Elkatoa!" And they whip the crowd into pride and mania with great flashes of blue.

An orgiastic chant of "Habesh, Habesh, Habesh" rises up to meet the pall of smoke over the city.

"They have raped our lands, raped our children, and raped our warriors in Kopach. They claim they want access to the forests, for their *ships*, and their *villages*." The speakers spit these words. "But we know what they want. Rape, pillage, destruction. They are *animals* who would imprison us, and rip from us our talents! Only

Habeshi are the true children of the All. And it is Habeshi who will drive the Sea People back into the ocean where they belong. Brothers, we *will* fight! We will destroy! We will win! Join the defense of the walls *now*!"

The intensity rocks me, even passing the edge of a square in a hurry, and I find myself brimming with the desire to destroy the Sea People.

But I manage to regain control, and leave the raging crowds behind, even as hundreds surge to join the Guard and pick up a sword.

I force a vendor into giving me a meat pie and a flask of wine, and take both with me up the long winding stairs. The thick wooden door stands before me, with sunset an hour away.

"Jazim, is that you?" the frail voice of my brother asks from the other side. He has heard my footsteps.

"Yes," I say, my hand against the large brass knob.

A clink of metal inside. "The Sea People are close, aren't they? I can hear it down below on the street: they're saying a great defense of the walls is planned. Jazim. The speakers are out in the squares. Jazim. Please. You have to let me go help them. The city needs me. Let me help, please, brother, please."

It is like my soul is being cleaved.

"Listen," I whisper. "I . . . know a way we can leave the city . . ."

There is a silence for a long moment. A hush before the storm. A tear leaks from me, then I jump as a body slams against the door.

"You filthy excuse of Habeshi. Traitor. Heretic!" the voice on the other side screams, and I drop the flask of wine. It shatters, red liquid pooling around my boots, then bleeding down the stairs. "It is the lowest ebb of the tide of Habesh, but like a tide we will come rushing back and sweep them back where they belong."

I am wobbly, breathless, and shaken. He is right. There is a natural order to these things.

"Just because it is hard, doesn't mean one shouldn't do it!" the voice screams.

True. Many have thrown themselves against the walls of Habesh. And there is no greater folly than running whenever something looks hard.

He is right, my brother, I think as the faint blue sparkles of magic around the door fade away.

I open the door.

It is full of shadows, this room, but my brother shuffles out from them into the setting sunlight. The loose folds of his skin roll, and the giant, rheumy eyes regard me with hatred for my failings. The clink of his manacles fill the stony walls with echos, and the chain drags along the dusty floor behind his left leg. It is a limb almost withered away, the life sucked out of it like the life had been taken from the rest of his body.

How much has he given to the city, for how long? And how has he survived this long?

His pride leads me to serve the consignorii. Puts me out of the tower every day with vigor. My brother: I love him almost as much as the city.

And he loves me back so dearly.

He rips the meat pie away from me, and gums at it with a messy sigh of contentment. "We must have our strength for the invasion," he mutters. "This city is the most beautiful thing in the world, and we must not let it be destroyed."

"We must have our strength to do the things we must," I say. I walk over to the balcony and look out over my city.

What did it mean to do the best thing for the city? Should I go back to capture the children? How long can we survive against the Sea People?

"You must let me out," my brother pleads. "Free me, let me go down to the squares. I will help others find their love of the city. Just like old days, brother, when I walked along the walls and gave courage and strength and pride to the defenders of Habesh."

I'm struggling with a chain of logic. An hour ago, my mind had been in a vastly different place.

My brother loves me.

And I love him.

He is dying. The city is at ebb. What is my brother killing himself by using up the last of his life going to add to all this?

Nothing. He has almost no life left to give.

I love my city, but I love my brother too, almost as much. And I have the strength to do something I've needed to do for a long time.

I turn back from the balcony, my fingers tingling, and he opens his mouth. "Jazim?"

"Hadim . . . I love you . . ."

I'm sobbing as I rip his magic from him. He collapses to the ground, shocked, and I catch him. His body is tiny, frail, and his skin loose. His large, drooping eyes stare at me in confusion.

"I'm so sorry," I cry as I carry him to the cot by the wall.

I'm a wretched heretic. The consignorii will kill me the next time they see me. My brother will hate me.

But he will live.

Maybe the city will too.

I hope the children do not wait too long for me. If they had ever planned to do so.

It is past the sunset. In the distance the night is lit by massive approaching fires, their orange flare reflected off the bottom of gray, foreboding clouds.

The Sea People are at the walls.

The ground shakes with their march, and the impact of their projectiles.

My swords are at my side as I leave the tower filled with an incredible love for my fellow Habeshi who stand to fight. I see the city with my brother's eyes: an ancient edifice to all that is great about this coast. The place where all eventually end up. Even the SeaPeople are drawn here.

Is there any greater place in the world than Habesh?

I think not.

This glorious city, this citadel on the coast where you can find anything you wish, buy anything you want. Here is where destinies are made, and stories created. Where lives are lived and legends made.

Yes, I think, as I prepare to join the defense of the wall, Habesh, you beautiful stinking whore of a city: I love you so.

THE SEAFARER

THE TEN SOLDIERS stopped their several days of running at the edge of the red stone cliff and looked out in awe over the gray ocean. A hundred feet below them the waves thudded against the rock and they inhaled the salt spray that slowly drifted up as a fine mist.

None of them had ever seen the ocean before.

"Hard to believe that we fought toward this for so long," Alej said. "And are only just now seeing it."

Even after they had stopped fighting, and started running, he had suspected he would never live to see it.

Horza, who had refused to edge any closer to the precipice with his chief, grunted. "We don't have much time," he said. "That scouting party will catch up to us."

Alej looked back. His men, in their dented and battered armor, stood scattered in a loose line from the coastal road to the edge of the cliff.

"So few of us," he lamented to Horza. "But I guess we were the lucky ones."

Horza spat. "That bitch was a god-gifted fighter," he said. "And Koraquan never stopped underestimating her abilities."

That bitch. Trust Horza to both insult and pay respect. They'd joined Koraquan's army, lured by the promise of a return to greatness. The Hundrapeans would rise again. They were told that they would swoop down on the city of Paika. The entire coast, Koraquan said, would be theirs.

The ruler of Paika had taken that city by force herself. She had led armies and destroyed many men, and Koraquan was just the latest in a long list of her enemies. She ripped their army apart thrice. Each time no less savagely than the one before.

There was a reason, Alej thought, that they called the ruler of Paika the Executioness.

By their last battle, Alej had become chief of the small band of men that had walked across snowy mountain peaks to join Koraquan, swept up by the promise of loot, battle, and glory. He'd barely managed to keep most of them alive, back against back, when their lines had been overrun.

They'd fought a bitter rear guard retreat.

And then they'd voted to leave. One of the many bands of stragglers deciding that Paika wasn't worth it.

The Executioness was too strong.

It was the northern wilds and hunger again for most of Koraquan's followers. Deadly bramble and icy tundra. Maybe even the wilds of the mountains.

But Alej took his men west, sneaking through the Executioness's lines where no man dared. They'd been spotted and chased. Now, exhausted, they were close to the end.

Alej turned and faced his men. "Thank you for choosing me as your chief, but I hope you find your true lives, now. Hurry and strip off your armor."

They helped each other unbuckle breastplates and armor. They threw them all over the cliff, with their Hundrapean swords after them. Anything that would identify them as Hundrap was swallowed by the ocean.

"The walled city of Rusajka is further west along the road," Alej said. "It's best if we split our coin and food now . . ."

"Horses!"

They'd mistaken how long it would take for the scout party to catch up. Four of the Executioness's ax-women swooped down on them. Without a word they all scattered, dropping packs for speed.

Orke, large and unwilling to give ground, stood in place and screamed at one of the women. He was spitted on the end of quickly thrown spear. He fell, and the food and coins in his pack spilled out onto the ground.

Alej ran for the protection of the rocks, then skirted them for the forests away from the road. The horses wouldn't follow him in there, he knew, for fear of bramble.

Alej approached Rusajka through the forested northern slopes. Bramble grew everywhere in them; sometimes it was hard to tell what was bramble and what was underbrush.

Let just the faintest brush of bramble tickle you, caress your skin, and you could die. The deep sleep would come for you, and you would likely waste away.

Accidentally let a clump of bramble touch you, and you died.

But it was better than being caught without a sword or armor by the Executioness's patrols.

The southerners claimed bramble was the result of magic use. But in the north, they called it Selvka's Curse and said that once, the great God Selvka enjoyed looking through the mirrors of his halls in the afterlife. Every mirror looked back down at human lives, which entertained him greatly. But generation after generation, the world's wickedness inflamed Selvka until he could stand it no more, and he cursed the world with bramble.

Some northerners swore magic had no effect on bramble, and that it would continue to plague man due to their wickedness.

Maybe, some admitted, there was more bramble around areas that used magic. But it was only because those richer areas were sinful and wasteful, and Selvka punished them more.

Alej had once believed it was Selvka's Curse.

Until his first southern battle. One where majistras cast spells and helped heal the wounded. After the first attack of Paika he'd woken up to see bramble dripping from the eaves of tents, and had to carefully step around it on grounds that had been completely clear the night before.

Alej crept slowly out onto a road and looked about, then risked using it for the last half mile of his approach to the city. He kept glancing over his shoulder as he walked toward the walls of Rusajka.

Rusajka was a blocky, walled city that jealously protected a great deep harbor cut into a cleft in the rocky coast. Alej paid the entrance fee in what little coin he had on him to the unimpressed guards. Now he would have to find a job of some kind or starve.

He could see why this city remained independent. Even with the Executioness's growing armies to the east, it would be hard to break these ancient, thick walls.

Rusajka traded with small towns to the north, and farms just outside its walls. Though judging by the stench in the air, fishing was one of its larger industries.

There were worse smells, Alej knew. His stomach growled with hunger whenever he passed food.

He spent two days wandering the city, looking for work among the thousands of shoved together inhabitants. He slept on the streets. His cloak kept him warm enough, despite an occasional chill wind.

To the west of the city's docks, shanties clung to the rock cleft, but there was no work to be found there. Alej stared at the thin beggars lying alongside the streets and winced.

On the third day Alej walked the docks, accepting polite declines as he asked after work among the forest of masts. There had to be fifty boats tied up to these wooden piers, he thought, with another thirty at anchor.

"Hey! You!"

Alej turned. The woman shouting at him wore a large, floppy hat and a furred jacket. She had a dagger strapped to her waist, and ragged leather boots. Her face was reddened from the outside air.

"Yes?" he answered.

"You're looking for work?" she asked. Close now, he could smell salt, leather and wood polish on her. Her forearms were wiry, her skin brown, and five earrings jangled in her left lobe. She wore five or six golden bracelets on each wrist.

"I am looking," Alej confirmed.

The woman looked him up and down. "Know how to swim?"

Alej considered that for a second, thinking about a river crossing in full armor, when his foot had slipped and the water had enveloped him, trying to drown him. He wasn't sure about working on a ship, or at sea. But the knot in his stomach told him he had no choice. He needed to eat. "Not well. But I haven't drowned yet."

Before he could stop her, she reached over and squeezed his upper arm, then pinched his chest. She smiled. "You seem strong. If you're willing to work hard, I can use you aboard my ship. You'll work the bellows. You won't get paid much, but you'll have a bunk of your own and two good meals every day. You look the sort that could use both. What do you say? We accept all tribes on our ships, stranger. We are a world of our own. There are worse places to make a life. We set sail for the Southern Isles once a year, and come back to Rusajka three months later."

Alej nodded. "My name is Alej," he said. "I am new to Rusajka. I don't know anyone here."

"Yalisa," the woman said. "Welcome aboard."

Alej looked at the water out behind her and automatically took a deep breath, as if he were about to dive in.

Sabina was the name of Yalisa's ship. Alej, along with several other grubby men from the shanties, had gaped at the size of the ship from their bench on the rowboat.

Two hundred feet long, he guessed. And so tall. The masts towered up into the sky, and what looked like thousands of lines and netting draped from crossbars far overhead.

Alej wasn't scared of heights, but seeing those masts rock, he realized that working in the bellows would be safer than clambering up those nets, like some of the sailors were doing.

Whatever the bellows were.

Yalisa, as she'd hinted, was the actual captain of this ship. When they got aboard she began to give orders with the casual expectation that they be followed. Everyone nodded and ran to.

A tiny shrimp of a man called Osilte showed Alej his bunk. It was a cubbyhole built into the side of the ship, with a curtain that closed it off for privacy. Four cubbyholes stacked on top of each other in columns, so that thirty crewmen could sleep in this forward section of the ship.

"Put your things in the locker beside your bed," Osilte explained. Then grinned. "If you want a lock, I can rent you one for some bronze pieces. Silver to buy one."

"I have no coin," Alej said. He took his pack and pushed it into the bed, then drew the curtain aside. "I own nothing of value."

"A true tragedy." Osilte pulled a lock out of his pocket. "You can owe me. Pay me back when the quartermaster gives you your wages."

"I don't like debts," Alej said. "That was how I ended penniless and hungry, walking the world."

"Your loss." Osilte pocketed the lock with a scowl. "Well then, let me take you to the heart of the ship."

They walked through tight, confined spaces, and then around a galley area where the smell of fried fruits and turmeric made Alej's stomach rumble. He hadn't eaten in far too long. He was weak.

Osilte opened a door, revealing a massive water tank made out of glass.

At first, Alej wasn't impressed. He had assumed sailors needed plenty of water for their long trips. Much like any army. He hadn't known that glass containers this massive even existed, but he assumed it had been made by magic.

Then he stepped further inside.

The tank held hundreds of gallons of water. But it was one of three tanks, he saw. Copper pipes ran from tank to tank, with spigots along the way.

Leather bellows allowed teams of workers to vigorously pump water from tank to tank. Water continuously moved through the tubes.

The first line of pumpers sucked water from a pipe that came out of the hull. They were taking in ocean water, Alej realized.

The first tank, brass bands gleaming in the lamplight belowdecks, bubbled and boiled with a purple fire that reached up through the glass itself and into the water. The air around it smelled faintly of magic: neem and parchment, old ink.

A man pedaled a spinning bronze disc by a leather strap connected to gears that creaked underneath him as he sweated away.

"This is the hydromorpheum," Osilte said. "*Sabine* makes water for the flotilla. Sweet and fresh, and drawn from the infinite supply that we are always floating in."

Then he pointed to a set of bellows that fanned the purple flame activated by the bronze disk. "That is your station."

The man pumping and squeezing the giant paddles of the bellows motioned him over. Alej grabbed the surprisingly soft leather handles and squeezed until his back protested.

Osilte chuckled as a set of bells rang. "That's the start of your watch. Keep pumping, and when they sound again, you will be done."

Alej pumped the bellows for several minutes. His wrists started to ache and his back began to seize. And he was still dizzy from hunger.

When he looked up to wipe the sweat away from his eyes, Osilte was gone. A foreman yelled at him to get back to the bellows.

Alej gratefully released the bellows four hours later as someone stepped in to take over. His fingers burned and he couldn't stand straight.

When he stumbled back to his bunk, the curtain had been opened and his pack ransacked. The dirty rags were scattered all over his bed, and his cloak missing.

Osilte stepped out from behind a thick post in the center of the room. "How horrible," he said with false concern. "Some ill-blooded sailor has decided to see if you had anything of value. It's a shame you didn't have a lock."

For a moment, Alej considered trying to break Osilte's face. Or smashing it against the thick post he'd stepped out from behind.

But working the bellows had left him weak, and he was still hungry after three days of fasting.

"There are many dishonorable men in the world," Alej said.

"That there are," Osilte said. "I must agree. By the way, bellowsman, tonight the western winds will blow and it will be cold. You shouldn't go on deck unless you have something warm to wear. Best to stay inside, where its nice, warm, and safe."

Alej watched Osilte leave with narrowed eyes.

There was a rhythm and a routine to hard work, one that Alej was well used to. Digging for sieges. Practicing with a sword. Using a sword.

But four straight hours of pumping strained even him.

Not enough to break, but close at first.

By the end of four days, his hands had blistered, then healed, then developed calluses. His muscles hardened after the end of the first full week, and he stopped panting.

But he was fed. And had a place to sleep. And that was enough.

With his first pay from the quartermaster, Alej caught a ride to shore to purchase a new cloak and a lock. Osilte was the second in command for the ship. It would not pay to end up in a fight with him.

As much as he would have liked that.

*

After yet another shift, well into the middle of his second week, Alej climbed the wooden stairs to the deck. The sun made him blink, but was welcome and warm.

At the front of the deck he threw a bucket overboard and pulled it back up using the rope attached to its handle. It brimmed with ocean water.

Alej pulled his shirt off and dumped it over himself, enjoying the bracing feeling. He would dry off in the sun and find a game of dice at the port side of the boat.

"Well now," said a familiar voice.

Startled, Alej opened his eyes to see Yalisa smiling at him. He hurried to pull his shirt back on, but she held up a hand. "In the Isles men usually don't bother to wear a shirt in the heat. Everyone up here is always bundled up. I forget what a well-muscled man can look like. What are the scars from?"

Alej pulled his shirt on anyway. "A mistake," he said.

Yalisa chose not to ask more about it. "I've seen you help row when going to shore. You're capable. You're also a cool-blooded man, which I need."

"Cool-blooded?" Alej asked.

"You didn't buy a lock from Osilte?" At Alej's nod she smiled. "Yes, well, usually the big ones like you take a swing. Osilte was a street fighter in the shanties of Rusajka, and he fights dirty. He doesn't look it, but I usually end up with a broken bellowsman who never again makes the mistake of clashing with my second in command. He's not too sure about you. Doesn't quite have you figured out in his mind."

"If you know about the locks, then will you make him give me my cloak back?" Alej asked.

Yalisa snorted. "Do you have any witnesses that can swear they saw him take it?"

Alej shook his head. "No."

"Then let it go." Yalisa pulled him close. "I am going to promote you, Alej. I need a messenger rower. Are you interested?"

This was not a hard choice, Alej thought. It would break his back less than the bellows. "I am."

She handed him a flask. "This goes to the captain of the *Akkadevi*. And only to him. Do you understand?"

Alej nodded. "I understand."

"We're having trouble preparing for our sail south," she grumbled. "*Jijabai*'s hydromorpheum has failed. Mine is the only one that works in the entire fleet now. I should be happy about the leverage that gives me. But no captain wants to risk sailing south with only one in case it breaks."

"Can't you fix it?" Alej asked, surprised.

"Do I look like a majistra to you?" Yalisa snapped. "Go deliver the message."

Alej rowed Yalisa's message to the *Akkadevi*. He'd never been aboard, and as far as he knew, it wasn't one of the three ships with a hydromorpheum inside.

Yet it was too large to dock in the harbor.

"Ho rower! Toss your painter up!"

He turned in his bench, shipped the oars, and threw the bow rope—the painter they called it—up at the man on the deck.

Alej tucked the message flask in his waistband and climbed up the ratlines tossed over the side of the *Akkadevi*'s hull.

A strong hand helped haul him onto the deck.

Alej delivered the flask, and while the captain was composing a reply, he wandered the deck looking for a dice game, or card game.

Instead, he saw his cloak.

He stepped forward and spun the man wearing it around. "Tell me where you got that cloak!" Alej demanded. And found he was facing Horza.

Horza's jaw dropped. "Alej!"

"Horza!"

"I almost threw you overboard," Horza shouted as they embraced. "I'm glad I waited to see what fool grabbed my cloak."

"I thought it was mine. Someone stole it."

They laughed, delighted to find they were still alive and had escaped the Executioness's patrol.

Horza leaned close. "Come with me, I have something for you."

They descended into the depths of the ship's holds, walking past barred rooms. Alej didn't pay attention to them until a tiny hand reached out and grabbed his sleeve, startling him.

"What is this?" he shouted, leaping back and looking inside.

A child of seven or eight years looked back at him. "I want to go home," he said plaintively.

Horza raised a hand. "It is not what you think. They are Paikan acolytes."

"Paika fell to the Executioness."

"Yes, but Paikan missionaries hail from the Southern Isles. They believe if they can teach enough northern children to abstain from magic, that maybe we can rid the world of the bramble's curse."

"But they're not here of free will?" Alej asked, as they walked past the rows and rows of children.

"Some are taken by warriors. Some are sold by their parents. Others seek the Paikan monasteries for a chance of a better life. None of them are abused. That is why I'm on this ship. I guard them. No sailor may touch an acolyte. Come on, keep moving, this is boring."

Alej glanced back as Horza pulled him along.

"You know who else is on these ships?" Horza asked.

Alej forced himself to look forward. "Who?"

"Jarka and Kvet made it to the city and also found work aboard the boats. Jarka as an oarsman. Can you believe that? He can't swim! He's terrified he'll fall over. Kvet, you know he can cook?" Horza laughed.

"Cook?" Alej could only think of Kvet and his bow, and the satisfied grunt one heard whenever Kvet aimed true.

Horza lived in a small guardroom at the end of the cages with three other guards. He opened a thick trunk and pulled out a large bottle of wine. "You must try some. It's very, very good."

"Horza, I still have to row back and deliver a message to my captain."

"Just a little bit. You can still row with some fire in your belly," Horza said, poking Alej in the stomach.

"A cup," Alej said, looking at it fondly. "For all we've been through together, yes?"

Horza pulled out wooden cups. "For all we've been through."

He poured a sloppy cup's worth, and Alej drank it.

Damn, he thought. It *was* good wine.

Rowing back taxed his abilities. He stopped at the wrong ship once. Maybe twice. His memory failed him in mysterious patches.

But back on the *Sabine* Alej tied up and slowly hauled himself up the ratlines.

He fumbled his way along the deck, looking for the hatch and stairs down to the bunks, but couldn't find it.

Eventually, giggling, Alej curled up in a pile of thick, barnacled anchor ropes and fell asleep, warm and content, holding the message flask in a close hug. He'd deliver it when he woke up.

It had been good to see Horza again.

Horza had seemed happy, he thought, falling asleep.

A face full of cold harbor water jerked Alej awake. Yalisa stood over him, holding the bucket. "Where is my gods-damned message?" she demanded.

Alej stood up, sputtering and wiping his face. Osilte stood just behind Yalisa, his face pinched and angry. And maybe a little bit satisfied.

Alej patted his waistband, but the flask wasn't there.

"It must be in the tender," he said. "Let me go look . . ."

"You were drunk, and you lost your message," Yalisa snapped.

"And on your very first trip as a message rower," Osilte added, voice dripping with scorn.

Alej frowned. He'd been drunk. But he hadn't lost the flask. That didn't sound like something he'd do. He could have sworn he'd had the flask.

"No," Alej insisted.

"No, you weren't drunk?" Yalisa asked, danger in her voice.

"Yes, I had too much wine. I met an old friend on the boat, and we shared cups. Something I will not do again," Alej growled. He focused on Osilte. "But I do not lose things in my care unless they're taken from me."

Yalisa cocked her head. "When you first came here, asking for work, you told me you knew no one in Rusajka. That you were alone. Now you drink with old friends."

"He fails you, *and* he is a liar," Osilte said.

Alej was hungover and angry, and snapped, "I *do not lie!* Horza and I fought at Paika. I didn't know if he had lived until I saw him tonight. He saved my life enough times I wouldn't refuse a drink with him. And as for the message," Alej stepped forward, but not too quickly, and pointed at Osilte. "I wager all I own in this world that *he* knows where it is."

Yalisa stepped between them. "He *does* know where it is."

Alej's eyes lit up. That bastard!

But Yalisa held up the message flask. It had been tucked into the back of her waistline. "He knows where it is because I am the one who found you passed out in your own vomit clutching it, and removed it to read it. And I'm the one that ordered him to come up and help me throw you off my ship. Osilte is good at those things. It's why I keep him around, even though he can be a bit rough on crew."

Osilte smiled. Alej bit back his anger.

"You shouldn't have taken him off the bellows. He is not trustworthy," Osilte said.

"I know," Yalisa snapped. "No need to repeat it."

But Osilte stepped forward and leaned over to her with sudden smile. "He *claims* he fought at Paika," he said, conversationally. "We can prove that lie easily."

Yalisa looked sideways. "If you wish, Osilte." She folded her arms. "Have your fun with him, then throw him off the ship."

Osilte left, and returned with two wooden practice swords. He threw one over to Alej, who caught it and shook his head.

That was the wrong thing to do. His pounding headache almost overwhelmed him. The deck shifted far too much.

"I left that life behind me," Alej said.

"Prove your words!" Osilte demanded gleefully.

So this was where Osilte figured he would get his chance to abuse him, Alej thought. The man looked overjoyed for his chance to beat on a hungover Alej.

Alej hadn't fought or practiced in many long weeks.

Well then, Alej thought as he moved the wooden sword in a quick pattern to get a feel for it, we'll see what still remains.

Yalisa stepped back, her arms still folded, and Osilte snapped forward.

Damn, but he was fast. A viper with a stabbing wooden sword that kept whipping through the air at Alej.

Alej had never been particularly fast. It took everything he had to keep out of the damn thing's way. Every parry required him to struggle to get his eyes to track the sword.

He hit and shoved Osilte back, to gain space just to think. It had been a long time since Alej had fought hungover.

Osilte stared at him, panting slightly. Alej's muscles were warming up, and old instincts trickling through him.

Alej might have lost his place on this ship and might be facing hunger on the streets of Rusajka again. But Osilte was going to regret stealing his cloak, Alej thought.

Oh yes.

He stepped in, swords striking, then kicked Osilte's feet out.

The small man stumbled, reached out to balance himself while still parrying, and Alej grabbed his extended hand.

Then he yanked him close and smacked Osilte in the face with an elbow while still holding off the wooden sword.

As Osilte staggered back, Alej raised the sword to crack Osilte's shoulder. Every time that man would hold something in his arm, he was going to remember Alej with a twinge.

All this had taken half a single breath.

"Stop!" Yalisa shouted.

Alej pulled back, and the blade only smacked lightly into Osilte's shoulder.

They both regained their balance, Alej swallowing a hint of bile that crept up the back of his throat and blinking blearily, Osilte holding his nose.

"Am I a liar still?" Alej demanded.

Osilte pulled out a piece of cloth and held it to his nose. "You don't fight from trained moves. You learned those things the hard way."

"You're lucky he chose not to take a swing at you over the lock, then," Yalisa said.

Osilte grunted. "If he can repeat that stunt, then maybe he should work for our shipsguard, not the bellows."

Alej tossed the wooden sword at Osilte's feet. "That life is behind me," he said. "I would go back to the bellows if you feel you can't trust me as a messenger rower. If you keep me. But I won't pick up arms."

Yalisa unfolded her arms, still eyeing Alej thoughtfully. "Go sleep off your hangover," she finally said. "We will talk later."

Osilte threw a polished sword, scabbard, and a shirt of mail onto Alej as he lay sleeping in bed. Alej scrambled awake and jumped out, knocking them all to the floor with a clatter. "Those days are behind me." Alej blinked as he looked down at his feet.

"I was there, I heard you," Osilte said. "And here is Yalisa's promise. We are meeting the Majistra of Rusajka and we need more bodyguards."

Alej leaned against the wall, struggling his way to fully awake.

Osilte grabbed him by the elbow, digging his fingers into the meat of his arm. "When the Executioness took Paika we lost our best port. The Executioness doesn't like Paikan missionaries. And hates the flotilla as well." Osilte looked around and lowered his voice to a whisper. "The Majistra here allows us to dock, but he extorts us with fees. Fees to cut down wood, overpriced instruments, and food. Only the water is free, and we are down to one hydromorpheum. He bleeds us."

"Are you sure he isn't a long lost brother of yours?"

Osilte struck Alej hard over the back of the head. Alej stumbled and spun.

That was enough. Beating the piece of filth with a sword hadn't taught Osilte a lesson, but now Alej would destroy him.

Osilte danced back quickly. "Touch me, soldier-boy, and you will end up hungry and on the street again."

Alej snarled, but stopped himself.

"Look," Osilte said. "Yalisa wants you to do this just once. She says you owe her for your drunken antics."

Alej picked up the chain mail and threw it at Osilte, hard enough to make the man stagger back and grunt.

"One time, for one mistake," he said. "But I'm not wearing that. If I fall in, I'll sink to the bottom of the harbor and drown in that."

Ten men surrounded Yalisa and two other captains for the trip up the stone steps to the foot of Rusajka's heart: the inner keep that towered over the harbor.

Thirty of the Majistra's guard escorted them up through the main banner hall, large enough to fit any of the largest ships of the flotilla inside. The masts would even fit underneath the tall stone arches.

The meeting took place in a great room with an oval table, large enough for ten to sit at.

One of the guardsmen sat and picked at his fingernails with a knife. A showy move, which, combined with the pointedly long wait before the Majistra arrived, was to remind them who was the petitioner, and who ran this city.

Osilte glowered at that. "Look at how he treats us."

The Majistra and Mayor of Rusajka, Chandak the Defender, arrived finally after an hour's wait. A fine cape of spun gold billowed behind him, and he'd wrapped his hair in green silks. His beard was oiled, and he smelled of fresh spices.

"So," he said, once the captains sat down. "You have come to beg for my help. And yet, for so long you have refused to let me sell any of your ship's water, little Yalisa. And now, it appears you can't even maintain your own magics. You have rebuffed and insulted me for so long it will not be cheap to get my affection back."

Yalisa's lip curled. "We pay you well for timber. We agree to buy all our stores and supplies through you. What more can you demand of us?"

Chandak's eyes gleamed. "You will give me a fifth of all your payments from the Paikan missionaries for delivering their acolytes."

The other two captains jumped up. "You *pirate*," one of them shouted.

"Tell us the price you want for the repairs in gold. We will pay it," Yalisa said calmly.

But Chandak wasn't interested.

One of the captains slammed the palm of his hand down on the table, and city guards reached for swords.

Alej tensed.

But Chandak saw the movement and waved a hand. The city guard relaxed.

"Go back to your flotilla," Chandak said. "You need a city to land at. If you give me this portion, I will supply your ships, I will help you repair your magical machines. You will have a partner. It's a dangerous world out there. I've changed our little understanding, and you are not in a position to really negotiate, are you, captain?"

And then Chandak dismissed them.

Yalisa watched him leave with disgust on her face. "He is no partner. He wants the fleet for himself."

Alej looked at her. "What happens if we can't repair the other hydromorphea?"

Yalisa sighed. "I don't know," she admitted. "We will have to make dangerous choices, then. The Majistra may yet end up owning us."

On the way back, Yalisa looked back at the city. "When you live on land, you will always have to deal with your neighbors. If they cast spells and choke your windows with bramble, it becomes *your* problem. You will have to stand it, or negotiate with them, or maybe just kill them out of general frustration."

"And it's different with you?" Alej asked.

"Yes. We can always move. We are free people. We have our own nation in every little hull. We take who we want aboard, and go where we want when our neighbors became too dastardly. It's time to sail, Alej. It's time to sail."

"Sail where?" Alej grunted. "The Southern Isles?"

"No, we still need working hydromorphea. What we need is a new port. We need to fix our hydromorphea, negotiate for better supplies. It's time to head farther west up the coast and find a better port."

"And what about me?" Alej asked.

"Stay, if you wish," Yalisa said. "But I will be the one that decides your role on our ship."

Alej glanced back from his oar at the Majistra's guards. If they recognized him again, alone and without a weapon, he wondered how they would react.

He kept pulling as he mulled that thought over.

The flotilla sailed at the end of the same day, and Alej with it, despite his worries about the dangers of the wide ocean. Ship hulls were scraped and decks tied down and tidied. Anything that might come loose inside the ships was secured. Miles of lines were checked over and coiled in neat stacks.

Ships sounded horns and flew departure signal flags from the masts. The red and yellow striped flags whipped in the wind as men hauled and cranked sails up into place.

The great, triangular wedges of yellow material shook, then billowed full of air until taut.

The anchored flotilla broke free and sailed from the harbor in clumps and staggered lines. Then the docked ships, pulled free by rowboats, shook their own sails out and followed.

Yalisa stood at the high rear cockpit of the *Sabine*. She looked back over the railings at the docks.

"They're watching us leave," she said, satisfaction in her voice. "I'll bet Chadak didn't truly expect that."

"In a week we'll be in Zebari," Osilte said to her. "They should be more than happy to take our coin. And we should have left for it six months ago."

Alej walked to the bow, thinking about the first time he'd seen the ocean, and how far it had stretched. Now that everything was stowed and the ship's sails were up, there was less for him to do. He could stand by the rail and watch the water foam and bubble past.

Osilte startled him by appearing just behind his left side. "Scared of the ocean, soldier-boy?"

Alej said nothing.

"We'll mostly be within sight of land," Osilte told him. "There are islands and rocks to steer clear of, but we'll mostly follow the coast west."

"Mostly?" Alej couldn't help himself.

"If it looks like there's a storm we'll head for open ocean," Osilte said. "Don't want to get caught near the coast in a bad one."

Alej nodded, and then turned green. "I . . ." he leaned over the side of the ship and threw up violently. Osilte started laughing.

Dazed, Alej looked back at him while spitting sick out of his mouth. "I don't understand. I've been living aboard for weeks. How can I be seasick?"

"You're out on the *real* ocean now, not sitting in a harbor. Now we'll see whether you are truly man enough to be on a ship," Osilte smirked.

Alej spent the next two miserable days clinging to the side of the rail. He kept his new cloak with him and slept on the deck rather than risk going below. Better to tough it out in the open air without making a mess he would have to clean up.

He paid no attention to whether he could see the coast or not, and didn't worry much about anything else.

But eventually the sea sickness passed and he could walk around the *Sabine* again. And eat.

In small portions at first.

By the fourth day, Alej felt like a human being once more. And that was when the storm caught the flotilla.

The white line of furious wind and water came from the distant horizon and far out at sea. It bore down on them so fast they barely had time to shorten their sails, or "reef" them.

Alej saw the ship across from them failed to do the same thing in time, and the fabric exploded into tatters almost immediately. The entire ship faded away in the white intensity of the howling squall.

For a day Yalisa and her crew struggled to keep the *Sabine* sailing as close into the wind as they could manage. The waves smashed the bow of the ship and swept constantly over the decks, terrifying

Alej. It felt like the ship spent as much time *under* the ocean as it plunged into the waves as it did riding on top of their crests.

When the storm broke, Alej saw the flotilla scattered to all points of the horizon. Two ships lost their masts and floated dangerously close to the ragged rocks of the coastline, saved only by the short duration of the storm and the large canvas bucket sea anchors they'd thrown over their bows to keep from being blown too fast toward shore. *Sabine* had managed to get several miles further out to sea, but now Alej understood why Osilte didn't like being close to the coast.

On the distant coast, a battered hull lay dashed against the rocks. One of the ships had failed to hold its own against the storm. Alej stared at it until Osilte yelled at him. "Get down to the hydromorpheum. Now."

Alej frowned. He was back to pumping bellows. But they had enough water in their tanks. The last thing the ships needed after a storm was water.

But when he entered the hold he saw the shattered pieces of glass, and the rotting stench of magic gone wrong made him gag.

The fleet could no longer make its own water.

"We need to salvage what we can," Osilte said. "Don't break anything more than we're already lost."

They sailed into the harbors of Zebari with their pennants flying and all the crew on deck, eager to see the new city.

It was larger than Rusajka, but not as impressive. There were no towering walls and turrets. Zebari sprawled lengthily along the low coastline. Shacks clustered the shoreline, and the rocky beaches were dotted with wooden fishing boats and drying nets.

"Yalisa wants you as a rower," Osilte said. "There will be shipsguard going ashore with us. Will you row?"

"I'll row, but I won't join the guard," Alej said, still looking out at Zebari.

"Yalisa says to bring your sword. You will be a rower, but even a rower might need to defend themselves if things turn bad on the shore."

"And what's the difference between a rower with a sword and a shipsguard?" Alej asked.

Osilte scowled. "You can cower away in the tender all you wish, soldier-boy, but you will carry a sword. Captain's orders. You know how to follow orders, don't you?"

Alej thought about the wrecked ship after the storm. "I'll follow orders," he grunted.

"Of course you will," Osilte said.

They rowed ashore to the largest of the docks where a somewhat official procession already gathered. The city's flags fluttered from tall staffs, and old men in black robes milled about.

More interesting to Alej were the tough-looking men in leather armor and tall, rectangular shields formed up at the start of the dock, facing a gathering crowd.

Yalisa and three other captains hailed the men on the dock as Alej and other rowers kept them several yards away.

"We're looking to trade," Yalisa shouted. "And for a new port. I am captain Yalisa of the *Sabine*." She introduced the other captains.

"Please, come to the docks. We would love to talk about trade," said one of the robed men.

Yalisa glanced back at Osilte. "What do you think?"

Osilte squinted. "They don't seem worried about us, but about that crowd."

Poor fisherman wearing rags watched them hopefully as they tied up and climbed out, and Yalisa and the captains began talking to the Majistra. Alej could hear snatches of the conversation from the tender.

"We need help with hydromorphic magic," she said.

"Oh, we would be delighted to help you," one of the robed men said. "Zebari once housed a great magical academy. However, we have little in the way of supplies, now. But many of our great Majistra can still assist you with whatever you have on your ships."

"You have no magical ingredients?" Yalisa asked, frowning.

"The city has fallen on hard times. The academy was . . . disbanded. Our former teachers are more worried with trying to rule the city as best we can since the Mayor fled in his own ship."

Hard times indeed, Alej thought, looking at the rag-wearing people gathering on the stony beach. Three hundred or so now thronged the seaside, watching them intently.

"We would like to offer trade," Yalisa said. There was a hopeful note in her voice. She had to be thinking that if Zebari had fallen on hard times, they would be able to negotiate good terms. "We need wood to repair damage to our ships and build new ones. I guess we can send out traders to seek magical ingredients, if you can help us . . ."

"We have no timber. I'm afraid you don't understand our position," one of the men interrupted. He made a sweeping gesture with his hand. "We are cut off from the other cities by bramble."

Alej looked at the gray hills in the distance, and realized what he was looking at. Beyond the city's edge, and the few farms that rimmed it, the land had fallen to bramble.

"We burned the forests, as it was choked with bramble. It made it easier to keep it back. But that has not stopped its march. We tried to keep the roads open, but we didn't have enough pitch to use for fire to burn it back, and we lost the battle. We keep the farms safe, and the Majistra hunt magic users to prevent them from cursing us with more bramble. We have held on thanks to our fishing boats, but they are getting leaky and old. We take wood from our walls and roofs to repair the boats."

Yalisa looked stunned. The captains equally so. She moved closer to the robed men. "Then what trade do you have to offer us?" she asked, puzzled.

One of the old men opened the palm of his hand. "Gold. We

still have lots of gold. We will buy *anything* you are willing to sell from your fleet." There was desperation in his voice.

A younger man in robes spoke up, his voice cracking. "We will be generous. If you could, maybe transport some of us. We will help you anyway we can. We will pay generously. Just *please* . . ."

He stumbled forward, and a coin purse full of gold fell forward and hit the plank. It broke open, and coins scattered. The man fell forward with a cry, trying to gather the coins up.

Alej heard a cries of suspicion surge through the crowd by the shore, and his head snapped up from staring at the shiny pieces of gold.

The crowd moved as one, shoving the shield men.

"Take us with you!" many shouted.

"Save us!"

"Show mercy. We also have coin!"

Alej moved forward and untied the painter, letting it drop back into the tender. Just as casually, he slipped back to his seat, getting ready with the oars.

"You, get to your oars," he hissed at the two other rowers waiting in their tenders. They were staring across the dock at the scattered gold, not paying attention.

The crowd shouted angrily. They wanted access to the sailors. They shoved even harder at the shields in their way.

Then the entire crowd moved as one to ram into the shields. The men pulled out their swords and shouted, but it didn't matter. Some in the crowd dropped, stabbed, but others stepped forward and overwhelmed them.

"Yalisa!" Alej yelled, slipping the oars out.

Yalisa leapt into the tender, almost burying the gunwhale under water. Osilte and three shipsguard scrambled in next, flopping awkwardly in as Alej began to row for all he was worth.

People were jumping into the water and wading out toward them, others swimming. Some jumped off the dock.

Alej pulled on the oars harder.

A woman reached the end of the dock carrying a child in her arms. It was no more than two years old. "Please Gods take him," she screamed, and threw the child at the tender.

Alej watched, horrified, as the child struck the water ten feet away and sank as it thrashed.

"It can't swim," Alej said, standing up and leaving the oars in their pegs.

He reached for the child with an oar, but they were too far away.

Osilte leapt into the water in a perfect, clean dive. He slid under water like a sea-creature, disappearing under the green.

The swimming crowd grew closer with every second, and Alej couldn't see Osilte anywhere.

"Where is he?" Yalisa asked, standing up as well behind him. "Damnit, Alej, where is he?"

Alej, still stunned at Osilte's actions, had no answer.

Several strangers reached their tender and clawed at the sides, trying to pull themselves in.

"Keep them off," Alej growled, still keeping his eye on the spot where Osilte had slid underwater.

He picked up an oar to shove the swimmers back, but Yalisa grabbed his arm. "You might break the oar," she hissed. "And then we'll be dead for sure."

She pulled her sword out and began clubbing heads with the pommel.

Osilte resurfaced in the midst of the other swimmers with a gasp, holding the child.

"Throw him rope," Alej snapped. Osilte grabbed it, and Alej began to row again.

They pulled five or six men with them who refused to let go, even with Yalisa screaming bloody death at them as they pulled Osilte up to the tender and aboard with the now-screaming child.

"Mama. Mama. Mama."

Osilte crawled to the bottom of the tender, vomited salt water, and lay on his side, panting.

Yalisa finally stopped screaming at the men on the rope. "Hold on until we're at the flotilla, and we'll let you aboard. Try to get on the tender and I'll cut your fingers off," she told them.

As they pulled their anchors to leave, leaky fishing boats launched from shore crowded with even more desperate refugees. The first to reach *Sabine* was a small coracle made out of what appeared to be animal hide and bones.

"Ho! Ship!" cried the rower.

The tiny vessel looked ready to swamp at any moment as the rower deftly moved closer to *Sabine*, and they tossed a rope to it.

The lithe rower slithered up and onto their deck.

He burst into tears when they let him onto the deck. "I can work for my passage," he cried.

Other ships were taking on what refugees they could, but Yalisa was gritting her teeth. "We only have what water is stored in barrels. We can't make any more. This is bad. How further west can we go before the water runs out?"

The man they'd pulled aboard, a skilled fisherman called Chatura, looked at Yalisa in horror.

"It's like this all up the coast," he said. "I used to live farther west, before I sailed. In the town of Aizawl. There they hung the Majistra," he said. "People reported on other people for using magic. There was blood. Some sailed out from the shore and never returned. There's nothing there for you but death and desperation."

They sailed south for the open ocean once more. Yalisa joined Alej at the stern rail, looking back at the gray, bramble-choked hills.

"I told you once that our ships were worlds of their own," she said thoughtfully. "We make our own water, use the winds to move, catch fish, and bow to no man."

Alej turned away from looking at the burbling wake of the ship. "I remember."

"I think I was wrong," she said. "Those cut-off cities, those truly were worlds of their own, and we're not that. We need good timber for our ships. Neem and parchment, brass tubes and glass and leather, and more, to create the spells that run the hydromorphea. It is good to have fresh fruit to eat, and news from traders. We are more independent, but we're still connected. I thought we could stop dealing with troublesome neighbors, but maybe we need to figure out how to deal with them after all."

"We're returning to Rusajka?" Alej asked.

"Yes," Yalisa said, with gritted teeth.

Later that night, while sitting outside and wrapped in his cloak, Alej heard scuffling and scratching on the deck. He found Osilte shoving a large trunk up to the railing. Without a word he joined in and helped Osilte lever it up, and over into the ocean.

It slowly floated in the direction of the desperate city.

"Will what's in there help them?" he asked.

Osilte looked at the chest floating in the *Sabine*'s wake. "Not much," he said. "But it's something."

"In the east they talked about the fallen Empire of Jhandpara, and its lost glories. I never thought I'd see something like this with my own eyes," Alej said.

"I am not your friend," Osilte hissed at Alej, as if in sudden pain.

"I'm not a threat to you, Osilte. I don't want your place. I don't want your woman. I don't even understand you. You harry me from day to day as if I'm some sworn enemy, and yet you risk your life for a child you've never even seen."

"Yalia's not mine, or anyone else's, to take," Osilte said. "She can make her own choices, like any other woman, northerner. It's the ship I am jealous for. Do you understand?"

Alej didn't.

Osilte sighed, as if talking to a child. "One day, Yalisa will leave for a different ship. Something grander. And I will have *Sabine*. That is what I want. Do you understand? This ship is my world and my mistress."

Alej thought he did.

Though the thought of serving under Osilte soured him.

The flotilla anchored off Rusajka's docks at dawn.

Yalisa joined the crew at the aft railing and peered through her spyglass at Rusajka's keep. "The Majistra's out on his balcony. He's waiting for us to land."

"He's gloating, no doubt," Alej said mildly.

"I hope he is. Come with me."

In the dim light of the captain's cabin, she folded her arms. "I'm here to ask for your help, Alej."

"You want me with a sword."

Behind her, the aft windows streamed bright morning light, making her a silhouette. "I've talked to your friend, Horza. He said you were a great leader. They made you their chief, which means you are as much a captain of men as I am."

"I became chief because so many died they had no choice," Alej explained sadly.

"That is not how Horza sees it."

Alej realized he was not going to be able to leave that world behind.

For a while he'd believed it was possible. Working the bellows, headed out to sea. He'd thought he'd severed a thread and was free to weave a new life.

But he couldn't sever it so cleanly. Those things he'd tried to bury kept resurfacing. Even in this distant, different life he'd decided to try and live. It was all connected, wasn't it?

"You want me to lead your bodyguards?" Alej asked.

Yalisa smiled. "I want you to lead the entire shipsguard, Alej.

This is your kind of fight. You have more experience leading men on the ground than anyone else. Can I trust you with that?"

Alej took a deep breath. "How will Osilte feel about this?"

"It is not Osilte's decision. It is yours." She held a red scarf in her hand and tied it around his right arm. "Do you accept?"

Alej let out the breath as he thought about the desperate crowds rushing the dock at Zebari. Thought about open seas with no water. And the creeping bramble slowly choking western cities from the lands around them. "I do."

The entire shipsguard landed in twenty long tenders, crammed with armored men glinting in the sun. All one hundred of them formed up on the docks, unopposed.

Alej, Osilte and Yalisa stepped forward to meet the thirty city guards that eventually approached the end of the dock nervously.

"Majistra Chandak will allow *fifteen* men, and only that number, to accompany your captains to meet the Majistra," one of the guards said. "No more."

"Pick your men," Yalisa told Alej.

Alej walked among the shipsguard until he found what he was looking for: Horza deep in the lines. "Who else is here, Horza?"

"Jarka and Kvet also asked to join the shipsguard when the rumor spread that you would be chief," Horza said with a smile.

"And who told them that?" Alej asked.

Horza shrugged.

Alej smiled. "Find them, bring them and ten other men that you think will serve us well. Do it quickly."

Within minutes Alej had a band of grim men around again. It felt strangely comfortable, like slipping into an old pair of boots.

He looked around at the remaining shipsguard, and lowered his voice. "You hold the docks," he said to them. "Once we are inside, that is your duty."

The shipsguard nodded.

Alej and his band detached and allowed themselves to be surrounded by the city guardsmen. They all wound their way through the tight roads to the keep.

Inside they were ushered up the winding spiral stone staircases to one of the halls with a balcony and windows overlooking the harbor. A reminder of the singular position the Majistra had in this city.

From here they could see the entire flotilla.

Alej could see that the ships were moving closer to the docks and shore, pulled by teams of rowers in tenders. Down by the docks, the shipsguard spread out, securing the roads and shore.

This time Chandak didn't bother making them wait. He'd been waiting all day. His face flushed with anger, and there was no pretense at politeness.

"You've come back to beg for the right to harbor in my city," he said. "The terms will be very, very different, captain."

Yalisa shook her head. "No Majistra, I'm not here to beg for anything. I'm here to take your city. It's time to change our little understanding."

Chandak laughed, taken aback at the total turn in conversation. But Alej didn't laugh at all; he was still eyeing the situation outside.

"You told me you would wait longer before telling him," he hissed at her.

She crossed her arms. "Majistra, you inherited this city. Your father hung the mayor from the battlements and took control. And yet, you've always believed the great walls of Rusajka and your own city guard left this city protected. But you've let the defenses facing the sea become overrun with shops and shacks. It's no longer protected from the sea. And now my shipsguard hold it."

Yalisa pointed out the great windows of the keep.

Alej ground his teeth. She'd told him, in the cabin of her own ship, that she'd negotiate with the Majistra as long as she could.

This was not negotiating.

She was goading the damn man.

"We are not really isolated, Chandak. I learned that. And if we're not disconnected from the land, then we need to control a port. We need to deal with you Majistra, instead of running from you."

"Are you mad? I have five hundred city guard, captain," Chandak said, bewildered. "You have a hundred shipsguard? You are outnumbered in this room alone two to one."

Alej had the hand on the hilt of his sword. Ready.

"Chandak!" Yalisa snapped. "Look out your windows and tell me what you see."

Alej looked at Osilte. Are you ready?

Osilte nodded.

Alej pointed at Horza, indicating that he should move his men up between Yalisa and the city guard. He also caught Kvet's eye, and jutted his chin at the door. They didn't want more city guard coming in. Kvet sidled off.

Jarka tilted his head at the city guard. A question. Attack now? Alej shook his head, but put his hand to his sword. Get ready. He pointed his thumb at the Majistra.

Jarka understood.

Alej was relieved to see the city guard as confused, or at least as stunned, as Chandak was.

Chandak turned to the windows, as had everyone else. Alej glanced out again.

The ships being towed into shore by rowers had beached themselves. City guard, merchants, and peasants watched from the shops and roads as people slid over the bows by ropes.

More ships raised their sails and brazenly tacked for shore at high speed.

"You are being *invaded*, Majistra. From the sea," Yalisa said. "There are more ship people armed with cutlasses than city guard. And we already have your docks and beaches. When was the last time you fought a battle face to face, Majistra? I doubt you even know how."

Chandak turned back, lips quivering. "Kill them! But save *her*."

Kvet slammed the door shut, startling the city guard, who looked over at him.

The shipsguard unsheathed their swords and attacked, armor clanking and swords sparking. Even with surprise on their side, though, Alej knew he stood a good chance of losing here. His men were experienced.

But numbers still mattered.

He let Osilte run in front of him to attack, and then looked for Jarka.

Jarka had held back, as Alej had wished. They nodded at each other, then together smashed through the city guard, barely watching their own backs and leaving Yalisa unprotected by the window.

A bold decision, if they failed.

They didn't engage the guards, just parried them long enough to move past them.

Someone screamed, and then stopped with a wet gurgle. But Alej kept his focus on his target.

Chandak raised his hands, blue light glowing from them as he realized Jarka and Alej barreled straight for *him* and ignored all else. "Do not think of touching me . . ." He started to threaten in a high-pitched scream, and Jarka's sword flashed so fast it was almost a magic of its own.

Chandak's left hand tumbled to the ground. Blood and blue light splashed from the severed wrist and pooled on the floor. The Majistra screamed and clutched his useless arm, trying to stop the gushing.

"City guard *halt*!" Alej shouted in his deepest, most authoritative command voice. The tableaux of butchery in the room froze, men looking back at him, refocusing.

Alej had his sword to Chandak's throat, who crouched on the floor, mewling and clutching his bloody arm.

"Drop your swords," Alej growled, in a voice that said he expected nothing less. "You have nothing left to fight for. Chandak isn't able to offer you a job anymore, and your life will be wasted."

A panting Osilte staggered back to rest on a table. Blood dripped from a bad wound under his arm. "Does he surrender?" he asked.

Alej looked down at Chandak. "Do you wish to fight to the death, Chandak, or surrender and gain your life?"

The Majistra looked up, his face an unhealthy pale. He shivered. "I surrender," he said in a tiny voice. "I surrender."

Yalisa helped Alej take Osilte to the top of the keep, where he looked out over the city with a smile. City guards had surrendered their weapons, and shipsguard had spread throughout Rusajka.

A few small fires burned here and there, where some had refused and fought the shipsguard, but it was over.

They had taken Rusajka.

"I saw this view once as a boy," Osilte said. "From this very spot. My great uncle was the mayor of Rusajka, and after Chandak killed him, my family was banished to the shacks after he took all our gold and houses."

"So you thought to rise to the keep again," Alej said. "And take revenge?"

Osilte shook his head. "I told you what I seek when we were at sea, soldier-boy. I left all that behind. I barely remember that life. What I remember most is the shacks, and knife fights for my life. Stealing and murdering and blood. When I joined the shipsguard and Yalisa took me as her first mate, I got a new life. I'm a sailor, Alej. I have no interest in land."

"I've given Osilte the *Sabine*," Yalisa said. "The captains have elected me to be the captain of Rusajka, and I accepted."

"I see," Alej said. He looked down at his armor, the sword, and sighed a little.

Yalisa moved closer. "I know you wanted to leave your sword

behind, Alej. But I had to have the best arms I could get. With you and Osilte by my side, I knew we would triumph."

"You trust me too much," Alej muttered.

"I'm a captain, Alej. I know how to spot a good man," Yalisa laughed. "We will need a new captain of the city guard, Alej. Will you continue to be my captain?"

Alej was tired of blood. But he liked to lead good men. And he didn't want to go back to the bellows, or working for Osilte on the *Sabine*. He thought about the thick walls he'd seen while coming into the city.

This would be a secure place. Few of his men would ever die facing an enemy from behind those walls. Not even the Executioness in the east could breach these walls, he thought.

He'd never be seasick again.

There would be good food, and housing. A house instead of a tiny slot of a bunk and a locker for his belongings.

There would be a place in the world for him, and people who depended on him.

"I'll be your sword," he told her.

Osilte threw a tight bundle wrapped in oilskin at his feet. "Now that I know you'll be leaving my ship, I have a gift for you."

Alej slipped the knot open, and unrolled his cloak. The one he'd first arrived in Rusajka with. He laughed. "Thank you, Osilte."

He wrapped the cloak around his shoulders and looked out over the cobbled streets of Rusajka. It was good to be on land again, even if it did feel like it was still swaying a little bit.

This, he thought, could be a place where he belonged.

THE BONEYARD

JAN DISCOVERED THE dragonet late in the afternoon, after most of the blue shift had clocked out of Pensey-Pump Fifteen, which was a strange thing as dragons had been extinct for four hundred years.

To be a digger, you needed to be strong enough to wield a diamond-tipped impact drill, steady enough to place explosives in a carved out hole, and smart enough to get the hell out of the way when the whistle blew. According to the For'Cap'n of the Shift, Jan was exactly . . . none of those.

Jan worked the rubble pits, an unglamorous assignment that meant running a pneumatic claw mounted on spider-walker legs to scuttle around the pits as he scooped up useless rock boulders and sorted through debris to see if there was anything interesting in the detritus.

He was good at it. Twice he had spotted mineral deposits in the rock, guessed when they had been dumped, and alerted diggers that they were near something valuable.

He was working through the remains of a vitrified hoard. Jewels and gold and trinkets. He was sorting them out when he noticed what he had thought was a gold-decorated egg sculpture on a flowery, wrought iron stand.

"What have we here?"

Jan swiveled the bucket over to take a closer look, and realized it wasn't solid. In fact, the small gold-lace on the outside of the stone was squirming. The egg rocked about in the metal scoop, then began to crack.

When Jan hopped out of the cab, knocking over his lunchbox, to get a closer look, a brilliant green and scaled horn broke through the gold thread. Yellow eyes covered in mucus blinked at Jan as he stared in shock.

Then the tiny, toothy mouth opened wide, and the reptilian face screeched at him.

A faint hint of sulfur filled the air between them.

Jan looked around. There was a policy that he should follow here, he knew. Past magical artifacts all went to the Ministry of Archeology. But this wasn't an *artifact*, it was an animal.

And recovered animals from dig sites were put down. He'd seen a team recover a reanimated griffin his very first month on the job. Later in the shift, a veterinarian had come in from Special Finds and put it down.

Reanimations were dangerous. They threatened modern life.

But a dragon.

Since the dragons died, and magic fell from the world, there had been prophecy about their return. Some believed it would start the end times. Others believed it would return the world to the glory days of heroes, magic, and great kings.

The tiny dragonet slashed its way out of the stone egg with sharp claws and stretched its adorable, useless little wings.

If Jan didn't do something, it would be put to death.

He opened his lunchbox and pulled out a strip of steak. "Hey, buddy, you hungry?"

The dragonet hopped onto Jan's arm, claws pricking his skin and drawing blood. It snatched at the strip of meat.

"We can't let you get put down now, can we?" he murmured.

*

Pensey-Pump Fifteen was originally a deep well and main pump for an irrigation system plan for the tri-satrapic area. But in the process of drilling down toward the water table, they had discovered a subterranean cave system, vitrified dragon hoards, and the remains of a pre-modern castle system.

Rook Inc took on the reclamation contract, and Jan had been apprenticing as a machinist. In theory he should have had a few more years under his belt before going under the earth, but there was money to be made here.

Because they were a small, rushed crew put together when the surprise hoard had been found, security was a bit lacking. Roan, the only guard working the metal detector and x-ray machine, merely glanced at the screen where Jan's lunch box rode the conveyor belt. He was looking for dark lumps that stood out, and the machine would also alert him if it noticed anything its algorithms flagged as jewel or precious metal.

The curved skeleton wrapped up around some bits of aluminum foil did not get flagged by the software, and Roan's glazed eyes passed right over everything.

Jan, knowing he was stepping over a very serious boundary, let out a deep breath.

"You're leaving early," Roan said. "You'll need to sign."

"I was feeling dizzy," Jan said. He'd alerted the For'Cap'n and gotten permission. He held up the slip.

Roan pushed a sign-out sheet over to him. Jan signed, and as he did so, the lunchbox rattled slightly. Jan looked up at Roan, but he was looking off down the entrance tunnel.

"Feel better," Roan grunted.

Seval screamed when she saw the dragonet. Her eyes widened with comprehension the moment Jan opened the lunch box and the tiny dragon leapt out. "This changes everything," she shouted.

His sister was not one for exaggerations.

"They would have put it down if I didn't," Jan said. "I just wanted to help it."

"Yes, but Father will freak when he sees this. You may have just become his favorite child."

"Not likely," Jan said.

"Oh, I wouldn't be so sure. Remember what our last name is, Jan. *Caster*. Last names come from the jobs our ancestors used to hold. We were casters, Jan. It runs in our blood. If magic is coming back to the world, then we will be able to throw spells. We're casters. It's our legacy. Few others can say that."

Jan Caster. *Your legacy*, his father had often called it.

Jan Caster worked the mine, digging around in the rubble for small bits of precious metals leftover from the older ages.

"I just didn't want to see it killed," he said.

"But you understand what you've done, right?" Seval practically vibrated with excitement.

Jan made a face. "I'm going to see if I can find the parrot cage in the attic," he said. "Don't tell Dad yet. You know how he gets when he's excited."

Seval thought about it. Then she slowly nodded. "Like bladder ball," she said.

"Right." If Dad got worked up about something he thought Jan might be good at, then was disappointed, the mood in the house soured.

Plan Weaver, one of Jan's friends from the collegium, took a taxi out to the house on the Day of Figs to share psalms, fruits and wine, then spent the day playing video games. *Ashes to Ashes*, *Sogon the Conqueror*, *Blades*, and then a turn-by-turn *Empire* simulator Plan was fond of.

It was half the day before Plan hit pause and pointed at the cage with the towel thrown over it. "I don't remember you having a bird for a pet," he said.

"Oh." Jan had kept the dragonet in there all week, feeding it meat scraps and bones. When he was back from work he would take the little dragonet out of the cage and scratch its chin, which it adored. It would lean back up against his forearm and trill happily, finishing the sound with a little puff of sulfur.

"Yeah, oh," Plan said. He stood up.

"No, leave it alone," Jan said. He moved to stop Plan, but the skinny collegiate was faster than him. A bladder ball sprinter, always popular at the collegium. Jan was sure no one missed him when he'd left to go to the mines to help the family make ends meet. Why Plan kept their friendship, he wasn't sure. He was afraid to ask, lest it break whatever hidden bond it was that kept them joining up on Holy Days to goof off together.

Plan threw the towel off the cage and froze. "By the Hundred Prophets."

"Yeah . . ." Jan wasn't sure what to say next.

"It's a dragon!" Plan staggered back, eyes wide and mouth open.

"Just a baby one," Jan said.

"It doesn't matter how baby or not it is," Plan shouted. "It's a trigger. It'll change everything! You remember your combined history classes, don't you?"

"Don't shout," Jan said. The dragonet had pushed itself up against the back of the cage and shook with anger. The tang of sulfur filled the room. "You're freaking Tink out."

"Tink?" Plan frowned. "You named your dragon Tink?"

"It's the sound his claws make," Jan said.

"You'll have more to worry about than the sound of his claws if anyone ever finds out about this," Plan hissed. "There are millions out there waiting for the Restoration. And they're true believers, Jan. Some of them are willing to do crazy things for the Restoration."

"We don't even know if that is true," Jan said. "Those things were written hundreds of years ago. Just because some prophet said that magic was bound to dragons and would return when they did doesn't mean it is true."

And just as he said that, Tink threw himself at the side of the cage and it vanished in a puff of blue smoke that swirled as the dragonet flew through it to perch on Jan's shoulder. Tink hissed at Plan.

"That looked pretty damn magical to me," Plan said, face pale.

Jan felt a tingling spreading down his arm. He flexed it and a ghost of pale blue energy ran up and down it.

Caster, he thought. And then his mind wandered to the historical novels he'd read about magicians riding out to save the land, doing battles for their sworn kings. Ancient fantasies . . .

"If Special Finds get wind of this, you'll end up in the stocks. Or worse," Plan said.

"That's why I'm keeping him in a cage."

"He's a dragon. He'll get larger. How long do you think that can last?"

"I don't know. I hadn't thought that far ahead." Jan sighed. Then he looked at Plan imploringly. "Can you research it for me?"

"You want me to get involved?" Plan looked horrified.

"Please."

"I'll see what I can find. I'll call you tomorrow."

Plan scurried out of the house to his older sister's borrowed moped. Seval watched him go from the living room. "You told him, didn't you?"

"He's my best friend. Of course I did."

"Idiot. He's a Weaver."

"What does his last name have to . . . oh." Jan stopped.

"Oh yes," Seval said. "He knows what might be coming. He's going to go right to Special Finds and squeal."

"We don't know that."

"You should tell Dad. If you'll tell Plan Weaver, we tell Dad. He's almost home."

Jan had locked his room door, knowing that his father was almost home. It was also why Plan had ducked out. Plan knew that, although Jan's father worked as a desk clerk for the city planning division, he did not want his Caster son hanging out with a Weaver, despite the fact that it was Plan who was working his way up through collegium and Jan who had struggled to find a path.

He watched out the window as his father passed Plan coming the other way. Dad shook his head as he pulled into their driveway and muttered angrily to himself as he walked up to the door.

"Hello, Father," Seval said as the door opened.

Jan tried to stare at her, willing her not to betray his secret. But Seval had *that* smile on her face. She opened her mouth, but their father paid her no attention. He dropped his briefcase to the floor.

"By the Holy Prophets," he said, eyes wide. "I always knew this day would come."

He dropped to his knees. Jan and Seval turned about to see Tink sitting on the back of the couch, watching them. The door to Jan's room was still locked.

Eyes brimming with tears, their father looked at them. "Where? How?"

Jan licked his lips, trying to think. Things were spiraling out of his control.

His father shook his head. "It doesn't matter," he said. "We have been preparing for this for so long. We always knew Restoration would come. I just . . . I could never have imagined it would be in my own house. There are people I have to call, things that need to be put in motion. Do not go to your job tomorrow, Jan. We will be taken care of. We are Casters. And we will cast again, damn it."

Ordinator Weaver opened the door, blinking and wiping at her eyes. "Jan? Jan Caster? Why are you banging on the door in the middle of the night?"

"I need to talk to Plan. It's an emergency."

Lady Weaver returned to the darkness of their large, stately brick home. "Come on," she shouted back at Jan. One of their servants also came out into the reception hall, blinking at the noise.

Jan followed them to Plan's room.

"It's my father," Jan explained a moment later as Plan waved the servant and mother off.

"Where's . . . you know?"

"In the car. Sleeping. The drive knocked him out."

"Your dad's car?" Plan woke right up. "He'll kill you."

"My father is an extreme Restorationist," Jan said.

Plan leaned over the table. "How extreme?"

"He says that a dragon is like a pilot light for a boiler, that we'll reignite the return of magic. He made calls to hidden Restorationists in government. They're just waiting to take us back to the true old ways."

The two friends looked at each other, and Jan could see that Plan also felt the tectonic shift about to happen.

"My family has come far in the last few generations," Plan said. "We were artisans, but never were allowed to own property. You read about those great people in history doing great things, but we were invisible to those books. Mud."

"It's like the stainless steel thing," Jan said, frustrated.

"What?"

"Edward Majister the Great had a display case of his most prized possessions at Castle Dawnfire. One of our country's greatest kings, and the most amazing thing that he treasured above his ability to lead and cast was a full set of stainless steel cutlery. They couldn't *make* stainless steel a few hundred years ago, and it was a super rare naturally occurring thing. So next to gold and silver goblets was his full set of stainless steel flatware, like the crappy ones I just purchased at the mega store for my cousin moving into his first apartment."

Despite the seriousness of everything, Plan smiled widely. "You *did* pay attention in combined history! And you're right. Think of how Ed the Great died."

"How did he die?"

"Dysentery."

"He shit himself to death?" Jan didn't remember that in class.

"Oh yeah. Read any history of the Third Renaissance and the nobles all die pretty ignobly. Hope the Red dies while on campaign of dysentery. Egon got worms. A whole bunch of nobles died of the flu. None of them washed their hands. They didn't know about germ theory. Didn't matter how rich or powerful they were, they died with boils on their skin, vomiting or shitting themselves into painful graves. Pre-modern conditions were horrific."

"Yeah. It gets easy to forget unless you study all that." Jan slumped forward. "But, we know all that stuff now."

"Sure, but if there's a return to the good old days, a civil war, you've seen what it's like in Lasoona. The services have collapsed there. They're trying to deal with cholera outbreaks in the middle of a war with bombs."

Jan groaned. "Did I already light things up? Was my dad right?"

Plan shrugged. "I don't know. I hope not."

"What are you going to do? After I leave?" Jan looked at Plan closely.

His friend looked down into his hands. "I have to call the authorities. I have to."

All this over a moment of weakness.

"Maybe I turn it over to Special Finds myself," Jan said. Then he could avoid jail. Maybe scientists in the government could bring back magic for all, not just caster families.

"What will your family think?"

Jan shrugged. He'd be disowned. His father would never talk to him again. Maybe the Casters would all refuse him his name. "Give me the rest of the night. Please."

"If you do it yourself, I can talk my mother into letting you move into the pool guesthouse for a few months until you get your feet under you."

"Thanks." Jan gave him a strong hug.

But, he thought, if he turned the dragon over now, Jan had a feeling he would have a roof over his head, and bars for doors.

Jan sat in the yard on a stone bench and fed Tink strips of beef jerky. The dragonet flew in spirals around the tiny yard, threading through the small red-leafed maple leaves.

His hands tingled again, and Jan looked down to see blue static filling the air around them. Some form of *potential* surged through his blood. *Magic.*

What could he do with this power? He knew more about the world than his ancestors had. Knew more possible things. What could he do with magic as well?

He glimpsed a vision of the future. A possible future. Riding the back of a full-grown Tink, the land flowing beneath him. A plane swooping at them, the chatter of gunfire, Tink bellowing fire, and Jan throwing magic at his enemies. Magic that could leap through chaff, dodge missiles, and destroy a modern battle jet.

You could rain fire down upon your enemies.

"I have no enemies," Jan said. "Just credit card debt, no car, and I'm living at home."

His worst encounter every day was Mira in accounting, who double checked his time cards.

A world of magic and fire and Restoration . . .

. . . or late night games of *Empire* with Plan, drinking beer at the local tavern, and maybe someday a promotion and an apartment of his own like his cousin.

Better a peasant today than a king yesterday.

Jan threw the last piece of jerky into the air and, as Tink dropped to the grass for it, he smacked the back of the dragonet's head with a shovel. The dragonet howled, but Jan did it again and again until the small creature finally stopped moving.

He buried Tink behind the orange tree, sobbing so hard he cracked a rib.

When he was done, mud stuck to his forearms where blue energy had crackled just an hour ago.

There were a few reporters in the yard when the sun rose and Jan got out of the shower. There was a man in sunglasses next to a black sedan.

Jan tapped one of them, a Caster that he recognized from one of the gatherings. "He's getting old," Jan said. "And he wishes really hard things weren't what they were. Go easy on him. He said he saw a griffin near Easterly Pub late one night, too."

Seval caught up to him at the end of the street, where Jan waited for a bus.

"There's a filled in hole behind the orange tree," she said, looking him over pointedly.

"Yeah." It was a single, neutral word, but it served as both confirmation and confession.

"Where are you going?" she asked.

Jan hugged her. "First to quit my job, then to Plan's for a while. Don't tell Father."

"He'll know you're there. But he won't dare step on that property. More likely, he'll be broken from grief. What are you going to do?"

Jan sighed. "We were always waiting for something to happen. How many generations has that been happening? I'm going to go back to collegium. And make something of the Caster name."

Seval surprised him by giving him a big hug. "Don't cut me out too, okay, brother?"

"I won't."

The bus squealed to a stop and Jan got aboard with all the other peasants. When the door closed, he waved goodbye to Seval.

Three years later, Seval gave him a basket of oranges as a gift on his graduation from the collegium with honors. They both cried, as the tart fruits tasted nearly divine.

WHEN ALL WAS BRILLIG

THE FIRST TIME I threw myself at the claws of the reaper, everyone assumed it was a mistake. Surely, said the reapermaster, she must have stumbled into its track. Though, we'd all been taught since we could walk to avoid the great creatures.

I had assumed it would carve me up, and those steel claws would shred me into a fine dust.

But instead, the godmachine delicately picked around me, its legs stepped over me, and when it was all done, I lay in a tiny island of grain swaying in the soft wind.

The reapermaster, who was sitting on the carapace, eating an apple and reading a book, saw the island. She shouted and pointed, then the village came to me and surrounded me, petting me to see if I was harmed.

"I'm unscathed," I said.

Only the soulkeeper, Uru, looked at me, his necklaces humming to him as he listened to the tone of my voice, his brass eyes flickering in the late day's sun. He *truly* looked at me, and he saw something that concerned him. It made his face sadden.

But the first time, Uru did nothing. Just cocked his head contemplatively as his dreadlocks tapped his shoulders.

So I did it again. For we were a free people.

*

The second time I tried, I ran straight for the thresher. There was no mistaking what I was doing.

I should have died, but instead the reaper screamed in horror, and every blade of the great machine came to an instant, shuddering stop. The metal hands pulled me away from the hopper, and I had a long slice across my shoulder that bled badly enough to drip over its arms.

"Ahadi," my cousin said, holding me in his arms while the Reapermaster consoled the machine. "What are you doing?"

But the question was rhetorical, and you didn't have to be a Soulkeeper to look at me and know what was in my mind. I felt shame, and the heat of it rose through me to break my surface as a single tear.

"You can feel the presssure, the toil, and the fear," said Uru. "And you should have come to me first."

The clean white surfaces and great glass palace hung over the Rupikiita River. He made tea from a solar orb and blessed it, set the dainty porcelain in my hands, and sat near me.

"I am not sick," I said.

"I never said you were." Uru regarded me, the tall cheekbones and their rusty skin twitching as he came to some sort of conclusion. A soulkeeper's verdict. "It is the miasma of an uncertain time. It is a part of the war. It is a weapon."

"What is?"

"To say that a heaviness of the soul is a tool of the enemy is to cheapen the emotions and experiences of the soul," said Uru. "Some people can become heavy with the weight of the world without the enemy's help. But in your case . . . in the case of others I've seen this year, it is."

"I feel weak," I confessed. "We need to keep harvest. We need to help the people who are holding the Great Line. They are sacrificing far more than those of us safe in the valleys."

"Even the creators at the line have to sleep, eat, have sex, play games, and make jokes. Or they would die. It is one thing to fight for survival. But you cannot stop being what you are in the middle of it, or you'll have nothing to go back to afterward."

I wanted to cry again, but that felt like I would have to go digging for the energy to do it. I was mud at the bottom of a dead well.

"My brother is on the line," I told Uru.

"I don't care," Uru said, shocking me. "Our job, right now, is you."

How long was the Great Line? A thousand miles? A million? It pulled people from its past, its future, from other worlds gauzily next to ours. When we took Ysny to the first camp, I saw what he called a skyscraper. Our steamhorse had blown its pressure stomach and reared back when it saw the building of steel and glass that was tall as a mountain. It flickered out of our reality when we turned a corner in the road, replaced by a walnut tree.

Ysny would join the mage corps. Standing with brothers and sisters in arms, their staffs high, throwing their minds against the chaos breach seeping through into our worlds.

The Entropic War could never be won, could it?

But they would hold the Great Line.

And we grew the food to feed our creators, who made order at the boundaries to hold the chaos back on the other side.

I missed Ysny. So much.

"There are rumors every day," Uru said. "Rumors that the breach has widened. The speakers claim that the Evening Parliament is leaving for another world. The Alliance had a falling out. I've even heard that the entire subcontinent wavered last week, and disappeared for twenty minutes. Its people came back, but were sick for days afterwards."

I had come to know worse things. And many of them were even true. The mountain lords had gone to their protected caverns. There was a draft for more creators. They were needed at the line.

The crops in Valley Two Hundred and Nine had failed.

Manna production to power the godmachines and instruments of order was down fifteen percent.

Just thinking about those things gave me a wave of despair, and as that happened, Uru sprang forward to blow powder from the palms of his hands at me. I coughed and swore at him as the air around me sparkled.

"See?" Uru said, leaning forward, his locks tinking against each other. "Do you see?"

There was a tendril of deadness in the powder, some absence that clung to me.

"We cannot know if the miasma is entropic in nature, and with the vagaries of a mind being vast, even a soulkeeper cannot say one way or another that it is the enemy that is bearing down on you and causing this. But, Ahadi, it cannot help. All of this cannot be helping."

"But this isn't happening to anyone else," I protested.

"You don't know that," Uru said. "You don't know who has made it through, who is yet to experience it, and who is now quietly living under the great emptiness. You cannot look into their souls. Not even I can. I can only try to make sure we keep them."

I did not want to hear that, because it terrified me even more. That so many other people might feel so tired, cored out from so much that they were less a machine than even the brass golems of San Urtep? I had been so deep within myself, I wondered how vast this epidemic was.

And surely, surely we could not keep order against the breach if so many were fighting even more desperate wars within themselves?

I had to reject it.

"I am not any weaker than any one else who is here in the valley," I said.

Uru sipped his tea, then rubbed his forehead in a tired gesture. "When did I ever say you were weak, Adahi? You are strong, and smart. Weakness has nothing to do with it. When someone snaps their leg in a fall, does weakness have anything to do with how they stand next? It does not matter whether it was the enemy that snapped your leg, whether you fell, or whether your bones were more brittle. What matters is that you let me splint the injury, and that you heal it. Or you will never walk right again, if at all."

It was a simplistic metaphor.

But it contained clarity.

"What do you plan?" I asked.

"I want to send you to a dragon's lair," Uru said.

We rode in the belly of a gryphon that smelled of sulfur, and then in a sling carried in the great talons of rocs. The great rift beyone the valleys fell away behind us. The eye-watering unreality fell away. The Great Line faded. Not in the way something in the distance did, but as if it never truly existed.

And away from the space of the Thousand Valleys we coasted over the strong rocks of Gibralter and onto to old London.

At Gatwick, after a change of clothes, we caught a creaky god-machine of some design called a seven-forty-seven, and that took us to the city of New York. And many leagues north of there, we came to the dragon's lair in the side of a mountain near a ski resort that was closed for the summer.

I should have paid attention to the wonders and wondrances of a strange time and place, the far-off fantastic. But I had retreated well into myself. I was numb. And I hated myself for leaving the Thousand Valleys. Leaving the line.

Uru gave me strange new beverages, and the food of another people. And it was ashes to me. Even the bar of Twixes.

*

I would like to say I made that journey after the second attempt.
I did not.

There was a longer story between that conversation and the
offer of the lair, and when I finally broke and asked Uru to take me
there. It was a war. A fight. A battle against the miasma.

Now I was less of a thing. The rot of a chemical fire in me that
had given me strength. For a time. The tremor of insomnia. The
ravages of a year of . . . limping on a broken limb.

Uru did not blink when I asked to go. Did not upbraid me for
taking so long. He and reapermasters and the village hugged me
and praised me and surrounded me with love so deep that even
down in the bottom of the well the mud stirred.

The reapers danced and followed me along the dirt road to the
soulkeeper's house. The massive farming machines even gifted
me with bread and ale that I threw out when the gryphon came
for us.

"Welcome," said the dragon. "You may call me Toni."

Long and slender, her scales glittered adamantine in the glow
of the cave. As we walked, Toni sinuously gliding ahead of us, she
told us about each item displayed in the walls. A coin given to a
beggar outside the chapel of St. Paul's Chapel in 1789. Gold from
the wreck of the Merchant Royal. A pearl tooth from the Visintine
Emperor Gax.

Each piece of her hoard had a small, papyrus note underneath
detailing provenance. Each item sat behind a glow of powerful
magic, as safe as if in a vault.

Toni showed them the spas, the sitting rooms, and the gardens
inside her lair.

"And this would be your room," she said.

A beach outside one window, and a forest with soft treefrog

song in another. A bed with soft curtains draped over the posts, fit for a queen. Marble floors.

"What do I do here?" I asked, scared to be left with the fifty feet of magical creature.

"All you have to do, is *be*," said Toni. "I guide the rest of it."

When Uru left, the half-mile thick stone side of the mountain sealed shut. I felt a tiny pang of fear as the dragon said, "There is nothing outside there. Nothing outside this lair exists now. It never has. It never will. Until I open it again."

"When will that be?" I asked, my voice breaking.

"Once a week, my assistant Janice goes down to a beautiful little town at the foothills near the lakes, and she buys fresh bagels from a deli with cream cheese that has *strawberries* in it. I can't wait for you to try them. You, however, are here until you need to leave."

I would have asked how that were possible, but dragons were older than gods themselves.

"What if I never get better?" I asked.

Toni wound around me in that disconcerting way that only a dragon could. "I told you. Nothing outside this lair exists now. It never has. It never will. So whenever you can, that will be the time. Remember, Adahi, this too shall pass. All those people out there fighting, some will come here. And some will leave here to go back to battle the miasma of entropy. The line will still be there. It always has been."

And the dragon Toni hugged me, a surprisingly gentle thing from a creature with battle-armor scales.

"I know this," the dragon said, "because I was once there on the line too, until it shattered for a moment, and a shard caught me. Then I came here to create a place of healing. I think, maybe I did more for the war here."

The dragon showed me scar in her flank. It was deep, and it had been soldered over in pure gold that flexed with her military scales.

"And now I am always here," she said.

"And those I let down, I abandoned?"

"Are they not happier to not bear the burden of worry for you? Have they not taken on their work with more verve because they know you are safe? Will you not do more, if or when you return, or even if you find a new path?" The dragon laughed. "And have you forgotten that none of that exists now that you are in my lair, a powerful singularity, the event horizon warped such that nothing leaves or enters without my will?"

With that, she had drawn up in the corridor, tall and vast, with fire licking her lips. She was not all hugs and softness, but strong in her admonition.

The dragon took my hand. I turned my back away from the universes that didn't exist now that I was in the heart of the dragon's lair. Away from the miasma, away from the news of entropy, I would be here to recuperate. Until I was ready to leave the lair and find my path again.

"Come," said the dragon. "Let us go to the beach and sun ourselves, and you will tell me about your war."

THE EMPEROR AND HIS TOTALLY AMAZING, AWESOME CLOTHES

I **DON'T WANT** to say that Hans Christian Anderson didn't tell the whole story. Hans was a noble collector of tales handed down from generation to generation all throughout the countryside. But one has to understand some of the complications with the narrative as it's been picked up and remembered.

There are many claims to truth of this story, and, as a scribe, it is my duty to head out and collect them. After spending several weeks canvassing the countryside, I submit this report to you in earnest.

We begin with the initial core story that you may well be familiar with, and it is this:

Many years ago, there was an emperor so vain and fond of new clothes that he spent all his money being well dressed. One day two swindlers came to town and let it be known that they could weave the greatest fabric in all the world. In fact, it was so fine that only those people who were stupid or unworthy of their positions could not see it.

The emperor, dazzled by the idea of dressing in the finest thread in all the world, allowed the swindlers, who pretended to weave the cloth but were really holding empty air, to trick him into making him a fine new outfit.

Then he paraded himself through town, as his courtiers and officers held empty air, pretending it was the train of his gown.

And then a child pointed at the emperor, and with the innocence of their age, cried out, "That man has no clothes on!"

That's roughly what everyone remembers, and to tell the story again, it seems like the spell is broken. The high, unworldly clarion call of the child pierces the entire sham and shatters it. The emperor is shamed, and tries to carry on down the street, but knows the truth of it all.

But that's not how the real world works, is it?

Gary (some names are changed to protect sources) is a distant relative of the child who spoke up in the courtyard.

"I wish she'd kept her little mouth shut, that poor idiot child and her family," he tells me.

We break our fast just outside one of the smaller villages in the periphery of the emperor's domain. As far as I can tell, Gary seems to shovel shit for a living, and his boots are stained with it. He wears a simple tunic, a floppy head covering, and has a simple, hard-working face.

Gary eats a single loaf of wheat bread and drinks watered beer.

"No good comes of yelling out at royalty what they ain't or what they is wearing," Gary continues.

Certainly, Gary notes, there are far worse things the rulers of the empire have done than walk through a town buck naked. Gary ticks off a list of crimes against serfs, inquisitions, expeditionary wars abroad, colonization on other continents, and rapes never brought to justice.

"A lap in your own skin?" Gary shakes his head and finishes his beer. "Hardly anything for us to get worked up about. If that kid had been raised with a lick of common sense, those weavers would have been paid in a few weeks and moved on, and we'd all of us had a good story to tell. Instead . . ."

He trails off.

Instead.

Gary sighs. "I knew it was a bad business when he stopped at the Victory Arch and whispered to the head of his guards."

Moments later men armed with crossbows beat back the crowds and dragged the little girl off in chains for sedition and inciting the crowds to riot.

After an evening spent trying cheeses down in the eastern boroughs, I found myself in the company of a member of the privy council smartly dressed in purple hose and a shimmering silk tunic. We ate sliced aged cheese and figs drizzled in honey.

We talk about the gazette that I write my reports for, long respected in four different countries in the region. My subject apologizes for not reading it several times before turning to the reason he has hunted me down to sup with me.

"I don't want to talk about the clothes, we have to focus on the child," the representative of the emperor tells me in between a tasting tray of southern red wines.

"The child?"

"Yes." He waves his glass of wine in the air. "Who was paying her to slander the emperor? Was she under the influence of anti-patriotic concerns?"

The emperor's court was under siege from the enemy, and that meant everyone in the country needed to come together and get past their divisions.

"But she was just a little child, surely—"

"Her parents took out a loan from merchants in another country. Another country, can you imagine? And her uncle travels across the border every month. Make sure you write that down. It's all very suspicious."

"How exactly?"

But he narrows his eyes. "It's suspicious. They could be taking money to cause unrest here inside our country."

"Are they?"

"They could be."

I write down that the emperor's representatives think that the girl could be influenced by elements seeking to cause unrest from outside the country.

There's something I have to do next that I don't want to do. But taking down a full account of what has happened requires it.

Chains rustle gently in the wind, and the cage swings slowly, thunking against the stone walls of the castle as I approach. The little girl inside shivers as the wind kicks up.

She eyes me warily, huddling deeper into a wet wool blanket that someone has given her. I give her a bundle of wax paper with bread and cheese inside, which she greedily scarfs down.

I've been told her parents are jailed as well. Her blanket, as well as food and water, have been snuck in at night by relatives who have to walk all the way in from a nearby town.

After some coaxing, the child warms up to me.

"He was stark naked," she says. The defiance in her tone wobbles a bit. She's been living in a cage for two weeks. But she does not withdraw the explosive allegation that the emperor was walking, nude, through the middle of town.

"All my life, I been taught to tell nothing but the truth by my parents, my teachers, and my priests. When I saw him walking over the cobblestones, he was nakeder than someone talking a bath. All I did was say it out loud, because I'll tell you this, everyone was muttering it to themselves."

"That's true, but, you know that this cloth is a special cloth," I countered. "Only certain types of people can see it. It's only for those who are unusually stupid or unfit for their office who cannot see it."

So many people forget that part of the story.

The child stopped gnawing on a piece of bread and eyed me critically. "I don't have a station," she observed. "So are you calling me stupid?"

"I make no such claims," I said, drawing myself up. "I am only a chronicler of events for the gazette. I write down—"

"Did you go see him?" the child asked. "Go see the emperor and write down what you see instead of talking to me."

After calling on many of the fine houses of the empire and being turned away, I finally am able to talk to a noble who knows how to grant me an audience with one of the weavers in question. This is the closest I can get to seeing the emperor for now, until the next time he goes on a parade.

The weaver wears elegant, imported silk, and insists on showing me the complex machinery that is involved in making the emperor's new clothes.

"I want to show you this," he says. "It's a Garibaldi Loom. Two hundred carefully oiled parts, the most complex, advanced piece of machinery in the entire continent. You can't deny it, right? You see the machine in front of you, correct? It was imported. Make sure you write down that we have a Garibaldi Loom."

The weaver stares at me until I write it down, carefully, in my notebook.

"This is a special cloth," the weaver says. "Only those fit for their office can see it. Do you understand what that means?"

The weaver holds his hands up in the air as if he's holding something.

"If you truly are worthy of your position," he says, his eyes glinting in the shadows of the workshop, "then you could see the beauty and craftsmanship of what I'm showing you."

"I—" I want to tell him I can't see anything.

"Or, and I can't imagine this applies to you, but, if you're stupid, you may not be able to see the cloth."

I am forced to defend my intelligence, explaining my academic pedigree.

"Of course you couldn't be stupid. Here," the weaver says, and approaches me. "It's a scarf. Let me put it on you."

He acts as if he's doing me the world's greatest favor as I'm made to feel like I'm in the circle of an exclusive club as the weaver drapes the scarf around me and nods approvingly. "Keep it. It is a gift to you."

At the door on the way out, I think the wind nips at my neck a bit, but I'm suddenly not sure.

"I mean, from the emperor's position, you have to imagine it," says Maximillan Weber, a noble in the court. "Stop getting hung up on whether anyone was naked or not. Imagine you're given a tool that allows you to determine whether or not people in your administration are worthy of their position or stupid. Wouldn't you use such a tool?"

Maximallan Weber, as far as I can tell, is not wearing anything at all. Which would normally be quite . . . alarming.

But to say anything out loud would be to suggest that I was stupid. That's the political atmosphere in the empire, now. So whether I think I am stupid or not, I cannot verbalize what I think.

Instead, I do my level best to lock eyes with Maximillan Weber's eyes and not look down as I take my notes for my story.

"Well?" he asks.

I cannot offer an opinion on a hypothetical, but stammer, "Some would say that it has not been proved that the threads can really do this thing."

"Have those people proved that the threads *can't* do such a thing?"

"It's impossible to prove a negative—"

"That's what *they* want you to think," Maximillan Weber shouts, standing up, much to my distress.

"Who?"

"The enemies of the state. Those dirty people. Foreign influences!" Maximillan gesticulates. "But the emperor didn't ascend to his position by being an idiot. He's playing a more advanced game than any of us. Always one step ahead. You mark my words, this disruption will reveal to him who his enemies are and the true state of things inside the borders. This will be a good thing. A great moment in our country's history."

I am escorted out of the mansion by Maximillan Weber's wife. The Lady Weber is draped in a voluminous evening gown.

She notices my look.

"I told my lord that I am far too simple a woman to dare wear threads that would reveal to the world that I married above my station," she says to me, with a cryptic smile.

My last interview about the matter is with the town crier, who stood on a raised platform on the day in question and saw everything. She fills me in on the times of day and the sequence of alleged events.

"Alleged?" She frowns at that word.

"Well," I explain, "I wasn't here, so who can say what happened?"

She shakes her head over the beer I have purchased for her. "Until the day I die, I will tell you he was naked. He was nude. He wasn't wearing any clothes. I saw his genitals."

Everyone in the tavern stared at us.

"I didn't," the town crier says emphatically, "want to see his genitals. Emperor or not, uninvited genitals are the worst."

"Some would say that the clothes could only be seen by those fit for their stations, or who were not stupid."

The crier laughs. "Why are you quoting them? They aren't here, it's just me and you. You're dragging them in here to create a conflict when right now, anyone in this establishment knows what they say, right?"

There's a hearty cheer of assent.

"Listen," the crier says, leaning closer to me. "You write this down and you write down what they say. But if it rained last night, and I tell you it didn't, and Jeffrey over there says it did, one of us is right, yeah? You should be figuring out who got soaked, not just taking care to put both arguments down on paper."

I am forced to say that she has a point.

"Besides, how do you justify putting children in cages over it all? Talk all you want about differences of opinion, but right now there's a child hanging in a cage outside a castle wall. If that ain't a failure of decency I don't know what is. All this talk about stations and stupidity just obscures a simple fact: he exposed himself to a lot of people who didn't want it. Doesn't matter what the threads are or how they work or don't."

And on that, the crier stood up and walked back to the bar, ending our interview.

So what then to make of the emperor's new clothes?

Well, I am just a scribe. I write it all down. You are the one who has to decide.

But I do know this: there are strong opinions on either side of the issue of the emperor's new clothes.

MR. SKIN'S HEART

TWO OF MANNY'S bodyguards kicked the door to my shitty, off-the-strip motel room door right off its hinges. I was waiting for them by the peeling door jamb with a taser. I jammed fifty-thousand volts of electricity into Paolo's neck and two hundred pounds of meathead dropped to the floor with all the grace of a bag of cement.

Jaqi, the other bodyguard, turned to me, exasperated. I dropped the taser when she punched me in the jaw so hard my vision flickered in time to the neon vacancy sign looming over the motel's parking lot.

"I don't like to hit women anymore," she said, reaching out a hand. She had a shotgun cradled in her other arm like it was her kid. "So quit messing around."

I groaned as I wobbled up to my feet. Jaqi, an aging medium-weight boxer, famous in her time for her vicious combinations, looked bored as she pulled a chair over for me.

"Sit."

I obeyed like a trained dog. Ass in chair.

"You know why we came," Jaqi said, pulling another squeaking desk chair over. She sat down across from me, the corners around her gray eyes wrinkled with crow's feet from the Nevada sun and etched with a weariness that made me want to apologize to her for making her day more complicated than it had to be.

"I can't pay it back," I told her, the truth leaping from my lips instead of the lies and pleas I'd spent the last two nights developing.

"Two hundred grand." Jaqi lay the shotgun across her lap. It made a point. "Manny can't overlook that kind of debt."

"I had a system that always worked when I ran tests," I said. I idly wondered if I could grab the gun from her.

Then I patted the numb side of my face. No way to run away from this.

Hell, Vegas was where I had run to.

Jaqi ignored what I'd just said. Too silly to dignify. Everyone had a system that worked, until it didn't.

"Manny has a way you can pay him back," Jaqi said.

"I won't—"

"You're not all that, college girl," Jaqi interrupted me, anticipating my next words. "Not for two hundred thousand. No one can work off that much that way. No, Manny has another use for you."

I could feel my heart hammer at my chest. I licked my nervous, dry lips. "What does he want?"

Jaqi leaned over as Paolo started to stir and groan. She petted him on the head. "A small piece of your soul," she said to me.

She'd told me not to take the money. She could have said "I told you." But that wasn't Jaqi's way, was it?

"Come," she told me after Paolo'd thrown up into the gravel by the parked Tesla. "Time to pay up."

I should have run farther, faster, the moment after I'd watched the cards come up bad as the slot machines chattered in the background. When that sinking, twisting feeling had risen up and swallowed me. That moment, that instant I'd realized I'd fucked up so bad I'd lost everything, and then some.

We drove away from the lights. I'd walked to the motel in a daze after that, past women in too-tight dresses and men laughing as they leaned out of limousines. Now we swept away from it all and toward the suburbs. The tall edifices, fueled by the failings of so many other transplants like me, fell away behind us in the mirrors.

Now it was all red-tiled roofs and clean white walls. Business centers. The edges of the city that lived off that beating center of flash and hope.

Manny lay in a bed in a small, boxy ranch house near the edge of a medical park. The machines crowded around him like boxy vultures, their light splashing across his palid face.

"What's wrong with him?" I'd just seen Manny a few weeks ago, loaded down with jewelry and sitting on an Aeron chair for his throne.

"His heart." Jaqi pulled the edge of a blanket back over one of Manny's feet. She pointed over to a corner, where a thin man lurked in the shadow. "Mr. Skin."

"Mr. Skin?"

The man's paper-thin skin soaked up the light as he stepped forward and grinned. "Has it been explained to her yet?"

I had visions of being left in a bathtub of ice and a bloody cavity in my chest as Mr. Skin stuck his hand out. A skeletal hand.

I refused to shake it. "What's happening?"

"Manny needs his heart fixed," Jaqi said. "And you owe him two hundred thousand dollars."

"You can't take my heart." Jaqi could knock me out easily enough, but I wouldn't die without a fight.

Mr. Skin wheezed. Laughing, I realized. "We don't want your heart, dearie. But we do need a piece of you to fix Manny's."

I looked at Jaqi. She looked bored. The same bored she'd looked when I'd arrived before Manny, just off my run on the tables. I needed a stake. Look at what I'd done with just the money I'd scraped together to leave the small college town I'd been trapped in.

My parents had refused to co-sign a loan. They couldn't afford it. Couldn't risk it if I failed. I'd seen the countdown toward having to leave start. I saw the future. A move back in to my childhood room, a job waitressing, and eventually a rundown house and car that always needed repair and a kid who couldn't wait to leave you and the small town you'd trapped them in. And over here, I could see a glimpse of the future I'd have with something different. Something big.

What else would you do with a math degree?

"Fuck you all," I said, looking around the room. "This is some weird shit."

Mr. Skin followed me outside as I sat on the side of the pool. He squinted up at the stars, then carefully unpacked a vape pen. He slotted a cartridge in and held it up. "Do you mind?"

I shook my head.

He clicked a button, and a cloud of peppermint wafted over our heads as he exhaled.

"I've been doing this a very long time," Mr. Skin said under the Las Vegas desert sky. "Nowhere better than here to be in my line of work."

He gestured toward the distant haze of neon lighting up the undersides of several nearby clouds.

"Are you a doctor?"

"No." He smiled. In the dark it looked feral and made me shudder. "You know better."

For some reason, I did.

"Jaqi said you wanted my soul." I couldn't look him in the face. It sounded ridiculous. Yet, the shadows, Skin's eerie face, and the whole night, it felt like it could be real.

Maybe there was something more than peppermint in that vape cartridge.

"Not all of it."

I laughed. Laughed at the absurdity of owing someone hundreds of thousands of dollars that had been lost in under thirty seconds. Laughed that I'd been dragged out here by some mobster's bodyguard. Laughed that Mr. Skin looked so serious.

"Who are you supposed to be?" I asked. "Rumplestiltskin?"

He blew peppermint smoke politely away from me.

"Yes," he said.

"Doesn't it stop working if I know your name?" I asked.

Mr. Skin nodded. "I changed my name, legally."

He pulled a wallet out from his tailored slacks. He opened it, and the driver's license inside peeked out of a clear plastic slit.

"You're covering the name with your thumb."

"My apologies." He moved his thumb. The license read JACK PARONSKAFT.

He pulled it out and tossed it into the pool where it fluttered to rest with dead leaves. Behind it was another license. TOM T. SKIN.

"I have lots of names now, all legally, with documentation. I've changed it so many times no one will ever track it down. Technically, I'm an LLC corporation, not even a name. And those shell corporations are nestled in shell corporations so deep it's just turtles all the way down." He held out a titanium card. A business card. It had no name on it, just an adress. "I made the mistake of someone finding out my name once. I won't do it again."

I looked at his dark eyes as I put the card in my back pocket. "You really think you're Rumplestiltskin?"

He shrugged. "Try me."

Something in his voice, an eagerness, chilled me. But there was a way out, wasn't there?

The same way out from the story.

"Can you give me money?" Like the gold she'd woven from straw to give a king? "Enough to get out of this situation?"

Mr. Skin's eyes glittered. "I can pay your debts. I can even stake you a little more to go back. I heard about your system. I think it's a good one."

"Ask about the price," Jaqi hissed, startling me. I turned around to see her watching us from the door, arms folded.

"Go back inside," Mr. Skin told her.

"What price to become the champion," Jaqi said. "What price to get your stake. What price to fix a dying heart."

"I am, always, fair," Mr. Skin said. "Always. I give dreams, I give life."

"You trap the desperate. The kids who get off the bus at the big city. The hungry. The mother with a sick child."

"What price will Manny pay?" I asked.

Jaqi walked over to stand between us. "The price for Manny's heart that you will pay will be less than the one Manny will have to pay. Skin just needs a small bandaid from you. But if you make a promise with him, that's binding."

"Let the girl make her own way in the world," Mr. Skin snapped.

"Come." Jaqi pulled me up to my feet. "It's time to do what you need to do."

I stood over Manny, and Mr. Skin lit a candle that he waved over the bed.

"Will it hurt?" I asked.

"No."

"What does it mean? To lose a piece of my soul. Am I going to die young?"

"You'll just feel a little less," Jaqi said as Mr. Skin leaned over Manny and tapped a pair of fingers to his chest. "A little less pain, a little less pleasure. A little less excitement, a little less dissapoint-ment. A little less of everything. It's just a nip, enough to save a heart, to hold it together, to let it beat."

I looked at Jaqi's weary face and realized it wasn't weariness in the corners of her eyes: it was just . . . less. And I understood.

She nodded.

"With your permission," Mr. Skin said, approaching me. He had a pair of scissors in his hand.

I didn't believe any of this. Did I?

If so, what harm would there be in letting them take some hair, chant something, and then move on. Shit, it was a deal to get out a two hundred thousand dollar debt, right?

"Go ahead."

Mr. Skin cut a small piece of hair. The smoke as he burned it on the candle lazed around the room, and everyone held their breaths.

"It has been done!" he announced.

"That's it?" I asked.

"That's it."

I felt . . . slightly relieved. But not as much as I expected.

Jaqi drove me back toward the city, and I watched the floodlit palms go by. "You believe Manny's really going to be okay? That this isn't some snake oil bullshit?"

"It's not the first time I've seen it." Jaqi slowed down for a red light. "Paolo had cancer three years ago. I gave him the card. Like the one in your pocket."

I bit my lip.

"I have a sytem," I told her.

"I know."

"I can't go back to that town. I can't . . . fade away. I want to *be* something."

"I saw my name in lights," Jaqi said. "I know. Kids from where I grew up, they could only dream of the life I lived."

And that's all she said until we stopped at the motel parking lot. She handed me a small stack of cash. A few hundred.

"It's enough for a plane ticket home," she said. "Or a good night at the tables. If your system's really that good, it's a small stake."

For a moment I sat there, looking at the worlds ahead of me.

Then I gave her the card from my back pocket.

"Give that to someone who really needs it," I said to her.

The ex-boxer smiled wanly as she took the titanium card. "I'd be happy to."

And then she drove off before I could change my mind.

THAT FARAWAY KINGDOM

WE FOUND THE hidden kingdom in the back of the basement cupboard that Grandma used as a pantry on New
Year's Eve. Grandma's eyesight had dimmed over the last decade
and she'd complained to my brother, Devaughn, about big mice
getting in there. "So be careful." We'd offered to go down and lay
some traps and retrieve some cranberries in a can for her.

The OG (our nickname for her), Grandma Celia, lived in a little
Victorian cottage-styled house that she'd raised five kids in. She'd
been in this area so long that it had fallen apart, been abandoned,
then been rebuilt by two different waves of immigrants, then gentrified). OG could barely wobble down the steps now, but she was
dammed if she was gonna move after all that.

But that wasn't all we were up to down in the musty old basement. My mom pulled me aside. "When you get down there, put
anything all rusted up in your duffel to sneak out."

It was a family New Year's tradition, trying to stop my grandmother from killing herself by botulism.

When we opened the generously-sized cupboard door, we
found a mouse in a trap struggling to get free.

It froze when the light hit it, stopped trying to lever free of the
trap with a sword in its hand, and turned to look at us.

"You feline turds," it hissed at us. "You broke my leg with this contraption."

Now, I'd always made fun of people who played the lottery. Those big hundred million dollar payouts blinked away in windows of gas stations and convenience stores all over the country, and when I worked a late shift at the Q-Mart, I saw some of my neighbors lose mad money playing number after number.

But seeing that little fellow with his tiny hat and feather, scabbard buckled around his waist, and sword in tiny paw, I knew what if felt like to strike it big.

We were going to be rich as fuck.

"We're gonna have to talk to Mom about how blind OG got," Devaughn said thoughtfully. "She can't even see the fucking portal to another world in the back of the cupboard."

To be fair, it was murky as hell down in the basement, and the portal shifted between the color of the brick and a darkness that my eyes just wanted to slide right on past. And it wasn't a big portal, just about three times as high as a mouse. Big enough for tiny woodland creatures, but not for any of us.

The captured mouse tried to stab Devaughn, dragging the mouse trap behind with his snapped leg, and we both jumped back as cans fell down at us.

"Easy, lil dude," I shouted. "We can help you. We'll help you!"

"It's true, I'm a nurse," Devaughn said.

"Well—"

"Nursing school," Devaughn corrected, with a glower at me.

The whole living room busted out in commotion when we got upstairs with Sir Mouse. OG tried to kill it with one of the four random volumes of the *Encyclopedia Britannica* that she had on her special shelf.

Sir Mouse was all gangster and stabbed Mom in the forearm with his sword, she said she would stomp the bitch, and I was about to shout at everyone to calm down, when Sir Mouse screamed, "I will be avenged!"

So when he leaped into the air, everyone took a step back and let him land on the ancient, always-steamed-clean but yellowed carpet.

"My leg!" the mouse moaned.

"That's one of those magical creatures." My mom grabbed the thick book away from my grandmother, who blinked at the ground.

"Those damn big mice been stealing all my food."

The mouse looked positively chastened. He attempted to stand, but couldn't. He whipped his hat off and bowed his head. "My apologies. My country is in the middle of a great famine, and we only tried to find food as best we could."

"You still can't just be taking other people's shit like that," my grandmother said.

Sir Mouse had a name. Hard to pronounce, but after a few tries we managed it. Squeepittikik. Hell, if folks can learn how to pronounce Tchaikovsky, people can take the time to get some rando mouse's name right.

Devaughn took Squeepittikik to the kitchen to get him splinted up, and the rest of us all huddled up.

"This is like finding an oil reserve under your house," my dad said, excited.

And there were companies that would pay big for the rights to it.

In Colorado, companies paid big money to a family that found a kingdom connected to their kid's closet where time went by more slowly than here. They shipped researchers through to set up labs and do research faster.

In Mexico City, medical companies were doing unregulated bio-testing on animals where laws didn't apply.

That wasn't to mention the massive royalties going to the Allsop family in Gurnsey for running an oil pipeline through their bedroom into Foasiy, a world where history left major oil reserves untapped.

Magical kingdoms were big money makers, with investment futures heavy on prospectors looking in every kid's bedroom corners for portals to other worlds that could be used.

The electric company in state had just put ads in the paper looking for a kingdom it could build a coal power plant inside of, and run the cables out to our world in. That way they could collect environmental credits for decarbonizing our world and offer up cheap power.

"I just want the mice out of my damn shit," Grandma said.

But my mom and dad had dollar signs bouncing around their eyeballs. To be honest, I was already thinking about rims and an apartment off campus.

Then we smelled smoke coming from downstairs.

Devaughn had set fire to the cupboard.

I put it out with an extinguisher while Dad slapped him upside the head.

Family holidays. They always came down to a moment like this.

But then Devaughn laid it down, and, even though my older brother kept fucking things up spectacularly, I had to see his point.

"We can't do them like how I heard you talking about," he said. "All those other places, they're getting used up, and hard. I did an internship in a housing projects for centaurs once. They'd been moved out and promised all of the modern world so that some folk could grow on their ranges year round and pop citrus out a portal right near downtown. But they're methed out and doing badly."

He didn't want to see the mice get fucked over.

So I did a number on my dad. "What about all that Ujamaa shit you're always talking about?" Lifting everyone up economically, not going all in on just the extraction, the colonization.

Devaughn saw my road and headed down it. "We don't want to be the colonizers, Dad."

"Not everything needs monetized," I said.

But Dad wanted to get his, and Devaughn and Dad always had a rocky relationship. They went around and around a bit, with Grandma chiming in from up the stairs that she didn't want the family fighting.

Finally OG tossed a can of soup from up the stairs at us.

"Gentle giants!" Squeepittikik shouted from up the stairs where he stood with the aid of tiny crutches Devaughn had made out of delivery food chopsticks. "Please! Stop your squabbles! The queen of this realm demands that you stop."

"Damn right she does," Grandma said. "Thank you, mouse."

Mom started laughing, and then I did, and we all calmed down a bit.

"I call for a conference to determine our futures," Squeepittikik said. "We will hammer out an agreement at yon table."

We all agreed it was a punk move to leave Squeepittikik's kingdom starving, so we ordered pizza that night as a quick boost to the people on the other side of the portal, waiting for Squeepittikik to come back. Grandma wouldn't let us give away any of her canned goods, so Mom made a late run out to a big box store. We weren't a rich family—it was all we could do to afford college loans for me and Devaughn. But Mom opened a store card with an awful APR to get four hundred dollars worth of dry goods. Lots of rice, beans, and peanut butter.

Squeepittikik went through on trip after trip, pushing himself to exhaustion.

We also ran a garden hose through the portal, setting up a source for irrigation and clean water.

Grandma's house became the center of a lot of interdimensional activity in the months ahead. Devaughn and I dropped out of school to manage the flow.

And slowly, things came back the other way. Gold from the mines of Asmok. Silver cutlery from gracious nobility on the other side.

There were some close days there with debt and trying to make sure no one discovered what we were up to.

Squeepittikik passed away on the fourth month. Came to see us an old mouse, wobbling with a cane (the mouse trap had always left him with a limp). Time, like in so many pocket kingdoms like his, passed differently than here. Squeepittikik was the prime minister of a nation-wide country, now famous for his efforts on our side.

We'd given them the encyclopedias. And then cheap tablets with Wikipedia on them. Things changed on the other side of that portal, Squeepittikik told us.

Dad worked with a whole division of mice that came to our side to take back solar panels and alternators to make water and wind turbines. They were determined to leapfrog us and skip the mistakes of heavy industry.

Next New Year's Eve things had changed so much, and yet, so little. The massive deliveries had stopped, so our secret underground delivery bunker was mothballed.

The massive water bills had faded.

Mostly we were the junction of a fiber-optic relay to the other world and an Amazon package delivery mailbox for things the other world found interesting. But even that had tapered off.

Due to our gold reserves, we were all millionaires.

But here we were, sitting in Grandma's living room, getting ready to toast in a new year again.

Squeepittikik's great grand daughter, Ominissak, joined us for a toast in the living room.

"I have an announcement to make," she said, after taking a polite sip from a saucer of champagne.

We all came to attention. Of late, the mice had pointed out investments for us to make that had panned out very well for us. Their kingdom was a magical place of healthy benefits for all citizens, and largesse. Their GDP per creature outstripped anywhere on Earth. But they weren't focused on just GDP. They were a magical kingdom that focused on the quality of life of every creature between a combination of advanced technology, good social policy, and applied magics.

If the portal in the pantry weren't mouse-sized, I would have crawled through it myself.

"I want to tell you that our magicians have figured out the portal will be closing soon. The rip in space and time is healing itself."

We were gutted. Over the last year, the tiny woodland creatures and their reports of life on the other side had become our lives.

"We are starting to pass your world in abilities, and some of our magical scryers have spent time in your basement looking at your world's future. I have a gift to pass your family: know this, work together to build the world you want to see, and you will be fine, even if you do not right away see the results."

And that was it, a blessing and a foretelling from the magical woodland creatures from the portal in my grandmother's basement.

Ominissak left us at around nine. Grandma picked up her cane and headed to bed at ten. "I could have told you all that," she said to us, before retiring to her room.

By midnight, the mice were gone and no longer in her shit, and life moved on.

We toasted for a new year, a year older, a year wiser.

THE ALIEN FROM VERAPAZ

AT FIVE O'CLOCK, agents working for ICE swarmed through the doors of a childcare center on 35th Street, across the road from Eastern Park, and arrested the children of a superhero.

Simeon got called in at six, when he was already on the Scozi Island ferry and thinking about passing by the store at the terminal for a pet six-pack of something as hoppy as he could stand to bring home and put on ice so he could watch the sunset in his backyard. Maybe he'd even sit there and toy with the idea of getting some of the awl grip done on the boat's hull, so that he could take the trailer up to the north end slip and get out for some recreational fishing.

But someone had fucked up, the phone started buzzing, and Simeon turned to look back toward the gleaming spires of the Financial District.

Nothing good would come of an all-hands-on-deck alert, he knew.

After letting the buzzing go on long enough to establish that someone *really, really* wanted to reach him, Simeon opened a battered old flip phone.

"Simeon," he said.

There was a pause on the other end. "You on the ferry yet?"

"Yeah."

"Shit." The voice Simeon was listening to was one of his superiors, a boss of a boss much removed and high up the hierarchy. Not someone he was used to hearing over the cheap phone. Bob somebody or the other. A red-faced, perpetually harried man in a well-tailored suit and a graying haircut that was aspirationally military short, even though Bob looked a century away from any sort of boot camp experience. "We'll send over a harbor patrol boat. Stay on the pier when you get there."

"That bad?"

"It's ICE. They picked up El Fantastico's children."

"They what?"

"They rolled up El Fantastico's kids in some sort of raid. We're trying to figure out what dickless judge signed the warrant, but they probably hid who the kids were from the robe. There'll be a car waiting for you. Unmarked Brick City unit."

The call cut off, and Simeon stared at the water from the railing. He would need to stop and get a big mug of coffee when they docked.

The harbor patrol beat the ferry in, and there was no time for coffee. The officer on the semi-rigid inflatable looked annoyed at being used as a taxi, but didn't take it out on Simeon, just gave him a bright orange PFD that smelled of gasoline and sat him down on the bench in front of the steering console.

Simeon thanked him and apologized on the other side. He scrambled awkwardly out with the help of the plain clothes officer waiting for him at the wharf.

"Thanks."

"Lars Erikson," the detective said, showing Simeon his badge.

"Simeon." Simeon pulled his wallet and showed his ID. They were gliding up between steel and glass office buildings a moment later in the detective's unmarked, boxy car.

"This the ICE thing?" the officer asked.

"Word already around?"

"My buddy Eddie said they took a super's kids."

"Something like that." Simeon watched a drunken cluster of dark-suited traders stagger out from a bar. Already blowing that Financial District money.

"Fucking baby-cagers. They tried to get the 43 to do some surveillance for them, chief refused, then sent us to watch them instead. Our territory, you know? Fucking cocksuckers, the lot of them."

Simeon felt a blow, the words an impact that left his chest tight and a swirl of reactions whipping past him, each one fading away as the seconds ticked by. He tamped anger and hurt down, looked over, and said calmly, "I'm gay."

"Yeah, okay," the detective said, not missing a beat. "That's the good kind of cocksucker, I'm talking about those *asshole cocksuckers.*"

Simeon let the rest of the ride lapse into an awkward silence.

When Lars stopped the unit and Simeon got out, the detective looked over at him. "You have to wonder: stealing a superhero's kids? That sounds like the origin story for a godamn supervillain."

"This is Brick City," said one of the officers standing outside the daycare center, *Incredible Minds.* "I can't believe they found El Fantastico's kids. I can't believe they took them."

Simeon joined the small cluster of uniforms inside after his ID was checked, and he was waved through. A young woman in a floral print dress sat on a chair in the corner of the room, her face puffy from crying. An officer was holding her hand and reassuring her.

"You're the liaison?"

It was a police chief asking. He looked nervous as hell, sweat dripping down the side of his face despite the soft kiss of the AC inside the old brownstone that had been converted into a daycare.

"I'm SRD, yes," Simeon confirmed, showing his ID again.

"Someone played 'not it' and you get the shit job here," the chief said, shaking his hand. "Superhero Relationship Department got called the moment we found out so that none of us had to . . . you know."

Simeon felt sick. "Does he know yet?" He didn't need to say who "he" was.

"No press, and no one has leaked, I think, or he'd be here already."

"When does he pick the kids up?"

"Any moment, according to her." The chief jerked his chin toward the puffy-faced woman in the back.

"Shit." Simeon wanted a coffee. Or a cigarette. Just something to do with his hands while he thought. "Where's the rep from ICE?"

"They left a statement." The disdain dripped from the chief. "'No person is above the law in this country, even one with powers. ICE was following orders and the law.'"

Simeon kept a neutral expression on his face. "Where are the kids? I need to be able to tell him where his kids are."

"ICE won't say. Undetermined location. But I have a friend who works the buses." The police chief scratched his forehead. "He really needed the job, been down and out for a bit. He got it out of dispatch that they have them in the addition to Collyhaven, the addition they made with that private prison company for holding illegals."

"Illegals like the children of an alien from outer space who has unlimited powers, can fly around the world, and shoot laser beams from his eyes?" Simeon asked. "That you now want me to go out and tell that we've locked his kids up in a cage upstate somewhere?"

The chief let out a deep breath. "A shit show, yeah. Will my men even be safe, staying here, or should we withdraw?"

"I don't know. What the hell is ICE hoping to accomplish?" Simeon groused.

"They're saying it's a deterrent. If even a superhero can't be here without papers, and the whole world sees this, then other people won't try to come here."

"Everyone knows that El Fantastico's parents sent him here to escape Cataclysm, who's sworn to kill him and his family. Breaking the kids' identity like this risks their lives." Simeon straightened up. "They're going to go after El Fantastico, too?"

"Yeah."

"How can you stop him from just going up to the jail and ripping it apart?" Simeon asked.

"I'm told that, if he finds them, the cages are wound with adamonite, from the pieces the Department of Homeland Security confiscated after the battle for Brick City, the first time Cataclysm attacked Earth. That saps his powers." The chief handed Simeon a folder. "You're supposed to give him this."

There was a "woosh" outside, a murmur of awed voices.

Simeon tasted acid in his mouth. He didn't want to do this. But it was the job, right? He hadn't grabbed the kids. He was just the messenger. He hated it.

He took a deep breath and went to deliver the news in person to the superhero, that ICE had taken their children.

El Fantastisco would be forever remembered for his role in fighting the Gruesome Five in the skies over Brick City, and all had cowered as the skies had roiled dark with awesome power in the first duel against Cataclysm, who controlled dark energy from his gauntlets of fury. But El Fantastico had also created a frozen ice dam to hold the water at bay against the tsunami of '83, and even dissipated hurricanes at sea so that they couldn't threaten the subways and homes near the beaches.

And that didn't count the thousands and thousands of small things, too many to count. Muggers stopped, bullets stepped in front of, bridge jumpers saved, and cats pulled out of trees.

During the blackout of '91, El Fantastico had lit up the sky over the city with his eye lasers. He'd been blind for a month afterward, depending on his finely tuned sense of hearing and clicks to navigate by sonar.

He never missed a day of protecting Brick City.

Why do it?

"Because when I had been thrown free of my own dying planet, you took me in," he told a reporter by the foot of the Statue of Liberty once. "Because, when powers like this are gifted, it is a great responsibility."

Now Simeon was looking at that same chiseled jaw, the dark hair with curls at the end, and those dark brown eyes. His cape, with the American flag stitched into it, brushed against the ground as he walked toward the steps.

"Mr. Fantastico." Simeon stepped forward, wondering if those eyes could see right on through the fake calm he tried to project.

"You're Simeon, from the SRD." El Fantastico stopped in front of him. "I remember you."

Simeon's knees wobbled slightly. "I'm sorry it's under these circumstances."

There were fifty years of clippings: El Fantastisco's exploits began when he was a teenager, and his powers had bloomed, but he looked like he was in his late twenties. He always had. That deeply tanned skin always looked flawless, the brown eyes ever curious and patient.

Even now.

"My secret identity has been uncovered," the superhero said. "So I skipped taking the F-train over and flew."

"How did you find out?"

"Super hearing. I overheard a tip line calling another reporter in my office that ICE had taken El Fantastico's kids. I'm guessing you're here to give me the bad news?"

Simeon wet his lips. "Yes."

He handed the folder over.

El Fantastico took it, wearily, and looked back at Simeon. "They're scared, in there. I can hear it on their breath."

Simeon nodded.

"Walk with me, Simeon. Let's reassure them, I don't want anyone shooting at me. There's a camera over there from the Post." El Fantastico's mouth twitched, an expression of disgust leaking through. "You know them, the ones who called my children 'anchor babies.' I would bet they're the ones who uncovered me and told ICE where my children were."

Simeon followed the caped superhero along the road to a bench in the park. El Fantastico sat down on the bench and pulled out a pack of cigarettes.

"You smoke?"

Simeon looked around, as if this was a prank, then took one. El Fantastico lit it by looking at the tip, his eyes glowing, and then lit one for himself. Together they took long drags as confused joggers passed by.

"Back in the 80s I used to do TV spots telling kids to not smoke for the Ad Council," El Fantastico said. "Truth is, my lungs eat cancer for desert and I like the taste. Nicotine's okay, too. I wonder if we had it back on the home planet?"

Simeon didn't know what to say. But the cigarette stopped his hands from shaking so much, so that was a relief.

"I find it a ridiculous element of just sheer chance that, had my pod veered just slightly as I tumbled through the Seventh Dimension, I might have landed somewhere like . . . Iowa, instead of Verapaz." El Fantastico blew out a long cloud of smoke that hung in the air above the path. "With corn bread, rural American parents, I could have had white skin and blue eyes as my genetic profile adapted itself to appeal to the people who found me. Do you think, Simeon, that my children would be locked up right now if that had happened, even though I still would have been an alien from another world?"

Simeon knew the answer to that, because ICE wasn't knocking on the door of Amazing Woman, or locking up British or Irish babies at Logan International. But the superhero whose parents carried him across the Rio Grande, led by a coyote, running away from death squads and crime, he was being treated differently.

He stubbed out the cigarette. "Look, I can't stop you from going after your kids. I can't imagine—"

El Fantastico interrupted him. "Do you have kids, Simeon?"

"No."

"Then you're right. You can't imagine. You have no idea. When I first got the call, the first time this happened, I thought about destroying them all. Every single one of them. Every uniform. They wouldn't have even had time to realize I was coming for them."

Those brown eyes were slightly aglow, either with anger or actual rays.

Simeon glanced down at the ground. Just a blink, and he could be vapor. El Fantastico was right, he didn't have kids. But he could imagine. And even just imagining, he could see the anger in people's faces at the idea of detained children.

"What do you mean, the first time?" Simeon asked, frowning.

El Fantastico took another deep pull from the cigarette, drawing it all the way down to just ash in his fingers that blew away in a slight wind.

"They shot me when I tried to rescue them, my powers sapped by the crap they'd put on the bars. You warned me, but I had to try. I barely lived. The caped vigilante, he refused to come with me. He's a billionaire playboy, he voted for all this. But the speedy guy came and got me, so I got away. And when I healed up, I flew to the sun and went back in time."

Simeon stared. "You can do that?"

"I can."

There was another long exhale from the superhero.

Simeon had a thought. "If you can do that, you can go back and warn us—"

"I've been doing that forever. What do you think all the truth, tolerance, and the American Way speeches were about? And yet, here we are again. Repealing the fourteenth amendment, taking back citizenship, the camps. I think, it's something you all have

allowed to happen and I am going to have to leave it. Even a superhero alone can't fight millions unless there are other millions
willing to stand by my side. I can't afford the bond payment they
want, not on a journalist's salary. They're cutting my position to
hire more online listicle staff."

El Fantastico stood up.

"So what now?" Simeon asked. "What should I tell the department?"

"Tell them that they could have stopped this. That you could
have worked together to stop it. But everyone stood around, doing their job, instead of stopping something that should never have
happened."

And then, El Fantastico was gone, jumped into the air, a small
divot in the asphalt where he had stood.

"That could have gone a lot worse," said a worried officer,
standing at the edge of the jogging trail.

Simeon wasn't sure.

ONCE "DEFENDER OF FREEDOM" SHOT WHILE FREEING
JAILED ILLEGALS.

Simeon didn't bother reading the article the next morning, but
the front pages all showed the same grainy security camera footage
of El Fantastico, his cape riddled with bullets, blood dripping down
the red and white bars, terrified children huddling under his arms.

The city was in shock.

The city was unsure. What would happen if Cataclysm ever
returned? Only El Fantastico had been able to stop him.

The future was suddenly uncertain. And the same ICE agents
who'd been interviewed saying that, under the new rules their jobs
were "finally fun again" were now reporting someone on 8th Street
tossed a bottle at them. And the beat cop nearby had refused to give
chase on foot to the perpetrator.

Simeon left his badge at home, crossed over on the ferry, and

took the north train to Collyhaven. It was packed with the sorts of
people Simeon had always regarded as drains on society. Coddled
students, do-gooders, the overly concerned.

But there was an old veteran in one corner with a sign that
said FREE THE CHILDREN, and a mother with two children. The
northbound was packed shoulder to shoulder, and there was a grim
camaraderie in the air.

"This your first one?" the mother asked. "Protest?"

"Yeah."

"Mine too."

The train rocked. Simeon thought about the fact that he would
be facing officers he knew, officers that he worked with on a daily
basis as he liaised between superheroes and the police force.

It wasn't millions, he thought, looking around at the train full
of people headed toward the Collyhaven Detention Center. But it
was a start.

A train full of small heroes.

THE SUGGESTION

SAM ANWANGWE WATCHED the reporter perched on top the aging Coca-Cola delivery truck bounce this way and that along with the rattling bottles. The sweaty American gripped the rails so tight that Sam laughed.

"It's like being on a ship," Sam said. "Surf with it, don't fight it."

But for the last ten miles, Brian Cooper had clung even tighter as the truck climbed and then slid down the other side of massive ruts in the dirt. When they finally reached Camp Mudima, Cooper hopped down and wobbled off down the dirt road.

Sam stayed back with the driver, Titus, and began stacking cases on a rusted old handcart with wooden handles so polished from years of use it practically gleamed.

"What's the American up to?" Titus asked as they both pulled the cart along the dirt road into the camp. Three hundred tents and two thousand Angolan refugees who'd crossed the border into Namibia as they waited for the fighting to resolve. Sam grunted as they got over the last hump before the dirt road became recently paved asphalt.

"He says there's a supervillain hiding in the camp," Sam grunted as they waved down one of the Peace Force guards by the check-in station, a rounded building made out of rammed earth and tires, then covered in a lime paste that gleamed white hot in the Zambian midday sun.

Once pointed in the right direction and having shown some ID, they wheeled the bottles into a cooled storage area back behind the camp's commissary, under the direction of a tired looking senior cook who smelled like relish and peanuts in a crisp, red and white dress that whipped about just above her ankles like a cape.

"In Lusaka, maybe," Titus said. "What would they want with the border? Besides, I told you already back at the bottle pick up, I know every one of the volunteers in Mudima. If there was some white man with powers here, I would know."

Titus laughed again at the idea.

They both stretched their backs back outside in the sun, and Titus thanked Sam for the help and left to drive back toward the distribution center.

"Have an amazing day," Sam called out to Titus as he walked back toward his truck. Sam smiled to himself as Titus started to whistle a cheerful pop tune they'd heard on the radio heading toward the camp.

Helping Titus on his delivery was, Sam thought, a small price to pay for a ride out in the bush. He absent-mindedly scratched at the long scar running up and down the center of his chest. It always itched in the sweaty heat.

The journalist, Cooper, had been looking to hire a local fixer who was going to take full advantage of the kid. In fact, Sam felt that the fixer Cooper had been about to hire would most likely take him thirty miles outside the city before robbing him and leaving him by the side of the road.

"Kaamba isn't his real name," Sam had shouted. "It's John. John—"

The fixer took off, and Cooper, wearing that ridiculous khaki shirt with far too many pockets, shook Sam's hand and thanked him.

"What you need to do," Sam said, "is pay one of the Coca-Cola delivery drivers from the warehouse to ride along, or offer to help unload. They'll be going anywhere you want."

"Camp Mudima."

Camp Mudima circled around Sam on the old tried but true spoke and hub layout perfected by Burning Man in the American Southwest, modified with some traditional Tanzanian fractal layouts that optimized the camp's functions.

Sam wandered around the camp, just listening to the stories he heard. Growing up in Durham, he'd seen so many pictures of UN tents, dirt roads, and defeated people sitting near them as they wondered what their future held besides more uncertainty.

Mudima looked nothing at all like that. The family housing were all molded bubble structures right out of a bad science fiction film, and they gleamed with fresh whitewash or geometric colored shapes.

The young couple in the nearest one to the left fled Angola when rebels burned the nearest town down. Their farm had failed, the drought ravaging through a country that had been balanced on a knife's edge as heavy weather roiled them. They'd been terrified of walking across the border, worried about their daughter's persistent cough, and didn't know what would come next.

For days they'd tried to evade border guards to get into Zambia. When they gave themselves up, hoping for some food, the same border guards they'd feared drove them to Mudima and waited until they were processed in and had been looked at.

"We didn't have to fear them," the father whispered to his wife as the guards left, stunned. They'd imagined tents and UN doctors, and being expected to leave the moment peace broke out.

"Of course not," the processing officer told them. "Everyone here is a part of COMESA, there's nothing illegal about crossing a border. Like the E.U."

"Like the E.U.," they had repeated.

"Here is your debit card. It starts you on food from the commissary. It's at cost. There are jobs all across the camp, and there's a listing on the central board that refreshes every day. You said here on the form you can repair coils and winding?"

"Yes."

"We could start you in the electronics repair facility. You do good work, you may go back to Angola with a hefty savings account in your MPesa. Do you have a phone? No, we'll get you one. You'll want it to keep up with the news."

The family, stunned, had been ushered to their small home just last night. Today they had to enroll their daughter in pre-school after a camp doctor, herself Angolan, checked her over and gave her shots.

There hadn't been a school within easy walking distance of their rural farm.

Sam heard a gleeful shout from near the edge of Mudima, interrupting any attempt on his part to find out more about the family.

The reporter, it seemed, had found his supervillain. Sam rushed down the road toward them.

"Do you mind if I…?" The pencil-thin man waved a bottle of beer in the air at them. "The brews they make here in the camp are good, but this is just a taste of home."

He sat on an Adirondack-styled wooden chair made out of what looked like carpentry scraps from the camp's workshop, cracked the top, and nodded at the reporter, and then Sam.

Sam smiled encouragingly.

Cooper took a small recorder with two angled microphones in the front and faced it at the supervillain, who said his name was Karl. The device looked like a pricey piece of equipment.

"So you are Kevin—"

"Yes," the supervillain said wearily. "I am Fuse. You found me. Well done, you."

Sam looked at the reporter. Cooper's smile could swallow a small animal.

For five years Cooper had been pre-writing obituaries for celebrities. He was the graduate of a renowned journalism school, top of his class. But in a dying field he'd not found the world-traveling adventure he'd imagined. Instead, he had a tiny apartment with a window that looked at someone's window air-conditioner, a fridge not much larger than his head, and so much educational debt Cooper imagined he would never be able to climb any higher than his current lot in life.

But he had a story, he thought. While digging through photos of a celebrity doing some aid work, Cooper spotted a face that had terrified him as a child.

"Be a good boy," his mom would whisper, "or I'll call Phreaker and have him reprogram you into someone better."

The idea terrified a young Cooper, who imagined himself stripped of free will, walking about like a robot because his mom had called a supervillain.

"You were Phreaker, the world's most powerful supervillain," Cooper said breathlessly. "You led the most dangerous team of powered people ever assembled. And during the Battle of Central Park you just walked away and were never seen again. Now you're here, in a camp, building houses?"

The most dangerous man in the world, Cooper told Sam right before they joined Karl in his hand-made hut. You'll be sitting next to the most dangerous man in the world.

If that didn't get him a better profile and job as a journalist, finding where Phreaker had gone into hiding, and why, then what would?

"I am here, in a camp, building things," Karl said. "You've correctly figured out what I'm up to."

Sam chuckled, but cut it off as Cooper glared at him.

"Who are you, again?" Karl asked.

Sam held up his hands. "I got Mr. Cooper out here. I'm his fixer. I'm very sorry, don't mind me. Just imagine I'm not really even here."

Karl nodded and turned back to Cooper, who moved on.

"What happened?" Cooper pressed. "What happened in that battle that convinced you to give it all up? A supervillain, turning their life toward service?"

"Villain," Karl said, and rubbed the top of his beer. "That word. Do you know the etymology?"

"It's French for peasant," Sam said.

Karl turned his head to study Sam closely. "You—"

"I'm sorry," Sam interrupted. "I did it again. Again, I'm not here, I won't intrude again. Carry on."

Karl slowly regathered his thoughts. "The word, it comes from the *villiens* who worked the land. The common people. Us. That's how I became who I was."

"The man who stole all the gold from—" Cooper started.

"Yes," Karl interrupted. "I did that. Yes. But name me a revolution where the victors didn't cancel debts or give out land. Inequality has always been the fuel of sedition, all the way back in recorded history, when it was Babylonians chipping the accounts away on stone tablets."

"Like a Robin Hood," Cooper said.

"The system hated Robin Hood," Karl snapped. "He stole from the rightful owners and winners. These heroes, running around getting their kicks off beating the shit out of some sad ass criminal stealing a necklace so his mom can get another round of antibiotics, that bondage-gear cloak-wearing asshole could be spending all that money they put into researching a new gadget for their tool belt into an early education program that takes ten times as many off the street."

"So you were going to give all that gold to the people?" Cooper asked.

"Fuck no." Karl laughed and took a drink from the bottle. "I was going to sink into the depths of iniquity and pleasure. I wanted what I thought the world owed me."

"So you *were* a villain." Cooper had a small notebook out, and he scratched several lines out as he waited for an answer.

"I was broken."

Sam leaned forward. There was something there, right on the

edge of Karl's body language. He wanted to steer the conversation there, but Karl started laughing. The sharp sound shattered the moment.

"None of that matters," Karl said. "You want to know how I ended up here, and it wasn't because of a realization or awakening. Nothing from my past will help you understand why I did this. What you need to know is all in the Battle of Central Park."

Fifteen superheroes facing off against twice as many supervillains. The devastation of one of New York's most treasured and sacred places. Sam let himself melt into the background to give Karl the space he needed to keep talking to Cooper.

"What happened in the park, besides the defeat?" Cooper asked.

"They had a kid in the fight." Karl shook his head. "Fifteen years old, still in high school, from Brooklyn. He took the subway to the fight after school, showed late but wearing a spandex jumpsuit with a big swirling spiral on it. Said he was the Whisper, or Mesmeri, something like that. All he had to do was whisper something into your ear, and you'd do it. And since the League let a child onto the battlefield, I plugged my ears with a set of plugs I got at a firing range so I could walk through the middle of the chaos and plunge my power glove into his chest to rip out his heart."

Cooper winced, then looked clearly guilty at not keeping his reactions in check. The fabled, and often useless journalist instinct to remain neutral meant he had an obligation to keeping the most interesting parts out.

"Do you know what that little shit did as he lay dying with his head on my shoulder?" Karl asked.

Cooper did not know, and said as much, and Karl nodded, quite satisfied with our shock and outrage.

Karl lowered his voice. "He pulled out my earplugs."

Both Sam and Cooper waited.

"And here I am," Karl growled. He shook the remaining droplets of his beer out onto the wooden deck and tossed the bottle into

a corroded, galvanized steel pail near the steps. One of the other
bottles inside shattered, and Karl sighed heavily.

"He told you to come to Zambia?" Cooper finally pressed.

"After he . . ." Karl looked over at a cooler by the edge of the
deck, wrestled with some inner demon, then rested his elbows on
his knees as he leaned forward. A penitent in a glaring sun. "I tried
to lie to myself. I said fixing the broken system would do far more
good than any direct actions I could take, I argued, but deep down,
I didn't believe it. Or it would have worked."

The most dangerous man in the world, inventor, maniacal
weapons master, the shadow that ended so many heroes' lives, took
a deep, tired breath as his shoulders slumped.

"It was a compulsion, deep down. Like the certainty you exist,
and that you like ice cream, and that small kittens make you smile.
I knew he planted it in me, whispered it into my ear, but I couldn't
fight it. The little shit had the last laugh. Because, no matter what,
I know that I was told to go out into the world and concretely help
more than I've hurt. And only when I've done enough to balance
the pain I caused before, would I feel I could leave."

Sam looked closely at Karl's hands. The scarred palms and
broken fingernails. The tremor of exhaustion. The thin muscula-
ture. Karl would work himself to the edge of physical failure, driv-
en by that small whisper ever in the back of his head telling him to
do more, more, more good.

"I think about that moment every day of my life," Karl said. "If
I had a power, I would have told my enemy to kill himself. End it.
But it turned out that every super the kid fought now works for aid
agencies, or runs halfway homes, or ended up retired to adopt an
army of needy children."

"How many did he do this to?" Cooper asked, the reporter's
gleam in his eye.

"Hundreds?" Karl shrugged. "I don't know, he was a kid in
some prep school, so he only had so many nights free to fight."

"He took away their free will," Cooper said.

"Don't look at me like that." Karl sat back and folded his arms. "Don't feel sorry for me. It's a good life, a simple life. I help where I'm allowed, I know my place in this world, I know what I have to do."

"Do you really believe that?" Cooper asked. "Truly? Because Phreaker said he wanted to bring about a more equal society. You turned your back on all your thinking?"

Karl nodded. "Let's be real here, how many dictators who promise to bring down inequality ever truly do it? I was arrogant to assume I could rebuild a system that complex through just my will, while the power tempted me. I know I'm doing more for the world here than I could have. Because if that was true, I wouldn't be here, would I?"

The interview continued as the sun slowly sank away and dusk crept into Mudima. A group of children playing soccer out in the carefully tended southern camp park mock-cursed the end of the play time, and their mothers yelled at them to come home, their whistles and calls bouncing off Mudima's many bright walls.

Karl finally stood after telling stories of the old battles, and anecdotes about the many pieces of the world he'd seen, disasters he'd helped clean up after. The interview, clearly, was over.

"I'd like to come by and get a photograph tomorrow when the light is better," Cooper said. "To go with the story."

Karl looked around the camp, saw nobody out, and nodded. He leaned over the pail by the steps and pulled out the shattered bottle.

Before Sam could cry out, before Cooper's eyes even widened in surprise, Karl struck like a cobra. The shattered blades of the bottle sunk deep into Cooper's neck, and Karl swept the dying journalist off his feet.

Cooper struck the deck with a wet thud, and Karl held him down until he stopped moving.

"Fuck," Karl said to the body in front of him. "Fuck. Why did you say that, kid. Why?"

He put a hand on Cooper's chest, rocked back and forth for

a good minute, and then stood up. He picked the body up easily. He'd had his skin stripped back and a robotic skeleton bonded to his bones twenty years ago so that he could compete with supers with powers. It once gave him super strength and speed, but time had run it down, and Karl moved jerkily down the path behind his house to a retaining wall.

Sam followed.

Karl dug out a shallow grave with a shovel leaning against a pile of bricks and gently lay Cooper down inside. He covered the body with dirt, and then walked over to mix some mortar.

"How long have you been standing there?" he asked, his back still to Sam.

Sam jumped in surprise. "You see me?"

"No. My eyes keep sliding away, like, there's something there that I can't ever imagine could be. It . . . comes from the same place." Karl slapped mortar in place, and then placed a brick with a still bloody hand.

"Maybe you are just—"

"You said: imagine I'm not even here," Karl said. "I remember that. But you didn't leave. I just . . . did what you told me."

The supervillain kept putting bricks in place and slapping mortar as he moved along the row.

"What are you, his son?" Karl finally asked.

"No."

"What are you doing here? Have you come to kill me for something I did, back then? It's okay if you are. I understand."

Sam watched Karl work and said nothing for a long while. Not until Karl finished the whole row and began to work his way back toward him.

"You should look at me, now," Sam suggested.

Karl did, and then returned to the work at hand. "You're not here to kill me, and you watched me bury that kid. What are you here for?"

"I came to release you," Sam said.

It had taken so long to find him. Just like the others, they were all so good and staying off official notice.

Karl stopped, the trowel held an inch over the last layer. His hand trembled. "Who are you?" His voice broke at the end.

"I was a sickly kid," Sam said. "Bad heart. Your punch, it ended his life, but it didn't damage his heart. He was an organ donor. And when I woke up, the nurses did anything I asked. But that was their job, so I didn't notice it. It wasn't until I was getting wheeled out to go home and someone almost hit Father and me that I understood. My father yelled 'asshole' at the driver, and I shouted 'go fuck yourself.' And after he hit the brakes and jumped out of the car he . . ."

Sam shrugged.

"Why didn't you stop me?"

"You were too fast, Phreaker. That skeleton of yours."

Karl started placing bricks again.

"Cooper didn't deserve that," Karl said.

"No one does," Sam said.

"You're right." Karl looked directly at Sam with large, pained eyes.

"I was going to free you, but then, you killed him, right in front of me. Even with that compulsion you've carried all this time, you still perverted the idea of balance in your own sick way." Sam grimaced. "It's not just whispers. I can see your memories. I can feel your story."

"I thought I would lose the chance to keep helping if he exposed me. And I have to help. I can't not do it."

"The killing was a choice, Karl. It showed who you really are, how you want to solve problems. Karl, you must never harm another human being again."

Karl nodded right away.

Sam thought back to an old novel in his father's bookshelf. "And you can't, through inaction, allow another human to be harmed."

"I will not allow that," Karl agreed.

"Goodbye, Karl," Sam said, and began to walk back up the path.

"He would have been proud of what you're doing," Karl said, not deviating from his bricklaying.

Sam left the supervillain moving another stack of bricks closer. But it didn't matter how many walls he'd built, Sam thought, they would never equal the value of a life like poor Cooper.

Sam felt horrible that he'd laughed at him on the truck. He'd taken advantage of Cooper to help him find Karl. And Cooper had paid for that. He needed to find someone to hint that Cooper would be found in the retaining wall. He deserved to be sent home.

Sam looked at a small notebook he pulled from his backpocket. It read: Jillian Swells. Botswana?

He left Karl bloodying his hands on the brick, mechanically moving one at a time, trying to rebalance the scales of his life one brick at a time.

There would never be enough walls to make that happen.

THE ATHEIST AND THE ANGEL

N OTHING GOOD COMES out of a five a.m. phone call, and
that's why my retainer hits six figures to get on the short-
list that gets through in the pre-dawn.

Additionally, I probably wouldn't have agreed to the retainer if
Theodora hadn't asked me for a favor. "It's a big client, and I need
the win, Jason. I desperately need the win."

She's still working off a debt. That asshole boyfriend of hers
ten years ago. She'd shot him. It had been her or him, he'd been
drunk and coming at her with a machete, but she's been working
off the reverberations of that kill ever since.

So I said yes to the retainer, and I answer the damn call as it
comes in. And drag my ass down to the location she gives me.

The body in the penthouse of the Jenga-block building near
Central Park looks peaceful. A well-built, middle-aged manager
type with salt and pepper hair, he lies on his back, cooling against
the Italian marble floor.

Theodora, the fixer, has already pulled his khakis up and but-
toned a pale blue oxford shirt up to the neck.

"Sorry to get you up so early, Jason," she says, not even bother-
ing to look away from her work. "I'm not thrilled. It's a shit way
to spend my birthday. The coroner won't find any marks or sub-

stances, no weapon. They'll be confused."

I've pulled on little booties, the same ones crime scene investigators will use so that they don't contaminate the scene. I'll toss the gloves in a garbage can outside downwind of the choking smell of the hot dog cart.

"Dee." It's too early to play guess the crime. "You have the scene handled, what do you need me for?"

She points to the bedroom.

I meander over and pull down the flimsy breathing mask for a better look.

"Oh."

The remains of an anti-celestial charm system still hang in the air, pieces of glyphs strung from the walls like spaghetti strands with a faint blue glow.

"A powerful defense system." I walk the edges of the room. "And something powerful enough to walk away after it triggered."

"The company spent mad coin on the safety measures in here," Theodora says from behind me, rolling a trunk into the room. She flips the top open to reveal rows of magical cleaners.

I turn back to examine the charm's remains. Scrape at some of it with a gloved fingernail. Sniff the fading residue. "Unicorn blood?"

"As an activator. Gunpowder for the spray effect. It was a bitch to clean." Theodora waves some sage in the air to loosen residue.

I look at her cleaning kit. "The killer wasn't expecting the charm."

"His soul was ripped out before the charm could even trigger."

"I'm not going to help you clean this up. I'm too expensive for that. Plus, this is bespoke." I pat my suit.

"That's not why I called you." Theodora uses a musical charm, a set of notes she blows out of an ocarina. The notes hang in the air and quiver between us.

She sucks the residue up with a small portable vacuum cleaner. As she follows the charm around the room, the machine swells like a puffer fish, struggling to hold in the potential energy inside the bag.

When she flicks it off I wait a moment for the sound to fade.

"So then why *did* you call me?" I ask.

Theodora makes a last lap of the room, checking that there's nothing left for anyone to find.

"Corporate wants this to look like a natural death. A stroke. After you leave, I install a new charm. Then we wait for cleaning staff in the morning to find him on the floor. But that leaves one small thing left untied."

"The actual killer."

"The scene is cleaned. But corporate still wants to know who did it."

"And why."

Theodora taps the side of her nose, but her smile is empty. "Corporate at least wants to know if it's trouble ahead."

"So they don't," I note, "actually give a shit about the death if it doesn't affect the company."

Theodora gets to her knees and pulls a new set of charm triggers out from her utility box. They look like open bear traps. One for each corner of the room. They glitter with silvered coating and werewolf fur.

"Come on," she says, grabbing my shoulder. "You'll want to be outside the room."

I step out with her and turn to watch her throw a doubloon under the bed. Pirate booty, with pirate blood staining it.

The traps snap, and the afterimage of a newly formed charm trap briefly sear into the back of my mind's eye.

"I'm a consultant, not a private investigator." I blink.

"Yeah, but we need you," Theodora says. She pulls a feather out of the inside of her vest pocket.

Fuck. I can see the outline of the issue ahead.

"Our killer's an angel." I take the feather and sniff it to make sure. The smell of myrrh hits me, stronger than patchouli. I cough.

Angelic for sure.

"Or a demon," Theodora says.

"Same thing."

Theodora rolled her eyes. "I miss your cynicism. I usually eat that shit up. But, we need you."

I move back to the door and remove my booties from the shiny patent leather Italian shoes I just had resoled. "Takes an atheist to catch a celestial."

"And since the apocalypse, I think you might be the only one left."

"Don't hate the player, hate the game." I grin. She doesn't want to, but she smiles back.

When the murderer can fly away, there are no tracks, I think.

But, other than the feather, we're up against a being that plays fast and loose with physical laws. And Theodora has already scrubbed the apartment clean.

She has a folder in her bashed up econobox car for me that she hands over after we slink out through a back entrance of the overly-ornate lobby. My stomach growls and I think about breakfast. It'll probably be a bagel on the run morning.

No, I can do better.

I pick through the folder.

"Forex trader?"

"Responsible for billions moving in and out. High profile, lots of pull."

"Think it's a sin thing?"

Theodora opens her door and looks across the top of the car at me. "I think it's an apocalypse thing, Jason."

I get in the passenger side, shoving old newspapers off onto a floor pasted with fossilized french fries.

"What are you doing?" Theodora stares at me through disheveled brown bangs.

"There's a deli a couple blocks up, but it's about to start raining and . . ." I gesture at my shoes. It's obvious I'm not going to walk there in the grime and dark water. "I'd call a car, but I have more questions."

"Everything's in the folder." She slams her door shut, starts the car.

"Everything they want me to know."

Theodora adjusts her mirror. "Jay—I did my bit. We're done now."

"Two blocks." I hold up a pair of fingers. I'm deep in the folder, dead to the world already. And I want the excuse to stay with her.

I'm being insufferable, but, I'm doing her the favor. Knowing me got the retainer and her services as a fixer. She knows it.

Theodora sighs, a distant sound to me in the moment, and we ease out into the chaos of traffic.

When I look up, a half hour later, we're in front of stained glass and soaring marble.

"I was hungry," I complain.

"And this will feed your soul," Theodora says with a raised eyebrow.

The Holy Name of Jesus Church. The nearest Catholic church. "Franciscans."

"I know some of the staff. They do good work over here. A full urban outreach program. Homeless ministries. The real deal, works and all. They'll be able to get you an intercession."

"I was going to do this after I ate."

"Go inside. Work the problem. I'll get you breakfast when you come back."

"Promise?"

"Honest to god," she says, hand on her chest.

These days, that's about as binding as anything.

*

It's not wooden pews and soaring arches. Father Khan walks me right on past all the airiness and light of a full on gothic cathedral and pink marble and off to his office.

I stare at a picture of the Virgin Mary.

Father Khan is excited. He's heard of me. But I'm here to get down to business.

"I'm looking for—" I start, but Father Khan holds up a hand.

"I had a visitation this morning, at the crack of dawn," he says. He's not excited to meet me, he's practically vibrating in awe. Apparently I'd been a little presumptive and full of myself when I assumed his liquid, wide eyes had been for me. "I have a message for you."

"I've been anticipated."

"It said the heathen would come for an intercession, but that I was to tell you it was," and here Father Khan faltered a moment and grimaced, "a *sanctioned* hit."

He reverently picked up a piece of paper folded over on itself, and carefully handed it to me. I opened it up and looked down at the angelic script. It glowed in the office's dim light.

"Well look at that," I muttered. The stationary came from the lobby of the apartment complex across from the dead currency trader. The angel had left a message with the nearest priest I would turn to for a formal request about the murder. Interesting.

I leaned back against the wooden and leather seat back. "What was the angel's name?"

Father Khan gave me a rueful smile and put his hands on his desk. "I am not going to be the priest that rats out a member of the heavenly host."

"Fair enough."

I stand up to leave. This was a fast dead end.

"Why?" Father Khan asks. "You value proof above all else. I understand that. I even understand how that kept you away from the church before now. But what more proof do you need than seeing the actual, literal signs of the apocalypse all around you? How can you call yourself an atheist now?"

I look back at him. He looks wounded, and a little bit worried. I know he asks out of a sense of genuine care. There is no need for faith now, no guarding against doubt when angelic beings fly over Broadway on their way to do higher biddings, dodging around the news helicopters.

"The *a* in atheist means without, and *theos* means god or gods. Greek roots." The first Christians were called atheists by the Romans, as they denied all the gods resident in the many cities. "I see the miracles and creatures. But I don't know what they are, and why they are. And if they are really doing the bidding of a single god, then I'm not sure I want to be involved. He's the god that killed all the first born in Egypt, and what the fuck did *those* babies ever do to him?"

Father Khan blanches at my casual heresy, and I instantly feel bad.

"Father, I don't know what is happening. But I know that demons have little hold against me and that it lets me help people here and now. I know that I do my best to be a good person, and that many of my friends believe a variety of different things that put their souls in jeopardy but who seem decent to me. If I'm going to be damned for that, I'm not sure I want to throw in with all that."

"But hell?"

"Maybe it's real, but I read the books." I smile reassuringly. "Lots of talk about how the wicked will go there. A lot of chatter from later writers about it, not much from the Old Testament and direct from God or Jesus about it. Besides, all the interesting people will be there."

I leave it at that. I notice that Father Khan has a tattoo. A misspent youth, maybe? I'm not going to harsh his mellow by reminding him about Leviticus saying tattoos doomed your soul.

"Plus," I say on the way out, "I'm British. At this point, I'm just trying to keep traditional secularism alive."

"Done already?" Theodora asked, looking up from her phone in surprise when I slumped into the passenger seat.

"Didn't need the intercession. The angel knew I was coming, left me priest-mail. Let's go eat."

"You look grumpy," Theodora says over beignets.

I lick sugar from my fingers. "Church after affects."

"You didn't catch on fire?"

"Funny. I think the old ones are pretty. I love the marble. But, I feel claustrophobic in them."

"Bad memories?"

"I'm not a bitter atheist." I lean back and consider whether to get a coffee or not. The city is starting up, suits coming into the bakery to get their morning orders. The hum of the city rises as the beast gears up for another day of hectic bustle. "I just have to be on my guard when I'm around the officer corps."

And I didn't like being used as a glorified messenger boy.

I order the coffee because Theodora's taking too long to eat. She eats like a squirrel, two dainty hands holding a pastry and nibbling at it.

"I'm sorry I suggested you," she says, realizing I'm staring at her. "They were tossing mad money around, and you go for cash over indulgences."

There's a heavy business in indulgences. In the Middle Ages priests sold them, creating a market economy for buying the forgiveness of sins performed. The entire Protestant reformation had, in part, bloomed out of the disgust over that.

With the apocalypse in full swing, Wall Street had securitized the shit out of them right away, making them the second currency of the new world we lived in.

I still used good old paper money, backed by the government of the USA, so I could buy all my worldly goods.

"I agreed to the retainer," I say. "Can't complain now. And I'm happy to do it for you."

The company wanted someone immune to holy and unholy influences, who worked for currency. And I had my own angle.

"They're dangerous to work for, our employers. You know that. I'm only doing it for indulgences. I have . . . almost enough." Theodora wipes her empty hands on her sleeves absent-mindedly. "Still, you shouldn't be working for them."

"Because it risks my immortal soul?"

She looks up at me. "You already do that with your beliefs. Why risk it further? I shouldn't have asked you to do this."

"Favor?" I ask. I point at the ribbon holding the pastry box.

She hands it to me and I pocket it.

"One more: give me one more ride on your way home?"

Theodora sighs wearily. "Corporate headquarters?"

"Yeah." She hates going to the belly of the beast. But I've been tasked with a holy writ and I don't feel like expensing a cab or taking the subway.

I get out and jog up the steps, each step splatting water onto the hems of my hand-sewn trousers. Through security and a scanner, each flanked by serious looking hellhounds that retch as they smell church on me. But there's nothing dangerous on me, so it's a phone call upstairs, then some more waiting around.

That's okay, I read some more folders in an ostentatious lobby, folding one leg over the other as I pretend this doesn't annoy me.

We have all the time in the world, don't we?

"Jason!"

Oliver Turner walks across the marble with all the grace of a panther circling prey.

"O.T."

"You're all the way up in the big boy lobby." Oliver has a grin as false as his perfect pearly whites.

"You sicced me on a dead trader," I say.

"Shhhhhh," Oliver says dramatically. "We're waiting for the horrible call about his untimely right now. We're going to be oh so shocked about it. Come into my office."

We walk past desks stacked with boring, white young men in identical suits working at moving ideas around. The problem with the apocalypse isn't that it's the end of the world. It's how long it takes, what forces are involved, and how you monetize them.

Wall Street futures commodities revolve around short time frames. Corn futures play out over two to three years. So you want to play with a date on when the next seal is unlocked, you could put money on that. Or maybe you want to boost the overall value in a massive damned souls tranche pledge to demons by vertically slicing them and abstracting their values? There's a person on Wall Street who can estimate that, sell a position, and look for the angelic buyers on the other side of the bet.

Oliver steeples his fingers and props his legs up on his desk. "What did you get for us? What's our exposure?"

There's a fire in the corner of his room. A perpetual pillar that licks at the air, but doesn't singe the walls. I feed the folders into it and watch charged white smoke swirl up to the ceiling and disappear into a void that my eyes slide past.

"He was trading against foreign currency movements," I said. "Putting a stake on a new breakaway state becoming a country, with its own money."

Oliver nods. This was in the folders.

I pulled out the small piece of paper given to me by the priest. Letters on it glimmer in angelic script. I place it on the desk between us, and Oliver looks down at it with a flicker of interest.

"The heavenly host doesn't want a new nation to appear, does it?" I say.

"They don't have the middle management for it." Oliver smiles. "Not since all that drama with Brexit and Catalan."

There are hierarchies to angels. Those hierarchies stack up. Human beings have *guardian angels*. Nations have *principalities*.

A principality is a powerful creature indeed.

"A nation without a protective principality . . ." Oliver licks his lips. "It's just so . . . vulnerable. Ever since the North American countries split from their mother nations, the greater war has been well fought."

Oliver gestures at the note. "Burn it for me, if you would? I'd rather not touch it."

I toss the angel's message into the fire, and the room shakes for a second as the fire struggles to absorb it.

"It was a sanctioned hit, so now you know what you're up against," I say.

"Same shit, different day," Oliver laughs. "But it confirms what our intelligence department estimated the response would be."

"All of this. It's not the end, is it?" I say. "It's just the trenches of some damn war."

Oliver looks out the window at two small figures falling out of a cloud, scrabbling at each other as they spin in the wind that tugs at their wings. "You're closer than you realize. You're always here, sniffing around. You need to read more religious texts, get into the really obscure shit outside the mainstream, and you'll do better."

"Duly noted."

"All of it," he repeats. "The older the better. Get out of the Zoroastrist influences into the really ancient stuff."

"That's not why I'm here today," I tell him.

Oliver makes a face. "Your payment's out on the table with the assistant. And yes, we made the change you texted us about. You surprised us. Jason Harper, taking indulgences after all this time."

I shrug.

Oliver leans across his desk. "So you finally believe we're here to drag you down into eternal torment?"

"I don't know what you are, or what they are," I tell him. "But that's not the game I'm playing."

"I hear prostitutes will only take pay in an indulgence that gets them ahead of the sin they're performing," Oliver says with an even wider grin. "You getting lonely, Jason?"

"It must madden you that I'm so hard to read." My lack of faith leaves creatures like Oliver hungrily sniffing the empty air. I'm Switzerland in their war, and yet, both angels and demons want my allegiance.

They'll never have it.

"Thank you for your services," Oliver says, as I let the door close with the faintest whiff of sulphur.

"I don't know how you're so calm after going upstairs like that," Theodora says with a shiver. "It always gives me the creeps."

"I know."

She lurches the old car into motion. I watch the skyscrapers slide by. An old man waves a "by GooD WorKs" sign back and forth through the air by the intersection. An angel with soaking wet wings perches on a balcony and watches us go by.

One of them murdered a man.

Old Testament angels. They were God's warriors. They slaughtered people, fought wars. And maybe, as Oliver hinted, they were all something even older.

"Big plans for you birthday night?" I ask.

"Renting a movie. Ordering in."

Theodora jerks to a stop.

I hand her the rolled up sheaf of indulgences, tied up with the ribbon from breakfast. "Maybe you should do something a little more reckless tonight."

There's enough in there to really blow off some steam.

She unrolls the papers and gapes at them. "Jay—"

I don't know if there's really some cosmic sin counter out there, or if there's a single act that clears it all. Theology argues about it. But if the indulgences give her a chance to start her life again after the hell she's already experienced, a hell that led to her trying to accumulate enough indulgences to feel safe again, well, she deserves it.

"You're a good person, Dora. You're a good friend. Happy birthday."

Right now, the world is still for the living. Even if all the apocalypse had appeared, we all had to live it.

How long did she need to suffer, truly, to pay off her debt?

If the priests are right, there would be time enough for that later.

ZOMBIE CAPITALISM

THE DOGS STARTED barking at the zombie in the pool long before Sheryl figured out what Zim and Garfield got the scent of. Zim, the German Shepherd, crashed through the picture window to scrabble out after it.

Sheryl yelled at the dogs to get back in the house as Garfield took off to join Zim at the chain fence around the pool.

Then she heard the zombie splashing about in the shallow end of the pool. It snarled when it saw her, and she couldn't quite stifle a small scream as she realized a rotting corpse had pulled itself through a hole in the pool fence. It had trailed blood and innards all across the decorative brick path, then collapsed in a cloud of black ichor into the crystal clear blue water.

Sheryl ran back inside and got the Remington Seven from the rack by the door, loading it and working the bolt by feel as she jogged to the back of the house. By the time she returned to the pool the zombie flailed around in one of the corners, not able to pull itself out of the pool. A long, black tangle of intestines looped around the pool cleaner had tied it up.

"Jesus Christ on a cracker." Sheryl grabbed Zim. "Damn it dog, you stay here."

She managed to get Zim's collar, but Garfield had scrabbled off counter-clockwise around the fence to wiggle through the damn hole. He arrowed into the pool along the zombie gut trail like the damn beagle scenthound he was.

Garfield ran around to snarl at the zombie as Sheryl got Zim's leash on him, clipped him to the fence, then ran over to the gate.

"Garfield, *get* over here!"

She fumbled with the padlock for a second. Garfield shrieked as the zombie got clawed, bony fingers into him.

Sheryl kicked the gate open and fired at the zombie. A chunk of shoulder blew away. She swore and worked the bolt again.

The second shot blew the zombie's head apart, bits of brain raining down into the pool. Sheryl pulled Garfield out of the water, carried him to the pickup, and got him into the passenger seat.

"Hilldale Vet Clinic," she shouted into her phone.

She was halfway to the vet before she realized she'd left Zim clipped to the fence, and called Kathy next door.

"No worries," Kathy said. "I'll send Jaden over. He can plywood up the window and take Zim in."

"I thought," said Cory from the vet's curved desk and two sleek computers, "that the National Guard had swept the town. What was the point of all those checkpoints around town? Fucking zombies."

Somewhere in the back, Sheryl thought, Garfield lay on a table under anesthesia. And that young vet from Chicago that didn't look like she could legally order a weak beer, or even drive a car, was trying to save him.

"Zombies, huh?" Cory said again.

Sheryl pulled her head out of her bloody hands when she realized he was talking to her. "What?"

"National Guard isn't doing a good job of keeping up," Cory said.

"They left," Sheryl said. She took a deep breath and blew her nose.

"They left? When'd they leave?" Cory looked horrified.

"It was on Channel Five," Sheryl said. "You didn't see it?"

"I've been working extra shifts," Cory said. "Trying to get ahead on my payments for steel shutters."

Sheryl had been seeing more and more of those go up. Bars on windows as well. She didn't like the look. The HOA kept sending out letters pointing out that it violated the community guidelines, but they just kept popping up.

Zombies trumped HOA rules.

"UTD won against the government." The judge on the case ruled that getting the military involved unfairly influenced the market. Ultra Tactical Dynamics, a company built just to provide zombie and zombie home defense products, would lose all its business if the National Guard defeated the zombie hordes. And that was anti-capitalist and un-American.

Second amendment rights trumped governmental anti-zombie actions.

"These are fundamental American rights," a blonde spokeswoman wearing aviator sunglasses told reporters at a press conference on the steps of the court, as Sheryl watched the news and chopped onions and carrots for a stew the previous night.

News reporters noted that the CDC wasn't allowed to track zombie populations starting next week, and conservative senators had advanced a bill to prevent funding for a cure.

"You should buy UTD stock," Zachariah told Sheryl at Bread-Worx the next day. "The dividend is growing, and the stock is flying high after the decision."

He'd been their financial advisor for three years now. Dale liked him. Zachariah was a high school buddy who came back to town after college with a business degree to take over his dad's business selling insurance and retirement.

Dale couldn't make the appointment, told Sheryl she needed

to go. What she really wanted to do was stay home and grieve Garfield.

Damn, she'd loved that dog.

Fucking Dale. He was probably off drinking at lunch. Sheryl hated meeting Zachariah on her own. He never took his eyes off her chest. She'd insisted on meeting him for lunch somewhere public to avoid the claustrophobic feeling of doing this in his office.

"They stopped the plague in France," Sheryl said, ripping off a piece of sourdough bread and dipping it in the potato soup. "What happens when this is all over?"

"We don't need a whole socialist intervention," Zachariah scoffed. "Got enough firepower right here for us regular folk to stop the horde. I saw Andy take out one of them in the hardware parking lot. Bang, right between the eyes. People got out of their cars to clap."

Some of the boys were talking about building blinds out in the woods around town to sit and hunt zombies with their rifles.

Zachariah had a whole prospectus for Cheryl to look over. A glossy brochure full of charts that showed zombie outbreak growth, personal defense sales, and featured UTD's unique "prep parties" sales system that set up individuals as distributors to sell defense projects on down the line. Like Tupperware parties, but for lawn spikes, shutters, guns, and bitching swords.

Dale loved going to town UTD parties.

"Listen, you see these videos online?" Zachariah asked.

He pulled out his phone and showed her a clip of three men in full camo gear on ATVs, all of them wearing night vision goggles.

"Watch this," one of them giggled, and tossed a stick of dynamite out into the dark. When it exploded, dark gore and body parts rained out of the night and everyone laughed.

Local government all over the country lifted limits on what hunters could use on zombies. YouTube was chock full of men filming themselves firing on zombies with all the arms they'd been hoarding since the NRA first started posting about the government coming to take their weapons.

"Okay, look, if you don't want to invest in UTD, how about something a little more exotic?" Zachariah leaned in and tapped the UTD brochures.

Cheryl sighed. "What's that?"

"You remember Randy?"

"Chemistry Randy?"

Zachariah nodded. "He's starting a safari experience for the city folk. You come out, do a few practice rounds on a shooting range, and then they load you into a open-topped bus with a wire cage and run you out into the countryside and you take potshots from the comfort of a vehicle."

Fifty thousand seed capital to help him get two vehicles with chopped tops.

Who knows how much they'd make?

"It's zombie capitalism," Zachariah said with a big grin. "And business is good."

"I'd have to talk to Dale," Cheryl said. She could barely focus, her eyes were watering every few seconds, and Zachariah was too focused on talking investing at her to notice that she'd been dabbing at her runny nose the whole time.

"He's good for it," Zachariah pushed. "He used to run the same business doing feral hog hunting. Same idea. You could hunt them with just about anything because they were spreading too quickly all over the country. We used to go out machine-gunning the things on weekends. Most legal fun you could ever have."

It looked like so much fun, but the bottom fell out because people started importing feral hogs up to other areas where hunters were all excited to start the process all over again.

And then soon you had feral hogs ripping through farms like a horde of locusts. They'd breed like rabbits. Local authorities would lift hunting restrictions. People would film themselves hunting with machine guns, and then the whole thing would repeat.

"Zachariah, I really have to get going," Cheryl said. "I have things to do still today."

According to the radio, stocks were up. Lots of companies building new things to deal with the zombie apocalypse. Construction was up. Walls, moats, shatterproof windows, heavy doors. The hardware stores were doing well. Everyone was taking out second mortgages or maxing out their credit cards.

The economy was humming along because everything had to change for the new reality.

CEOs reported that things had never been better. The NAS-DAQ at new highs. S&P 500 hitting new records.

A shambling corpse stepped onto the road. Cheryl screamed and swerved. Never swerve, she thought. Her car insurance agent told her that. Just hit it dead on and keep moving. Call the 1-800 number on the back when you got home.

Do not park the car in the garage, leave it at the end of the driveway.

Dale always mocked her fuel-efficient hybrid. Maybe he was right, maybe she needed a big pickup that could climb over a zombie and keep going.

The edge of their two acres needed spikes. And Cheryl needed Dale to dig a moat. She'd called about the steel shutters, but they were back ordered three weeks.

Funny, the magazines Dale had all featured heavy weaponry. But nothing about ditch-digging and defensive features.

Cheryl dug a hole near the Japanese maple at the property marker. Garfield's favorite spot. He'd sit there and watch the road, waiting for them to come along the curve, then race his way out to the driveway to pace the car up to the garage.

She wept as she returned to the car and pulled the still form out from the trunk. Garfield's body sagged in her arms as she walked out over to the grave and slid him in.

"You deserved better," she said to her dog.

The zombies came through two weeks later. They wore brand new camo, and many of them had vests with the logo for Randy's new zombie sightseeing company on them.

"Figures," Cheryl muttered as she looked out her non-shuttered windows at the undead running across her lawn, ripping up the daisies and boxwoods. "DALE!"

Zim started barking up a storm downstairs. Dale shouted at the dog. Then the dog shrieked and Dale ran up the stairs, eyes wide.

"Safe," he gasped.

She kept a shotgun by the bed, always at the ready, since Garfield died. Cheryl aimed it down the stairs and fired.

Dale came back with a smile and an AR-15.

Together they stood on the landing and gunned the creatures lurching up the stairs at them apart, one by one, until the walls dripped with gore, the banister fell over, and the stairs creaked with the weight of the dead.

When it was all over, Cheryl sat in the ruination of her carefully remodeled kitchen.

"We fucking crushed it," Dale shouted, getting himself a bottle of bourbon and stepping over a corpse.

Cheryl shook her head. "Dale, I'm tired of this."

Why did it have to be so hard? Why couldn't they all work together? Why did everything have to be extracted? Paid for? Lobbied for? Why was she sitting here surrounded by all these bodies, her dogs dead, when there had been perfectly good soldiers surrounding the town earlier?

Quarterly profits.

Dale wouldn't get it. He'd just won. And where was Cheryl going to go? Fucking Europe? She was an American. Her family was here. Her friends were here, her community was here.

Cheryl sighed and grabbed a mop. Tonight she'd clean. Tomorrow, she'd talk to the bank about a zombie disaster relief loan so they could start rebuilding the house, even though they were already up to their eyeballs in debt.

Maybe it was time to buy a little UTD stock.

STORY NOTES

THIS SHORT STORY fantasy collection is bookended by two zombie stories. I have a complicated relationship with the zombie concept. Coming from the Caribbean, the zombie is usually a stand-in for certain attitudes about the "other." A mindless horde spilling over the border from the south . . . the history of the zombie is entwined with the jumbie, and zumbie from Western Africa. And the mythology certainly seems to have grown, from my cursory academic reading, in the aftermath of the Haitian revolution. Western fear and imagination twined around Haitian Vodun to become this strange, scared echo of a religion that was present around me growing up. And yet, as a young Caribbean kid, I gathered around a TV with friends to be scared and grossed out by your standard flesh-eating western zombie just like any other teenage kid.

As a writer, though, it amuses me to grab the westernized zombie and use it to interrogate the world that it lives on in. In "A Different Kind of Place" I'm not writing about zombies, I'm writing about small towns in the Midwest and their attitudes about vaccination and community and the willingness to harm their own people to spite those from the "big city." In the final story, "Zombie Capitalism," I listened to a podcast about wild boar loose in the southern US destroying farms, and came across the fact that the boar were being spread around conservative areas of the US despite the horrible damage they were doing because gun nuts got excited about being able to hunt them after seeing videos online of farmers desperately trying to kill them off to protect their livelihood. I realized, before the 2020 pandemic, that zombies would overrun a certain segment of the US even if a cure were offered. As in any good zombie story, it's not the zombies that are the problem, ever, it's the people.

I really wish these stories hadn't called it so well. I thought I was being too hard at the time. Sometimes, as a writer, you hate being right.

The third zombie story, "Trinkets," was an early story of mine written for a themed zombie anthology called *The Book of All Flesh*. Because I felt the Caribbeanness of zombies had been stripped away, I went into the story trying to tell a Caribbean tale, while knowing that I had to play with a westernized type of zombie. I tried to reclaim zombies for the islands, even though it was an early story of mine. Did I succeed? I can't quite tell, but it's a shivery little tale that I think shows the complexity of my identity: a bi-racial Caribbean boy who loves classic genre elements and is influenced by both his history, his roots, and his wildly nerdy love of genre.

Another story from my period as a baby writer comes as a result of Nalo Hopkinson, who asked me if I had a story for an anthology of Caribbean fantastic fiction she was putting to bed in a week. A senior in university, I'd just returned from the Clarion writing workshop and been told about Nalo's fiction there. A Caribbean writer making a career! I thought it was impossible and that I'd been insane to try it myself. I emailed her right away to say hello and she invited me to submit a story to her anthology.

"Of course," I said in an email. "But I need a day to polish the story to show you."

Reader, I had no story.

But Nalo said a day would work, and I pulled an all-nighter working on "Spurn Babylon." I poured myself into that story, pulling on the emotions I'd felt reading about the *Henrietta Marie*, a slave ship found off the coast of Florida in the 1970s. In the 1990s, when I wrote this, some early efforts to create a museum for what divers found aboard the ship had just started. I knew that Charlotte Amelie harbor in St. Thomas had ships buried in the mud, and the idea of a slave ship surfaced after a hurricane grew into this story.

Nalo had rewrite suggestions, of course, and I right away confessed to her I'd written it in a night. But she accepted it, and it was one of my first three professional short story sales. I still find the imagery haunting.

It wasn't just that story. I generated two more stories for Nalo. "Death's Dreadlocks" came from a story I heard as a child about . . . Death's dreads. "Four Eyes" came out of trying to again capture a slice of St. Thomas as I had in "Spurn Babylon."

"Four Eyes" ended up in another anthology that Nalo edited. "Death's Dreadlocks" is a story that I debated over including here. I love the concept, and I'm eternally unable to find where that story I heard ever came from. But the Africa I painted in the story is an example I point writers I mentor to as an example of how stereotypes are bricks that we keep adding to make a wall of simplistic narratives.

My brick made sense within the universe of the story, but it added to that wall in the wider, real world. The complicated nations of Africa, the wide variety of nations I've come to know and people I've come to meet, deserved better than the usual pick-up trucks and famine that the story evoked as an easy background. I apologize for that. Part of being a writer is owning the mistakes, learning from them, and working to do better.

What's weird as a writer is that story, even if written twenty years ago, still remains. Do I pretend I never wrote it? Or do I add it and contextualize it?

The title story "Shoggoths in Traffic" came about because of one particular confusing mad-cap GPS adventure on my way to an event. Late, frustrated, and after two loops around a medium-sized city I'd never been in, I pulled over and wrote "the devil's GPS route" in my phone's notes program. When I started a Patreon, I turned to the idea right away, glad for an excuse to tackle the concept. It was reprinted in a Year's Best anthology, one of the first Patreon stories to do that, I believe, and in *Lightspeed Magazine*. LeVar Burton also picked it to read on his podcast "LeVar Burton Reads." As a teenage, geeky fan of *Star Trek: The Next Generation*, someone blown away by *Roots*, and who watched a ton of *Reading Rainbow*, as PBS was the only station we got on the boat we lived aboard in St. Thomas, hearing my words in LeVar Burton's voice wasn't even something I could have dreamed of back then.

"Brickomancer" also lives in the same universe, or at least it does in my head. I keep seeing more modern conundrums that I point out, with a laugh, as "obviously the result of occult patterns," and wonder if I have a novel ready to grow out of those two stories.

Maybe . . .

If LeVar agreed to read it I would drop everything I was doing to throw myself into it!

Go back in time and kill baby Hitler? Why not? But when face to face with a child who hasn't yet done the horrible things in his future, could you wield the knife? "The Placement Agency" is a daycare facility outside of time and space where the Keeper of Souls houses all the mass murderers of timelines that it has gotten rid of . . . in a way that it feels ethically appropriate.

But how do you take care of these tykes?

So, one of the things I found out upon moving to the US was that a lot of people didn't know much about Buffalo Soldiers. Many of them didn't realize how non-white cowboys were. Generations of Hollywood westerns white-washed a rich and diverse history. In "Sundown" and "The Scar that Stains Red the Gulch" I tried to throw light on some of that, particularly the real life story of Willie Kennard, a bad ass beyond anything Clint Eastwood or John Wayne ever portrayed. The events Willie mentions in "Sundown" before he encounters the aliens are documented.

They really happened.

The fact his story hasn't become immortalized in a movie yet is criminal.

The stories after this now slip for a while into the mode of second world fantasy, which I love. "Tides," "The Widow's Cut," and "On the Eve of the Fall of Habesh" all play out in worlds that never existed, separate from our own. It's a classic mode I've admired ever since I first encountered *The Hobbit* in third grade.

"On the Eve of the Fall of Habesh" began as an experiment in simple world building, trying to imagine a system of magic that had been industrialized, and much like in our own world, I wanted to explore the price the machine of industry takes on its people.

"The Seafarer" came out of the secondary world Paolo Bacigalupi and I created for our novellas "The Executioness" and "The Alchemist," which joined two more novellas many years later to become the book *The Tangled Lands*, which won the World Fantasy Award, much to my shock. We used that world to explore the tragedy of the commons, using magic as a metaphor. Bill Schafer of Subterranean Press commissioned the story for *Subterranean Magazine* after doing a gorgeous limited edition of "The Executioness" as a stand alone novella. I loved getting a chance to jump back into that world with "The Seafarer" and its sailors.

The last of the second world stories, "The Boneyard," takes a world that continued on into industrialization. I'd been reading a history of the Renaissance and been struck by how many times great princes died so horrible of things like dysentery. Even a world that had once held magic might not be interested in bringing it back.

"When All Was Brillig" came out of the great funk I felt around me in 2019. A tangible, chewy darkness that felt like it crept around a land and overwhelmed so many friends. This story formed out of my wondering what fighting something looked like, but literalized.

I'm not sure it landed the way I wanted with readers, but writing it felt important. Much like another story that also formed out of the political atmosphere of that time: "The Emperor and His Totally Amazing, Awesome Clothes" came from a comment I made to a friend while watching a movie where the hero just has to get the news out that a horrible thing is being done by a corrupt ruler. It's a trope. Often a movie ends with the printing press running news of the conspiracy.

But how naive to keep repeating this narrative. Because if you exposed the idiocy of the ruler, chances are their supporters don't care. Reporters keep tripping up on this, I think. They keep thinking finding the story will bring down the leadership.

The world has moved on from that and we're still adapting, alas.

"Mr. Skin's Heart" is a stunt story. The most common question a writer gets is "Where do you get your ideas?" I gave a presentation where I promised to show the audience how I worked. I arrived at an art studio with no idea what I would write and explained how ideas build on other ideas, and how writers flip and twist the obvious to have fun with it and develop a story from a simple seed. It's not just a great idea that you need, but it's the execution and character that take it to that next level.

After I gave my quick presentation, I had the audience give me cliches until one of them leapt out at me. We then brainstormed the idea live, twisting it about until it became interesting, and then I sat down and wrote the story live on a laptop with a projector in front of them over the next couple hours.

"See," I said at the end, when I read the story back to them. "Ideas come from anywhere, including you. It's putting the butt in the chair and writing it, that's the hard part."

*

"That Faraway Kingdom" came out of my love of portal fantasies—those stories where someone from this world steps through into a whole other secondary world. C.S. Lewis, with the wardrobe into Narnia and the time differential, has always dwelled in the back of my mind.

For this story, having a talking mouse wander into a human house on Earth and change the fortunes of a family as the civilization on the other side becomes an advanced civilization as the family grows up cracked me up.

When I stop and think about comic book heroes, a fantasy genre all on its own, I keep poking at some of the foundational assumptions buried in them. In "The Suggestion," I wanted to explore some of implications of a super power that allowed verbal control of other human beings, and in "The Alien from Verapaz," I wanted an answer to what if the US treated Superman's family the way it treated those poor kids at the border they caged, if Superman had landed just a little bit further south.

I am not a believer. Many of my friends and family are, but I'm something of a secular humanist. And some of my reasons for that lie in the questions of the story "The Athiest and the Angel," where I try to imagine an atheist hard-boiled detective that meanders around the period after the rapture, comfortable in their own skin, and doing their best to follow their values and help their friends.

Also, demons would totally infiltrate futures markets and Wall Street. Don't @ me on this, you know it's true.

In fact, as I write this, I start to wonder if this story might not be related to "Shoggoths in Traffic" and "Brickomancer," now that I think about it here. It's all connected, isn't it?

And that isn't a bad moment to end these story notes on,

realizing that I keep coming back to certain themes from story to story. A Caribbean perspective, an immigrant's desire to braid the stories of the past and my present, an interest in examining the implications of power structures in our modern world. Throughout all these stories, I can't help but return to those questions as I look out into the world and then back to the page.

I hope they provoked some thought. At its best, fantasy lets us reexamine the world around us, and poke at its assumptions by looking at it through new lenses.

And I hope, also, that these tales entertained.

Because ultimately, fantasy promises to take us away from this world for a moment. So even though, like a magician, I've taken the curtain away to show you how I move the levers around, if I did my job well, a reader should have been transported somewhere else.

If even just for a moment.

And then come back thinking about the world today with a slightly new light.

ACKNOWLEDGMENTS

I OWE DEBTS of gratitude to so many for making this collection happen. The first is to the many editors who have commissioned or accepted stories from me over the years. Without them the stories would never have happened. Nalo Hopkinson and John Joseph Adams both helped me take many of the stories inside this collection up a whole level. Bill Schafer and Yanni Kuznia also commissioned several of the stories in this collection, for which I'm grateful.

Many of these stories come from my Patreon, a way for readers to help authors by directly subscribing to them. If you'd like to get stories from me in your inbox as well as essays and other random acts of creation, you can find my Patreon via my website at www. TobiasBuckell.com. But I'm eternally grateful for my supporters there. They've helped bring over forty stories into the world that I wouldn't have written otherwise.

I'm also grateful to my agent Hannah Bowman for helping come up with the plan to make this collection a reality, and to Patrick Swenson, my editor at Fairwood Press, for including me in on ideas for the awesome cover concept and doing so much work on editing these stories.

And lastly, my thanks to my local idea crew, Chris, Ross, Brandon, and Ray, who let me bounce ideas off them week to week as I talk about whatever shiny new ideas are popcorning around in my head.

ABOUT THE AUTHOR

TOBIAS S. BUCKELL is a *New York Times* Bestselling author and World Fantasy Award winner born in the Caribbean. He grew up in Grenada and spent time in the British and US Virgin Islands, which influence much of his work.

His novels and over one hundred stories have been translated into twenty different languages. His work has been nominated for awards like the Hugo, Nebula, World Fantasy, and the Astounding Award for Best New Science Fiction Author.

He currently lives in Bluffton, Ohio with his wife and two daughters, where he teaches Creative Writing at Bluffton University. He's online at http://www.TobiasBuckell.com and is also an instructor at the Stonecoast MFA in Creative Writing program.

PUBLICATION HISTORY

"A Different Kind of Place" originally appeared in *Apex Magazine* (2018) | "Spurn Babylon" originally appeared in *Whispers from the Cotton Tree Root* (2000) | "Shoggoths in Traffic" originally appeared in *Lightspeed* (2017) | "Death's Dreadlocks" originally appeared in *Mojo: Conure Stories* (2003) | "Brickomancer" is previously unpublished and appears here for the first time | "A Prayer to Berlinetta" originally appeared on *Patreon* (2018) | "Four Eyes" originally appeared in *New Voices of Science Fiction* (2003) | "Trinkets" originally appeared in *The Book of All Flesh*, Eden Studios (2001) | "The Placement Agency" originally appeared on *Patreon* (2017) | "Sundown" originally appeared in *Dead Man's Hand*, Titan Books (2014) | "The Scar That Stains Red the Gulch" originally appeared on *Patreon* (2019) | "Tides" originally appeared in *Ideomancer Unbound* (2002) | "The Widow's Cut" originally appeared on *Patreon* (2015) | "On the Eve of the Fall of Habesh" originally appeared in *Subterranean Magazine* (2013) | "The Seafarer" originally appeared in *Subterranean Magazine* (2013) | "The Boneyard" originally appeared on *Patreon* | "When All Was Brillig" originally appeared on *Patreon* (2019) | "The Emperor and His Totally Amazing, Awesome Clothes" originally appeared on *Patreon* (2019) | "Mr. Skin's Heart" originally appeared on *Patreon* (2019) | "The Faraway Kingdom" originally appeared in *Patreon* (2019) | "The Alien from Verapaz" originally appeared in *Patreon* (2018) | "The Suggestion" originally appeared on *Patreon* (2020) | "The Atheist and the Angel" orginally appeared on *Patreon* (2020) | "Zombie Capitalism" originally appeared in *Motherboard Magazine* (2020)

OTHER TITLES FROM FAIRWOOD PRESS

CPSIA information can be obtained
at www.ICGtesting.com
Printed in the USA
LVHW020236240622
721996LV00002B/240

9 781933 846187